ALLEGIANCE of BLOOD

First published in Great Britain in 2019
Mark Turnbull

All characters in this publication are fictitious and any resemblance to real persons, living or dead is purely coincidental.

A CIP catalogue record for this book is available from the British Library.

ISBN: 978-0-9556353-4-2

Cover design and layout by
www.chandlerbookdesign.com

Printed in Great Britain by
4Edge Limited

INTRODUCTION

Since the age of ten I've been fascinated by the Wars of the Three Kingdoms. I've always wished to write about the period, and in my own small way, bring its events and people to life once more. My aim has been to create an entertaining plot, woven with historical detail, which allows the reader to truly feel as if they have been transported back to 1642-43.

Acknowledgements

I'd like to pay tribute to the fantastic organisations that are guardians of this era, such as *The English Civil War Society*, *The National Civil War Centre – Newark Museum*, *The Battlefields Trust*, *First Marquis of Montrose Society* and *The Sealed Knot*, to name but a few.

Thanks also to my wife, Kate, for being so very supportive, and the many others who have helped me, such as my 'book club' buddy Keith Crawford, editor Julia Underwood, 'The 1642 Tailor' and Rawdon's, Tyldesley's and Winchester's regiments of The English Civil War Society. Lastly, I'm grateful to John Chandler for producing a great cover that sums up the book so well.

www.allegianceofblood.com

In memory of
Frances and Maureen.

Chapter 1
23 October 1642

The image of a small casket filled his tortured mind. Not much more than a foot in length, it lay upon the earth beside him. Inside was his stillborn daughter, as cold to the touch as the naked blade of his sword, and as grey as her small headstone. His entire body felt paralysed as the tormenting memory finally faded, to be replaced by images of his wife, Anne, and his son, peering down upon him. His wife's eyes were red with tears that burnt her silky skin, causing him much anguish, but Sir Francis Berkeley could barely manage more than a pathetic whimper.

Mother and son soon vanished as well, this time leaving nothing but the scudding clouds above him – the blackest he'd ever seen – with edges tinted grey by the sliver of moon they masked. It was as if they were conspiring to keep hidden, for a little longer, the terrible consequences of the first battle between King and Parliament.

Wails like those of starving gulls circled this frozen Warwickshire battlefield to pick at Francis's remaining sanity. Fear had him pinned to the ground and the night sky pushed down to smother him. He begged for a speedy release, if he was not dead already; set to join his baby who'd breathed her first and last some two years past.

The moan of a voice calling for help was certainly not a haunting hallucination, but very real. Like a criminal in a noose, Francis seemed to have been cut down and spared at the eleventh hour. Although lasting only a moment, that was all it took to be sure that lifeblood still ran through his veins.

Chapter 2

The blind hell in which Francis had been lost for several hours exploded into an array of stars, like silver studs pinning the sky into place. He was surrounded by irregular and silhouetted shapes that turned out to be the dead and the dying. This realisation had him desperately trying to get onto all fours, although his body would not budge, and the frosty grass stabbed at his cheek like a phalanx of miniature pikemen. Seized by the icy earth, his brain's desire for movement created only a torrent of pain and an intense cry.

Francis's yell enlivened others, from high-pitched shrieks to the moans of tormented souls, drawn from their broken bodies to heaven. The noise thrived upon the crisp air to haunt any still alive amongst the dead that carpeted the Vale of the Red Horse.

Driven by abject fear, his frozen fingers clawed out. Blood seeped from a cut inflicted by the unwitting caress of his sword, although he sensed barely a dull throb. Soon though, it would congeal, exposed to the elements that were picking off any soldier who'd survived the chilling battle between fellow countrymen.

Civil war had that very morning soaked this field with blood. It had spared neither Royalist nor Parliamentarian. The day had also seen Francis dismounted, engaged in hand-to-hand fighting and surrounded by beasts and riders. It was somewhere amidst this melee that he had been felled; not by a sword, he now gathered, but by an anonymous, half-inch musket ball. Its smooth surface, scored by a moulding line around its circumference, had flashed with silvery pride prior to tearing through Francis's red breeches and taking a glancing bite out of his thigh. Unable to properly feel his limb, he was filled with anxiety over the wound and whether a ball or any fabric might have lodged in his leg, which could spell amputation, or even death.

He wrestled to raise himself enough to see the slopes of Edgehill, the original position of the King's men, atop which a dancing fire caught his eye. He'd not been abandoned. The Royalists seemed still to be on the field and this gave him hope, more than he'd experienced in all his twenty-five years. A faint flicker of light, bobbing in the distance like a ship's lantern, made him certain that a comrade in arms had broken away to search out and rescue him.

* * * * *

Nathaniel Harbottle was not a soldier. In fact, he could only be loosely described as a Royalist, which is why the ghastly battlefield he so gingerly stepped across made his stomach churn. He did not care for the aims and motivations of either side, his own being merely to blend in and appear loyal to the King, which current circumstances made none too easy.

The moon averted its gaze, an owl hooted at him, and the only protection afforded throughout was the dark of night itself. Such darkness also brought its perils and, when his foot became entangled, he lowered his dull lantern, only to recoil in horror at a human arm hooked about his ankle. It was as if the earth had peeled back to reveal a graveyard of disinterred bodies and mangled faces. Their lifeless eyes caught in Harbottle's candle made it flicker at the sight.

"I'll not fall foul of your mistake." Harbottle held his head high to avoid the hollow gaze of the latest corpse he had to step over. *I choose survival rather than King or Parliament.* His thoughts were not with the dead but the living and, in particular, a certain Parliamentarian with whom he'd agreed a rendezvous.

"Over here," Captain Richardson said, emerging from the gloom like a wraith.

"Couldn't you have chosen somewhere a little less gruesome?"

"This is war, man," Richardson replied.

"A war against whom," Harbottle hissed. "when Parliament claim to be fighting only to rescue the King?"

"Spare me the politics." Richardson clearly just wanted to have done and get away.

"I've been ordered to pass on this request for the return of the Earl of Lindsey." Harbottle held out a letter.

"What?" Richardson released a mocking laugh. "The King may get his commander back in a coffin, for the surgeons have long since given up."

"Just take it to the relevant authority." Harbottle thrust the letter at him again.

"Is there any other information you wish to share?"

"Only that the King's heart is not up to another battle on the morrow," Harbottle kept his voice low, glancing at the bodies as if any one of them had the potential to eavesdrop.

"Well, well." Richardson replied. "The Earl of Essex will be much interested to hear that. Watch they do not suspect you."

"Rest assured, they don't. Otherwise they wouldn't have entrusted me with this little errand."

"And what of Sir Faithful Fortescue?" Richardson asked about the Parliamentarian commander who had his men fire their pistols into the ground at the start of the battle and then ride forward to join the Royalists.

"Jumped beds like the whore that he is and still lies with the King's men."

"You might wish to tell Fortescue's new master that we have reinforcements arriving tomorrow," Richardson suggested, omitting to add that they were from Cambridge and wouldn't arrive before evening. "Staunchly loyal to boot."

"Very well." Harbottle requested the man commend him to Lord Essex. "Should I find out further information useful to you I'll let you know."

"At a good price, I'm sure you will," Richardson said as he took his leave.

"And a good night to you, Captain."

The October frost chilled Harbottle's bones just a little more than it ought, and he couldn't help but wonder whether he could go on jumping between sides. Turning to retrace his steps, he afforded one last glance to check that nobody else was in the vicinity, for he had the sensation of being watched, and the thought stirred the hairs on the back of his neck.

Chapter 3

The body beside Francis was racked with rigor mortis, permanently holding its last contorted expression; a look of horror that would only vanish with decomposition, cell by cell. Certainly, the wide-open mouth and taut skin from its last cry for mercy vividly encapsulated what must have gone through the soldier's mind in the final seconds of life.

Shock and the bitter night had similarly frozen Francis's own features. His face was so cold that nothing of his consternation over the corpse and the arrival of two men could materialise in his expression.

"The King's sleeping in his coach," said one. "He's determined to stay with his men, but they won't fight again in the morning."

Upon the betrayal of more intimate details relating to the King's cause, Francis realised the need to act dead if he didn't wish to end up so. Understanding of what the two men were about made it abundantly clear that he was in as much danger now as he had been during the battle. So frayed were his nerves that he feared the white face of the body near him, with a glow like the moon's, might somehow give him away. If even the faintest flicker of the lantern should meet Francis's glistening eyeballs it would be his undoing.

"Should I find out further information useful to Parliament, I will let you know," the second man added.

The speech escaped on a cloud of frosty air and caused Francis's eyes to open. He watched the men, whose candle gave them a glowing aura and, to his horror, the bespectacled one looked back at him. Francis must have been seen and had overheard too much, yet he could only close his eyes once more against the inevitable. His nervous state muted his senses, and he did not register the receding footfalls that left piercing quiet in possession of the night. Francis could not tell if it was forty seconds or forty minutes that passed before he next opened his eyes, so still was it that time itself seemed frozen.

"This one 'as a ring," a gruff voice gleefully noted in near proximity.

Looters. They would slit Francis's throat for whatever valuables he possessed. The silver lace stitched onto his crimson woollen doublet was itself more than sufficient to seal his fate. He thought of his precious wife and regretted not being able to look into her emerald eyes one last time to tell her how much she meant to him. How in nearly three years of marriage she had made him happier than he could ever have imagined possible.

"Please God, let it be him," a female voice stifling tears was right over him.

Francis glimpsed a silk cloak and gathered hood that framed a face most angelic. There was no accounting for why such an angel would be wandering in such a place other than that tonight was no ordinary night.

"Madam." He couldn't tell if the word had escaped his lips

until she lowered her lantern, handkerchief over her mouth. "Please ..."

"What's going on over there?" Captain Richardson, not having strayed far, demanded to know the lady's business with brandished sword.

"I'm looking for my husband, sir, and God be praised, I've found him."

"King or Parliament?" Richardson asked.

"I am of neither and mean no ill to anyone," she replied and pointed at Francis, appealing for assistance to get him to his feet. "Oh, won't you help? Aren't we countrymen when all's said and done?"

"I dare say he'll survive," Richardson said, observing Francis's injured leg without so much as a grimace of his weathered brow.

"I'll pay you as much money as you desire," she pleaded.

"Captain Richardson at your service, madam. I fight for Parliament, but also for honour, therefore keep your money," he remarked upon kissing her hand and then knelt to pull Francis to his feet. "Now be off with you both." Richardson soon got back on his way and there was no doubt that, but for her intervention, this would have been Francis's last night upon earth.

Light headed and nauseous, Francis put an arm around the lady and could initially focus on nothing save her sweet breath, so far removed from the stench of war. Her very proximity instilled life into him and his hand, taken by hers, prickled with warmth while his heart glowed over such a selfless act.

"Pray, tell me why you rescued me?" Francis asked.

"My dear husband is missing, so why should I not at least save another man's life?"

"I owe you a debt of gratitude I fear I can never repay."

Francis let out a cry of pain and slowly hobbled forward.

"I had thought our nation forsaken, yet that kind man proved God's love still abounds in us, no matter what our allegiance," she said.

Francis wondered where in this catastrophic mess her husband could be – dead already from the savage fighting, or the looters' next victim? A question that provoked a shiver as he recollected the pair he'd overheard plotting to jeopardise the King's cause.

Chapter 4

Robert Devereux, third Earl of Essex and Captain General of the Parliamentarian army, paced his grand tent, its hem tugged at by a biting breeze that sought refuge from the horror outside. To make it infinitely worse, his serving boy had gone missing with his pipe, the object dearest to him, especially in such a time of unprecedented stress.

"Fetch Sir James Ramsay," Essex snapped.

"His whereabouts are uncertain, my lord."

The white ostrich feathers of Essex's hat almost took flight when he swiped it from his head in a rare flash of anger. It was one thing to actually oppose the King verbally, but to lead an army against him was high treason. Since the age of ten he knew fine well the consequences of that, his father's head having rolled for the same. Now here he was with everything to lose and "Black Ramsey", the commander of his left wing of cavalry, had also vanished, much like the fellow's men after their cowardly charge, which was yet another matter to deal with in due course.

"Scour the countryside for him."

Essex imagined how Prince Rupert must have mocked the performance of Parliament's horsemen. It was into this furore that Sir Philip Stapleton stepped, the commander of Essex's cavalry reserve. The same man who had prevented the total rout of his army that day.

"General, we've received a most curt order from the King," Stapleton, a no-nonsense Yorkshireman, said. "He insists we release Lord Lindsey."

"An exchange of prisoners?" Essex had fought alongside Lindsey in Holland when he and the Royalist general were young bucks. "How are Robert's wounds?"

"He's gravely ill, yet still persists in accusing his guards of treason," Stapleton replied.

"Have my own surgeon sent to him." Essex waved off a messenger with a swish of his marshal's baton, as well as the King's request, over which he would not be harried. "Now, we have other business to discuss," he said, leaning on the table. "Have you seen Ramsey?"

"No, my lord, but I do have some good news for you ..."

"About time I had some," Essex declared and began to pace again. "Has anyone found my damned serving boy?" He poked his head out of the tent, feeling every bit of his fifty-one years, and his rosy cheeks were prickled by the frost.

"Colonel Hampden's two thousand men are marching to us as we speak," Stapleton revealed.

"Good news? They won't be here until after midday tomorrow." Essex shook his head. "We'll have to retire from the field to patch up our army long before that. It would serve us well if, as is believed, the King is ready to negotiate."

The Lord General's mood was not improved by Stapleton's lip, which curled in response to any talk of withdrawal, let alone negotiations.

"I venture to suggest we resume the fight as soon as day breaks and drive the enemy from the field. If we don't defeat the King in battle, then we leave the road to London open to him." The fiery candlelight lit up Stapleton's dark eyes and the gold embroidery decorating his cow-hide buff coat. It was as if his opinions were just as interwoven into his character.

"I am already resolved upon our course of action," Essex replied.

"Your Excellency." Captain Richardson requested permission to enter. "There is word that the King's troops are to withdraw to their original positions and will not attack again."

"Is your source to be trusted?" Essex took heart, for his men could not stand up to a second assault. Yet he was equally concerned that the Royalists' impotence would only prompt further calls for him to renew the conflict himself.

"In as much as his information has always been most accurate in the past," Richardson replied.

"A man who betrays those to whom he professes loyalty is capable of betraying anyone," Essex said, using this double-edged sword to keep his subordinates at bay. If negotiations might bring victory where this battle could not, then he was all for opening dialogue instead of a second assault.

"May I point out once again that we would be finished if the King is allowed to reach London?" Stapleton said, persisting with his opinion that even if the Royalists weren't in any fit state to renew the contest, they showed no intention of retreating. "General, I heard you fought pikestaff in hand with the common soldiers of your regiment."

"As should any good commander," Essex replied. It was care of his men that firmed his conclusion that they must leave the field. Better to safeguard his troops rather than remain here out of stubborn pride and allow the King, from the heights of Edgehill, to watch like a hawk for the best time to swoop.

"The men are passing your act of bravery around as though it were a bottle of the finest ale," Stapleton recounted. "It fuels their desire to defeat the enemy."

"I fight for our cause just the same as any common soldier," Essex declared and stamped his feet to warm them.

"My lord, you sent for me?" His chaplain arrived with both hands clasped together as if praying for the night to be over.

"Stephen, I have no time to write an account of today's events. Do me the favour of preparing a paper recounting the battle and send it to Parliament, as they will be anxious for news. And send also Lord Wharton and William Strode to give them verbal assurances of our complete victory."

"Victory?" Stephen's pause questioned the very notion.

"Aye, just that," Essex said and looked him in the eye. "As if it were written in the gospels."

Before any more could be said, Essex's boy was escorted in with his pipe, promptly clipped around the ear and then sent packing again. A suitable pause ensued, allowing the Lord General to fill the bowl with his finest tobacco and linger over the lighting of it.

"Our forces will draw up in the morning and face the King again." Essex relented, but held his pipe firmly by the neck. "Though we shall not instigate any attack and, if they make no move, we shall promptly withdraw."

Essex saw no point in further bloodshed, having today held the King's forces in check. He had proved his own and his army's worth, which might well end the war through a negotiated settlement with a suitably contrite King Charles the First.

Chapter 5
Four Days Later

As they traversed the heart of Banbury Castle, even Francis felt lacking in stature next to the six-foot-four Prince Rupert. With two formidable curtain walls circling the fortress like a target, King Charles had scored a bulls-eye when, swept along by his victory at the Battle of Edgehill, the castle surrendered upon his approach.

"So, you used to serve in the London Trained Bands?" Rupert seemed very interested in Francis's inside knowledge. "When did you leave the capital?"

"Following the mob's attack on my home, Your Highness," Francis said, trying to keep up with the pace of the King's nephew. "January, forty-two, not long after His Majesty also left."

"I may require your expertise to help reinforce my case."

The forthcoming council of war and an unexpected barrage of criticism for his proposal to strike at London consumed Rupert. When Francis, who was falling behind, failed to reply, he turned. "Ah, I forgot that those damned rebels took a piece of your leg."

"Given half a chance I'd have it back from them," Francis replied.

"Essex, the old fool, has retreated to Warwick Castle to lick his wounds." The Bohemian Rupert verbalised his ire in perfect English. "Leaving the way to London wide open."

"Then surely we should seize the opportunity to take the city?" Francis had a mind to recover what was left of his home and possessions.

"We should indeed, although I fear convincing the *learned gentlemen* of the council may not be as easy." Rupert resumed his march and folded back the scarlet cloak that had not been off his back since Edgehill. "Pray wait here in case I require your assistance."

"At your service," Francis said, stifling a grimace of pain caused by the long walk. He watched the Prince enter council and give a sweeping bow to the King, who sat at a grand table with his other military and civilian councillors around it.

Once alone, with some urgency Francis sat in the niche of an arched window to attend to his leg. He savoured the caress of the cool October air, and a far from unpleasant smell of wax and red lead intermingled with saffron from his dressing.

"I propose we march on London straightaway, whilst their army is in such disarray." Rupert put forward his point so strongly that Francis could still hear his voice outside.

* * * * *

Within the chamber, Rupert watched the Earl of Bristol survey proceedings like a proud stag preparing to do battle with a young pretender.

"If we are to adopt such an idea and send cavalry riding roughshod across the capital," Bristol warned, "then surely this will defeat the object of our political aims." He looked at the other councillors and continued before anyone could interrupt. "It is my opinion that such a resolution would set every Londoner against us and not endear our cause to the people at all."

Exasperated, Prince Rupert raised a hand and said: "If we do not move on London we will have a protracted war." He fixed his gaze squarely upon the old man. "Would a speedy end, and therefore fewer casualties, not endear us to the people?"

"Your Majesty," Bristol said, turning to the King, who had thus far withheld all judgment, "might it not be prudent to send to London emissaries of peace rather than death and destruction?"

"Peace?" The Prince was not one to be side-lined. "Have we come this far only to surrender?"

"With the greatest of respect, His Highness may not be familiar with the ways of the English." The opinion slipped from Bristol's mouth as if he were addressing the monarch, and not Rupert, the General of the Horse. "And the Prince is also young." He clearly wasn't one to do things by halves. "Who is to say his furious cavalrymen won't get out of control and set the city afire?"

"By God!" The accusation had Rupert on his feet. "It is manners that have been cast to the flames by such slurs." He could well understand why, in years past, Bristol had spent some time in the Tower at His Majesty's pleasure.

"I beg you show more restraint, Your Highness," Bristol said with an unctuous, pleading expression. "I simply deliver my opinion, as do you, on this most vital of points. To take a rash decision could cost us the war."

"The Prince is a proven commander and gifted leader of men," Sir Jacob Astley interjected.

King Charles placed a pondering forefinger upon his cheek and the auburn flecks of his moustache, and with a nod to Rupert, seemed to signal his faith in his nephew's ability to achieve what he proposed. But the hesitation that followed hinted at the King's concerns regarding his own reputation and accusations of tyranny that pricked his conscience anew.

"Give me three thousand horse and foot as a flying column." Rupert had no time for doubts. "I could purge Parliament and bring an end to this conflict within weeks."

This image roused the seventy-year-old Earl of Forth from hibernation. "With Essex's men out of the way, they have little left to defend the city," the old general agreed.

"Victory by conquest is always hollow." Bristol's monotonous voice chimed in. "We should be battling soldiers, not civilians." His caution was adopted by others, who warned of the risk an attack posed to London's prosperity and commerce, not to mention the many private concerns held there.

Rupert's call for personal interests to be laid aside garnered little support, and his mounting frustration at such opposition to a logical, military decision certainly did not influence the council. King Charles's melancholy eyes watched, waited and weighed up the evidence from beneath heavy eyelids without him once intervening. It seemed he would not take Rupert's bait, most likely because of the Queen's warning that his nephew was headstrong. But neither did he appear to trust Bristol. The King's pearl earring glinted as he turned to his nephew, who suggested that civilian councillors had not enough grasp of military tactics. Next, he turned to Bristol, who retorted that generals did not appreciate the political ramifications. The King soon leaned forward, and with the fingers of both hands neatly interlinked, he secured a respectful silence.

"Gentlemen, thank you for your opinions," the King said without stammering, despite being torn asunder by both sides' losses, all of whom were his subjects. "I am of the opinion that an attack on London would most assuredly secure victory over the traitors in Parliament, but it would lose me the hearts of my subjects." Accordingly, he gave the order that the army should march for Oxford. "That city lies within a suitable radius of London and there we may consider how best to defeat the rebel army in the field."

* * * * *

Footsteps echoed from the corridor and a man emerged and approached Francis, his boots and cloak spattered with mud. Pulling off his leather gloves and removing his felt hat, he stroked a hand through his thick, black hair and enquired whether Prince Rupert was within.

"He is, sir, but as you may gather, preoccupied at present." Francis noted the expressive eyebrows rise in relief as, with a nod, the man waited patiently. "Are you with the army?" Francis leaned on his lacquered cane and stood to engage in further discussion, if only to pass the time.

"No." The man's large eyes came to focus on Francis.

"Weather playing havoc with the roads?" Francis asked.

"Aye, though the rain helped me stay awake as I rode."

Francis formally introduced himself, but the fellow only gave his Christian name, Nathaniel in return. There was something about his swarthy features, and even the way his pencil moustache seemed ready to abandon his thin upper lip, which niggled at Francis as if he'd seen him somewhere before, although where and when, he had no idea.

Before any more conversation could be had, the council

dispersed, led by Prince Rupert, whose face was flushed carnation pink and his brown eyes bronzed with disillusion. Behind him the flow of councillors diverged like a stream to give the Prince a wide berth, except for Lord Bristol, who strolled past dabbing his mouth with a scented handkerchief.

"Wait until a protracted war devours your wealth, my lord." Rupert's warning prompted no reaction.

"Weaken their case by patience and reason, Your Highness." Old Forth, on the excuse of his gout, stopped to offer Rupert some advice. "It is much more effective than biting at their heels. All is not lost with one battle." He was well versed on that, having served in the Thirty Years War.

No sooner had Rupert thanked him for his wisdom, than Nathaniel bowed and announced he had news regarding the enemy.

"Very good, Harbottle, come and acquaint me with it," Rupert instructed.

When Francis approached the royal, Rupert notified him that they were not to march on London, a discussion which opened up etiquette and enabled Francis to enquire after another role. "I may not at present be able to fight, but I could still command within a garrison town."

"Our most pressing need is to bring Essex to battle." Rupert led both men out through the corridor without furnishing a suitable answer.

"Master!" Francis's young serving lad, out of breath, ran up the moment he stepped outside. "Her Ladyship says that the King has had enough of your time and entreats you to return home."

"Does she indeed?" It was the Prince, not Francis, who answered the boy's outburst. "Then tell the good lady that Rupert of the Rhine grants her husband's freedom."

"Your Highness, you're my hero!" The lad had followed the royal's exploits since his first victory. "Is it true you jumped onto your horse at Powick Bridge and charged without coat or armour on your back?"

"My apologies," Francis flushed with frustration. "His tongue runs on wheels."

"Tis true what you heard." Rupert ruffled the boy's hair. "More's the pity that those upon the council do not possess your enthusiasm."

The boy's features jumped the moment Rupert's large hand gave him benediction.

The Prince turned to Francis and reiterated the certainty that hostilities would resume once realisation dawned that Parliament would never relinquish any of the powers they had seized. Then with a smile, he commended Francis on the loyalty of his nine-year-old servant and in the same breath all but assured Francis's future by saying he would do what he could for him.

Chapter 6

A blur of bronze flashed before James Jackson's eyes. With every flicker of black tail feathers he struggled to focus on the bird he'd picked as they wrestled together in a jumbled mess of aggression. The gamecocks looked so alike and moved so fast, flapping their wings and bounding at each other with their stick-thin legs. This posturing scattered sand from the floor of the cockpit into a haze, while excitement mounted during a brief period of the birds' separation.

"Get at him!" James's waving fist did not break the deathly stare of the cockerels, who, with wattles and combs cut down, lowered their heads like hardened street fighters.

"Tear him apart!" Nathaniel Harbottle hung over the wooden fence that kept the three-deep spectators at bay and grabbed James as the game birds closed in again.

"Mine has his wits about him," James said, pointing a plump finger.

"Unlike you, who's settled on the loser." Harbottle's narrowed eyes watched how his bird stubbornly brought the other to hesitation. "My golden Unite will give me a nice return."

"You bet a whole twenty shillings? Have you taken leave of your senses?" The birds' jagged metal spurs glinted in James's eyes. "The bugger scratches like a scorned woman."

"My intuition never lets me down," Harbottle said with a confident sigh. "I always back the side that prevails." His assertion was proved when his cockerel leaped and clawed the other to the floor and the spur found its mark amidst the fury. "Shame your cock isn't up to it."

"I've had no complaints in that area," James said, at the very moment in which his bird's breast was sliced open, amid piercing squawks.

Blood flicked across the arena. One man kissed a charmed bunch of feathers hanging about his neck, while another threw a half-eaten chicken leg at the loser.

"Spare me the details," Harbottle said and calculated the odds.

"Easy come, easy go." James shrugged, turning his back on the pit, for he much disliked the gruesome ending. But, to Harbottle's accusation that he couldn't stand the sight of blood, he shook his head. "I've fought bare knuckle. I'm as used to blood as I am to a bit of spilled beer."

"You mustn't spill much of it then." Harbottle glanced at the fellow's gut.

James brandished his fists and declared: "I've rearranged the features of many a man for less."

"Enough of your blustering," Harbottle said, having heard these assertions before. The only thing he wished to arrange, he told James, was business, having not come to London for leisure alone. "Now pay your debts and let's get on with it," he prompted, taking out a clay pipe, lighting it with a taper and sucking on the long, thin stem. Harbottle had information about the Royalists to pass on. From the sliver of tobacco in the small bowl he drew the sweet taste of success.

"I don't have enough on me to pay my debt in full," James said, holding out three silver coins, the agreed sign that he wished to hand over a new cipher for their correspondence. To this offering Harbottle made suitable public complaint which James followed by suggesting the man visit his home that afternoon to collect the remainder. "But do not mention it to my wife if she answers the door."

"She doesn't approve of your gambling?" Harbottle asked.

"Elizabeth approves of nothing nowadays unless it's first been sanctioned by one of God's vicars and then the Archbishop of Canterbury himself," James lamented. This inane banter, a conduit that had disguised all that needed to be said for now, brought an end to their business.

Chapter 7

Francis watched the raindrops splash against the window and slide down the pane, leaving streaks that distorted his reflection. His oval face, slender nose and large eyes were framed by a mop of light brown curls, though the fine hair of his moustache was lost in the dank view.

Sometimes, his life, his purpose, seemed equally blurred by the all-consuming war. The horn of a passing sow-gelder emphasised his own neutered state. There at the bedroom window he would have sat for another half an hour, watching people go about their business and considering how to pull himself out of his dilemma had Master Hathaway, the physician, not arrived.

"Terrible weather out there," Hathaway commented as he gently placed some bottles and a bowl onto the table. After five minutes of fussing, he handed over a concoction he'd made earlier that day. Francis drew the brew to his nose and sniffed. "That's right, tip it all down."

The physician's paternal tone, frustrated Francis beyond all measure as he attempted to do as Hathaway advised. After a sharp spasm and a rush of wind, he regurgitated what he'd eaten that morning – lampreys, red wine and all – into a nearby earthenware bowl from the bottom of which decorative figures of Adam and Eve peered back.

"Is it finished?" Francis groaned.

"From that end at least," Hathaway said, swirling the contents with satisfaction, and he was still examining them when Anne entered.

"A letter has just arrived," Anne said, and she held it out. "The messenger was very well dressed, so might it be important?"

This news prompted Francis to cut short the physician's visit, despite Hathaway's counsel for the use of laxatives. The man began to pack up his belongings while Francis's stomach once more became unsettled, but this time due to apprehension over the contents of this letter.

Francis had pawned his best silk suit to pay for these lodgings, which, pre-war, were hardly fit for animals. But Oxford was like a giant sponge, unable to withstand the influx of those following the King, leaving every nook and cranny rented out and bringing it to saturation point. The streets surged with rivers of urine and waste, both human and otherwise, and munitions production spilled into public buildings. Yet, by comparison, its colleges were squeezed dry of both funds and students by the army. As fast as typhus tried to drain the city, the holes were filled by newcomers. Yet, despite struggling against the tide of these conditions, Francis could do little but sink or swim, for proximity to the King's person was everything. For Francis, the money earned from his suit entered one hand and passed out the other, to purchase just a little more time to find the opportunity he so needed.

"Come on, open it," Anne urged as soon as Hathaway had left the bedroom. She watched as Francis broke the red seal and unfolded the letter, taking barely a couple of seconds to scan the writing.

"I'm to accompany the army. We're to march on London!" Francis clenched a fist. "If that goes well, it may only be a matter of weeks before we regain our home and fetch Henry back."

"You really think so?" Anne embraced him and laid her head on his chest. "We must repay your sister's kindness for keeping him safe in the countryside."

"We must pray the King takes London."

Holding Anne in his protective arms and kissing her curls, he could hear hope in her melodious words. Henry's face had not lit up her eyes for the last eight of his twelve months of life and this hope seemed to fill a fraction of the emptiness she had suffered since the boy had left. She had admitted that moment had been almost akin to the loss of their first, stillborn child.

Now Anne rushed after the physician and stepped onto the street to call after Master Hathaway, even using his Christian name, desperately entreating the man to return and ensure her husband began his vital journey in the very best of health.

"A change of heart, Sir Francis?" Hathaway said as he once more entered the bedroom, stroking his fine cobwebs of hair into place. "You'd do well to take this tonight." He extracted a small bottle from his bag and gave a gentle tap to its stopper.

"He will if he knows what's good for him." Anne placed a hand upon her husband's thigh.

"What's in it?" Francis asked.

"An elixir known only to me and our Blessed Saviour." Hathaway turned to Anne. "You must understand, Lady Berkeley, that when your husband was wounded, he lost more than blood." The doctor spoke at length about the imbalance of Francis's humours, for not only were his blood and phlegm out of balance, but most assuredly his black and yellow bile too. "Make sure he has several chamber pots on hand."

Anne thanked the physician and saw him out. She returned with a cup of distilled oak buds to freshen Francis's mouth, after which he eased her against the painted flowers and curlicues of the wall, and his lips met hers. She stroked his cheek and offered to assist with any ailment he might have, his acceptance readily given by tracing down her neck with an abundance of kisses.

"Good job I didn't give you boiled spearmint," she said with a smile that accentuated her almond eyes and rapid breaths that saw her bosom swell.

"I've no need of aphrodisiacs," he said and led her towards the bed.

"Stops wounds from healing too." Her hand caressed a newfound ailment swelling in his breeches.

The tender touch of her delicate fingers, skimming the stubble of his jaw, banished every battlefield nightmare. As he sat upon the wool-filled upper mattress, she stood before him and traced the contours of his biceps through his white linen shirt, lifted the garment over his head and discarded it. However reluctant she may have been to have him go to war again, tonight he was going nowhere. She pushed him onto his back. Her slender legs, adorned with linen-thread stockings and the pretty garters he found so irresistible, stepped out of her petticoat. Ample incentive to return, she told him with a coquettish smile, by making sure that he took good care of himself and brought back their dear son.

Chapter 8

"Washing clothes again, are we?" James entered the kitchen, unbuttoned his breeches and urinated into a pot in front of his wife while whistling to the tune of his golden trickle.

"If not for me you wouldn't have a clean shirt on your back, Mister Jackson," Elizabeth said, grabbing the pot and sloshing it into a large buck tub along with the rest of the family's urine.

"So you keep telling me," James replied, her admonishments one of his few sources of amusement these days.

"We have six children to clothe, if you haven't forgotten." She had the maid avert her eyes from his appendage and sprinkled wood ash into the buck tub to which their linen was added, and then used a pole to give it a good stir. "Because your godliness is well past administering to, I will at least attend to your cleanliness," she said and motioned for James to take one end of a pole draped with what she had washed earlier and carry it into the garden.

"How about just attending to my stomach?" His grumbling that there was only cold meat again was as busy as the blustery wind, and as sharp.

"Go wash well, sayeth summer, for with sun I shall dry." Elizabeth ignored him and sang like a morning sparrow, joined by her maid. They laid laundry over the rosemary bushes to infuse it with their sweet smell. "Go wring well, sayeth winter, with wind so shall I."

"I know what I'd like to wring," James muttered and stalked away to answer a knock at the door. An expected dull knock of Harbottle the Cavalier. "You're like a vulture."

"And I'll swoop down on you until I get my money," Harbottle told him.

"Come in then," James said, closing and locking the door behind him. "The women are busy outside," he explained and escorted Harbottle straight through to his private study.

"Now, the cypher." Harbottle got to the point. "Otherwise I cannot send Parliament any more of my special letters."

"Did you convince the King's officers that London is unassailable?" James opened the decorative box that held the family bible. He reached inside to fidget with a false side, behind which was hidden a small paper that he extracted and handed over.

"A bastion that will oppose them to the last man, my report said." Harbottle secreted the cypher into a pocket inside his doublet and accepted some decanted wine.

"My masters in Parliament will be most pleased to hear that," James replied and handed over two golden Unites, "as I trust you are with this. Now, where's your Prince Rupert these days?"

"Arguing that we should attack London whilst Parliament's army is away." Harbottle finished his wine. "Speaking of which, does Essex plan to dally in Warwick like a milk maid for much longer?"

"He'll have his army back to London soon enough," James said, remaining tight-lipped about everything but his favourite Rhenish wine.

"Maybe he's died?" Harbottle's playful jibe stemmed from the fact that the Lord General carried his own coffin along with the army. "That would explain why he's vanished."

"He's very much alive." James pointed at Harbottle with his glass.

"Then has he got a woman secreted in Warwick?" Harbottle persisted.

"Away with you!"

"Ah, I forgot, after being cuckolded by two wives, he's done with women," Harbottle said.

"At least he hasn't substituted women for his dog, like Rupert." James chortled and, anticipating where Harbottle's humour was leading, got in first with a question of his own. "Does the Prince look set to get his way over assaulting London?"

"The King's men are only biding their time in Oxford." Harbottle leaned forward and stroked his thin black moustache. "But King Charles doesn't wish to enter London over the bodies of his people. At least that's how I think he phrased it."

"Murdered enough already has he?" James recollected his father's imprisonment for non-payment of an illegal tax. "He either starves them to death to pay for his art collection or finishes them off with his religious reforms." His insides churned with resentment as well as with hunger. The same pangs as those of his childhood, when his poor mother had shed tears of anguish alongside those of her hungry little boy over the struggle to put food on the table. "Damn the King!" He turned to the plate of cold meat that Elizabeth had left.

Harbottle raised his hands and said, "I might be in the service of the King, but I'm no Royalist either. His money puts food on my table, as does the little extra I receive from Parliament."

"Then you might have to start sharing your meals with me." James tossed aside some particularly gristly beef.

"We could be sharing peace soon enough if Parliament agree to send emissaries to the King." Harbottle sat back. "Do your masters have an appetite for it?"

"Peace negotiations serve a multitude of purposes but peace itself generally isn't one of them," James retorted. "We'll see how much it is truly desired after Lord Essex brings the army back to London."

"Well, I'd best leave before he arrives." Harbottle stood and excused himself. "I'm away to purchase a silver locket for my dear wife, because my sole loyalty lies with her," he said, expressing pity for all men forced to accede to society's demand to take sides.

"There's no choice needed. Parliament is the only guardian of our rights." James couldn't help but feel a little frustrated at men like Harbottle, who tried to float like gulls above the froth-capped waves of allegiance, diving for any opportunity that presented itself.

"Parliament is too greedy for power. One tyranny would simply be substituted for another if they prevailed." Harbottle said.

"*Bonne chance*, Nathaniel," James said, showing him to the door. "Keep your king holed up in Oxford as long as you can."

"Might not be so difficult considering he's employing cripples," Harbottle replied.

"Cripples?"

"Aye, some fellow named Berkeley, shamelessly chasing Rupert around for employment." Harbottle laughed. "Although hobbling might be a more appropriate term."

"How strange."

"Well, I shall write to you when I learn anything new. In the meantime, I'll be in Brentford for a week or two," Harbottle advised him.

"Ah, Pocahontas used to live there." Such jocular chatter furthered the image that James desired to portray. "You know, that savage from the New World," James said, while opening the door and looking out onto the streets of an old, and as yet unchanged world.

A new existence was precisely what James dreamed of, where men could worship freely, roam freely, and be free from oppressive rulers. How could someone as educated and sincere as his childhood friend Francis Berkeley support a tyrant? He recalled Francis's ridiculous assertion that the King had already made numerous concessions, and that Parliament's demand for control of the army, which had always been the monarch's, was taking it too far. But, as a soldier, no wonder his friend thought that.

If it was true that Francis was struggling for employment, he might now see reason and come around to James's way of thinking. They might even work side by side; such a wonderful thought would also mean that Francis wouldn't end up perishing on a bloody field, for that would no longer be his arena of war.

Chapter 9

Rupert of the Rhine's grand banner led the Royalists along the London road and towards Brentford. His coat of arms were quartered; the black and white befitted his clear-cut foresight and the blue and gold his rare splendour. Clustered around the King's nephew were senior officers and regimental commanders, who looked on as he removed his red coat and replaced it with one of grey, more in keeping with the misty shroud that hung over the countryside.

Sir Francis Berkeley was among the Royalist officers, although a gentleman volunteer with no official rank, a fact he'd taken care not to mention to his wife. He had also been careful to remain close to the Prince, who now trained his spyglass upon a house at the crossroads. With celestial shafts of sunlight attempting to penetrate the fog, the dark timber bones of the building looked to hold nothing in their grasp but enemy redcoats.

"Sir Richard Wynne's house," Rupert announced.

"And Denzil Holles's regiment fresh from London if I'm not mistaken," Sir Thomas Salusbury said in his melodious

Welsh voice and eyed the enemy. "My regiment can send them back whence they came."

"Nay, Sir Thomas, I have a greater honour in store for you," the Prince replied and signalled to a trumpeter, who duly raised his instrument and let out a series of vibrant rasps. "Your regiment will have opportunity aplenty to win back what reputation it was deemed to have lost at Edgehill."

"Most gracious of you, Highness," Sir Thomas said, as a sizeable contingent of Royalist cavalry made ready to charge.

* * * * *

Trumpets shrieked at the five hundred cavalrymen of the Prince of Wales's regiment. The breath of anticipation from man and beast seemed to replace what little mist had been burned off by the approach of morning, and now Francis and his colleagues headed into the unknown.

Over his yellowy cow-hide coat with two layers at the sleeves Francis wore back and breastplate armour, which rust treatment had turned a russet colour. His black hat was cocked at one side with a red ribbon and black leather boots unfolded up to his thigh. Yet he was reduced to a shadowy figure of his former self as he entered the haze of a different plane, wondering who would re-emerge and who would vanish forever. Their noisy approach to Wynne's house gave seven hundred Roundheads a rude wake-up call.

Francis took his horse up to a trot and then a canter, adding three hoofbeats per stride to a unified pounding that made England tremble; fifteen hundred such hoofbeats as the whole regiment advanced. Steady and determined, they moved to a gallop and rapidly closed the gap to the crossroads ahead, leaving a wake of flying sods behind, and the rebels with little time to prepare.

The fog, the speed of his beast and the adrenaline pumped memories of Edgehill around his head and numbed Francis as he leaned forward on his down-stuffed saddle. Wynne's house loomed up dripping with enemy redcoats. The Parliamentarians formed a line with one flank covered by the building's imposing presence which was fronted by a line of green hedgerow. Through the hedge pointed the narrow eyes of a hundred muskets, watching the Royalists and waiting for the horsemen to come within two hundred yards range. But the Roundhead's light artillery pieces stole the glory and pumped out shot in golden explosions that flashed like lightning. Their barrels called on the muskets to echo their onslaught.

At three hundred yards, the Royalists did not rein in their horses to make use of their carbine pistols. Instead, following Rupert's orders, Francis and the rest cantered right up to the lines of Roundhead musketeers and lashed out with swords, only levelling their two-and-a-half-foot pistol barrels when at point-blank range. Francis cut down one foe with his basket-hilt sword, sliced another and soon the enemy ranks began to collapse into a jumbled mass, confused and beaten.

Francis continued to yell at both his horse and the rebels, and swipe, slash and stab with his double-edged sword. The purpose of his cries was not merely to push his mount onwards, or break enemy morale, but to keep his mind from lingering too long, for that would bring certain death.

"God damn you!" Francis cried, his swordsmanship abruptly arrested when his three-foot blade became lodged in the butt of a musket held up in self-defence. He struggled with his weapon and came to a standstill, rebels swarming around like bees and cracks of fire snapping at him from every window. An enemy soldier seized Francis's leg to pull him down and, although the man was quickly despatched by another Royalist, it prompted Francis to jettison his weapon and follow the Prince of Wales's regiment, which wheeled off to regroup.

With half the rebels' total force at the house, Sir Thomas Salusbury's Royalists now received their special orders. Rupert sent them south-east to take the battle to Brentford itself and cut off the enemy manning the house from the other half of their number in the town.

Clutching his baton as if it was the honorary law degree conferred upon him by the King, Salusbury drove his men in the direction of Brentford End and its bridge, as if they had a legal right to it all. With four times the enemy's number, Rupert's side-lining of the house made the rebel's position there untenable. He looked set to successfully divide and conquer.

Parliamentarians began to haemorrhage from the house at the crossroads upon this turning point, and their crimson ranks streamed headlong towards Brentford End, as if realising the bloodletting that must occur if they did not get there before Salusbury's Royalists.

Turning his horse towards the town, Francis and the Prince of Wales's regiment pursued the dislodged enemy. They killed any enemy stragglers, passing a number of orchards and cutting down all rebels ripe for the picking. With Brentford End on one side of the Thames, and the old town on the other, linked only by a small bridge, they drove some rebels into the river to drown. The Parliamentarians fortifying the crossing were thrown into disarray by their fleeing colleagues, who clattered up to them and clambered over anything that stood in their way.

Francis had now come as far as he could. Brentford End's narrow streets hampered the horsemen and they waited for the

Royalist infantry to close up to the bottlenecked bridge. It was defended by Lord Brooke's purple-coated Parliamentarians – an apt colour in view of the choked crossing – who fired intermittently when not masked by their retreating comrades.

Salusbury's Royalists, with pike and musket, got straight to the job before them. Seventeen-foot wooden poles levelled at the rebels in a bristling wall of iron tips that aimed to gore faces, necks or armpits. Musketeers prepared their guns. The repetitive ritual of loading began; first pouring powder into the barrels, followed by the musket ball and wadding, ramming it home and then firing it at the enemy. When they withdrew to repeat the process, fresh men replaced any component of this cycle that was killed.

"Sir Francis Berkeley?" A soldier asked, and conveyed the order that Francis take command of a company of pikemen up ahead, the previous incumbent having had his brains blown across his men. Francis dismounted and readily joined his new band, where the relentless onslaught for over an hour finally dislodged the Roundheads from the stone bridge, sending them in retreat up the incline of Brentford's single street.

Chapter 10

Nathaniel Harbottle watched his wife sleeping. Margarita's dark hair and its tight ringlets lay at her shoulders and contrasted against her white smock. He stroked some aside to reveal her olive skin and placed the lightest of kisses upon it before gently rising from the bed. From the small truckle bed on the floor, his son's light snoring prompted Nathaniel's smile. He turned to the backstool and took his folded clothes and carefully left the room.

Once in the little study he pulled on some grey breeches and put on a purple doublet, hooking them both together by means of discreet clips from his waistband. Standing at the window of the house he'd especially rented in Brentford, he pondered the instructions of his Royalist masters for what seemed like an age and then fastened the heather-coloured ribbons at his knees. Today he would take a break from observing the Roundheads' troop movements, but not solely because of the mist smothering the windowpanes. The twelfth of November was his son's tenth birthday, and the boy and his mother had only arrived yesterday.

He fastened up the last of his doublet's twenty wooden buttons, turned back to the room and gave thanks for the contentment of knowing that everyone he held dear was together under the same roof. From the purse on his belt he extracted the key for a chest, opening it with a click-clunk and lifting the lid. There, lying on a thin bed of letters relating to his private business, was a backsword. No ordinary one though. He lifted it out and laid it on the table, brushing one hand over it.

"Father!" Tom said, walking in and embracing him.

"My son." He kissed the boy's sandy curls. "I have something to mark your special milestone," he said, and then retrieved the sword and held it out in both hands, gesturing for the lad to look. "Passed down from my father and his father afore him and goodness knows how many generations prior to that."

"And now you're giving it to me?" Tom called his mother closer, and she came forward with a smile at his joy, if not at the choice of gift, which she'd only agreed to because of its family significance.

"Yes, it's yours now," Harbottle said, although it took more prompting before the boy took the leather-covered wooden scabbard.

"You'll teach me how to use it?" Tom asked, running his fingers over the hilt's floral inlay of silver, then the copper-wire grip, until the pause made him look up.

"All in good time." Harbottle alluded to the constraints of war, but not the most severe constraint of all: his own lack of swordsmanship. What neither wife nor son knew was that, at a similar age, Harbottle's own father had begun tutoring him in the art but the man's lack of patience had left deep wounds of insecurity and a cut to Harbottle's arm, the scar of which he bore to this day. This, along with the memory of being told he had to learn the hard way, had meant that Harbottle did not learn at all.

"Do you fight often?" Tom frequently questioned his father's absences. "Are you an officer?"

"Were it not for me, the King's army would have been ambushed or defeated long ago." By stating what was not even a quarter-truth, Harbottle sought to avoid both of his son's questions. To answer them would have necessitated lie being heaped upon lie when one was bad enough. Besides, how could he even begin to explain that he had helped, as well as hindered, both sides? In the employ of the King, but on the secret payroll of Parliament, he was one of the few men who could answer "both" to the immortal question on everyone's lips: King or Parliament?

"When the war is over you'll teach me how to wield it?" Tom asked.

"Aye, I promise," Harbottle said and held his son's shoulders. "And peace is now being discussed by both sides, so we may not have to wait long."

"Your father is a man of his word." Margarita beckoned her son. "But, pray never become a soldier, you hear?" she insisted.

"Don't you want to take it?" Harbottle asked, as Tom gently placed the blade back onto the table and stepped back.

"I shall save it until I train with it." Tom resolved, and his mother ushered him out of the room.

The rejection cut Harbottle to the quick. From beyond the grave his father's botched tutorage returned to haunt him.

"You are braver than any man I know, Nathaniel, but pray don't raise his hopes unless you have the time." Margarita whispered. "Come downstairs when you're ready to eat."

Harbottle briskly tugged his chest open and snatched one letter from it. He walked to one of the wooden beams that vertically striped the wall and pushed a fake panel. It opened up-over, and he slipped through the gap in the wall and into a tiny priest's hole behind, placing the correspondence in a small casket for safe-keeping. He then passed back into the room and made ready to join them downstairs for warmed ale and oysters though all hunger pangs had vanished. At that moment his wife dashed back into the room and when he went to steal a kiss he noticed her fulsome lips quivering.

"What's the matter?" he asked, and then what sounded like a thunderstorm broke overhead.

Margarita pointed to the window, put a hand to her chest and exclaimed, "They're here."

"Who?"

"Prince Robber," she said, using the Roundhead's name for Rupert, "and his demon dog!"

"What?" Harbottle couldn't comprehend it. "When last I left Rupert, he and the King were at Reading." He darted down the narrow stairs and through the hall to open the door, half expecting to meet the Prince at the threshold, but discovered instead an array of Parliamentarians shoring up the defences in the street. Word that the Royalists had been sighted on the London road came to Harbottle on many a passing lip, prompting Margarita to fetch Tom.

"Whatever shall we do, Nat?" she asked with increasing desperation.

"We'll be fine." Harbottle assured her of his alibi that he was here on King Charles's business. "Though you and Tom need to hide," he said, locking the front door and leading them up the creaking staircase.

"Aren't the King's men our friends?" Tom asked.

"Friend or foe can often get confused in the heat of battle," he warned, with an instruction to bar the door to the priest's hole from the inside.

Margarita took his arm and begged him to stay with them, surreptitiously voicing her worst fears that the Royalists might realise the truth of his dealings with Parliament. He looked into her eyes and promised not to be long, explaining that he had things he must attend to first and headed off to the kitchen to stoke the fire.

Chapter 11

Brentford's single street was one mile in length and extending out from one side of it were wharfs which joined the River Brent. It was via this artery of water that the commerce of London flowed back and forth, which had fed the town's growth and the beating heart of Syon Abbey.

The first positive Francis noted about the street was that there was only one direction in which to attack. It had taken an hour to dislodge the Roundheads from the bridge and, having just crossed, he formed up his company outside Saint Lawrence's church as the retreating enemy scurried up the street. The second benefit of the simple layout sprang from the fact that he could observe the Roundheads' precise movements, and very quickly noted a further defensive position perched on the crest. Some rebels darted into approaching houses giving warning, if any were needed, that the town would be fought over building by building.

"March on!" Francis had his infantry delay no further and, with resolute steps, the Royalists passed The George tavern in their pursuit of the enemy. Weight of numbers would no longer be an advantage in such close and confined quarters, and this would, instead, be a test of endurance.

Francis's unit closed up to a Roundhead company that stood firm like a roadblock, covering their comrades' retreat and horizontally presenting their pikes to point the Royalists back to where they'd come. The Roundheads were supported by musket fire, which made it all the more imperative to see them off as quickly as possible, and Francis's company packed tightly together, shoulder to shoulder, in the face of them. Pausing only to fire off chants and fierce roars, it was as if the Royalists were leashed beasts, struggling to break free and be at their rivals. Sparking adrenaline enveloped Francis, despite being at the rear of his men, and he made all manner of demands that they stick together.

The strength of the compact square of Royalists relied on not having the slightest gap between each body. Those at the rear shoved and pushed those in front with all their might and each line bore down upon the next, and on Francis's command, they advanced with supporting fire from Royalist muskets. The Roundheads pushed forward to meet them, until in a frenzy of weapons both sides hurled themselves at each other. Finally came the clash as levelled pikes locked together and both sides almost merged into one mass.

Push of pikes brought a great tangle of torment from those run through by the deadly tips and anyone trampled underfoot, while the pikes of each side tensed and groaned under the pressure that forced them skyward, as though springing up in resurrection. Dead Royalists remained propped on their feet, pressed up against their colleagues who sweated, bawled and forced themselves forward in an attempt to break the Roundhead formation. Francis cried out as much encouragement to his phalanx as humanly possible in the din, and so the impasse continued for what seemed like an hour of heated claustrophobia. He was blind to anything outside his company and deaf to the world. It was the timely addition of more Royalists from the rear, crashing onto the ranks of their weary mates, that caused Francis and his men to lose footing and begin to advance. They tripped and stumbled across the ground vacated by the Roundheads, who back stepped and then broke into retreat.

After catching his breath, Francis had his men on the move again with instructions to follow the fresh Royalist units, who were making good on this success. They passed Dove's Tavern and the Lion Inn, all of which were empty, but closed up to the narrow street of houses that flashed and smoked like a passageway to hell. Two and three-storeyed timber buildings offered a perfect line of sight to the crest, which was the enemy's strongpoint. Francis's future, like that of every one of his men's, depended upon the soldier to his right and left. Within the last half-mile stretch, a way of life took over that narrowed his world down to this band of eighty comrades.

"Don't leave them in possession of any one of these hovels." The lieutenant-colonel's instruction sent Francis and his men funnelling up the street where every window bristled with gun barrels. Royalist pikemen led the way, with musketeers at their backs, firing at enemy snipers above. As the block edged forward, some infantrymen broke off to clear out the houses they passed to safeguard their rear.

"Cut through the alley and down to the wharf." Francis sent two men to see if this could offer a discreet means to advance and outflank the rebels. As they departed, the back of a nearby musketeer exploded, leaving an exit wound the size of a baby's head, and the soft splatter of warm blood peppered

Francis's face. The blur of death and buzz of war that rang in Francis's head was now compounded by cannon fire from the street's summit and he hesitated.

One of the Royalists retrieve their company standard from its last bearer, who writhed on the ground with his leg a mess of shattered bone. As they hoisted six-foot tall flag once more to the heavens, the painted taffeta slapped in the wind as though challenging Francis to respond.

"Berkeley's to me!" He called for a dozen men and took them to the first house on the right. One kicked in the door and Francis burst inside with pistol brandished, lighting up the defenders in flashes of fire that unleashed his sword-wielding infantrymen. Francis hurried to the perimeter of the room and ran through a sniper whose musket rested on the window ledge. Another Roundhead turned his musket about and swung it, only stopped by a well-aimed pistol ball.

"Clear upstairs." Francis sent a couple of men to the upper floors. "And put as many blades through as many rebels as you can."

He ordered the remaining lads to spread out and check the downstairs rooms, and they headed off like terriers sniffing out rabbits. Francis brandished his sword and followed, but a fiery glow coming from the bottom of one door attracted his full attention.

Chapter 12

The dried-up old door rebounded off its hinges with the full force of Francis's shoulder barge, and beyond its shuddering frame was the noise of cracking kindling. He rushed into the room, expecting to find rebels setting the place afire, but was surprised to see only one person at the end of a long table. The man stood at the same moment that Francis entered and hastily cast a sheet of paper into a hearth, framed by a fire-surround of blue and white Delft tiles, where several other pieces of correspondence blackened and burst into flames.

"Who are you?" Francis levelled his sword and glared down its length.

Declining to answer, the man grasped some remaining letters and attempted to consign them to the fire, although a couple fluttered free from their fate and landed on the stone floor. Before anything more could be done Francis reinforced his order with the tip of his blade.

The smouldering, inky-black secrets of one letter and its red glow burned into Francis's curiosity. The momentary illumination of the writing just prior to its destruction took his attention for barely a second. But this was long enough for the man to grab a pistol from the chair he'd been sitting on.

"Get back!"

"You're from Banbury?" Francis recognised Nathaniel Harbottle.

"You fool." Harbottle's eyes widened. "I'm on the same side as you."

"What are you doing here?" Francis demanded.

"That's Rupert's business, not yours."

"Then why so much panic at his approach?" Francis judged the desperation to destroy these documents to be highly suspicious.

"Who knows what will happen." Harbottle went to burn another. "They cannot fall into the hands of the rebels."

"Leave them." Francis was having none of it.

"Drop your sword!" Harbottle thrust his pistol forward with impatience.

"Shoot me and you'll alert my men."

With Harbottle's instruction and the desperate glare in his eyes, Francis became certain that what was happening here was decidedly not in the King's best interests. The inlaid brass of Harbottle's doglock and its sixteen-inch barrel had Francis reluctantly agree to lay his blade upon the table. But the sword had barely touched the surface before Francis quickly swung it back at his foe, and only narrowly missed.

Harbottle kicked Francis's weaker leg, sending him to the ground in a heap. It was while he was there, looking up at the man, that a memory sprung deep within Francis that hadn't stirred for some time, perhaps even at all since its inception. A troublesome memory accompanied by prickly anxiety, for within this maelstrom emerged the recollection of Harbottle's spectacles and his glowing features on that same field of Edgehill on the night Francis had lain wounded.

"You?" Francis forced himself to get up.

"You're persistent, I'll give you that," Harbottle said.

"From Edgehill ... I always felt I'd seen you before," Francis cried.

"What?" Harbottle's pistol trembled in his grip.

"In the dead of night, meeting with the enemy," Francis recollected.

"After years of watching others, I see I have been spied upon myself." Harbottle paled with realisation. "A secret that will die with you." He squeezed the trigger, only for a flash of yellow and a hiss to taunt him upon its smoking misfire.

Francis seized his sword and sliced at Harbottle's leg; a streak of crimson filled the gash. Before the blood had time to soak into his beeches, Francis punched the man in the face and then in the stomach. Harbottle, winded and with a broken nose, careered backwards into a shelf of pewter plates that jangled across the floor around them.

"You betrayed every man who lost his life that day." Francis caught his breath and grabbed the remaining letters. "Cowardly son of a whore." Clutching them in his other fist he held them up in vindication of all the lost souls of Edgehill who'd been sold out by this self-centred dog. It took all of his restraint not to skewer Harbottle on the end of his sword that instant.

"I'm no such thing." Harbottle panted, claiming that swimming against the popular tide took much more courage. "My family's future will not be dictated by attachment to one of two corrupt factions."

"Perhaps you'll soon come to realise the futility of your two-faced strategy."

"Your battlefield memories are little more than the ramblings of a lunatic," Harbottle replied.

"I suspect these letters contain more than mere ramblings." Francis warned that Harbottle would soon be swinging from a noose. "A constricted throat will put an end to your betrayal of the King."

With the appearance of his subordinates, revealing that the street was rapidly being cleared of rebels, Francis's prediction took a step closer to reality. Every passing day of peace negotiations had seen royal dominance loosened bit by bit, because every fresh day brought Parliament's field army closer to London in its bid to defend the city. Brentford's fall evened out the balance of power, but what remained to be seen was whether Francis could tip the scales against Harbottle and prove the man's duplicity.

Chapter 13

"We have visitors." Colonel John Hampden pointed across the fields of Turnham Green and at the King's army of Cavaliers.

"And truly half our size, if my eyes don't deceive me," Lord Essex said, referring to reports he'd received that the enemy numbered only twelve thousand.

"Praise God we beat them to the capital," Hampden replied and glanced at his regiment of greencoats.

"Draw the army into battle formation." Essex's features remained as grey as his hair. "This encounter will be pivotal to Parliament's survival."

"Do you think they'll attack?"

"You've heard how Rupert burnt Brentford to a cinder?" Essex asked with a frown. "We can't take any chances with London."

"The King stands no chance when we have the capital at our backs supplying us." Hampden pointed a thumb over his shoulder.

"London is empty, it seems." With a sniff, Essex eyed the common folk who had come out here in droves. "They eat and drink as if they're making ready to watch a play."

"It can do no harm. Perhaps their presence demonstrates we have the populace on our side," Hampden suggested.

"Perhaps, but civilians only ever get in the way." Essex was in no mood to be swayed. "Send them back to the city and back to work, and have our own provisions distributed to the troops." Essex's orange sash billowed around him in the wind. "Let them fill their bellies."

"We shall soon see if the King has an appetite for battle," Hampden's small, round eyes looked as perceptive and calm as ever they did. "If he does not, we must drive his army from this field, otherwise our negotiating hand will be compromised."

"Our hand in these peace negotiations is safe as long as we simply prevent the enemy getting anywhere near London." Essex took out his telescope. "No need to battle for the sake of it."

Across the one hundred acres of open land, Essex could see everything. He looked east towards Stamford Brook, and then north to the hedges that led to Acton and Chiswick Commons, where he decided to form up his army near Saint Nicholas's church. To the west, the smoke of Brentford's last breath spiralled as a warning of what would happen to London should the Royalists get past him.

"The hedges are full of enemy snipers," Philip Skippon said, jabbing a pointed finger northwards. "By your leave, I'll take my boys and drive them out."

"Agreed, take your trained bands and see them off," Essex replied, wishing to safeguard his position. He accompanied Skippon back to the eight-thousand-strong London regiments, watching closely as the forty-two-year-old commander explained their task with a dynamism that would have made all the difference had the man been present at Edgehill.

Calling first on the courage of the London Trained Bands, Skippon implored his boys to heartily pray and fight together. "I will run the same hazards and fortunes with you." He bid them remember that their cause was the defence of themselves, their wives and their children. "Come my honest, brave boys, pray heartily, fight heartily and God will bless us," he declared, riding past and sealing his promise to be at one with them.

"In a single sentence he has summed up everything the common man fights for." Even Essex felt imbued with a desire to grapple with the enemy.

"He's written a manual full of inspirational advice for his soldiers," Hampden ventured his opinion that there were a number of Essex's officers that should read it.

"I'll offer him a command in my army before the day's out." Despite not possessing the ability to convert his deep-seated emotions into momentous words, Lord General Essex rode from one wing to the other, inspiring awe by his mere presence. On his great black horse of sixteen hands, he rode first to the left wing and along the front line, where the cavalry cheered and huzzahs spread like wildfire. Passing onto the centre and his infantry, he was welcomed by cries for "Old Robin" and heartened by the army's determined stance, such as the bed cords he observed, wrapped around waists as spare match cords for muskets. Finally, with his great orange sash slapping his back like the hand of his proud father, he swept onto the right wing, also made up of cavalry, and met with his Lieutenant General of horse.

"They are in good cheer," Balfour noted, watching as the Londoners peppered the hedges with shot and caused the Royalists lining them to take flight.

"With good cause." Essex observed how the lines of his army stretched much farther than the enemy's. "We could outflank them in one deathly embrace."

"Then might I suggest we make good our advantage?" Colonel Hampden asked, barely taking his eyes off the King's standard. "My regiments could secure the high ground to the north."

"Let our troops confine themselves to attacking their meat, cheese and beer." Essex shook his head. "Blocking the King's route to the capital will weaken his position, whereas gambling upon a battle risks all the cards Parliament holds," he reiterated, though didn't verbalise his concern about the bulk of his army being merely raw recruits.

"Remember Boudica." Sir John Meyrick, with a body shaped like a pear and cheeks as rosy, judged weight of numbers an unsafe deciding factor. "Eighty thousand against ten thousand Romans," he said. Having first fought alongside Lord Essex twenty years ago in Holland, he well knew the man's leanings. "I say let them initiate battle, for it is they who need to get past us."

"With the greatest respect, we've cleared their snipers, so we should make good our advantage with a full assault." Hampden put forward that to hesitate would simply erode the army's morale. "All of Christendom will assume we refused to engage the enemy out of fear."

"A fair point," Essex said, holding fast to his own opinion, but appreciating the need for a show of force.

Accepting Hampden's suggestion to seize the high ground, Essex sent the colonel back to his greencoats, who, with eager roars, set off in good formation to a thunderous drum beat. They emerged from the centre of the Parliamentarian army and headed northwards across the field, ever closer to Acton Common. The resulting gap left in his army's line troubled Essex even before Meyrick pointed out the dangers of their force being split in two by a well-timed enemy charge.

"Rupert will pull your army apart as easily as an old woman unpicks her knitting." Meyrick nodded at the shadowy masses of the Royalist cavalry which began to edge forward before Hampden's men had covered one hundred yards. "He won't pass up such a golden opportunity."

"Instruct Hampden to return." Essex rescinded his order in the face of this warning and cursed his earlier self-doubt. While the messenger chased after Hampden, the strains of a trumpet fanfare drifted across the morning air and spurred hundreds of Prince Rupert's cavalrymen onwards. Like a great arm, they darted forward from the King's force and extended towards Essex's army, ready to punch a hole through them.

"You see my concerns about risking everything," Essex said, turning to his officers.

Yet Rupert's cavalry fist drew up short of Hampden's troops. They contented themselves with firing pistols and then wheeling about to return to their original positions. It was now the turn of their artillery, which spat cannonballs in a provocative gesture that proved the King's aim of luring the Parliamentarians onto the offensive. Essex quickly made this point to the newly returned John Hampden.

"We've shown them our innate weakness," Hampden declared in frustration.

"We have avoided their trap, more like!" Essex would not accept any debate, not least because Rupert was off again, spilling across the field. The Lord General's eye traced the Royalist's path, which led straight to the raw and untested men of the London Trained Bands. "They just need to hold their nerves," he muttered.

"Present arms, damn you!" Meyrick watched the London auxiliaries until they lowered their pikes at the oncoming enemy.

"Send an officer to instruct all men to stand firm on pain of death," Essex ordered, wiping his furrowed brow. "Let no man move unless they have my express permission."

Soon, none of Essex's force had any reason to move when Rupert's cavalry reached the end of their leash, turned about and headed back to their master, leaving Essex to bitterly denounce such a game. But he knew it to be a most dangerous game indeed, for the King's nephew was taunting his army, hoping they would turn tail, or impetuously attack, and either way leave vulnerable holes in their lines.

"You were right to be wary of them, Your Excellency." Meyrick smiled and leaned in close.

In the fading afternoon light, evening began to draw in and the King's entire front line finally began to ripple with movement due to a general withdrawal from Turnham Green, which saw the soldiers vanish like apparitions. Exorcised of the demons before them, Essex's men cheered, shouted insults, sang psalms and roared with an equal measure of defiance and jubilation. Amidst this relief, a cavalryman approached the Lord General to inform him of only twenty-five Parliamentarian deaths.

"Gentlemen, we should remember this as the day we saved the greatest city in the world," Essex announced triumphantly, whilst happily overlooking Constantinople and Paris as being no match whatsoever.

Chapter 14

Francis stood atop the tower of Saint Lawrence's church, looking out over Brentford and towards Turnham Green. The cool breeze sharpened his wits and conveyed the distant noise of battle. It kept him in constant contact with events two miles away that were crucial if he was to succeed in taking back his son and his home. The tower also afforded him a live plan of the town, better even than Moses Glover's recent map of the town.

As temporary governor, he'd received a stream of reports here, ranging from the state of the rebel prisoners, the cache of captured arms and ammunition, behaviour of the townsfolk and last, but by no means least, the latest regarding Nathaniel Harbottle's stubborn refusal to talk.

"We'll be in London by morrow, Jack," he told his deputy.

"Aye, God willing," Jack Mandeville replied.

"I thought I issued an order that the wounded be taken to the marketplace?" Francis stood, laid his hands upon the Kentish ragstone and took stock of the turmoil in the street below.

"We're sorely stretched, sir."

"I need two men to ride out to the London road and keep an eye on comings and goings," Francis commanded, and an officer was dispatched to see to it.

"Governor, sir." A sergeant saluted and picked his way across the parapet like a wary sparrow. "You enquired about civilian casualties; a total of seven perished," he said, looking back to the door and moving on to news of a woman they had plucked from a priest's hole. Following his signal, a soldier brought her closer, although she fought his grasp.

"Get your hands off me!" She brushed hair from her face. "I will not have any of you manhandle me ..."

"She refuses to reveal any details about herself." The sergeant interrupted her. "Maybe she's a Catholic, but what's certain is that she has a filthy temper."

"What do you expect?" She demanded to know the whereabouts of her son.

"Good work discovering her, Sergeant," Francis said and, turning to the woman, introduced himself. "Now, who are you, madam?"

"Where is my son?"

"Do you know where her child is?" Francis asked the sergeant. Finding that the boy was still held in the priest's hole, he ordered mother and son to be reunited. "Now, madam, your name?"

"Margarita." She sang better to his tune.

"I can understand my men's suspicion if you will not explain yourself. Now, your surname, if you please." Francis persisted.

"Johnson. A Protestant, and a loyal subject of His Majesty."

"Why were you hiding?" Francis had so far found the woman to be sane and no apparent threat.

"I was hiding from the beasts that are your men," she cried. "Do you condone them doing this?" She opened her arms to show off streaks of dried blood that circumvented one of them.

"She tried to slit one of our lads' throat with a child's sword. We simply restrained her." The sergeant's sunken eyes narrowed. "We also found this in a small casket," he explained and produced a letter which had been refolded numerous times.

As he unfolded and straightened out the parchment, Francis was met with writing where occasional words had been replaced by a series of numbers. "In which place did you say you found her?" he asked.

"The house next to the Boars Head Inn."

"From now on you will be treated with due respect as long as you are honest with me, madam," Francis said, realising that the building in which she had been hidden was the one where he'd discovered Harbottle.

"I thank you, sir," she replied with a polite nod.

Francis, almost certain of his hunch, held out his hand and said, "Now, your locket, if you please."

"What? I took you to be a gentleman."

"Merely a wish to look at it," he replied and watched as she lifted the pendant from her neck but kept it tightly within her grip.

"I place my life and my trust in you." She opened her fist reluctantly.

Francis picked it up and examined the silver casing, where the inscribed letters M and N flourished within engraved, vibrant flowers. He prised the clasp open with his thumb and a satisfying click revealed a miniature portrait of Nathaniel Harbottle. The artist had perfectly captured the man's black curls and large, expressive eyes which seemed to plead for her safety. She was clearly the man's wife; a fact which necessitated not just the imprisonment of Harbottle's physical being, but also his image, by closing the door of the tiny silver cell and pressing the front.

"Madam Harbottle," he said whilst looking her in the eye. "I will keep this and return it to you in a few days."

After a pause, Margarita nodded with an understanding of the predicament, in which she, her husband and son were beholden to Francis. She said nothing to deny his assertion of her identity, nor made a scene and left quietly, thankful that soon she would have her son by her side. Not long afterwards Francis left to find the captain who he had set to work in decoding the documents he had seized from Harbottle's clutches.

"I've deciphered the most common characters, so it should just be a matter of time now," the captain said.

"Take this one too, for I suspect it might be of more importance given the lengths taken to hide it." Francis handed over the parchment. "I need an update this evening." He wished to play as full a part as possible in protecting the King's cause from danger, and he instructed Jack to assemble a court in which he would question Harbottle. As darkness fell, Francis was determined to expose the truth, because without it he would never be able to fathom out the level of treachery afoot.

* * * * *

Two houses were burned down during the battle for Brentford. As the last wisps of smoke evaporated into the approaching November evening, and blackened timbers cracked against its ever colder onset, the church window flickered like a beacon. The candles in the aisle laid bare a world of stark contrasts. The bible laid on a table in front of Francis was darkened with age, yet its gold-leaf lettering sparkled as brightly as the day it was applied. The light also fell into the severe creases of Francis's brow, highlighting his unrelenting opinion of the soldier now before the court accused of stealing from the church after their victory.

"The sights of battle turned my mind," the soldier pleaded, barely looking up.

"God preserved you in the fighting and you repaid him thus?" Francis asked. "The King has decreed that such a crime should be punished by death."

"I beg you, spare me for the sake of my wife and five children."

"In view of your confession, you'll not hang," Francis replied, instead sentencing him to ride the wooden horse with muskets tied to his feet.

"God bless ye, sir."

As a clerk entered the punishment into a ledger, the soldier had most likely never thought he'd be relieved at the prospect of being perched on top of a right-angled joint of wood.

Now it was Harbottle's turn. He stepped forward with his hands tied behind his back and paused to examine the people present. His thick, black hair and inquisitive eyes attracted the attention of all while the roles and responsibilities of the court were read out in a monotone voice.

"Governor, eh?" Harbottle said slowly. "Was that the only position left for a physically defective officer?"

"Still as cock-sure as ever, I see." Francis pulled at the ribbons that bound the letters he'd taken and hoped to loosen the man's tongue just as effectively.

"Wait until Rupert hears about the fool who tried a fellow Royalist for carrying out orders," Harbottle said with an unrelenting expression.

"I'm trying a man who has no loyalty to anyone but himself," Francis replied without taking his eyes from what he was reading.

"I need not answer to someone whose authority here is but temporary," Harbottle judged.

"These de-coded letters have already answered for you." Francis scanned the translation underneath the numerical code.

62 40 11 23 7 is still away at
- - A R - E -
12 17 47 12 7 13 with his boys
O - - O R -

Francis re-read the words that his man had attempted to decipher, although they were proving difficult, judging by the amount of dashes, and he clearly needed more time. Time which Francis did not have for Harbottle was correct about his tenure in Brentford. What struck him was that one of the sets of numbers could spell out "Oxford".

Pray keep me informed of events near you and
do all you can to delay 124

"What, or who, does one hundred and twenty-four refer to?" Francis held the letter up.

"Perhaps the recipient's age?" Harbottle suggested.

"Who wrote these letters and why are they coded?"

"Merely family correspondence." Harbottle didn't relax his fixed stare.

"You were destroying them in panic lest they fall into the wrong hands," Francis said, raising his voice and pointing at the accused.

"A fabrication," Harbottle replied calmly. "Your men looted my belongings and now you're looking for a way to excuse their actions."

"You passed secrets to the enemy on the night of the battle of Edgehill!" Francis found this unforgivable.

"Another fabrication," Harbottle replied with a demand to see Prince Rupert. "I'll see to it that you never hold a commission again. I'm here on the Prince's business and you have put that in jeopardy."

"You accept that these letters were in your possession?"

"Aye, private correspondence regarding finances." Harbottle's mouth and his thin moustache seemed on the verge of a smile.

Francis leaned over the table to look him straight in the eye. "Of which you have no worry, being in the pay of both sides."

"I will not answer such slanders."

"My men discovered something very interesting secreted away in your lodgings." Francis waited for a few crucial seconds and then revealed the third letter. "Do you usually hide family correspondence in priest's holes?"

"I've never heard such nonsense," Harbottle frowned.

"Am I to resort to asking your wife for the truth?" Francis asked.

"My wife?" Harbottle's large eyes widened.

"Aye, you heard me. Margarita seems an honest woman."

"What has she got to do with this ridiculous affair?" Harbottle demanded.

"Quite a lot, considering she lingers in a dank cell at this very moment with claims of rape upon her lips." Francis sat back, desperately hoping that this lie would break the man's will.

"It's beneath even you to fabricate something so utterly abominable." Harbottle's voice was deep, his nostrils flaring as he struggled with the rope binding his wrists.

"Unfortunately, it's the truth," Francis said. "And, although you don't normally place much importance on that, for once you must face it."

"Be a man." Harbottle urged with increasing desperation. "Don't bring my wife into your ridiculous game."

"It's too late," Francis replied with a glare. "You did that the moment you betrayed the first of the King's secrets. We found her in a priest's hole with your son, though nine months from now he may have a half-sibling."

"Enough, I say!"

"Your treason has caught up with you," Francis insisted.

"I will kill any who has laid a finger upon her."

"Both are safe as my prisoners." Francis held up one hand. "But as you so rightly point out, I could be relieved of my post at any moment. Therefore, you would do well to deal with me before it is too late."

"Trickery!" Harbottle insisted.

"We'll see." Francis produced the silver locket. "Do you think this a trick of the eye?" He allowed the chain to dangle though his fingers.

"Margarita." Harbottle squeezed his eyes closed and gripped his fists until his knuckles whitened and his shoulders hunched. "I never imagined that anyone could ever be so callous as you."

To Francis's warning that he would die a traitor, Harbottle's face screwed up with hatred. After hesitating, he begged for the safety of his wife and child and watched intently as Francis laid the locket on the table and arranged the chain with precision.

"Tell me about these letters and you can watch them walk free," Francis wished for nothing more than to release the woman and child.

"I cannot trust the word of a man like you," Harbottle replied.

"Then you shall have it in writing." Francis took up a quill, signed a document for the release of Margarita Harbottle and her son and pushed it in front of the prisoner. Harbottle had barely read every word when Francis set upon him again with demands for the identity of number one hundred-and-twenty-four.

"I have your word?" Harbottle sighed and took the paper. "James Jackson. He is a contact of mine."

"James Jackson?" Francis baulked at the unlikely coincidence.

"That's what I said." Harbottle tightly held the paper.

"He's your master?" Francis was left wondering if it could be the same James Jackson he'd known since childhood. He missed Harbottle's reply as he read over the letter again and it then dawned upon Francis that the handwriting bore all the hallmarks of being his friend's.

"Sir Francis?" Jack broke the tense silence.

"A moment." Francis wished to consider the Pandora's Box that was opening and how, with one simple name, the tables had turned. Unknowingly for Harbottle, but turned so much that through association, Francis himself had now become linked to this network of treason. Allowing this to continue would place his friend James in jeopardy, but just as equally, terminating the matter to save him would be a betrayal of the King's cause; something Francis had initiated this trial to prevent.

"Prince Rupert commands this garrison to withdraw forthwith and join the main field army!" An officer and some men stepped into the church and put paid to all proceedings.

"Withdraw? We are not masters of London?" Francis introduced himself.

"I'm afraid not, Governor," the man replied, explaining that tomorrow they were to march for Reading.

Tomorrow's journey would be very long indeed. The road would lead Francis all the way back to the house in Oxford – not his home – and leave his son farther away than ever. Anne's hopes would be dashed. Yet, in the corner of Francis's mind, a fuse lit that led directly to his conscience and it would fizz over the truth about Harbottle and James.

Chapter 15

"Bring the children," Ned Hungerford commanded his wife and opened the family bible to turn to a preselected page. Lucy, however, did not move. Instead, her shadow remained cast across the table that he had made with his own hands, not long after his awakening to God's love.

"Husband, what ails thee?" she asked.

"This conflict betwixt King and Parliament." The visit of an army recruitment officer to Kings Lynn had unnerved Ned. "I fear it will swallow us all." He had thanked the Lord that, fortuitously, he'd been toiling in the fields at the time.

"That's something for the citizens of London to worry about." She shunned the war out of a desire to protect her family.

"Wife, you speak as though you are head of this house and like those women I hear chattering at market," he replied, having had enough of their views about all men who hadn't yet danced to the army's drumbeat.

"I meant no offence." Lucy kneeled beside him. "But merely wish to point out that we are far removed here."

"Your brother isn't, though, which is why we have his son." Ned frowned at the noise of their nephew crying again. One of Henry Berkeley's piercing cries when he greedily demanded milk, and far too much of it, leading him to vomit and then wail once more for his own way.

"Francis has always been the soldiering type," Lucy said, stopping short of further defending her brother when Ned raised an eyebrow.

"Rise up and fetch our boys." One of Ned's hands trembled with frustration above the linen coif that covered her black locks. Yet still his nephew's shrieks filled his ears even when Lucy went to attend to the boy. The bible's bold, black letters seemed to rebound off the page in their revulsion of the infant's gluttony and Ned realised his chance to cure the child and eliminate the qualities in him that were offensive to the good Lord. Henry had perhaps ended up here for that very purpose, and Ned could prove his love of the Almighty by infusing the boy with the same devotion.

"Father." The appearance of his two sons wearing pious expressions, suggested they had spent the last few hours studying the question he had posed them. The youngest angelically raised his eyebrows.

"Have you both proven to the Lord that you have kept the Sabbath for his glory?" Ned asked.

"Yes, sir."

"Then recite the words I had you learn," he instructed, raising his voice over the screams of his nephew, which finally began to abate.

"Christ suffered for us, leaving an example that we should follow." John stood straight with hands behind his back, copying the posture of his father he'd observed in church.

"Excellent, now tell me how you have both suffered in your short lives," Ned asked with a nod.

"The time when the bigger boys tried to drown a cat and, because I protested, they beat me with sticks." John looked at his father's serious expression for signs of approval. "Yet I got about my work in the house without complaint, for Jesus suffered more than that for me."

"And God healed your wounds because of your good grace and prayers." Ned reminded the boy that cherishing the Almighty would bring salvation.

"I have one about my hand ..." The youngest began, only for his older brother to interrupt.

"No, don't use that one, Brother."

"I will use it if I like, for 'tis my hurt to talk about." Isaac's lip pushed up in stubborn disregard. "When I hid behind the cow to jump out and scare mother it stood all over my fingers ..."

"Enough!" Ned snapped. "I warned you to think hard about this, and instead you give a flippant example of idleness. Your mother is busy and hardworking while you, boy, simply act the fool."

"But, Father, I think God laughs sometimes, too." Isaac trembled.

"How dare thee!" Ned leapt to his feet and cracked the boy around the head. "You shall never talk about our Creator in so blasphemous a way again." He watched the lad flee, cover his head, and go to ground under the table. Such behaviour could not be allowed to re-occur, prompting Ned to reach for his little whip.

"I am sure he meant nothing by it, Father," John stepped forward.

"Do not taint yourself by excusing what rolls from this wicked boy's tongue." Ned commanded Isaac to come out.

"Those who want to love life and see good days should keep their tongue from speaking evil and their lips from lies."

"Boys, leave us." Lucy entered to usher them from the room and it was only Henry and his frowning face that distracted Ned. Every crease represented the petulance that streaked the child's character and, with renewed crying, his face turned pink and then almost crimson. His wide-open mouth revealed a tiny, trembling tongue that formed the fuse of a wail that exploded right in Ned's face.

"You know why your brother has ended up involved in this war?" Ned asked.

"I know nothing of his reasons," Lucy replied, insinuating that neither did Ned.

"Greed and the love of material wealth, which is why the Lord hath directed his child to be removed from him," Ned said.

"Please, Husband, my brother is not some evil sinner."

Ned stared hard at Henry and said: "He stretched out his hand and touched him and said unto him, be clean." The boy interrupted his guardian making the sign of the cross by seizing one finger.

"He's not even one-year-old," Lucy reminded him, after yet another Sunday had passed by in nothing but devout worship.

"The best age to cleanse him from sin." Ned glared at the bairn, whose whinging seemed like a plea from his tormented soul. A soul which had become tarnished like an old cooking pot and needed scouring of all residue.

"Ned, sometimes I fear you think more of the Lord than your family," Lucy said.

"On the contrary, I think constantly of my family's salvation and how we can earn our place at His side," Ned replied.

"The child cannot understand."

"His face is red with petulance. Can't you see?" Ned had to turn away.

"Can we really pass judgement on a baby?" Lucy asked.

"God judges us all."

Lucy took his hand between hers and rubbed the tough skin as if she was trying to rekindle the warmth that had burned low between them. The same love that had impelled him to elope with her all those years ago in spite of her overbearing father.

"Marrying you meant that my Father disowned me, Ned, yet your love was worth that loss. And when Mother died not long afterwards, it was you who pulled me through." She laid the tip of her little finger over a half-healed cut on his hand and expressed her wish that his tormented mind be released from such religious shackles.

"If I am tormented, then it is His will." He examined the bible once more. "Don't you feel God's bounty, Lucy?"

Ned noticed Lucy's eyes well up and goosebumps of sorrow appeared on her arms. She was not usually the emotional type, but when she verbalised her wish to once more feel the bounty of Ned's love, he knew not what to say. And before he could respond, she left the room.

"O' Lord, wilt thou not help your blind disciple see the way?" A deep breath had barely fallen from Ned's lips before an array of sunbeams penetrated the small window, which was open to the elements. Shafts of light invaded the house like a multitude of pikestaffs to defeat all his doubt. Ned dropped to his knees, face down in the scattered straw, and basked in the Lord's glory, not daring to look up again for several minutes. When he did, the light had faded, but his sense of rejuvenation would remain for a long time to come, as if the Creator himself had peered into his tiny home to shower him with love.

"Let me have your command in the passage I happen to alight upon," he said, inserting one of his thin fingers into the bible at a random point and opening it, only for his excited eyes to scan the writing. "Tell me why you singled me out."

Put on God's armour so that you can make a stand against the tricks of the devil. We aren't fighting against human enemies but against rulers, authorities, forces of cosmic darkness and spiritual powers of evil in the heavens.

He read the words again, and then a third time, barely breathing, for they held the answer for which he'd been searching. How his heart burst with happiness at such a clear sign that the Almighty still had faith in him, when others did not.

Therefore, pick up the armour of God so that you can stand your ground on the evil day.

"Lucy, come quickly! The Lord of Hosts hath given me his command." Ned fell into hysterical laughter.

"What's going on?" She questioned the outburst.

"Divine guidance." He assured her with both hands extended into the air and recounted the direction to take up arms against the King. She repeated his words and rested one hand on her chest, unable to comprehend what this would mean. "Listen," he said, poring over the passage once more. "Stand with the belt of justice as your breastplate and put shoes on your feet so that you are ready to spread the good news of peace."

"But doesn't that speak of peace?" Lucy asked.

"You do not understand. This is an instruction; a call to arms." He gave a dismissive shake of his head and continued to the next line. "Above all, carry the shield of faith so that you can extinguish the flaming arrows of the evil one."

"Perhaps I don't understand, Ned."

"That refers to only one man, he who wages war against the people of this nation," Ned said, and then tears came to his eyes.

"You have always been so averse to bloodshed and war." Lucy's protests were met with more scripture.

Take the helmet of salvation and the sword of the Spirit, which is God's word.

Ned's ecstasy equalled Lucy's complete sense of desolation, as if he had drained all her positivity and filled it with worry. Lucy expressed her concern and asked what would become of their family, and her brother's, if they were on opposite sides of this conflict. Ned did not answer and did not hear, nor would his answer have been very positive even if he had. Henry's renewed tears made Lucy sigh. The boy's presence would be the first battle stemming from Ned's newfound allegiance, which forged from the dying rays of a sunset, brought an end to this chapter in their lives.

Chapter 16

The damned saltpetre men had the street in uproar. But wasn't the whole realm in the same state and this simply indicative of it? Complaints abounded at the way they had dug up soil floors in search of compressed bird dung or urine-soaked earth, leaving their spoil heaps piled all over the place like giant molehills. The uproar brought about by the war was the very topic that Francis and Anne had taken a stroll to discuss in the hope that fresh air would aid clearer thought about their future, and that of their son's.

"We have the authority," the saltpetre men insisted.

"You've already been here yesterday," one householder replied.

"We'll be back tomorrow if you don't shut up!"

"Go dig in the King's lodgings and see if he approves."

People milled around the wooden cart and the great, stinking mound that topped it. It smelled so bad that Francis considered there to be no need to use it to manufacture any gunpowder, for one waft of its raw state would floor an entire army. The saltpetre men brandished their shovels and stormed the next property, warning that resistance would lead to prosecution. Francis and Anne took the opportunity to side-step the commotion and head into a narrow alley off Holywell Street. Yet the water trickling the length of this lane was far from holy, with a man adding to the flow right now, and the pair quickly made for the chink of light at the other end and stepped out onto a square which teemed with people.

"A travelling troop of players?" Anne avoided the other option.

"Afraid not." Francis omitted mention of the gallows that poked above the heads of those in front, its rope swaying from the breeze in rehearsal of its coming purpose. Like Anne, he was in little mood to see this and they took every opportunity to manoeuvre their way through the excitable and belligerent citizens of Oxford.

A father lifted his young son onto his shoulders. Another group climbed hastily erected platforms, creating a gap that allowed Francis and Anne some quick movement. Others had come prepared with food, adding their own merry chants to the growing noise that reached its zenith upon the arrival of the accused. First came a clatter of applause from the metal-clad wheels of the cart across the cobbles, and then the prisoner was taken, shackled at the wrists, up the steps and onto the wooden scaffold for all to see.

The scaffold seemed to float amongst this sea of people with the gallows like a single mast. This was the prisoner's final destination and he looked out across those baying for his blood, while a chaplain in a black hat stood ready to navigate his soul to the next world.

"Give your confession of sin." The clergyman's features were paler than his white robe and as severe as the bible he now pointed.

"Harbottle?" Francis stopped dead and, still clasping Anne's hand, drew her close.

"God will find me innocent of any crime," Harbottle repeated after being jeered. "He judges us all." He looked around the crowd, causing Francis to turn away.

Nathaniel Harbottle appeared wasted, only half the man he had been when facing Francis in Brentford. Every facial feature that should have been plump or rounded was now sunken or in shadow. Even his swarthy complexion had been sucked from him and his thick, black curls hung limply across hunched shoulders. But despite the prisoner's appearance, Francis shivered with apprehension beneath his finery.

Harbottle slowly kneeled in prayer. His mere presence dug into Francis's deepest and most personal thoughts. All of the fear, guilt and anxiety accumulated during this conflict, suppressed within him out of necessity, were now raked up. As with the saltpetre men they had left behind, Harbottle scraped, tore at and prodded every level of Francis's demons.

"Almighty God, Father of our Lord Jesus Christ, maker of all things and judge of all men," the clergyman said, and raised his hand into the air. "We acknowledge and bewail this man's sins."

Might they know I still have his letter? In his now unravelling state, Francis regretted not burning the one he'd retained on leaving Brentford.

"I have done nothing but serve both the King and his Parliament." Harbottle now seemed desperate to be heard and understood.

"You have been tried and convicted of the foul villainy of treason." The officer of the guard conjured up the crowd's chanting to drown Harbottle out.

A desire to spare his friend James's name from being brought into the trial had been Francis's reasoning for withholding the letter of evidence, sparing not only James, but also Francis's personal association with him from coming to light. Admittedly, Harbottle's confident assertion that he could talk his way out of it all had convinced Francis, but the one thing neither man had reckoned with were the gentle persuasions of the rack and what it could extract from anyone. Clearly some truths had been tugged out of Harbottle. Fear of what the Royalists now knew, or thought they knew, was what struck Francis.

"Let us acknowledge the manifold wickedness that this traitor has most grievously committed by thought, word and deed against the King's majesty." The rousing sermon puffed the preacher's plump cheeks.

"Like the King, I fought to free Parliament from the clutches of a few controlling men. And like Parliament, I fought to free the King from evil counsellors ..." Nathaniel looked around as if hoping that someone, somewhere, would record these last words if only for the sake of his son.

Francis craned his neck above the rippled folds of a bald man's head, while Anne tugged her fur stole about her shoulders.

"Have mercy upon him, most merciful Father, for thy son, our Lord Jesus Christ's sake." The prayer continued as Harbottle climbed a small ladder and the executioner went to put a bag over his head. But Harbottle refused to be covered, desiring to look his accusers in the eye.

"Sometimes I wonder whether Henry is actually better off staying in the countryside with your sister," Anne said to Francis in view of this horrific sight.

"Grant that we may all avoid his treason and hereafter serve and please thee in newness of life, through Jesus Christ our Lord, Amen," the preacher said.

The wintery sun shone from behind the clouds to momentarily blind everyone and leave the scaffold silhouetted, as if God too was withholding favour from the spy. Francis felt the looming black scaffold, stamped upon the sky, was drawing him closer.

"Tis a mercy that His Majesty has not had him drawn and quartered." One man remarked, judging Harbottle entirely worthy of having his entrails pulled out of his belly before his own eyes.

God have mercy upon his soul. Francis's thoughts went to Margarita and young Thomas, whose lives would never re-emerge from the shadow that was about to be cast over them. The executioner, whose black hood gave him an ethereal appearance, slipped the noose around Harbottle's neck and adjusted it ready for its deathly embrace. A drumbeat had only just begun, and the executioner barely gone to take hold of the sides of the ladder, when the condemned man suddenly leaped off.

As Harbottle dropped, the crowd's shocked gasps momentarily killed all heckling and he seized back control of the last, crucial moment of his life. His body sank backwards. The rope tightened about his neck and, running rapidly out of length, jerked him like a puppet, with a strained groan as the wooden frame took his weight.

"He's done it himself!" An old hag screeched that Harbottle had cheated them all in the same way he'd cheated the King.

"Hold him!" The hangman hurried over, trying to lift Harbottle by the legs, and save him for a second attempt, in which he could succumb at the designated moment, by the hands of justice.

"Jesus Christ!" Francis grimaced at Harbottle's courage and the horror of the spectacle, which showed just how expendable they all were for the greater good. Also expendable was the crowd's natural compassion and emotion, both of which were quite easily dispensed with by those who glared at the prisoner during the confusion, and the woman who was now hurriedly mounting the scaffold. As Harbottle jerked and convulsed, she grabbed his feet and tugged with all her might. The hangman held back, considering it too late, or simply respecting the last wishes of the widow-in-waiting. She dropped to her knees, screaming and wailing like a banshee, pulling on his legs, clasping his breeches and calling out her love for him. Two soldiers closed in, but by then she had at least made sure that her husband's suffering and indignity would not be strung out. For her effort she was rewarded with a musket butt to the head, sending her to the planking in a heap, just below the intermittent writhing of her husband's feet.

The people at the front of the multitude pressed forward waving fists or shouting threats, the very sight of which led to the clergyman's hasty withdrawal from the scene. Having stirred up the crowd into such a frenzy, he was unwilling to put his trust in the Lord's protection. The hangman also departed because the prisoner would be dead in less than ten minutes anyway.

"The poor, poor man." Anne shook her head.

Francis could acknowledge his own disgust with no more than a grunt as he considered how easily his own life might also be squeezed out at the end of a knotted rope.

"Dancing a fair jig, eh?" A man nodded his head at the prisoner and then turned to Francis. "Now, how about some oysters, sir? Twelve pence a peck and ideal to enjoy the ending," he asked, putting down his wooden cart and wiping his hands on his dirty apron.

"I've no appetite." Francis placed a protective arm around Anne and headed home, not able to stomach the reality of his own part in bringing about this traumatic scene. To shoot someone on the field of battle, in the heat of the moment, was one thing, but this was entirely another. What he had witnessed filled him with misgiving, which would not die with Harbottle, and he resolved to immediately hand in the letter he'd kept.

Chapter 17

Pounding of a lone drum echoed across Kings Lynn like the word of God chanted over and over, calling upon Ned to enlist.

"Think of your family," Lucy whispered her own appeal, not wishing the two boys to hear. "I can't bear the thought of losing you."

"My sweet, you ask me to cast the Almighty aside," Ned said with a shake of his head. "To obey God will save my family."

"What of the children and their religious instruction?" She omitted mention of herself for, ever the realist, she knew he wouldn't stay for her. The tall, slim man before Lucy was only familiar in appearance. Gone was the humorous but tender character who would do anything for her and who, when they were together, made it feel as if they were armoured against anything that life could throw at them.

"We aren't fighting any normal enemy, but rulers, forces of cosmic darkness and spiritual powers of evil." He quoted the scripture the Lord had shown him, and which now seemed to be his guiding light.

"Well ..." Lucy sighed and turned away from him, deep in thought. "When the fire of war eventually consumes us, I shall turn to your bible for advice."

"Please, Lucy." He quickly fastened the remaining wooden buttons of his doublet. "Support my decision, and one day I will help you understand."

"Just go, Ned," she replied. "Do not take any unnecessary risks, I bid thee." She felt unable to even plant a kiss on his lips and, as she went to walk away, he stopped her and took a diamond-shaped pendant from about his neck, inscribed with 'JL' for Jesus's love. He pressed the small religious token into her hand and tenderly closed her fingers about it. Saying nothing in response, she tightened her fist around the malleable tin, which weakened in her warm grip. She called the boys forward to take one in each of her arms.

"Remember to send that letter to thy brother, for his child cannot stay here any longer," Ned said, and stepped out of the door.

"I'll deal with it." Lucy's expression betrayed her loathing to give Francis a deadline to collect Henry, less still to hand him over to the care of the good Puritan preacher if it wasn't met.

"Being the son of a known Royalist, he stains our door like a cross of the plague," Ned said as he turned to her.

Lucy focussed on his narrow, thoughtful eyes, their softness accentuated by light brown eyebrows. She wished to remember every bit of him: the way his face tapered from his forehead, down to a small chin and his gentle appearance. Something in her eyes must have resonated with him, for he embraced her and not only that, but stroked her cheek in the way he had on the day of their marriage. He began to walk, following the path he'd set his heart upon.

"God be with thee, Father," their eldest shouted.

"Keep thy brother from evil, John," Ned called back and left Lucy for the first time in seven years.

The parting brought back memories of the day Lucy's father had cut her out of his life, after she married without his blessing. Since that day, she had expressed a desire not to share anything with her father; neither feelings nor experiences and most especially not any of his stubbornness. Yet it began to dawn upon her that she had been as stubborn with Ned just now. As a result, she relented and called after him, but he was too far away. "I love you!"

"God will hear thy words, Mother," John reassured her and, although Lucy's sparkling blue eyes were full of tears, it was not a jot to do with relief that the Almighty would hear her.

"Does this mean John is now the master of the house?" Young Isaac decided that his six-year-old sibling would make a rather good job of it.

"We must do all in our power to assist mother," John urged.

"I shall." Isaac took her soft hand and held it as if he was swearing fealty to her. "I'll watch for the bad man that angers father and make sure he doesn't keep talking to you."

The lad's naive sentiment budded straight from his heart like creamy climbing honeysuckle amidst a garden of herbs. Innocent and non-judgemental love was the purest and most beautiful form of all, and Lucy tried more than anything else to cultivate it in her boys. Their examples made her certain that she would find forgiveness in her own heart for Ned.

* * * * *

The way to the town square was muddy and clung to Ned's shoes as though Lucy were dragging at his heels. His footprints rapidly became small pools as standing rainwater seeped into the impressions and a bird landed to drink in it after escaping the bustle of the marketplace, which was where Ned was headed. Once there, he found an arc of people gathered around a table and a large drum, presided over by a sergeant with drumsticks. It seemed as if he were preparing to dissect a body, but instead he pounded out a beat that brought the crowd to life.

"We're looking for God-fearing folk wishing to take up arms in defence of our laws and liberties." The recruiting sergeant's pitch rose at the mention of the Almighty before diving into deep, rattling gravitas when he asked if Lynn had any such men. His voice carried far and wide to hound volunteers, weeding them out of every alley for his wily, darting eyes to catch sight of. And then, like a hound at a fox, he'd have them. "Who wants to see Irish Catholics cross the seas? Are we to turn our cheeks while they massacre more Protestants?" His predictions turned his large, round face magenta as he stepped closer to the array of townsfolk. With a mouth curled and contorted with determination, he gave a pikeman the cue, who thrust his ash pole forward and made the tightly-knit civilians recoil in shock.

"Can any father risk their children being skewered on the end of one of these?" The soldier assumed a posture out of the drill book and jabbed the tip at the throng.

Faced with these gut-wrenching questions, the crowd began to simmer. The unrest sprouted from the stirrings of terrible imagination and a mutter of discontent rapidly spread in the guise of what they'd do to any Papists that strayed into England. The sergeant stroked the spikes of his stubbly jowls and considered whether Catholics were here already. Then just as quickly he returned to the table, laid a sheet of crisp paper on the drumhead, dipped a quill and left a pause. This few seconds' silence was taken up by his pikemen, who began at each end of the crowd. They let children try on their helmets, whispered stories to young men of the girls waiting for them in every town and village and spoke of valour to mothers, the old and the infirm, all of whom needed protection.

"Down with the Papist whoremongers!" A group of women shouted, one of whom shoved her husband forward to sign up and in doing so, secured the shilling promised by the sergeant.

"Being part of our ranks, united against all danger, is the only way to protect your family," the sergeant shouted out.

"By what authority do you press men into the service of Parliament?" An old man stepped forward.

"Ah, good question." the sergeant stalked right up to him. "We serve the King and his Parliament."

"Yet the King raises his own troops in opposition and the law stipulates that men can only be pressed into military service by his command," the man explained.

"Your name, sir, afore I answer thee?" The sergeant straightened his portly frame.

"Ambrose Delaney."

"Our authority is the Militia Ordinance which has passed through Parliament, Ambrose," he replied, looking at the townsfolk. "Now, why would any honest, law-abiding Protestant even question such a thing?" He put his arm about the old man and led him to the drum.

"I don't believe the King assented to the Ordinance," Ambrose pointed out. "Therefore it cannot be law."

"People of Lynn," the sergeant called and waved a soldier closer. "Do not lose sight of the true peril we face, as this man has." He repeatedly prodded Ambrose's chest. "The evil ones who misguide the King use this argument every day."

"There are many evil ones across this land," Ambrose said, but a sharp twist of his arm prevented further comment.

The sergeant committed the old man to one of his soldiers with an instruction that he be shown a copy of the ordinance, repeating for good measure that he should understand the impact of every word. Next, the sergeant proceeded to read from the Book of Common Prayer to once more secure the crowd's undivided attention.

"Sir, I come here to do God's will," Ned said, relating to the sergeant's Christian devotion. "Let me put on God's armour so that I may make a stand against the tricks of the devil." Beads of sweat formed on his forehead.

"Above all, carry the shield of faith so that you can extinguish the flaming arrows of the evil one." The sergeant continued the thread and placed an arm about Ned. "Here's your first weekly two shillings, though I promise you and every man who joins us that there's more to be had than that." The last words, which saw many a man step up, rolled off his tongue with a phlegmy rasp.

Ned took a quill and formed an inky cross next to his name. The silver shillings were the shiniest he'd ever seen, and the sides were still rounded without any hint of being clipped by opportunists who melted down their pickings. The King's profile glared back at Ned, although the eyes had been worn away to leave what looked like empty, soul-less sockets. The petulant mouth and prominent chin of this imprint further inflamed Ned's desire to fight against the evil one's religious policies and secure freedom of worship. Ned pocketed the coins as the crowd began to drink and make merry, while old Ambrose Delaney's feeble moan went unheard as his opinions were beaten out of him.

Chapter 18

Hanging over the balcony of the theatre and looking down on the fight that had broken out in the pit, young John's head seemed, to any who entered the box, as if it had been lopped clean off. Precisely that view confronted Francis and Anne upon finding the lad after having navigated hordes of theatregoers, numerous pedlars of food and a variety of people simply using the place to carry out business. They hadn't worried about getting a seat, as John had been sent to occupy two as soon as the doors opened.

"That boy tests my patience," Francis muttered and then called out, "where are the seats you were meant to reserve?"

"Forgive me, sir." John raced over to the couple.

"You've forfeited your pennies," Francis told him.

"But I've been here since the doors opened at noon, as you instructed, sir." John received his mistress's usual support with her hand resting on his shoulder.

"That's three hours," she told Francis with a tilt of her head, and before the boy left, she promised him an orange from one of the pedlars.

Anne suggested once more that they need not incur the expense of the visit, finances already being tight, but with a kiss on her hand Francis insisted that they mark her birthday. So, while she sat in a green baize seat, he dropped to one knee and unfastened from her shoes the wooden platforms which had protected them from the dirt of the street. The characteristic act of gallantry brought a rosy glow to her cheeks and, as his fingertips brushed her silk stockings, a smile to his when imagining the garter above them.

"What's the play called?" Anne distracted him from all naughtiness following the entrance of a stout man and his son, full of complaints about how busy the streets were and the numerous delays.

" 'The Sisters', by Mister Shirley. The one we wanted to see at Blackfriars last year." Francis took his seat as the newcomers occupied theirs beside him. The atmosphere was tempered by the mild and calming music of a viol on stage. Each slide of the bow across its gut strings, and its manipulation, adjusted both pitch and tone of the soothing birdsong melody, but it was not enough to drown out the men's continued complaint.

"Did you get bothered by those sheep being driven to the slaughterhouse?" The man asked.

"No," Francis replied.

"Damned abattoir will stink tonight, enough to put one off one's food."

"I don't doubt it," Francis said and, hearing Anne cough to stifle her amusement, was hard-pressed to suppress his own. Even the fellow's eyelids were so plump that they gave him a permanently tired expression, while a neat line of beard in the centre of his chin seemed to point the way to his mouth, from which came a further revelation.

"Still, the good news is that the sheep were the rebels'," he declared.

"The rebels were dressed as sheep?" Francis couldn't help himself, being in a jovial mood.

"No," the man thundered, "they were owned by Sir Michael Mills, a local roundhead."

"He's father's neighbour," Anne said, sitting forward.

"Confiscated by our raiding parties." The older man grasped his meaty fists together to emphasise how they'd been wrested from their owner. "They're paying house visits to all rebels in the surrounding area."

A storm of worry rolled across Anne's green eyes, which darkened as concerns about her parents and, in particular, her father's political views, tossed about in her mind. To Francis, drawn into that same tempest, his father-in-law's decision to allow a Parliamentarian detachment to camp on his land, and to make public donation, needed no mention. Dashed was any hope of escape from the unenviable task of assisting Anne's parents.

"Can you protect them?" The music reached a crescendo as Anne took Francis's hand.

As if James Jackson was not enough, Francis now had another problem to contend with and he replied, "I'll see what I can do."

"If you can save one thing, let it be my mother's jewels," Anne asked.

"Tobacco, tobacco, sing sweetly for tobacco ..." the music and high-pitched chords of the fellow on stage provided a suitable backdrop for Francis to ponder his options. The song, Anne explained, was the one her father used to sing to her as a child. Its subject more than likely one of his vices, alongside drinking and gambling, Francis assumed.

"Tobacco is like love ..." The viol added its earthy rhythm to the singer's assertion. "Love makes men sail from shore to shore, so doth tobacco ..." The lyrics prompted a great rattle of laughter from the pit.

"Tobias Hume has gone quite mad since writing this." The large man let out a puff of air from his cheeks.

"He's promised the King twenty million pounds in gold and silver coin for his cause," Francis said, and he felt the need for several pipefuls of his own when considering his son's separation as yet another of his pressing worries.

"Love makes men scorn all cowardly fears, so doth tobacco. Love often sets men by the ears, so doth tobacco ..." With the last few words, a painted sunset scene was lowered into place with the aid of a rope. Candles danced provocatively behind blue glass, giving the appearance of stars, while through the open roof above, the real stars looked down upon these impressive imposters. The audience wowed and gasped at such props. A fake milestone was moved into place, which the candles perched on the end of the thrust stage vainly attempted to illuminate. Before Francis could make any further attempt to read it, however, a journey of his own opened up with the entry to the box of a well-dressed man who introduced himself as Sir William Legge.

"Sir Francis Berkeley?" The Irishman asked. "His Highness Prince Rupert requests your attendance forthwith."

"He wishes to see *me*?" Francis's thoughts immediately turned to the letter he'd handed in to the authorities not a day before.

"Just so." Legge dabbed his forehead under a rich, chestnut wig. "He too is in the theatre this evening."

Promising Anne he'd be back soon, Francis followed Legge, who enquired where he was from and how long he'd served the King. After Francis explained that his soldiering days had begun in the Bishops' Wars with Scotland, a light crease came to Legge's brow, as though he'd known this all along, and he revealed that he had served in the same conflict.

Chapter 19

The stage jutted into the centre of the theatre like a thermoscope testing for any change in the audience's temperature, who sat around it in a semicircle. Four bedraggled bandits stood on it with their leader, Frapolo. In the actor's hands was a proclamation - a reward for Frapolo's capture - and, after reading it aloud, he held it to his forehead like a handkerchief and eyed each one of his henchmen in turn.

"Am I not your sovereign and you my subjects?" Frapolo questioned their loyalty. "Have I not by stratagems so oft preserved you?"

"Most excellent, Frapolo, a little human frailty may be pardoned," one gang member replied, suggesting it was natural to be tempted by such a reward.

"To obtain it you do lose your honour, live branded and pointed at in the street. There goes a rascal that betrayed his prince or cut the throat of his comrade." Frapolo considered the loyalty of his band. "We cannot tell whose heart is treacherous."

* * * * *

Prince Rupert, from his box, shook his head at the notion of thieves squabbling about loyalty and honour, and questioned whether they even possessed such qualities. A sardonic smile lifted one side of his mouth bitterly at the recent betrayal of King Charles's cause by one so close.

"If any here defy our laws, I'll shoot him." Frapolo drew a pistol and held it upright upon his chest like a newborn.

"Hang laws and those that make them," an outspoken gang member replied.

"I will not have you thieve amongst yourselves." Frapolo verbalised his idea to have his band take religion in order to bind them together in their crimes.

"I'll be of no religion."

"What man is he, who hopes to drink, to whore, to escape the wheels, rallies and gallows and be of no religion?" Frapolo turned to every section of the theatre upon each point, one hand rising higher and higher with incredulity.

"You would think Shelley had just written this after watching Harbottle's treachery play out." Rupert turned to his brother, Maurice. "Frapolo is right, by God, you can't tell which heart is treacherous." He looked on as the band of cutthroats held up a young traveller on the highway, only to find he had little plunder. The loud chants of the robbers drew his attention back to the play.

"Knock out his brains!"

"Pistol him!"

"Cut his throat!"

"Accept me to your tribe and spare me, gentlemen, for I have knowledge of where great money lies hid," the young traveller said, pleading for his life.

"Where is this treasure, sirrah?" Frapolo stroked his long chin, giving a sideways glance to the audience.

"But two days ago my father received six hundred pistoles and I can direct you to the cedar chest in which they are secured. Where I'm kindly used, my heart is honest," the young man replied, much to the audience's mirth.

"The little rogue." Sergeant-Major-General Astley squinted down at the actors, as if still an eighteen-year-old in the Azores, trying to spot the Spanish fleet. "I'd have him flogged, if he were my son."

"You'd fell him like one of your trees?" Rupert laughed at the old soldier, who'd declared war on the oaks that obscured the trajectory of the cannon he'd placed for Oxford's defence.

"I've not seen Lord Astley so cross since that night outside Breda, when we crept out of the Dutch trenches and right up to the very walls to listen to the Spaniards planning their attack," Maurice said, recalling the siege of the Spanish-held city.

"Had anything happened to either of you ..." Astley said that their mother, the Queen of Bohemia, would have gutted him. "She never wanted any of you to be soldiers."

"Rather she never wanted any of us to be captured by Catholics," Rupert corrected, being the one son to have fulfilled her worst fears. "Besides, I'm sure that 'Honest Little Jacob' would somehow have escaped her wrath." Rupert used his mother's pet name for Astley.

"I much prefer sergeant-major-general, thank you," Astley replied as Colonel Legge entered their box.

Rupert turned to Legge and rose from his place as if he were waiting for a suitable distraction. Now on his feet, the Prince's appearance provoked applause and foot stamping from what seemed like all four hundred people below.

"I don't understand how they follow this play, for they seem to watch my every move." Rupert was quick to escape their adulation.

The Prince was informed that Sir Francis Berkeley had been located. When the man was duly shown in, he noted how Berkeley bowed stiffly and could not help but question whether or not his heart was treacherous. Behind him, the audience laughed at Frapolo's judgement that one of the sister's chests was worth rifling and, with a wry smile finding his lips, Rupert began his own performance.

"Sir Francis, I've not had a chance to see you since Brentford." Rupert smiled. "I have heard many good things about your actions."

"I am always at your service." Francis's whole body seemed to squirm, right down to his toes curling in his boots.

"Discovering that treacherous rat, Harbottle, in his nest was a great service," Rupert said, announcing that he would come straight to the point. "The letter you handed in and the deciphering offered us valuable information." As if he were merely searching for a tradesman to carry out some menial chore, the Prince enquired whether he could make use of Francis's services, a request that brought ready agreement. "You knew Harbottle was a double agent, yes?"

"Aye, Your Highness, I'd gathered as much when I began to question him," Francis replied.

"Well, from those letters we managed to gather the name of his contact; one James Jackson." Rupert gave a cough. "A name that may not be completely unfamiliar to you?"

"I grew up with him in Colchester, although I have not seen him since I left London and declared for the King," Francis answered without hesitation, leaving the Prince with the opinion that he'd been expecting the question.

Recalling the young man in the play and his words that if kindly used he would be honest, Rupert smiled and thanked Sir Francis for his candour, enquiring whether he and James were friends still. The answer was offered up as a fact – that they were enemies in the eyes of the war, as were so many friends and family members. In other words, an affirmative. Rupert considered his own, wretched eldest brother who was far too open towards Parliament.

"Your bonds of friendship with Mister Jackson have become crucial to His Majesty's cause," Rupert said.

"Crucial?" Francis's face paled, as if his heart had sucked all his blood to its core for self-preservation.

Lowering his voice, Rupert asked, "Are you willing to put loyalty to the King above all others?"

"Most definitely." Francis's brow knit at the very notion of betraying both the King and his honour.

A decision so quick, Rupert knew, that could only be proffered without fully considering the many facets that comprise a man's honour. Rupert also knew that when looked at from certain angles, like a freshly cut diamond, honour and loyalty offered very different aspects to every beholder. He did not elaborate upon what was required and instead turned and looked back towards the stage. "There is some information that James Jackson possesses, of which we are in great need. Colonel Legge will deliver further instructions," Rupert said, and when Francis took the cue to bow and leave, his silver medal caught the Prince's eye. "You fought in the Bishops' War?"

"Yes, Highness. I sold everything I had to buy a commission in the cavalry," Francis explained.

Rupert raised an eyebrow. "So, you're familiar with the way His Majesty has been denigrated by the Parliaments of both Scotland and England?"

"That I am, sir," Francis replied. "If I may, Your Highness, could I ask a humble favour?" He continued upon Rupert's gesture. "Would it be possible to command one of the companies who are visiting the rebel estates hereabout and help gather in a harvest for His Majesty?"

"Granted." Rupert approved such a minor request without much consideration. It meant nothing to him who rode out to loot the homes of rebels, yet by granting it he had made Sir Francis indebted to him, which was never a bad outcome. With that, the Prince returned to his seat just as many below him were leaving theirs. Shoving through the benches, a stream of people exited the theatre before the end of the free first act.

"You still think Berkeley was trying to hide that letter to cover his friend?" Maurice whispered.

"No doubt of it," Rupert replied.

"He could well be involved in Harbottle's treason?"

"We cannot rule that out," Rupert admitted, "but I will test his loyalty for certain." He turned to Legge. "Keep a close eye on Berkeley and all the comings and goings at his house.

Chapter 20

She'd cried enough tears to fill the German Ocean and after her second attempt at crossing it, Henrietta Maria, Queen of Great Britain and Ireland, had finally made it home after a year's absence. The anchor of her ship splashed into Bridlington Bay on the Yorkshire coast, despite bleak forecasts in both weather and horoscope. But never once was she put off by anything, especially when she had set her mind to it, and more so, when it meant being reunited with her husband.

With quick steps she danced across the deck of the Dutch flagship and ran to the rail to examine every inch of the English landscape. Beneath the scrubbed planking were arms, ammunition, money and men that she had brought all the way from Holland to aid her husband. One year of scrimping, saving and bartering, as well as anxiety and frustration during her war waged against Dutch officials and their government, who were not best pleased at her presence in their midst.

"May you scatter my enemies, Oh Lord, and be both my guide and safeguard." She fired one of her renowned scowls westward, where in the expanse of ocean her Parliamentarian pursuers lurked.

"Your Majesty." The Dutch Admiral Van Tromp gave a sigh of one ready and willing to hand a particularly petulant and demanding child back to its parents.

"My thanks for your good care of my person." Henrietta usually spoke her mind, but in this, the hour of her victory, she put her true feelings aside. However, this suppression prevented her from looking him in either of his oversized eyes.

"You honour me with such praise and I thank the Almighty that you're safely back to England," Van Tromp said.

Of that I do not doubt! She thought.

"Now, I must find out where Parliament's ships are." Tromp pondered his journey home.

Their ships?

"Is anything wrong, madam?" Tromp noticed a change in her expression.

"They are the King's ships." Her irritation burned through the wintery chill that hung about her cheeks. "Our ships, which have been stolen by traitors."

"My apologies, madam. A slip of the tongue."

"Besides, you've nothing to fear, for your countrymen have declared their neutrality."

"I cannot speak on behalf of my country." Tromp excused.

"Oh, you do not need to, Admiral. Your government have always made its intentions perfectly clear."

"The English Parliament accuses us of being hostile," Tromp said.

"Hostile? If they knew how rudely I was treated by your ministers and how the Dutch East India merchants refused me loans, then Parliament could never claim you to be hostile." Her tapping foot imitated her increasing heart rate.

"But if I may venture, Majesty, our traders have served you well." Tromp clasped his hands behind his back and pondered the royal jewels she had pawned. "The Prince of Orange also allowed your followers to stay with you in Holland."

"It's a good job the Prince is my son-in-law, otherwise your States General would have had my attendants expelled," she said, unwilling to have anyone play down what she had been through. "Just how could they consider banishing trusted members of the Queen of England's entourage?"

"If my nation has offended you, then I apologise, but I am sure this was not the intention." Tromp deftly defused an escalating situation.

"And there was that absurd little official who tried to impound my munitions on the basis that I had no licence," she asserted, while searching for signs of the Earl of Newcastle's escort party.

"Your Majesty." Tromp stepped closer.

"Yes, Admiral?"

"I imagine the enemy must be confined to Hull, due to this adverse wind," he suggested.

"If they are it's certainly the Lord's doing." As was her survival of the storm that had wrecked her first attempt at returning home. Huge waves had seen her servants strapped to their beds with hysterical fear, while she steadfastly refused to be cowed.

"Quite," he persisted with a cough. "The Lord is also providing me with an opportunity to return home." He revealed his wish to leave the next day.

"Can you see any of Lord Newcastle's men?" Her weary eyes stung from the salt air. Without giving Tromp time to answer, she desired the opinion of the Duchess of Richmond and beckoned her closer.

"I'm afraid not, Your Majesty." The Duchess shielded her eyes from the dying sun, which scattered a path of golden ripples from Bridlington right up to the ship's hull.

"Oh, Mall, having come so far, I am still stuck on this accursed ship," she moaned to her surrogate daughter, who had been raised in the royal household. Together they paced, such was the Queen's inability to remain still.

"Madam, remember that fretting brings nothing but a fresh wrinkle. If you need proof, look at the Hollander," the Duchess said in reference to Tromp, who removed his hat to reveal a bald pate with long, straggling locks at the side.

"His furrows are well earned," the Queen conceded, "for his father was blown apart by a pirate's cannonball and he captured by them."

The Queen's thoughts of her own father, stabbed to death whilst held up in Parisian traffic, were short-lived when the Duchess clapped her hands together. The source of the interruption was some cavalrymen riding onto the quay and prompting Henrietta to hurry back to Tromp, her dark ringlets bouncing with excitement, to request she be rowed ashore in spite of the cautious protests of Henry Jermyn, her Master of the Horse, who argued that they did not know the loyalty of the arrivals.

"They do not look like the Roundheads." The Duchess watched the leading horseman leap from his steed, rip off his hat and wave it in circles of excitement that were far too flamboyant for any dour Puritan.

"All of Yorkshire is held for His Majesty." The Queen emphasised her husband's strength, as if because of this, there could not be one man in the entire county who would wish her harm.

In no time, she had stepped onto the quay, pausing as if taking it all in, but in reality finding her land feet again.

It took no time to recover her forthright manner and she referred to the lateness of her escort, only to be assured that Lord Newcastle would arrive shortly.

Her lodgings on the quayside itself were pointed out to her. A short walk, thank goodness, for Holland had inflicted headaches, toothache and various coughs and colds upon her weary body. But as a general – leader of the officers she had recruited – she would show her vulnerability to none but her intimate circle. The populace of this small fishing port cheered their latest catch after she was brought ashore. A brief glance at the drab people was enough to see the joy her presence had brought them and assure her that she was amongst loyal subjects.

"Don't you think we should stay further inland?" the Duchess asked.

"If we did that, my munitions and supplies would be syphoned off by all and sundry," the Queen replied, entering the lodgings and resting on a chair in the parlour. "I must keep my eye on them."

"What if the rebels' ships come closer?" the Duchess asked.

"Tromp's presence will put paid to any of that." The Queen's doll-like lips pursed above her diminutive chin at the suggestion that the rebels would dare threaten her. "However, let us have the cargo unloaded."

"There's lobster if you wish to eat, madam." Jermyn's fussing was met with a nod, and his mistress lifted her lace sleeves to examine the bruises on her arms, testament to the roughness of her failed first voyage.

"A general can give good orders if he eats well, my merry band of followers." She rubbed one nasty weal and, although willing it to go away, would have it do so only after everyone had noticed it.

"May we call you She Majesty Generalissima?" Jermyn suggested with quick wit and a ready smile, both honed at the gambling table and used to secure winnings of all kinds.

Such a title had the Queen instantly standing to accept it, all of her four and a half feet being duly crowned, declaring her wish to be known by that name whenever she was with the army. Imagination sparkled in her earthy, brown eyes. Tired eyes, which soon prepared to dream about the potential exploits of Her She Majesty, who would ride to her husband's rescue with two thousand cases of pistols, one hundred thousand pounds in coin, enough arms for near ten thousand men and experienced officers, and volunteers to their cause.

Chapter 21

Patrick Hall, its red brick as stark as his mother-in-law's flame hair and rouge-laden cheeks was renamed, at her insistence, after the Irish saint. Its former name, Fortuna House was hardly appropriate either, considering his father-in-law's gambling. Yet, all of this aside, Francis and his thirty men rode up to a formidable piece of architecture, reminding him that the unreliable old man was once a successful merchant.

"A fine house," Sergeant Fisher said, clapping his hands.

"Station men all around the place until I see how willing the owners are to contribute to His Majesty," Francis instructed.

"Patrick Hall?" The sergeant mused. "A Papist enclave by the sound of it." His eyes narrowed at the sandstone mullions and doorway, from which a man emerged with gesturing arms.

"Sirs, why are you come?" George asked.

"We are from the King, sir, to collect for his cause. Are you willing to donate?" Francis fixed him with a look and stated his name and rank.

"Nay, nay, he has had enough from me in taxation." George's jaw was fixed with a stubbornness that had increased with age, and his eyes looked questioningly at Francis.

"We will not be leaving empty handed." Francis dismounted and, with two men in tow, headed for the entrance assuming that the letter he'd sent ahead must have gone astray.

"You are going to ransack my home? Is this how the King's men behave?" George asked. Thankfully for Francis, he seemed to recognise that something was afoot and made no personal references.

"You'll be lucky to retain your liberty if you obstruct the King's business." Francis took off his gloves and hat as he stepped over the threshold and considered how best to make George aware of his real intentions.

"I know a senior Royalist and shall complain strongly to him," George said.

"I'm sure he would help you if he were here. But you are a known supporter of the rebels," Francis replied and listed his donations to their cause, insisting he provide in turn for the King. Their boots clinked across the black and white porch tiles which, devoid of furniture, echoed George's assertion that they had nothing of value. Into the hall, and Francis stopped in the centre to look up at the walls, although no paintings hung upon them. The beams stood out like bare ribs, starved of adornment. A few pewter dishes lay scattered on the table along with a small block of cheese, the sides of which George had trimmed as finely as if he'd shaved them with his razor. There was a chest against one wall in which Francis found nothing but old candle stubs, some linen and more dishes.

"We melt down the remaining wax and reuse it," George explained.

"Check the kitchen and pantry." Francis sent off one of his men, desperate to find enough worth taking to assuage the hunger of war and prevent any comprehensive search that might turn up the jewels of Anne's mother. On into the parlour, where the wooden panelling glowed from the flames in a large fireplace, and Francis picked out a single silver plate, and on the small side table, a silver scented pomander perforated with holes and decorated with swirls. He assumed it to be Mary's and dreaded the moment he uncovered her in his search, which continued as he paced back through the rooms and towards the stairs.

"Where's your gold and silver coin?" Francis couldn't help but hide his frustration at the task before him, as well as his naivety over the complexities of it.

"I have only the wages for the servant," George replied.

"You must have more. What about sheep, how many?" Francis asked.

"Twenty, we took the rest to market," George said.

"Take some men and round them up," Francis instructed his soldier who, chewing on mutton, had returned from the pantry to report that there was little of worth other than some wine. The man then followed Francis upstairs while the other was stationed on the door.

"My wife is sleeping," George complained.

"She can continue her slumbers if you just hand over a donation," Francis insisted and held out one hand with desperation. "A suitable amount and we'll be on our way."

The fifteenth-century staircase creaked in protest at every step and George vowed to take his complaints directly to the King. When Francis asked him to be quiet, George insisted that if they were to take his property they should have his opinions too. Even the doublet on George's back had had its gold embroidery unpicked and sold. The top of the staircase opened out onto a corridor in which Mary stood framed in a doorway, her features as clear and striking as any of Holbein's portraits.

"So, you've stooped this low, Francis Berkeley." Mary exclaimed.

"Silence!" Francis barked, in no mood for more opposition considering he was risking his reputation to assist them.

"You will not enter a lady's bedroom." Her shrill voice denigrated George for not dispelling the intruders and she took hold of each side of the doorframe.

"Take her to the pantry and keep her there until I've finished." Francis seized the excuse to get rid of both her and his soldier so that he could talk to George.

"She's Irish, sir," the soldier noted.

"Aye and proud of it." Mary's nose crinkled with scorn.

"A donation to His Majesty is what we have come for." Francis told her.

"We have nothing for King Charles, except the contents of our chamber pots," Mary screeched. Her outburst earned a strike across the face.

"Lay no further hand upon her; we're not savages!" Francis yelled at the soldier. "Gag her instead." He deemed this fit for her own safety as well as his.

"Unhand my wife!" George protested.

Francis bade George follow him and went into the bedroom, to be hit by the smell of clove-studded oranges clustered upon every surface. Giving time for his man to lead Mary away, he took George by the shoulders.

"This is intolerable, Francis!"

"Didn't you receive my damned letter?" Francis looked him in the eye to get his undivided attention.

"No."

"I'm trying to help you," Francis said.

"Help?" George began a coughing fit upon the very word.

"Aye, I wrote to tell you to hide Anne's mother's jewels," Francis explained. "My purpose was to limit the devastation of this visit by leading it."

"Ah, I've not received any letter." The relief pushed deep wrinkles back across George's cheeks and up his forehead. "Then punish that man of yours for his assault upon dear Mary."

"I will, but just give me some money, or anything of average value and then we can be gone," Francis pleaded.

Carefully dropping to all fours in stages, as though he were descending a mine shaft, George tapped on the floorboards and lifted one to reveal a pouch which he opened and poured out beside him. The rich tinkle of golden angels, each worth ten shillings, continued until one third were freed, but before George could secrete the remainder again, Sergeant Fisher and two soldiers hurried in, as if enticed by the noise, to report that the sheep had been seized.

"I knew you'd make him crack, sir," Fisher said, and grabbed the bag.

Those suffering from scrofula were always given a golden angel by the monarch upon being cured and the loss of his coins sapped George's colour and left him a shade of dead Spaniard. Fisher, bag in hand, now pointed at a painting of a young woman and had the other soldier retrieve it, cut the canvass out of the gilt frame and gouge at a small ruby set into it.

"Not my daughter." George hovered over the portrait and looked down at Anne's childhood features. "That was her mother's." he addressed Francis and pointed at the extracted gem.

"Let me see," Francis instructed and, taking the ruby, ordered his men to recover the other angels from the floor. He then sent Fisher to get the lads ready to move on to the next property. "We'll get a sack full of real jewels from there, rather than fakes like this!" After the sergeant left, Francis returned the sentimental ruby to George under the pretence that it was nothing but a mere garnet.

With the jewel in his father-in-law's trembling grasp, Francis fell under the scrutiny of young Anne's gaze and her satin cheeks seemed flushed by the outrage committed upon her family; more so at Francis's inability to prevent it. Her ringlets were soon all that was left visible when George held the painting to his chest and cried out that they were finished. The money was his life savings; their only means of subsistence; he insisted again and again that they'd now need help. With nausea climbing to the back of his throat Francis considered whether the continued security of Anne's mother's jewels was enough of a success to outweigh the emotional damage caused to them all.

Chapter 22

"Your Majesty."

These two words were repeated slightly louder each time until, on the third occasion, they took on a desperate tone the likes of which she was most unused to.

How dare they disturb me, Queen Henrietta thought.

When her stinging eyes opened, they found Jermyn kneeling by her bedside, his profile growing in detail with every weary blink, and behind him the Duchess of Richmond stood with a shawl wrapped about her. Their candle-lit frowns brought back memories of when she was informed of her father, Henry IV of France's assassination. She sat up with a start.

"What is it?" she demanded.

"Ships have been sighted," Jermyn said.

"Where are my munitions?" The Queen took a proffered silk shawl from the Duchess, folded the green material around her shoulders and prepared to check on her precious cargo.

"Four enemy vessels have been spotted off the coast," Jermyn warned.

"Have my munitions and arms been unloaded?" she asked.

"Orders have been given to secure what has not been brought ashore already," Jermyn replied.

"What time is it?" She knew that she'd never get back to sleep.

"Just before five of the clock."

"Those cursed rebels will not give me any rest," she complained.

"We must move!" The wide-eyed Duchess fretted at the Queen's lack of understanding, while Jermyn's mop of sandy curls shook so much they could not hide his panic.

"Move?" The Queen raised an eyebrow. "They would not fire directly upon me..." An unearthly rumble interrupted her. The cottage trembled at the truth of the situation, and a whistle of artillery had her dog, Mitte, flee into the corner of the room.

"We must go immediately." Jermyn was as protective of his royal mistress, as the Queen was of her munitions.

"Dress me, Mary," the Queen commanded.

"There is no time," Jermyn replied.

"Go as I am?" She complained that such a half-dressed flight might be construed as a sign of fear. A second roar of naval cannon and a series of crashes soon had her jump to her feet. Dust raced across the wan light of Mary's candle, minute debris rained about them and the structure shivered right to its foundations. Henrietta donned a cape, pulling up the fur-edged hood, and the trio hurried through the house and outside.

"Curse them!" The Queen saw four distant warships enveloped in the morning mist. Their jumbled forest of masts and rigging seemed to point through the fog and up to heaven, while the groans of the hulks as they adjusted to the swell were like those of the undead.

"The ditches further inland will be safe," Jermyn said, urging the women to run as fast as they could. The only indication that they were heading in the right direction was the incline, which pushed at their calves.

"Mitte!" The Queen cried and turned about, notwithstanding Mary's screeching, to head back to the quayside.

Mother of God, protect me! Henrietta leaped back through the doorway as a cannonball splashed through one of the cottages, scattering fragments of wood-splinters and glass. Inside, the house was so dark it seemed as if her eyesight had completely given out, and she felt her way like a blind woman, screaming her pet's name. Above her, the morning clouds desperately tried to patch over the hole in the roof and Henrietta spotted the terrified gleam in Mitte's eyes as she crouched down to scoop the dog to her bosom.

No sooner was she back outside, and away from the musty air that stuck to her throat, than she was met by Mary. Linking arms, they hurried back to Jermyn and slid into a trench lined with her attendants, one of whom, Sir Richard Warrington, gave her his cloak for added warmth.

"Are you hurt?" Jermyn asked, but his petite mistress ignored his concern and glared over the parapet at the vile creatures who had just tried to murder her in her bed.

"Queens of England have never been drowned, nor I believe have they been blown apart. I was quite safe, and I knew it," she said.

"Someone else could have risked their life for the dog," Jermyn replied.

"To think I wrote to the King saying I needed the air of England, or at least the air where he was," the Queen said. Despite the four ships, the poisonous air and the fear that abounded in the cover of darkness; in spite of the fact that a portion of her subjects were willing to obliterate her, and her continually poor health, she had never felt more alive than now.

"The tide will be going out soon." Warrington said. "The rebels' time here is numbered.

"Why does Tromp not fire upon them? He's has had plenty of time." The Queen pointed an accusatory finger at the Dutchman's shady vessels, but nobody was willing to answer. She suspected nobody dared.

"Tromp will excuse himself due to the fog; I'll lay ten pounds on it." Jermyn characteristically took the chance to have a wager.

"Then let us pray that London is turned over to us soon." She eagerly regaled her closest attendants with news of a plot to capture the capital. As morning drew nearer, her positive news lifted morale, and with great excitement she revealed that the Tower would be captured along with certain leaders of Parliament and the Lord Mayor. Newly-built forts around the city would be overrun, and all from within. All of it led by loyal nobility, citizens and officers, aided by a network of agents who were undermining Parliament's hold on the city every day.

Chapter 23

To Sir Francis Berkeley
Oxford. 26 March 1643
Sir,

His Highness, Prince Rupert of the Rhine, commands you travel to the town of Reading, where, between 13-16 April you will find James Jackson. You are charged to make contact with him. The means and persuasion you employ is left to you to craft, though it must be without mention of the King's business and must appear entirely natural.

The success of making sure such a meeting occurs is imperative. You are required to impart specific information by employing subtle and cunning subterfuge. The information you must convey will be passed to you verbally by the bearer of this missive. It will please His Highness to be acquainted with your proposed methods before you leave Oxford.

The Prince is confident of your ability and appreciates your numerous services to His Majesty. Though an intercepted letter which you penned to your father-in-law in advance of a visit by our troops under your command came to his attention of late, he is willing to overlook this said letter and be satisfied that it carried no dishonour or betrayal, if you succeed at this task. Wherein, he would rejoice in considering you for a permanent military posting within his own regiment.

Col. Wm Legge

Chapter 24

Fourteen men milled around the medieval King's bedchamber in the Palace of Westminster, although the bed had long gone, and the function of the room had long since changed. Now home to the Committee of Safety, formed one year ago, their part in laying to rest the autocracy of King Charles was pivotal. Their responsibility was to direct both Parliament's war effort, and its army, under the command of the Earl of Essex.

"Couldn't a better location have been chosen?" Henry Marten's black eyes scowled at paintings of the four Evangelists seated on lions, which still rode the wall. He would exorcise the room of every whiff of royal pampering if he had his way, just as the mob did in 1267 when they broke in here. In his opinion it should be each of that mob's images celebrated on the walls and not popish biblical scenes.

"They say Edward the Confessor died in a chamber on this site," the Earl of Northumberland remarked to Lord Pembroke.

"Someone should tell those fellows they're no longer required." Pembroke smiled, admiring the exquisite, knightly guards who looked down from the walls as if searching for the four-poster and their master.

Aristocratic arseholes. Marten's lip curled in contempt, and he prayed for the day when their kind would be nothing more than flaking remnants, side-lined to the corner of a dusty old room.

"Old Testament, I believe, Mister Pym." Northumberland drew attention to the stunning painted narrative that ran around the chamber walls.

"Really?" Pym gave some eight-winged seraphs a cursory glance.

The late arrival of one member marching through the eighty-foot chamber gave Marten an opportunity to satisfy his dry wit. "Welcome to the royal palace of King Pym!" Marten raised his hands.

"This is no time for merriment, sir," Pym said and nodded to the scribes, whose quills were poised to etch into history. He then paused a moment, as if in pain. "Today our purpose is to further debate an alliance with our brethren, the Scots." In his West Country accent Pym called for the need to make the Scots see that they were equally threatened. "The King's evil councillors are enemies of both the English and Scottish Parliaments."

Do we target the snakes, or their charmer? Marten for once held his tongue, because the committee would not be ready to tolerate such talk. Yet.

"What will be the price of Scotland's support? Their religion being imposed on England?" This question drew the concern of the five members of the House of Lords and the ten from the House of Commons.

"Would we also be accused of treason and of prolonging the war by inviting the Scots into England?" Northumberland asked the other Lords, who, despite their inferior numbers, sat in prime position at the table.

"I am positive no peer will go to Scotland to further such an alliance." The Earl of Holland shook his head.

"Have you all given your opinions to Lord Holland, my lords?" Pym's small, fox-like eyes landed upon each one in turn. "Is he the voice of every one of you? The voice that I should take special and significant note of?"

The only change to Lord Essex's bearing was an increase in puffs of tobacco smoke; the spreading plume seemed indicative of his many thoughts on the matter. "I am a general and not a diplomat," he said, remaining neutral.

"Your Lordships?" Marten pushed the others.

"My governorship of the Isle of Wight takes up my time," Lord Pembroke replied.

"My Lord Northumberland?" Marten was quick to take aim at this particularly foppish, vain and snivelling coward who was forever running to the King with proposals for peace. The man's large, flaring nostrils were probably sniffing out another way of coming to terms with his royal master.

"Inviting a foreign power to invade the kingdom is treason." With each word, Northumberland methodically drummed his fingers on a letter lying on the table in front of him.

"I'm certain that the House of Commons can provide suitable men to carry out this most sensitive and crucial of roles." Pym left the Lords exchanging glances at the very thought of being side-lined.

"Do you not understand our concerns?" Northumberland asked.

"Any who disagree with a Scottish alliance disagree with what we are fighting for. Freedom of worship and an equal say in government are at stake." Pym raised his stocky frame and stood, leaning over on the table as if weighed down by the news that he now chose to share. "Does anyone present know of a plot to capture the capital?" Gasps, murmuring and coughing resulted. Such an inferred accusation bit at the ankles of the faint hearted, herding them back into the fold.

"A coup?" Lord Holland's jaw dropped.

"What are their aims?" Viscount Saye and Selle frowned deeply.

"I know little of the detail as yet," Pym replied.

"There are many who would prefer us to have peace at any cost," Marten declared, his black hair stuck to his sweaty forehead. But this time his words were uttered with Pym's prior agreement.

"Who speaks of peace at a time like this?" Pym took the lead given.

Marten turned to Northumberland, who had tried to kill the war twice in this manner. Would he be prepared to finish their cause by involvement in a coup?

"Peace is to roll over like a dog and expose our bellies to a fifteen-foot pikestaff." Marten declared.

"Just as some will not be happy until our entire nation has devoured itself. When all is said and done, we need a balanced monarchy and Parliament working together in harmony, for true danger lies outside this realm." Lord Northumberland referred to the Dutch, whose fishing fleet constantly raided English waters, or the Spaniards, who were a synonym for enemy.

"I don't wish to see us all consumed, Lord Northumberland, but I do think that one man should be devoured to save the rest of us. However, the said man should have his crown removed beforehand, lest it cause any indigestion." Marten gave a sarcastic smile.

"Henry, pray hold thy tongue or have it cut out." Pym winced, as if sensing the wounds such extreme radicalism would inflict upon their unity.

"I hope, Mister Pym, that such a remark is simply the lunacy of one man." Pembroke looked for reassurance. "If an equal balance of power can be gained without further bloodshed, why not pursue that?"

"Denzil Holles lost a third of his regiment at Brentford," Marten rose from the table to stand near the window, where images of Justice trampled Pride. "All our soldiers will have died for nothing if we hand power back to the man who causes all our woes." Marten's wide nose sniffed at the very thought. "He should be the last casualty of this war."

Pym raised one hand, calling the scribes to halt.

"Who is this traitor that is allowed to mouth such villainy?" Northumberland asked angrily.

Marten, still standing, eyed Northumberland, whose floppy hair fell across his whole brow to hide any furrows of serious expression. The peer held a letter between his fingers and its contents piqued Marten's curiosity. Therefore, he plucked it, as easily as if he'd extracted a flower from a garden. Protests abounded. Northumberland growled like a vicious dog and Marten walked away, opening the paper and scanning the contents for evidence of involvement in this plot. Northumberland, cane in hand, got to his feet and the peers raged. But all Marten could discover were a few fine words to Northumberland's second wife, and instructions concerning his five daughters.

"This is an abominable outrage!" Northumberland was upon Marten in an instant. Raising his cane, he cudgelled the man's head once, and then twice. "The King is correct, you are an ugly rascal and whore master!"

The sergeant-at-arms got between the pair to arrest Marten, and it was some time before calm returned.

"My Lords and gentlemen, if peace is what you seek, then we will indeed send a proposal to the King, despite my opinion of its futility." Pym was able to silence all opposition with this concession. "I do this because we fight for freedom of speech and I respect your opinions. But if our approach is rejected we have no alternative but to fight on to victory with Scotland by our side." He'd already drawn up a list of conditions; tightly worded points which he was quite sure left no room for manoeuvre, and which the King would certainly be hard-pressed to find comfort in.

"Peace we may pursue, but the proximity of the Royalist garrison at Reading threatens the safety of London." Lord Essex added military foresight to the agenda. "Readings capture would hamper any plot against us."

This intelligence reinforced Essex's position as commander of the army, and he sat back with satisfaction as Pym gave the operation approval. Soon the whole Parliamentarian army would descend upon the town.

Chapter 25

"Best tankard in Reading that is, sir." The serving girl nodded.

"That so, eh?" Francis took two shillings from his purse. "Then bring me some of Reading's best cheese and bread too." She stroked his hand as she took the coins.

"Said that to me not fifteen minutes since." A man slammed his pewter flagon down beside Francis. "Only one with a lid, too, sir!" He recounted her words in a high-pitched voice. "She'd make a better merchant than me."

"James, by God!" Francis stood immediately and looked his friend up and down.

"Steady now, no kisses." James raised a hand to Francis, turned to the girl, who was just leaving and slapped her backside. "You on the other hand …"

"Your eyesight must be suffering by now from all this ogling!"

"Then I'd gladly go blind, for there'd be no point having sight if I couldn't behold a fair maiden from time to time," James replied.

"Not sure she's a maiden," Francis said, and they gave each other a short, manly embrace, intermingled with many slaps upon each other's back.

"Best maiden in Reading!" James chortled. "Anyway, what the devil are you doing here?"

"I'm off to Kings Lynn to fetch Henry."

"He's still there?" James frowned. "With that boring brother-in-law of yours?"

"I've never had the opportunity before now." Francis justified to himself as much as to James.

"You'll have missed a great deal of his development; he'll be grown up."

"Probably ready to enlist." Francis groaned at the truth of James's statement. "And what are you doing here?"

"Make a better commander than you, he will." James shoved his arm. "Why are you not in military dress?"

"I don't have a permanent post. I was wounded at Edgehill," Francis explained.

"So I heard. You risked everything for the King and he leaves you destitute?" James shook his head. "Parliament has vacancies," he said, leaning in close.

"I'm surprised you've not taken up one of them. Now, why are you here?" Francis tried for a second time to get an answer, as was frequently the case with James, who'd sidestep questions. "You do know that this is a Royalist town?"

"I'm not fussy about which side I sell uniforms to." James tilted his head. "Therefore, I must proffer my thanks to the King for starting the war and giving me such trade," James whispered. "But mark those words, my friend, for they'll be the only time you hear me being complementary about him." He eyed the maid approaching with their food and helped her place it on the rickety table.

Francis watched his friend's antics; he'd never changed. It felt quite wrong to know that he had some information to impart to James surreptitiously. In fact, the details were not very detailed at all, but a cryptic jigsaw with the main pieces missing: that an Alderman of London was in constant touch with the King, but since Harbottle's death, this communication had stopped. Nothing very remarkable on the one hand, but by that same token, its unassuming manner could equally carry far reaching consequences, upon which Francis tried to avoid dwelling.

"Aye, I have stockings." James had meanwhile got the girl interested, but pushed the need for her to try the stockings on, claiming not to know the size of his very last pair.

Francis's friend's portly stomach shook with excitement as she let him check the circumference of her thigh through her skirts. His long, flat eyebrows, like mizzen yardarms of a ship, rose with his swell of excitement. Delicate lips, with a cupid's bow as defined as any woman's, gave him a ready smile that lit up his face, framed by blond hair.

"Thank ye, sir." She agreed to meet him in his lodgings.

"Give my name, John Chandler, and they will permit you entry," James said.

"She serves *us* food, yet *you* have her eating from the palm of your hand," Francis smiled.

"She can eat anything off me she likes." James leaned forward, took a swig of his spiced beer and let out a sage and rosemary-edged hiss of satisfaction.

"Is that so, *John*?" Francis emphasised the alias just used.

"Saves any problem at home with Elizabeth. You know how it is." James raised one hand.

"No, not really." Francis shook his head. "Mind, I'm surprised you leave London at all. You were forever hanging around Parliament for the latest gossip."

"Plenty of it going on at the minute."

"Talking of which ..." Francis waded straight into the task before him, to be done with it sooner, rather than later. "Have you heard about the King becoming friendly with a London Alderman?" He watched James's bottom lip push up in a negative. "Well, supposedly, their letters stopped abruptly a week ago."

"Really? Do you know the alderman's name?" James asked discreetly while nonchalantly brushing down his doublet.

"No, but if you ask me, it has something to do with a spy who was hung around the same time." Francis asked if he'd heard of someone called Harbottle, although his friend only offered a shrug. "Well, the letters stopped when he was executed."

* * * * *

Captain Sidney stood outside of the inn on Duke Street flanked by two guards from the garrison and, once Eliza, the serving maid, appeared, he left them and walked with her. She was well known to him from previous times he'd stayed in Reading and once they were a suitable distance from the inn, he stopped and turned to face her. Even the dark of night could not obscure her pretty features.

"Did you manage to overhear anything?"

"Aye." She told him that one of the men had given her his name as John Chandler. "But the other had earlier greeted the same man as James."

"Good work!" It was just as Sidney had hoped, having trailed Sir Francis Berkeley all the way from Oxford on Rupert's orders. The man had unwittingly led Sidney right to the very nose of the elusive James Jackson; had allowed him the chance to observe Jackson with his own eyes, to lift the veil on the spy's identity and begin to make a mental record of his appearance.

Sidney's large hand took Eliza's waist, his muscular arm easing her towards him, though his strength was unnecessary because she closed up willingly. His lips caressed hers and asked her to meet him that night. He would have her as his wife some day for, despite her station, she was witty and sharp, caring and kind. But right now he had business to attend to and even her charms could not prevent his return to the guards.

Entering the noisy establishment, Sidney pushed past a table of gamblers and one in particular who was on his feet, moaning that the unlucky dice must have been fashioned from the bones of a rebel sheep.

"Arrest them both!" Sidney pointed at his targets but remained at a distance, and his burly soldiers shoved customers aside to close up on two men who stood in surprise. Both protested and demanded to know what was occurring as they were manhandled and bound by the wrists.

"You must be mistaken," Francis insisted. "What's the meaning of this?"

"You forget you're merely a civilian, and not one to give orders," Sidney replied as the pair were brought closer to him.

"On whose orders are we seized?" James's demand was answered by Captain Sidney pointing a thumb to his own chest. He did not budge, but instructed the soldiers to separate the men and throw them into gaol, where he would speak with them both later.

"What's the charge against us?" Francis tried in vain to reason.

"You'll regret this!" James roared with fury.

James's threat came back to Francis when, the following day, he was not graced with Sidney's presence. Instead, a roar of thunderous cannon and a sparking panic permeated even the dank gaol, increasing the drip of stale water from the corner and sending the rats to ground. The gaoler railed against the Roundheads, who, it seemed, had arrived with their whole army to lay siege to the town.

Chapter 26

John Pym's eyes opened from a fitful slumber. They stung as though the April sun had burned them and he rubbed at the swollen skin under each one, which nowadays was soft and a lighter hue than the rest of his face. Waking brought an almost immediate need, and he struggled to his feet, lifted his nightshirt and sat on the oak close-stool just in time.

"If it's my destiny, Lord, to be thus afflicted, pray let it not detract from your cause."

The warm April day did nothing to help the stench of a second deposit, which was revolting. As ever, footsteps outside concerned him, because his health concern was known only to two others. He called out. A tap echoed at the door followed by the sweet voice of his servant boy – one of those two people.

"May I take that, sir?" Isaac pointed at the chamber pot as his master stood.

"When do the night-soil men arrive?" Pym's mind went to the amount of waste building up in his basement.

"This evening, sir."

"You're a blessing to me, Isaac. God be with you," Pym said.

"God's will be done." The boy's reply warmed Pym's heart as he put on his black suit.

"I pray His will is done at Reading too." Pym splashed his face with rose-water and left his gaze lingering upon the plaster ceiling. This solitude was interrupted by the faint echo of a joyful laugh. Not any old laughter, but that of Lucy, Countess of Carlisle, his beloved mistress. A laugh which spoke directly to his needs and desires and gave warmth to his swollen stomach, as well as prompting him to hurry to the mirror that hung, canted forward, to check his greying moustache and beard.

"My dear John," she said upon entering and planting a kiss upon his cheek, thus foiling his plan to save her from the odour.

"Let us walk in the garden, my lady." Pym ushered her back to the hall, where Lucy took her pomander, hanging from a ribbon about her waist, and sniffed its perfumed contents. He held up one finger and stepped outside to call for Isaac. But the boy was one step ahead, already gathering in Pym's linen drawers, which had been drying on the briar-rose hedges. Once he'd done that, the Parliamentary leader led Lucy into the glorious sunshine of this secluded haven.

"Note my pink cheeks, John, prettier than your roses if I do say so." Her assertion caused a chuckle to escape him and he took both of her hands, marvelling at her beauty.

"I do not know why you need such flamboyant artistry, for you are pretty enough."

"Artistry?" Lucy giggled at his Puritanical ignorance and rejection of fashion. "Van Dyck may paint me, but not literally, I'll have you know. This is from Spanish Paper."

"The colouring of which comes from the blood of the cochineal beetle ..."

"I have no desire to know!" She linked his arm. Quickly changing the subject as they walked, she complimented the colourful, rectangular flower beds covering the garden like vibrant Turkish rugs. They followed the gravelled path to a small avenue of trees, the tops of which had been clipped and entwined to provide a covered walkway.

"You're tired, John?"

"Nay, I am fine," he replied.

His reply prompted an uncharacteristic frown from Lucy, whose delicate lips were perpetually poised on the verge of humour. "You cannot hide anything from me." She gently traced one finger across the worry-line on his forehead.

"I was working late on some letters." He remembered the hourly calls of the night-watchman, who was his only companion during regular bouts of insomnia.

"I hope that is the truth and you do not have another lady?" she said.

"I've no interest in any other." This extended even to his own wife. "Although many glorious peacocks fawn over you with their rich feathers."

"My lords." Isaac's voice carried on the warm air. "Pray wait and I will find my master."

The words led Pym to curse the interruption. Lucy wafted him with her painted fan that caused images of cherubs to fly before him with every flutter.

"Master Pym, a word if you please." Lord Holland's approach forced him to step forward from the avenue and hold a hand to his brow to cover his eyes.

"My lord, to what do I owe the pleasure?" Pym asked.

"I hear Parliament has recalled the Earl of Northumberland and the peace commissioners." Holland looked down his nose.

"We had been negotiating for over one month and got nowhere," Pym said.

"The King had agreed to disband his armies." Holland insisted.

"Only if we allowed all expelled members to return to Parliament," Pym replied – every one of them staunch Royalists, he knew. "And moved Parliament to some location twenty miles outside of London." He scoffed at such unrealistic terms. "Nor did he agree with any of our other proposals." Pym listed abolishing Bishops, giving Parliament power to appoint all officers of state, and command of the nation's armed forces, while also having the King's supporters put on trial.

"A little more negotiation could have built peace on solid foundations," Holland replied.

"God has decreed that we must fight on!" Pym's patience with Lucy's former beau was now gone.

"Good Christians fight to save lives," Holland said.

"In that case, your Queen is damned, for she has brought arms and munitions into this nation to prolong a war against our people and, in an intercepted letter, instructs the King not to make peace." Pym glared. "For which she should be impeached.

"Impeach the Queen?" Holland spluttered at such an unthinkable course.

"If still you baulk, then I have nothing more to say to you than good morning." Pym clasped his hands behind his back, turned and left them as quickly as the sun scattered the few clouds that attempted to overshadow it. It was at this point that Lucy emerged to add counsel of her own, having made sure she listened to the whole conversation.

"Do you not risk alienating them, John?" she asked.

"The time has come when men must stand firm against a return to the King's tyrannical government. I've appeased the peace party long enough and have now proved the futility of negotiations," Pym replied.

"You take too much on your shoulders," she fussed.

"I *must*," he replied, "for unless we secure the Scot's help we will be finished."

Chapter 27

A twenty-pound round shot rolled to the bottom of a culverin's fourteen-foot-long barrel with a deep rumble. As it came to rest on a bed of hay, a ramming stick quickly followed it, to make sure the barrel was free of debris.

"Give fire!"

The concentrated explosion forced the ball back the way it had entered. It was blown out of the mouth of the cannon at a forty-five-degree angle towards the western approaches to Reading, and across the route of Pangburne Lane. Whistling across Old Street, between the watchful gaze of Saint Mary's church and Reading Priory, The Free School was firmly in its sights.

Barely three days into the siege, the hot cannonball passed through a wall in the manner of a spectre and left a hole in just the right place to cause a topple. Like a house of cards, the wall tumbled onto the neighbouring building and had some of that crash into the street below. The noise of this near miss made no impact on Sir Arthur Aston, the King's Governor of Reading, who was preoccupied with smashing the will of the man before him – yet another spy that had been found in his town. His brutal determination was such that he would have the fellow's cooperation at any cost.

"Now, you traitorous son of a whore, we have a task for you." Aston stood in front of James Jackson, who was bound at the wrists and seated on a small stool.

"I don't take orders from you," James replied.

"I warn you, I am not to be crossed!" Aston slammed his hairy fist onto the table and sent books and paperwork scattering. But Jackson was not to be cowed, therefore Aston turned to the man's friend. "Mister Berkeley has done us a great service by helping us discover your identity." He smiled a wide grin. "But that doesn't exonerate him. You'll both suffer if I don't have your compliance."

"What he says isn't true, James." Francis desperately asserted.

"Listen to the two little lovers." Aston glanced to Captain Sidney. "Perhaps we should bugger them with a red-hot poker if they don't do as I say."

"As long as you don't harm his hands," Sidney said, pointing to James.

"Oh yes, we need those, don't we?" Aston instructed James to write a letter to his masters in London. "Tell them the King has put a stop to the Royalist coup in London."

"I will not." James was resolute.

"I've just hung one of your kind." Aston's bushy, black eyebrows dipped.

"And I'd like to hang all of your kind, you catholic dog," James replied. The slur saw Aston smash the back of his hand against James's face, sending him to the ground.

"Enough!" Francis stood, his own hands also tied. "You'll pay dearly for this when Prince Rupert hears about it."

"He's not interested in the likes of you, Mister Berkeley," Aston said.

"I'm a knight of the realm." Francis stepped closer.

Aston remained silent and paced to the mirror, where he meditatively stroked his moustache and beard and, for half a minute or more, he did nothing but admire himself in silence. It was as though he'd just dressed after rising that morning and was preparing himself for the usual nine o'clock inspection of his garrison. Almost as if he'd forgotten all about the brutal task at hand. So, when he released a loud laugh and finally turned back to his prisoners, it was enough to have every ounce of dread in Francis's body suddenly drop to the pit of his stomach.

"You are no equal to me!" Aston boomed, and he reeled off his own military record, first in the service of the Tsar of all the Russians and then the King of Poland against the Turks. He strung out the name of Gustavus Adolphus - of Sweden, insinuating that Francis was ignorant - and then made a great show of his present service to King Charles. Next, he eyeballed James. "I once had a man flogged in Poland for looking at me the wrong way."

"Last chance." Sidney yanked Francis's bindings and forced him back into his seat. "Write the letter." He placed a quill and parchment on the floor next to James.

"I'd rather sign my own death warrant." James spat on Aston's boot, folded down beneath his knee.

The thick globule clung to the black leather under the lace decoration at the boot-top. It trickled slowly down, as if to escape the observation of Aston's bulging eyes. His spurs gave a faint jangle of warning as he drew back his foot and kicked James in the stomach so hard that Aston grunted like a wild beast. James curled up into a ball, writhing in pain, but unable to cry out. Unable to breathe at all. He couldn't even open his eyes before Aston grabbed his collar, dragged him to the fireplace and dropped him in a heap in front of it.

"Remember he needs to see to write." Sidney's warning was given as casually as if he'd counselled the Governor about the food at a local inn.

"I guarantee nothing." Aston kneeled beside James, carefully donned one leather glove and flexed his fist several times in succession. He grabbed James's blond locks and forced his head slowly towards the flames.

The heat seemed to leap from the fire and adhere to James's face and, like a leech, began to suck it dry. James cried out. He kept his eyes tightly closed, his left cheek exposed to the fire's dance, which flickered higher and higher and reached out to him with carmine, streaking arms.

His skin smelled like burning leather. As blisters formed, his vocal chords screamed with torment, while in his ear the crack of the embers exploded as if he were up against a firing squad. A bullet would be a mercy. Even if he wished to give in to Aston's demand, he couldn't verbalise it because of the excruciating pain. Francis's angry roars, his demands for mercy, made not the slightest difference to his friend's plight, but were met with a blow in the face from a blunt object, and Francis's nose erupted into a bloody mess.

"Governor!" Sidney cried, but at that moment it was unclear what had prompted the interruption.

Before anything further could be said, a whistling sound made Aston jettison James and all four men felt a shudder. Above them, the roof timbers caved and broke to fall about them like a felled forest. Tiles scattered in a downpour of masonry. Across what remained of the chamber, a racing invasion of dust, debris and smoke swept all before it and hung heavy in the lungs of any still breathing.

Chapter 28

Aston's chamber was no more, but rearranged into a tangle of wreckage and for the second time in six months, civil war left Francis lying amongst a landscape of rubble. He could not breathe properly through his painful nose. Dazed and barely conscious, he could be forgiven for mistaking the scattered wall stones around him for hills with pointed wood shards, church steeples and the dust and plaster merely a covering of snow. And Francis like a wounded giant, the russet colour of his doublet looking like it was saturated with dried blood

Part of the chamber wall pointed accusingly to the sky, which glared back in dark menace. Drops of falling rain attempted to refresh Francis's face and a breeze blew from his body the fine layer of the building's fabric that had settled upon him. To his right, a gap in the wall took on the guise of a canvas depicting the countryside it looked out upon. Missing from it were the fifteen thousand Parliamentarian troops surrounding three sides of Reading and ready to encircle it.

Francis's throat felt as if, coated with a layer of grit, it had dried, contracted and cracked numerous times. He coughed and the resulting swallow clung at the movement of his Adam's apple. Struggling to his knees, he paused for a moment to adjust to the dizziness and scanned the place for danger, having not forgotten Aston's brutality.

Thankfully, the man seemed to be dead. Lying on his back with arms outstretched, his black hair was a mess of blood, while roof tiles lay around his head. Upon getting to his feet, Francis spotted Sidney, who appeared to have been cut in half, his body crossed by a huge roof timber. The increasingly heavy droplets of rain diluted pools of blood that had gathered in his closed eye sockets.

Francis's bound hands would be his downfall, and he looked around for a means of escape and found shards of window glass jutting from a frame. Edging backwards to the largest piece, he began to rub the rope against it, catching his wrists many a time, until his hands were at last free. At this point Sidney's small dagger came into its own; he took it and searched for James. The opportunity this stray cannonball had afforded the pair was apparent and, with mounting agitation, the urge to escape became all-consuming. Their captors, probably the only two people in the town who knew Francis and James's identities, were forever silenced.

The fireplace's open mouth drew Francis's eye and he made his way across the uneven floor to find his friend lying face down in front of it, as though in supplication.

"Are you all right!" He shoved some rubble aside and, after a few attempts, gently moved James and cut his bindings.

The tormented moans were enough to satisfy Francis that his friend was at least alive. But then he caught sight of James's face, which in an instant almost made him reverse that judgement. The skin of his cheek had adopted a devilish red glow like the embers that had burnt it, brown and burnt like leather where it had lifted from the underlying tissue, and his ear reduced to a mess of gore, having lost its form. Morphed into a hideous mound, the ear stood out amidst what resembled volcanic lava, the likes of which glistened where it was not tinged with dirt.

"James!" Francis yelled.

"Aston?" James's voice was hardly a croak.

"Dead, both of them."

"Go," James insisted.

"I can't leave you here." Francis made to lift him.

"I'll be fine ..." James winced, waved for Francis to stop and with difficulty, told him to go to his room at the inn and look between some exposed wall slats where he would find a travel pass. Before Francis could argue, James reassured him that once Parliament took the town, he'd be with his own side again. Reassuring himself that James's wounds were not bad enough to kill him and vowing to do all he could for his friend, Francis left the place via a spiral staircase which slipped out on to the street.

While the garrison contended with the enemy, he headed to the south of the town where the dispossessed had gathered with the aim of at least surviving until the end of the siege.

Chapter 29

With his realm split in two, the slits in King Charles's helmet further divided up the landscape before him. His sight was improved by the lifting of his visor, but the split in allegiance was without any solution that was as quick.

Before him stood the north side of Reading, from the Abbey on the left to the priory on the far right, and both peered out over the top of a formidable wall. Within the town were three thousand of the King's soldiers. These men were more valuable to him than the town itself, for with them he could always recapture Reading. Yet without them his army would be further outnumbered, and his chances of taking London put back by several months if not to the end of the year. Not to mention the demoralisation their loss would wreak.

"Let the word of battle be 'Queen Mary' after my dear wife," he instructed Sir Jacob Astley, who'd also ridden with him from Oxford.

Sitting upon a white steed, the King eyed the route between the town wall and his relieving army. His eyes didn't get far down the slopes outside Reading before landing upon the rebel army encircling the town, and in turn encircling the enemy was the River Kennet. This tributary of the Thames prevented the King from simply sweeping down and driving off the Parliamentarians. A stone bridge clinging to each side of the riverbank was the only way his soldiers could get at the rebels, but sitting bolt upright in his gleaming, black armour, the King was not too concerned by this.

"Only two regiments of theirs stand between your army and victory, Your Majesty." Lord George Digby's eyes sparkled as blue as the Kennet when the intermittent April sun played upon it.

"We'll smash through the rebel's lines and extract the garrison." The King could imagine it now: his men attacking the rear of the enemy and the garrison rushing out in a frontal assault. Those enemy soldiers that did not get crushed between the two would flee for their lives, while the garrison and his men headed in triumph for Oxford.

"Surely, if we broke the siege we could retain the town too?" Digby put aside the fact that the monarch's relieving force was only a third of the size of the enemy's. "Such a victory would break their morale." His golden locks were as rich as the pickings he suggested. "Perchance they could even sue for peace."

"Alas, we do not have enough men to engage their entire army," the King said, but, despite his words, he still found himself drawn to Digby's sanguine appraisal.

"Your presence alone is worth ten thousand troops!" Digby pointed to the great banner royal, borne on the shoulders of twenty men.

The King's narrow, tapered standard fluttered in the breeze, its long tail flashing with colour like a comet signifying the royal presence. The flag of Saint George began the blaze of glory, followed by crimson, lions rampant, crowns and the royal coat of arms, as well as the words impelling all who beheld it to "give unto Caesar his due". Cloven at the end, like a snake's tongue, it threatened to bite any whose heart was poisoned towards the monarch.

"You think it possible to drive off their entire force?" The King pondered.

"If you serve up a hot breakfast to the two regiments before you, that must send the rest to flight," Digby maintained subservient eye contact. "Your force could camp under the city walls; that would safeguard them until reinforcements arrived."

"If only you were in good health, my lord," the King said, ruing the man's inability to join the fray. Digby's relentless optimism was like a breath of the purest air, not unlike Scotland's air where, in Falkland Palace, the King had drawn his first breath.

"Not being able to fight for your cause pains me more than my wound." Digby grimaced, and doubly so upon the arrival of Prince Rupert. "Your Highness, I was just talking to His Majesty about the hot breakfast we'll soon give the rebels."

"Then you had best withdraw and leave us to it." Rupert bowed his head to the monarch. "The army is ready ..."

"Withdraw?" Digby's double chin retreated further.

"Well you are in no fit state, my lord." Rupert began to discuss the six thousand Royalists poised for action in the face of a rebel force of over fifteen thousand.

"I won't be commanded to withdraw in such a peremptory manner." Digby expressed frustration at the prince's high-handed disregard of his person, despite his past services. "I shall join the attack regardless of my injuries, and use my walking stick as a lance if needs be."

"A most noble gesture." Stifled amusement glistened in Rupert's eyes. "Though such action is surely more suited to one of the fine plays you write."

"It is best you stay here rather than risk your life, Digby, for you are too important to me." The King's well-timed order allowed the peer to save face.

"Then regretfully, I obey, being of true allegiance to Your Majesty." He gave a measured bow of his head. "But the next opportunity I have to fight for you will be as a volunteer and not as a colonel." He offered his immediate resignation.

"I will discuss this with you once we are back in Oxford, my lord." The King could not afford to lose a man of such experience. "My nephew meant no ill, of that I am certain."

"I hear Lord Digby's heart is set upon a political career, so his resignation comes as no surprise," Rupert said upon the man's departure, but his statement was met by a cold silence.

The Monarch pointed his gold-tipped baton towards the enemy, his order relayed by the cries of every officer throughout the relief force. And so the royal troops moved off towards Caversham Bridge in a light drizzle that did not dampen their desire to vanquish the rebels.

As he followed behind his troops, King Charles eyed Harrison's Barn, where the enemy was ensconced. The earth about it was pock-marked by dark holes from cannonballs that had ploughed it and horse's hooves that had ridden roughshod over it. The cracks of musket fire increased, orders were fired around the men and the fervour of battle took hold.

"We must cross the bridge before they can take up position and oppose us," Rupert said, watching the two enemy regiments attempting to head the Royalists off. He secured the necessary permission from the King to take a vanguard of musketeers, and they set off at a good pace, ushered on by iron shot from their own artillery which hurtled overhead. This intermittent pounding encouraged the King's men as much as the rattle of the drums that beat out the English March.

King Charles kept close to his men, for his presence was indeed invaluable, even if it did not equate to the full ten thousand that Digby had quoted. Observing the leading soldiers approach the bridge, to be welcomed by enemy sharp shooters, his gaze went to Reading and back again. He felt certain he could make out activity from the walls of the town, but so far he could see no such action at the gates. His troops slowed and formed a line five abreast, to cross the river under a barrage of fury spat at them from the Roundheads. Despite Sir Thomas Blackwell's new recruits returning that fire, the Royalists clearly had a hard task ahead. If a charge from Aston's garrison was needed to tip the odds in their favour, then now was the time for it; the moment was clear to any man of a military background.

The small sphere of King Charles's telescope was trained upon Reading, but the gates remained firmly barred. There was not so much as one puff of smoke, nor a single fiery explosion of musket shot from the town in support. His sights returned to the bridge, where pikemen crushed across it. Their vertical pikes at this distance resembled nothing more than strands of wheat, blown here and there by rebel firepower – lead shot darted across them like mere pollen and left dead Royalists hampering their colleagues advance.

"Is Fielding not deafened by our twenty-four pounder?" King Charles was focussed once more on Reading, whose garrison hibernated like cowering dormice. If Aston had not been incapacitated, this situation would never have arisen. Fielding, his deputy, had best move now, or all the King's objectives would be scattered alongside the bodies of his troops and subsequently buried with them. The only excuse his mounting anger could put forward was that a mutiny had broken out in the town. And a mutiny it certainly was on someone's part, for Fielding well knew what was expected of him because a messenger had swum the river to personally deliver the royal orders.

"Give the musketeers priority over the pikemen," Rupert instructed, in the hope of gaining mastery in firepower. "I will ride to them, Uncle."

The rain became heavier, and the sky ominously darker. The King's steed adjusted its footing and tugged its head against the bridle as the Roundheads' artillery opened up and sent a shot ricocheting across his path. Artillery which now threatened the divinely appointed monarch of England, Scotland, France and Ireland.

"If Richard Fielding does no more than watch my brave men get cut down, I shall hang the rogue." King Charles drew his sword and spurred his mount towards the mass of men near the crossing, where Rupert's black banner shivered at the cold realisation that treason must be afoot. "Let us see if they dare remain idle when their sovereign is engaged in combat!"

A flurry of hail rattled against the King's helmet and drove him to a roar of frustrated anguish. Like a caged beast, he was trapped on the wrong side of the water, unable to secure enough of a foothold and facing the full might of the rebels. Any small pellets of frozen water dissolved instantly upon meeting his hot forehead and the inevitable advice that his men must retreat from the field was a dagger stabbing at his back. The pain of treachery was more piercing than that of failure. He'd never felt such disrespect and pure disregard for his person since the eve of war, when Hull had refused him entry and barred its gates before him.

It would not be long before Reading had to fling open its gates one way or the other, and when that time arrived, no matter how long it would take, he would wreak God's retribution upon every last traitor nestled within the place.

Chapter 30

The bells of Saint Lawrence's tolled ten slow chimes. For the Parliamentarians who lined up outside Reading, each one was like an impatient rap upon the gates because by now they should have taken possession of the town.

To the Royalists who were vacating it, winding their way through the streets, the tolls were reminiscent of a funeral march. Governor Aston, who had only been concussed and left unable to speak for most of the siege, was carried in a litter at the head of the procession. Its crimson hangings, the colour adopted by the King's officers, cried out his utter loyalty to the monarch seeing as he could not.

The opinions of Reading's populace pealed as much as the bell tower, some cursing the catholic Aston, some blessing the Parliamentarians, but most counting their losses and simply denouncing all warfare.

The wooden wheels of the Royalist wagons lumbered along the uneven ground full of Aston's wounded. For most of the siege they had been his in name only, for command had been vested in Richard Fielding, his deputy, and it was he who had opened up negotiations for surrender, despite orders to hold out. It had also been Fielding who had withheld his support of the royal relief force on the basis that, having already verbally agreed surrender terms, he would not break his word. But soon the last word on Fielding's chivalry would be with the King.

Four cannons trailed after the carts like dogs at their heels. Pulled by draught horses and oxen, and carving deep ruts out of the road, a belligerent one-ton saker jarred against a rock. Temporarily halted, the colourful pennants of the marching men also came to a standstill. Musketeers stopped swinging their rests and drew up, while the smoke from their smouldering match cords no longer dispersed on the air as quickly. All drumbeat was silenced too.

"Let's get moving," Fielding said. His men, leaving with arms, ammunition, honour and prestige, were attracting the wrong attention from all sides. The rebels railed against such honours bestowed upon a vanquished foe, while the people bandied it about that this had been secured only by Fielding's treason. When the gates opened, the Parliamentarians lined both sides of the road ahead, jeering and making all manner of insult and Fielding's men, it seemed, would have to run the gauntlet.

"Catholic dogs tearing back to their bitch!" One rebel referred to the Queen.

The Royalists made no further delay, and with a multitude of threats of their own, the officers implored their men to hold fast and ignore the provocation. The King's men were yelled at, spat at, pushed and shoved and some had their weapons and belongings seized. Lord Essex, Parliament's commander, insisted that his men honour the terms of the treaty and let the garrison pass unhindered. But in the end chaos reigned, and Aston's troops were forced to get out as best they could, slipping through the press of rebels who made off with anything they could get their hands on. At this point most civilians drained away, like the blood in Fielding's face, for they could sense the aggression of the Parliamentarians, who snarled and tugged at their leashes like mad dogs.

As the Royalists emerged from the gates by any means they could, the victors hurried into the town amidst a din of dishonour. At this point Francis took his chance and also exited the town. When challenged by a parliamentarian officer, sight of James's travel pass and the atmosphere were enough to secure approval, albeit with a strongly worded command to get on his way. He needed no encouragement. Where he was making his way to, on the other hand, was something he had long considered this past week, as he lay low in the makeshift camps of the homeless. He was on his way to Henry.

* * * * *

"Praise God." Francis's tired eyes caught sight of the worn carving on the milestone. The town of Lynn was barely five miles away and he turned to the horse he'd purchased to give it words of encouragement. His calm, soothing voice attracted its expressive eye like a shiny, brown marble that reflected the respect Francis had so far demonstrated. With a pat on its neck, they slipped into the tranquillity of the shaded wood where trees on either side leaned in close and from their lofty heights echoed the most pleasant birdsong. With a russet coat, black breeches ties at the knee, and a plain, linen shirt and collar, Francis aimed not to draw attention to himself.

This tranquil paradise welcomed Francis with the excited burble of a stream, while shafts of light winked through the leafy oaks to twinkle upon its waters. He led the mare down a bank from the path to the water's edge, where, with his encouragement, she quenched her thirst in Leonard's Beck. Inhaling the sweet and earthy scent of the wood, Francis kneeled down, cupped some water and splashed his weary face as the horse snorted its thanks.

From the solitude came panting and rustling which Francis missed, but his horse lifted her head and pricked her ears, turning to him with a soft nicker. Jangling footfalls heralded two men leaping from the undergrowth to run right up to the horse and mount up one after the other.

"Hey!" Francis bellowed as the first man dug his spurs into the horse's belly, so that they were off across the beck before anything could be done. "Come back, you bastards!" He gave chase, splashing through the water after them. But he stood no chance, even if he hadn't slipped and fallen to his knees.

"You!" Two soldiers emerged with drawn swords. "Where have those Cavaliers gone?"

"The God-forsaken pair who just stole my horse?" he asked and pointed after them.

"And what's your business here?"

"I'm travelling to Lynn, I have a Parliamentary pass if you'd like to see it." He began unfastening his purse to get it.

"No need." The other continued pursuit of the two men and instructed his colleague to follow.

Francis quickly made his way through the forest, more than ever alone without his mount to listen to his innermost anxieties, the first of which was a need to make Lynn by nightfall and seek out Lucy. He also ruminated over the reason why Royalist soldiers were being pursued; cavalrymen at that, judging by their spurs and the way they mounted up so easily.

He thanked God for James's pass, the thought of which brought his friend to mind again. James's courage and selfless act of bestowing it on Francis made him pray to God that he was all right. All further thought was banished from his mind upon hearing the clink of metal, an army of scuffling feet and the drone of voices, which made him flee to the undergrowth. He crouched on the damp grass while, on the path above him, the marching ceased, and someone stepped to the edge of the bank.

"Ah, that's better." The man groaned a sigh of relief.

Francis, squinting through a clump of fern leaves, was confronted by a jet of urine that sprayed over him as the soldier arced it around and watched the result of his handiwork.

"Oi, there's a man here!" He saw Francis. "Are you for King or Parliament?" he asked while tucking himself away.

"For Parliament and the freedom of this nation." Francis's assertion did not stop a corporal hurrying forward.

"What's your business?" The Corporal levelled a halberd and aimed the sharp point at Francis.

"My horse was stolen back there. Two of your lads are chasing the thieves."

"You're wet," the corporal observed with a frown. "Come 'ere."

"Aye, I chased the dogs as they made off, but to no avail." Francis began walking up the incline towards him.

"Where you from?" the Corporal asked.

"Colchester," Francis replied, opening the purse attached to his belt.

"A fugitive from Grantham, more like." The Corporal put words in his mouth.

"I'm loyal to Parliament." Francis took out his pass only to find it damp.

"Corporal, what's going on here?" A tall, gaunt man approached.

"Says he 'as a pass from Parliament, but this is all smudged. Looks like a poor excuse for a Cavalier to me." The corporal judged.

"If you do not think it genuine, we'll take him to Lynn with the others," the officer instructed, but then stepped forward and stared hard at Francis from under the brim of his felt hat. His small eyes, almost squinting, a delicate look about his lips and the manner in which he nervously scratched his nose with his forefinger, were enough to suggest that the man was none other than his brother-in-law, Ned Hungerford.

"Well, well, your name, if you please?" Captain Hungerford smiled in recognition.

"James Jackson." Francis averted his eyes.

"A likely story. What of this document?" Ned asked of his subordinate.

"Of no use but to wipe my arse with, sir." The Corporal handed over the unfolded paper whose writing was beyond all recognition and which Ned tore in two.

"If I could have a private word, Captain?" Francis wondered at the untold difficulties his presence could bring Ned, and whether this would be enough to make his brother-in-law rethink his arrest.

"Sir, he's already been bound of late, there are scars on his wrists," the soldier said. "Judging by his nose, been in a brawl too."

"God's true grace has shown favour to us by handing me yet another Royalist." Ned gave a smile to the heavens.

"I desire but a moment of your time, Captain, for I am here to see my brother-in-law," Francis persisted.

"Very well, just one minute, and we shall remain in view of my men." Ned said. When assured the prisoner's fresh bindings were tight, he invited Francis to follow him for a few paces. "Right, what do you wish to say that's so urgent?"

"To declare that I am not James Jackson is to declare that I am your Cavalier brother-in-law." The use of the derogatory term for a Royalist made Ned's eyebrows wilt and conjured up images of marauding Spanish horsemen from which it was taken.

"This is merely a test of my faith," Ned whispered. "An ultimate test that proves my allegiance to God over any allegiance of blood."

"What of Lucy? You'd hand her brother over?"

"It's for her own good," Ned replied.

"Your veneer of piety masks a streak of vindictive hatred. Does God give you two faces, one with which to worship Him, and the second when you cause pain to others?" Francis asked.

"You've no right to lecture me on the ways of Our Saviour," Ned said.

"Look, if I leave Lynn, I can take my son with me and remove the source of your anguish." Francis changed tack.

"And you claim I have two faces?"

"You have hidden and protected the son of a prominent enemy." Francis fixed him with a determined glare that had Ned adjust his footing. "I can take him away and your dirty secret will be resolved there and then."

Such a threat caused Ned's small, hazel eyes to momentarily flash with green envy.

"Corporal, take this man to the back with the others."

He had no need to be Cain to Francis's Abel, for God clearly favoured Ned without any shadow of doubt. As well as putting the child into Ned's care, the good Lord had now seen fit to also hand the father over to his guidance.

Chapter 31

Rich Pickings. A man in a threadbare ivory-black doublet looked at the crowd gathered in Kings Lynn's market square and his small stoat-like eyes picked out each and every purse in sight. With a quick glance at the narrow streets leading off the square, his baggy eyes soon ascertained which one was busiest, and which would offer enough cover.

"A fine day." Sir Hamon Le Strange and his eldest son clip-clopped slowly through the street. As much a familiar sight as Saint Margaret's Minster, the Le Strange's had been established here since the Norman Conquest. Most people of the town were known to him; from the gossiping Mary Reevington and her downturned mouth, which only changed direction when she had a pipe stuck in it, to Henry Howard, the oyster seller who had just fathered twins and was now selling his wares from morning until night.

Sir Hamon's long face and longer nose were as white as the milk of Jacob Tyler's ass, which he led door to door, promoting the health benefits for babies and the infirm. Yet upon spotting that stoat of a pickpocket again, after having threatened to whip him if he ever returned, Sir Hamon's blood was up. He instructed the constable to give chase, his own eyelids taking on a pink hue around their edges, but otherwise he remained outwardly unruffled. On he rode, his hair brushed back like the windswept grass of the sand dunes leading to The Wash. Bolt upright too, because as sheriff he represented the law and must therefore be as straight as it.

"Master Tillier," Sir Hamon greeted the local blacksmith. "Has your forge been pillaged since I replaced the last constable?"

"No, praise God." Tillier held up his tongs as a means of excusing himself and getting back to work.

"Most pleasing." Like an owl, Hamon's eyes seemed to observe all around him without movement of his head. A very wise owl. And an effective Justice of the Peace who could outwit any criminal, as well as a pillar supporting law and order in these uncertain times of war.

While they rode, Sir Hamon afforded his son a story regarding Margaret Blackwood, whose father ran one of the taverns and was considered the most beautiful woman in Lynn. The scene occurred, he explained, when the local Parliamentarian commander was supping there and boasted that the town was a bastion of loyalty. "The young lady offered a kiss to any whose heart was loyal to His Majesty and would drink a toast to him," he said, revealing that the result had been a rowdy clashing of tankards in good King Charles's name and the commander's angry arrest of the girl. "A sad state of affairs when folk can't even express loyalty to their king."

"Doesn't it have more to do with her beauty than political opinions?" His son followed his father's eye, which had now turned to the South Gate of town.

"Speaking of Parliamentarians ..." The expressive bone structure of Sir Hamon's brows signified his severe disapproval. He tracked the noise of marching men as they appeared and made their way over the bridge crossing the River Fosse and onto to the grand gate, whose façade of white stone shone like marble.

"They'll not be paying tolls for what they bring into town," his son said.

"It's Lynn that pays the price every time with these soldiers." The rival military authority haunted Sir Hamon's gaunt cheeks.

"It's still too early for any of our plans," the younger man counselled.

"The appropriate occasion will present itself in good time," Sir Hamon replied.

When eventually the procession of troops emerged through the arched gateway and into its shadow, Sir Hamon turned his horse to face them and viewed the column of prisoners. Not the usual poachers, that's for sure, but Royalist soldiers, he'd been informed earlier. But one captive's stride and bearing drew his attention, as though the man was of a more refined character than his bedraggled appearance suggested.

"A moment, if you please," Sir Hamon called the captain over, who stood peering up at him.

"How may I be of service?" Ned asked, stifling a groan.

"What do you have here?" Sir Hamon enquired before any fabrication could be concocted.

"They are Royalist fugitives, sir," the captain answered and then looked back at his men to escape the questioning glare.

Hamon stroked his very fine, brown moustache and then asked, "Are there any officers?"

"No, sir." Ned's expression was of one who cursed the tenacious way the justice handled his duties.

"And just how do you deduce that?" Sir Hamon wondered.

"Sir, we have orders from the colonel to round up all enemy suspects ..."

"The colonel, the colonel," Sir Hamon repeated under his breath with a tedious sigh. He peered again at the prisoner he'd singled out, whose gait was far too proud for a common soldier, and wondered whether the appropriate occasion he spoke of to his son might have just presented itself. "Are there any officers, man?"

"We round them all up regardless of rank," Ned replied.

"That's not what I asked you, Edward." Sir Hamon's long face looked down at him. "That man is an officer," he said and pointed his little finger at Francis.

"His manners are terrible, sir." Ned could do without any interference with his brother-in-law, especially from Le Strange, for who knew where that might end up.

"Gentlemen do not always have manners," Hamon said and his brows dropped again. "It certainly seems as though he swam here."

"We found him near Leonard's Beck…" Ned was cut off for a second time.

"I shall question the man. Fetch him to me this evening."

"But, sir, as much as I respect your order, I have to report to the colonel." Ned attempted to extricate himself.

"That is my express instruction. Bring him to Clifton House." Hamon noted that the prisoner did not change his stance and was quite collected.

The Justice was done with Ned and left him looking up open-mouthed and, although no words were upon his lips, his eyes reflected his every opinion on the matter. Sir Hamon had a plan, and he rode away in deep discussion with his son. So deep in fact that, most unlike him, he missed the constable, who had apprehended the thief with the nasty little stoat eyes.

Chapter 32

Sir Hamon le Strange stood looking out of the window. He eyed Captain Hungerford's reflection in the glass as the man brought in Francis, his shackled prisoner. After instructing Hungerford to return in thirty minutes, Hamon watched him leave with hesitation in his step and a second's delay before finally closing the door gently with a soft clunk. He felt sure this reflected nervousness on the captain's part. All was not as Hamon had initially thought. His earlier suspicions seemed interlinked with much more than he could fathom at present.

"Please, come closer." Hamon invited the prisoner to stand with him. The man's slow footsteps echoed on the wooden floor and Hamon noted the close proximity to him in which the prisoner stood. "Beautiful, is it not?" Hamon pointed to the sunset's crimson ripples and the golden orb that seemed to have been pitched into the centre.

"Aye, very." The prisoner appeared to focus on Hamon's ash blue silk doublet and the golden embroidery which sparkled in the candlelight, while the vestiges of daylight slipped beneath the horizon.

"Well, stranger, let me introduce myself," Hamon said, and gave his name before carefully adding his offices in hierarchical order. "Deputy Lieutenant of Norfolk, Justice of the Peace, and former Member of Parliament." He omitted mentioning his secretive Royalist sympathies. "Now, would you be so kind as to furnish me with your details?"

"James Jackson, sir."

"Are you a soldier, Mister Jackson?" Hamon raised his delicate eyebrows, not for a second believing the name he had been given. He observed the stains on the man's russet coat; mud and some blood specks. Then his light brown hair, which although messy was of neat cut.

"No, sir, this is what I was trying to tell the captain. I am a merchant."

"By your accent, a relatively local one." Hamon ventured.

"I'm from Colchester, my lord. Why is such a grand person as you interested in me?"

"When you came in, Mister Jackson, I pointed out the sunset," Hamon said, turning to face him. "The way the indigo clouds overlap gives them such a deep hue." He explained that the clouds' conspiracy to hide the splendour of the dying sun could never fully succeed. "Did you notice that phenomenon?"

"I'm afraid my mind was more taken by why I'd been summoned here."

"Well, when I saw the captain bringing in his brace of prisoners today, not one of those strung out around you could overshadow your presence."

"A compliment indeed," Francis acknowledged.

"You're clearly not their commander, for they did not look to you, or take any special note of your movement." Hamon slowly began to reveal his suspicions and made note of the prisoner's reaction.

"The captain is positive I am a Royalist fugitive."

"He has his own demons." Hamon would come to Captain Hungerford later. "I do agree with him that you're a fugitive."

"I don't follow your meaning."

"I'm fairly certain you're a soldier." Hamon strolled to the table and twisted a grape from its stem. "An officer at that, for your posture is far too regimented for a merchant," he said, inviting the man to sit with him and offering the bowl of grapes. And then Hamon smiled at his reminder that his hands were bound. "What goods do you trade?"

"Wool."

"Ah, our mainstay too." Hamon took pains to describe Lynn's need to levy pontage on all wool brought into the town. "The funds are essential to keep our roads in good repair. Though, with the drop in wool's price, it's a wonder you manage to make a profit. How much is the going rate now?"

"It varies, but quality is declining," Francis replied.

"It varies?" Hamon's long gaunt features were emphasised. "I have entertained such untruths long enough." He stood and started pacing slowly and deliberately, for he often thought better on foot, and he thought very logically about the amount of detail that jarred. He stood behind the prisoner's seat. "Are you married?"

"Alas, no. The quality of good women is declining faster than that of wool."

"I see." Hamon noted the way the man touched his index finger with his thumb at certain times; the briefest of movements, which to anyone else would have gone unnoticed. "Tell me, my dear wool merchant, is Colchester still filled with Dutch weavers?" He already knew this to be so.

"Aye, and their Bays and Says cloth cannot be beaten." Francis seemed quick to respond. Nor did he move his fingers.

Hamon sat down in front of him with a contented sigh. "I see you speak the truth about that fact at least." He nodded with approval. "My three score years on this earth, and having presided over the trial of many a criminal, have given me the experience of knowing when the truth is presented to me." He ventured that his skill was so well honed it was as if he had a sixth sense. "You know the captain?"

"I have never been here before to make his acquaintance."

"He also tries to distance himself from you." Hamon unravelled the whole affair with the greatest of satisfaction. "Are you related?"

"Of course not."

"Well." Hamon leaned forward with his long, thin fingers interlocked beneath his chin. "You're a Royalist officer, raised in Colchester and related to the Parliamentarian Captain Hungerford. No wonder neither of you care for each other," he said with a long and drawn out hum. "The last question in the puzzle must be why you are here and what unnerves the captain so."

"All nonsense."

Hamon stroked his wispy, fair moustache and went on to open the cover of a silver watch. Amongst the painted animals and flowers, he looked at the hands; another ten minutes before the captain was due to return.

"You're not related to him by blood, for you bear no similarity." Hamon decided to think aloud. "Neither are you named James Jackson," he said with a long and hard stare. "Who might you and the captain share as a relation?"

"Enough of this tomfoolery!"

"Madam Hungerford," Hamon said calmly. Her image danced in his mind, imprisoned there from the moment he first saw her; eyes as striking as her character and full lips, just like the prisoner. "Why, you even share a perfectly rounded chin that God seems to have added as an afterthought."

"What do you want of me?" The prisoner stood up.

"Your dear sister I'll wager?" Hamon remained seated. "You have three fine nephews."

"I do not have a sister. Your assumption, based on the opinion that I have a woman's chin, can't be further from the truth."

"People in this town can get whipped at my behest," Hamon replied with narrowed eyes. "Your sister wouldn't be half as pretty were she stripped to the waist, tied to a cart, pulled through the streets and whipped."

"You would be prepared to do that to an innocent woman?"

"I would hang her." Hamon corrected him. "Now, I wish to know your real name," he said and, before the man could reply, Hamon held up one finger. "Listen very carefully." He looked the prisoner in the eye. "If you are honest with me, I will respect that."

"I am Sir Francis Berkeley." Francis decided the best option would be to comply, hoping that, as a fellow knight, he might ensure Lucy's safety and that of her children. "I ask you again, what is it you want of me?"

"A knight of the realm?" Hamon shook his head and let out a short burst of laughter. "Not even I guessed correctly at your rank. But may I suppose also an officer in His Majesty's army?" The question garnered a slow nod from Francis. "Then you are exactly who I am looking for."

Hamon gave his word that he would free Francis, but insisted as he sat back in his seat, that when freed, Francis should completely espouse his service to ensure the continued wellbeing of the captain's wife. "I need you to deliver a message to the King and his council," he revealed and picked up a quill and began scratching an exquisitely neat order. The words, in tightly looped script, signed with the large 'L' of 'Le Strange', sat on the paper like a magnificent swan.

"I'm allowed to go?" Francis asked.

"You are to be exchanged for a Parliamentarian officer." Hamon paused. "When you're free, you'll take a letter to the King along with this as proof that you come from me," he said, twisting a ring from his little finger and handing it over. "But mark me, I expect a reply to my letter, otherwise I will assume that you have broken your word."

"Upon my honour, I shall deliver it." Francis looked him in the eye.

"Prior to your departure, I will arrange for a messenger to hand you the letter in question," Hamon explained, looking down his long nose and warning Francis that this should remain of the utmost secrecy.

Barely a minute later, a knock echoed at the door. "Sir Hamon, are you ready?" Ned asked, his words breathlessly tailing off.

"I'm satisfied that the prisoner can be released in due course, Captain." Hamon stood and paced slowly back towards the window as they left. In the dark glass he saw his reflection, the one man who could truly govern Lynn; the latest of a long line of le Stranges, ready to rescue the town from the rebel fist that squeezed it dry; head of a dynasty whose position and ethos of loyalty naturally meant that his sympathies lay squarely with the sovereign.

Chapter 33

Tears streamed from Anne's eyes. No longer teardrops, but a unified cascade that ran down her rosy cheeks. Each eye was tinged with redness and swollen, her tear ducts streaming in absolute abandon and, above them, every one of her long eyelashes merged in watery union. But it had not started like this. Far from it.

When her eyes first beheld her beloved son, they had widened with happiness and her pupils dilated so much that the emerald green was all but enveloped. She stood frozen, unable to comprehend this moment after praying for it so long, and now it was here she feared she would crush Henry with her loving embraces. She had too much love to give and an inability to control it; one of the many reasons she began to sob. She broke down in a maelstrom of sadness and joy, bitterness and relief, which made her shoulders hunch.

She sobbed until she had so little breath left she was forced to inhale sharply. This was the moment she took Henry to her bosom, kissing him all over, feeling his hair against her face, his warmth and the softness of his skin against her cheek.

So they remained, her tears wetting his head until he released a moan of protest at this maternal cocoon. The simple sound moved Anne to laughter at the relief of being able to hear any noise that fell from her son's mouth. Henry was home.

Francis's embrace of his wife and son was indicative of their world. They remained without any thought of food or drink for most of the evening, playing, hugging, kissing and laughing the hours away as Henry examined his parents and every bit of his new surroundings before giving the briefest of smiles.

"Dod!" Henry said, prompting delighted laughter and parental encouragement for more. It took a while, but when he did make another utterance – the same word – he repeated it several times.

"What are you saying, my darling?" Anne cupped his cheeks.

"Ray dod."

"You're a talkative little man." The boy took Francis's hand and seemed to look about in search of something or someone. The word led Francis to ponder anything that sounded remotely similar.

"Is this what you're looking for?" Anne took Henry's little straw soldier, which his cousin Isaac had made. But it did not satisfy him.

Francis watched Anne's concern grow and took her hand. He appreciated her distress at not understanding their son, nor being able to fulfil her motherly role and instinctively give her child what would make him happy. Francis felt her body prickle with warmth and watched her eyes well up.

"Your straw man?" Francis tried again in vain.

"Come and embrace your mother." Anne lifted the child and held him close, but he wriggled and kicked.

"Dod!"

"God?" Francis frowned and Henry let out a whine that developed into a flood of tears. The Almighty's name instantly had Francis think of Ned Hungerford, wondering what he'd done to the poor boy.

"Fetch that girl," Anne instructed, "he must be hungry."

"Aye." Francis hurried across the bedroom, slipping on the rush mat and bumping into the rocking chair, which moved back and forth in equal desperation. He headed across to the room where Jane Aylesworth was quartered and, opening the door, he called her name.

"Sir Francis!" She quickly tried to cover herself, but had nothing to hand.

"Oh ..." He drew up in shock. Her breasts, as smooth, silky and curvaceous as two drop-pearl earrings, were all he could focus on for the second it took him to understand his mistake. Her hands now covered her browned and engorged nipples. She turned her back to him, took her nightdress and lifted her arms to bring a curtain down over the peach cheeks of her rounded bottom.

"Jane, my apologies ..." He didn't know what to say and turned to leave, almost forgetting his purpose. "My son is hungry."

"Did you find her?" Anne asked upon his return to the bedroom.

"Yes." Francis closed the door and, turning his back on Anne, took a moment.

"Is she ready?"

"I think so," Francis replied.

"She should be able to hear how hungry he is." Anne's expression was chiding. She held Henry in her arms, paced around the room as though she was dancing on nothing but light cirrus clouds, and successfully managed to temper the lad's hunger with love, care and attention. "I will speak to a midwife tomorrow to find out if I am able to feed him."

"Fine." Francis had no notion of such complexities.

"She's so young." Anne suggested Jane be sent back home to Norfolk. "We can do without the expense if I can take over."

A tap at the door interrupted them and Jane timidly stepped into the room as if she were walking across a frozen lake; careful not to break any part of it lest she be consigned into icy depths. With a shawl wrapped tightly about her, she barely lifted her gaze from the floorboards. Nor did Francis, who went to the corner and poured some wine, for his throat had become quite dry.

Upon sight of the wet-nurse, Henry yelled with delight. He seemed to be the only one overjoyed to see Jane and held his hands out to her. As Jane took Henry to her room, he calmed quickly.

"Are you all right?" Francis sat on the bed next to Anne and placed an arm around her.

"When I finally get him back, he prefers some slip of a girl," Anne said with a sigh. "A comely little lass she is at that." She lay on the bed. "Even her milky white skin seems to echo the fact that she can give my son precisely what he needs."

Francis lay down beside her and touched her trembling body. She would not and could not sleep, so he held her in his protective arms, considering how, with their wishes fulfilled and family reunited, such a milestone still had the capacity to cause pain. As he drifted into a fitful slumber on the wool-filled mattress, he remembered that, secreted between that and the straw-filled paillasse beneath, was a leather satchel containing Sir Hamon le Strange's vital message, which would also have to rest until morning.

Chapter 34

Prince Rupert's hand slid impatiently across the vellum map of Bristol, smoothing the calfskin out with a crackle. Dressed in a terracotta-coloured silk suit following a meeting with the King, he removed the matching cloak draped over his left shoulder, ready to get down to business.

"Summon De Gomme," he said, judging his Dutch military engineer's advice to be invaluable.

"I hear the rebels don't have enough troops to man all of Bristol's defences." Sir Richard Crane, captain of Rupert's lifeguard, noted.

"Nor does the Governor have enough boldness to govern the entire city." Rupert leaned over the plan and looked down his aquiline nose.

"May I enquire, is the plan still to join forces with your brother's western army?" Crane asked.

"Aye, his Cornish men are some of our bravest," Rupert replied.

The Prince tilted his head while pondering and prodding the map. Bristol's ringed walls – the north studded with five forts – resembled a constellation of stars. To the south the Rivers Avon and Frome provided a natural defence. They flowed into the city from the south west and temporarily parted ways before re-joining again, and channelling out of the eastern side. This formed an island in the centre from which Bristol castle looked down upon the densely packed streets of this inner sanctum.

"The south is less heavily fortified." Crane placed all four fingers of one hand right under the line denoting the wall.

"Yet it is more concentrated with buildings," Rupert said, already preferring the north. "They will also, no doubt, fortify the church there."

"I see. Whereas to the north, once we break past the forts, we are in relatively open ground?" Crane caught on immediately.

"Exactly so," Rupert replied, without the need to point out the benefit to cavalry movement, or the fact that the forts could then be cut off from the town. "Now, how much powder have we managed to prise from Lord Percy's grip?"

"He claims there are only one hundred and twenty barrels, half of which are marked for the King's field army and our garrison towns," Crane said, turning to the Prince. "A mere fifty for us."

"Fifty?" Rupert's piercing eyes glared back at the map. "I have to capture England's second city, a port that will open up routes to Ireland, with fifty barrels of gunpowder?"

As he paced Saint John's College library, the Prince's dog lazily followed, and each of the forty-two alphabetically arranged bookcases they passed seemed to stand to attention. Rupert called for Monsieur De La Roche, whose fireworks he now saw the need of and, upon his arrival, De La Roche swept off his hat in a cascade, somewhat like his renowned pyrotechnics.

"*Votre Altesse.*"

"*Ah, Monsieur, combien de feux d'artifice avez-vous?*" Rupert wanted only the precise numbers that he could supply.

"*Il-y-a des pétards et grenades. Je pense qu'il-y-aura quatre charges de chariot.*"

"*Très bon,*" Rupert considered four cartloads of petards, grenades and fire-pikes to be a most useful addition to his force and an unexpected surprise for the enemy.

"Pardon my English, Highness, but with them you could be a second Guido Fawkes and blow up Parliament's army ..." Although, at the word 'Parliament', Boye began to bark. The yaps of the little white poodle echoed throughout the one-hundred-and-ten-foot chamber, unused to any such outburst.

"All right, Boye." Rupert bent down and patted the plump dog. "He despises Parl… or should I say, that London Assembly, as much as I, monsieur," Rupert said.

"So I see." De La Roche watched in fits of laughter as Rupert went on to shout the name of Parliament's leader – 'Pym' – the command having Boye cock his leg.

"Meneer De Gomme," Rupert said in welcome to the Dutchman, who was confronted by a dog making ready to urinate; a Frenchman in hysterics and a Prince of the blood on his knees. "I drag you away from the defence of Oxford for a great purpose," Rupert said, escorting him to the map. "Be so kind as to take a look and tell me where, in your opinion, the best points of attack would be."

"Certainly, Your Highness." De Gomme's keen eye took a few minutes to assess the gradients of hills, and the lines of streets and rivers. "Quite impressive earthworks to the north, though not as good as Oxford's." His bottom lip curled into a smile. "Six-foot high, with five-foot ditches in front of them," he noted. Yet despite this, the north still looked more favourable. "My research has found that these two forts in the north have a significant gap between them which may be out of range."

"My thanks for your quick and clear advice." Rupert appreciated the efficiency of such foreign professionals, vastly different from many of their stuffy English counterparts.

Rupert was notified at De Gomme's departure of Sir Francis Berkeley's humble request for an audience and he granted it, for the man had been missing since the surrender of Reading. Governor Aston, though recovering, was still suffering from concussion, and Captain Sidney was no more, so Berkeley could fill in the gaps about his task.

As he waited for the man to be shown in, the Prince looked out of the window at the summer's day. The June sunshine always had a capacity to transform. The grass took on a gold-green tint, the leaves of the trees waved at the warm breeze and it was as if all was well with the country. Certainly it was a land thoroughly deserving of Rupert's teenage remark on first visiting England; that he wished to break his neck so his bones could forever remain here. At the time he never foresaw that many Englishmen would one day wish to do just that. He turned to the doorway crowned by the arms of the library's founder, Bishop Williams. Upon Berkeley's entrance, Rupert could only wonder at the excuse for his absence these weeks past and whether the man had fulfilled the instructions allotted to him.

"Your Highness." Francis carefully removed his hat, satisfying etiquette by keeping the inside out of sight, and bowed.

"Sir Francis. I expected you to be in a wooden casket the next time you entered Oxford," Rupert said, raising his head high in displeasure at the lack of contact.

"My sincere apologies, sir, I was caught up in the siege of Reading." Francis held his hat in front of him as though it could deflect the prince's wrath.

"That was over with before the end of April," Rupert replied. "It's now June."

"By your leave, sir, may I explain what happened?" Francis asked.

"Did you fail?"

"No, Your Highness, I conveyed the information to James Jackson," Francis replied.

"To your friend," Rupert interjected, purposefully keeping up the pressure.

"I was afterwards arrested by a Captain Sidney, though I know not why."

"You were the only person aware of the false information we were feeding to Jackson. There could be no risks," Rupert explained.

"I hope that my past services to His Majesty vouch for my loyalty." Francis hesitated.

"Point duly noted, Sir Francis. Now, where did you get to after the surrender of the town?" Rupert asked.

"I went to fetch my son," Francis said in reference to his sister's care of the boy. "The eastern counties are becoming ever more misguided in their loyalty to the rebels and this caused me grave concern for his safety."

"And how did you travel there and back unmolested?" Rupert raised his eyebrows.

"I stole a pass from a rebel," Francis replied. "As well as my son, I have brought back some military intelligence you may find useful." He manoeuvred a ring from one of his fingers. "This is from Sir Hamon Le Strange and I have a letter too." He handed them both over.

"I see." Rupert held the ring up to the sunlight and then broke the seal and opened the letter.

To whom it may concern,

I ask you to forgive the manner of this letter. It is sent via this man, who identifies himself as Sir Francis Berkeley and he has proof positive of my identity. Kings Lynn is ready to be true to its name and declare for His Majesty.

We ask for your military support to ensure that we become the first of many towns in East Anglia to cast off our rebel oppressors.

Our defection would offer the King's armies in the north a safe route of passage to London and I humbly submit myself as a candidate for governor of the town, once I have had it turned over to the King. As soon as I receive your assurances, I shall act.

Boye sniffed the pieces of wax that fell to the floor, but finding them of no interest transferred his curiosity to Francis's latchet shoes and red soles. Rupert's attention was stolen from the letter by the dog's wagging tail and the rubbing of its head against Francis's leg.

"He has a keen nose for false rogues," Rupert said, which added weight to his opinion that Sir Francis was as plain and uncomplicated as the whitewashed walls of the chamber.

Rupert turned and paced to the bookshelves deep in thought. Shafts of sunlight fell across the books chained to their housing and the thousands of dust particles gravitating towards them. The defection of Kings Lynn would similarly draw the attention of the enemy, and their troops, and if this was to occur at the same time as his assault upon Bristol it would be fortuitous. But not only that, the rebels would also be pulled away from Newark, which, with its control of the north road, would be a vital part of the Queen's route south with her munitions.

"It seems I doubted you, Sir Francis." Rupert was ready to offer him a permanent captaincy in the infantry. "Now that the matter of your son is resolved, it should be to your other family that you give your entire focus." Rupert alluded to the army. "We have a coming siege that will tip the scales in our favour."

* * * * *

Barely four weeks later, Francis's second family had a new arrival in Queen Henrietta Maria, who brought with her various brother officers in tow. It was to Wroxton Abbey that Sir Francis had accompanied the army, and where King and Queen were reunited. Although Bristol had not yet been besieged, Wroxton Abbey certainly was, but by Royalist officers and gentlemen who danced and feasted under a canopy with music and merriment at the Queen's safe arrival.

But one of their number was in no mood to make merry. Sir Richard Warrington's smile upon seeing Sir Francis Berkeley more resembled a snarling dog such were the jagged teeth that poked out of his wrinkled mouth. Teeth that he bared at his former subordinate in as jealous a manner as Rupert's dog Boye, who, being hand-fed by the King, warned off any who got too close.

King Charles feted his wife magnificently, holding her hand, kissing her and looking longingly into her eyes as if they were married that self-same day. Nobody could tell that eighteen years of marriage had passed; eight children had come and three of them gone. Their near-daily correspondence during the seventeen long months of separation was well known and the only thing overshadowing this loving reunion was the continuing state of open warfare that had now existed between the King's subjects for eleven months.

Barely any at this point in the celebrations considered the war as the Queen's vivacious shrieks of laughter heralded the entrance of Henry Jermyn, her Master of Horse with her dwarf jester riding on his back. Coupled with these antics were Boye's, sitting up on his back legs and begging at the name of King Charles, and the Queen's excited stories of Dutch woe; rebel bombardment; storms at sea; her ailments and finally her prized munitions.

Many noses were put out of joint by her arrival, chief amongst them Prince Rupert's, who was now branded as too headstrong. Numerous others looked to the Queen for patronage, themselves all but sitting up on their hind legs. Jermyn, she had put forward for a peerage; Lord Percy, the post of General of the Ordinance; Sir Arthur Aston, Governor of Oxford, and Sir Richard Warrington, an officer's commission, to name but a few.

In thirteen days' time the fresh commissions of Sir Francis Berkeley and Sir Richard Warrington would bring both men together in the dank, early morning sky beneath Bristol's forts for the first time since civil war broke out.

Chapter 35

With large controlling hands sprawled across one of Bristol Castle's sandstone crenellations, and his plump fingers gripping the masonry like a minister in the pulpit, Nathaniel Fiennes looked down upon his flock. His face was as square as Bristol Castle and his eyes as if they'd slid towards each ear to allow room for his broad nose. One pupil might be slightly higher than the other, but he was still Parliament's governor, and his eyes still perceptive. He watched the cannons being removed from the ships in the harbour; the vessels' brass hearts going on to be transplanted into church towers, behind gates and in main streets for defence.

The four turrets of Bristol Castle were regular haunts of Nathaniel's, for up here he was closest to God. Forget the pomp of churches and the vast cathedral. It was right under the Almighty's gaze that he felt most calm, his head at its clearest and, with Rupert's fifteen thousand Royalists outside his gates, what better place to conduct the defence?

"Saint Mary Radcliffe's has artillery atop the tower, sir." Captain Bagnal praised the building's ability to hamper any attack on the southern walls.

"It'll do more of the Lord's work now than it ever has." Fiennes' puritanism was as ingrained as the weather-beaten patterns in the stone. "In fact, I'd prefer to load the Bishop of Bristol into the muzzle for the first salvo."

"We don't have the Bishop, but our forts have one hundred and fifty barrels of gunpowder to feed their bellies," Major Wood said and looked towards the two great northern hills, upon which those forts were nested.

"If only I was stocked up on soldiers too," Fiennes replied. He lamented having half his garrison absorbed into Sir William Waller's Parliamentarian army, which had lost them all in defeat two weeks ago. "Soldiers, to hold back the Cavalier hoards and their devilish Prince."

"You still have two thousand brave troops under your command." Wood barely paused. "And remarkably strong forts and earthworks. The populace is loyal, and let's not forget, Rupert has a distinct absence of siege weaponry."

"Do not underestimate him." Fiennes' troop of horse were the ones who had experienced the first of Rupert's famous cavalry charges.

"As long as we don't underestimate ourselves," Wood replied; his words as plain as his black, Puritan's garb and short hair.

"I am a realist." Fiennes crossed his arms. "Our walls are medieval, and the city is crossed by two rivers which will hamper the movement of our own men." After giving his opinion that this was the hardest city in England to defend, he sent the officers back to their command points.

"The enemy are already doing battle with disease." Wood's manner had been prickly ever since the governor replied to

Rupert's summons to surrender. Fiennes had told the Royalists that the town could not be relinquished until he was brought to more extremes.

One of Fiennes' forts to the north, whose palisades crowned Brandon Hill, offered a view of the ant-like enemies who had worked busily all day setting up gun posts and making probing attacks. Rupert's men had never stopped throwing up fresh defensive positions and, from his outdated ones, Fiennes was left most apprehensive. Barely thirteen weeks of governing the city had brought him to such a state. Not that he wasn't prepared to lay down his life for God's cause – he wasn't afraid – it was concern at the task before him. Nor was Bristol quite as secure from within as it should have been. He'd taken over after arresting the last governor for complicity with the King.

"You are but human, my Prince, and I have God on my side." The only one to hear Fiennes was a crow landing on the corner of the tower with head darting one way and then the next. Its black feathers were as dark as the night that came on fast and seemed darker than most nights, as if God had averted his gaze from what was imminent. Flying over Bristol's southern wall, the bird glided over Saint Mary Radcliffe's, whose tolling bells pealed out a warning that the Royalist troops were on the move.

Landing just in front of the steep ditch beneath the city wall, the bird hopped around, unperturbed by the King's Cornish soldiers, whose advance stopped as fast as it had begun, and who soon returned to their original positions. Governor Fiennes' garrison, however, was duly kept on constant alert throughout the night, so much so that the dull, clanging bell had them wishing they could also take flight.

* * * * *

In the dark of night, a dense human forest of Royalists stood to the south of Bristol, but the nightly pall could not lay to rest the ferocious tempers of the Cornish. Their colonel, Sir Nicholas Slanning, stood with his men, who were eager to grapple with the city's defenders after yet another feint attack. And, although merely a ruse to keep the Parliamentarians on high alert, this impotent play-acting gripped the hearts of every Royalist. Their adrenaline spiked, anticipation soared, but having to draw up short of the city and then trail back to their lines took its toll. Certainly, some might understand the tactic, even appreciate the necessity of it, but it wasn't possible to trick the enemy without tricking themselves too. The Cornishmen's disappointment did not simply disperse when they eventually turned back and resentment bubbled every time.

Now at three of the clock in the morning, Rupert's officially planned assault was still many hours away and the Royalist artillery lit up the sky with flashes like molten iron, leaving Slanning's men itching to forge the real attack. The cannons fired at sprawling Saint Mary Radcliffe's, which stood between them and the city walls; the largest parish church in England was now stuffed with a full congregation of Parliamentarians and three of their guns.

"Captain, ready for the next feint?" Slanning checked.

"Aye, sir, but I'm not sure they are," he replied, pointing at the conscripted Cornish miners – or 'tinners' – who stamped their feet in the manner of unruly steeds.

"English sons of whores." One Cornishman echoed the bitterness of being forced to leave their families and enter England to fight alongside Englishmen, against yet more Englishmen.

"Listen to me," Slanning called to the front ranks. "This is but another ruse only. Pass this on to those behind you." He looked at the array of flowery, white ribbons in their knitted wool Monmouth caps.

The eight hundred Cornishmen set off again towards Bristol. Wind blew in their faces in a bid to temper Slanning's men; the central tertia, flanked by Colonel Basset and Buck's regiments to their left and right.

The Lord's prayer was taken up by the men as they marched; its tempo increasing with the speed of every footfall. However, no Cornishman was willing to forgive any Parliamentarian that they trespassed against.

"Slow down!" Slanning used every breath to demand restraint, but the advance continued apace, and the beat of drums was lost in the growing furore. Curses, chants and frustration replaced order. Rapidly it became clear that there was no going back this time and, with Bristol still in darkness save for the moon and the light flickering at the windows of Saint Mary Radcliffe's, the Royalists were unleashing their deathly attack three hours earlier than planned. But deathly to whom it remained to be seen, for it would not be a co-ordinated attack as Rupert's northern contingent was unaware as to what was occurring in the south.

"To the walls!" Slanning saw no other option than to make the best of it. The tertia of three thousand men converged upon the city's nine-foot thick walls, whose silhouetted turrets resembled devilish horns and their crenulations, vicious teeth. The monster that was Bristol was now fully awake and thumped out artillery barrages of its own.

Flashes of fire taunted the Royalists, rapports shook every star in the sky above them and whizzing missiles whispered their names. Some of Slanning's men were cast into the air along with earth and stones, but still the rest rolled on.

"Ditch!" The cry repeated, although the warning was not able to prevent some tumbling into the seven-foot gap. Bristol's cannon roared in mocking laughter as the whole Cornish army was forced to halt, to clamber into the three-foot-deep fissure in the earth and then out again. The Royalists were little more than cannon fodder because siege equipment had not joined the advance of what should have been only a feint. Finally, the ditch had brought the men to heel where their commanders had failed.

Bristol's twenty-five guns thundered in chorus and the flashes picked out the late arrival of the Cornish carts packed with siege ladders, faggots and the woven brushwood fascines employed to make paths across the ditch. Thirty minutes after their premature attack, the three thousand Royalists struggled in the night, without cover, against a hail of death that compromised everything until two huge explosions rocked the city.

The duo of Rupert's demi-cannons vented a tremor that spread right across Somerset and, apart from mimicking the Prince's towering rage, the gigantic detonations signalled the all too premature start of the combined assault on Bristol.

Chapter 36

"March on, lads!" Francis had his company on the move so quickly that they were still only half-awake. He'd been resting with the northern Royalists when the demi-cannons shook every stone in the rocky earth around them and blasted plumes of crimson and orange skywards as though Van Dyck had daubed a ghostly paintbrush across the heavens. Francis wore a white band tied about his neck, a colour that adorned all of Rupert's men in some way as they commenced the full-scale attack.

"The devil take those Cornish!" One of the men cursed.

"He may have already." Francis drew his sword. "But he won't be taking us," he yelled as his company advanced, part of the four regiments under Colonel Wentworth's command.

"To the hill!" Lieutenant-Colonel Sir Richard Warrington ordered. "But no heroics, Berkeley," he warned as Francis passed him.

Cursing the incompetent old man under his breath, Francis couldn't even see Bristol. Two hills ahead of him obliterated sight of everything, and their dense silhouettes were broken only by the rebel forts crowning each one which flickered with gunshot. Fireflies of musket balls and comet tails of soaring roundshot rained down upon the Royalists. These missiles tore through many of Wentworth's men before they'd even closed up to the right-hand hill, topped by Brandon Fort. The high ground was once home to a twelfth-century chapel. Now the eighteen-foot square wooden palisade echoed only to chants of war, and the approaching Royalists were on a pilgrimage of a very different nature.

Once at the base of the mound, Francis's company was in the thick of it. Without respite, Wentworth's troops attempted to fill with tied brushwood the ditch running around the base of Brandon Hill, but they had insufficient fascines. A similar situation had the rest of the northern attack grind slowly to a halt.

* * * * *

An earthwork wall, with a ditch at its front, sprang from the west of Bristol, circled the north side and stretched around to the east of the city. It linked each hill fort into a pendant and its central jewel, Windmill Fort, had drawn Prince Rupert's eye. His attention was not on the fort, but the Royalists who were being picked off as they attacked uphill and, unable to cross the ditches, now broke into retreat.

"S'wounds, do you run?" Rupert couldn't believe his eyes. His three-pronged attack in the north, a devilish trident that should have brought Bristol down, was blunted.

"Highness, they have no equipment with which to bridge the ditch, for its wider than we anticipated." One of the officers explained.

"Cowering behind there won't help, be damned!" Rupert spurred his horse and pounded towards the stream of men going to ground behind a stone wall. Pikemen, like giant hedgehogs, hoped to hibernate until a better climate presented itself. But Rupert of the Rhine's wrath, and the heat of his rage, warmed them up to make a further attempt to take the Windmill Fort.

The Prince drew up before the troops and circled his horse, soon joined by his standard bearer and a posse of officers. "Follow me!" His cry pounded the soldiers as much as the artillery and his determined presence bowled over all defeatism.

Rupert led them back towards Windmill Fort. If needs be he'd have them fire round after round until the fort and its palisades were reduced, splinter by splinter; to mere stumps of rotten, wooden teeth. But as the Prince led the troops on, his horse buckled, and it went down with a shot to its eye. Rupert, extracting his feet from the stirrups, jumped off the horse and marched away without so much as adjusting his pace. Colonel William Legge rode over to give him his own mount in replacement.

"My Prince, are you injured?"

"Of course not," Rupert replied. "Tell me, what of the other two northern attacks?"

"There's no breakthrough anywhere." Legge shook his head.

"Wentworth's?" The Prince asked of the attack upon Brandon Hill.

"Pinned down."

"Grandison's at Priors Hill?"

"Lord Grandison was shot in the leg, unlikely to survive. Colonel Owen shot in the face," Legge explained that the men were spent and had no senior officers.

"The Cornish?" Rupert was desperate for any encouraging sign.

"All three colonels killed and their regiments forced to fall back, I'm afraid."

The young royal roared with frustration. A costly hour this had been in terms of everything; valuable officers, men, reputations and the expense of ammunition and powder. These facts had left him in no doubt that Bristol simply had to fall to him this night, if it was the last thing he did. With far too much already lost for the night to end in defeat; like a gambler, he threw in everything.

* * * * *

"This way, men!" Francis had his company follow other Royalists making for the centre of Windmill and Brandon hills. A crevasse between them that led right up to the earthwork wall that ringed the north of Bristol. Through this valley, Colonel Washington's dismounted dragoons were rushing, truly untouched by any cannon.

"Remain with me!" Sir Richard called after Francis, who ignored him.

The taffeta standard of Francis's company called his eighty men together in great, arcing waves, and he led them over the uneven ground ahead and towards the earthwork. Rumbles from the rebel's artillery shook the ground, while a series of blinding flashes disorientated the Royalists. Coupled with the skeletal fingers of stone that poked out of the hard soil, Francis and many others found it difficult going in the dark of night.

Yet they made it between the two hills which were out of range of all artillery. This ground was not torn up like a trapdoor to hell. Windmill Fort may have been right above them, but hurrying on beneath its nose put the men well below the trajectory of its cannon and they closed right up to the perimeter of Bristol. Jutting from the earthwork wall was a defensive, triangular spur like a bow of a ship, its deck housing a small artillery piece that soon foundered amidst an explosion.

Francis called on his soldiers to head straight to the wall, which stood taller than most men, in front of which was a ditch five-foot-deep by six-foot wide. It was in the ditch in front of the spur that Colonel Wentworth himself and some men threw grenades over the top. With swords and hands, pikes and halberds, they poked and hacked at the wall in a bid to break through it. Drawing up in a line with the enemy forts to their backs, Francis had his men provide covering fire to the commander.

"Prime your pieces!" His musketeers poured powder into their pans and blew off the excess. Into the barrel went more gunpowder and a lead ball, followed by a tap of the butt upon the earth.

"Place your wadding!" Francis had his men ram paper wadding into the barrel with a scouring stick and, once done, the guns were fired at any target presenting itself.

Two hours after the attack commenced, fortifications and buildings began to develop a golden edge as dawn came like an alchemist's spell. A barn that masked Francis's men from the fire of Brandon Fort behind them, loomed out of the darkness, as did the earthwork wall that stretched off as far as anyone could see. It felt as though every man was waking only to discover that the horrors of the night had been real.

"Gather up those posts." Francis took a handful of men and made use of some broken storm poles that had once jutted defensively out of the earth. Other Royalists set upon a wooden cart, beat it to bits and used its planking to bridge the ditch at a narrow point.

Francis and his men furiously stabbed their sharpened weapons into the earthwork wall. Their hands almost bled with the repetitive cut and thrust. Jab after jab of poles, halberds and swords, along with digging and clawing, gradually took its toll on the dense earth, and a segment began to break. The front part fell away, and the same weapons carved, chopped and hewed to further open up the breach.

A pink streak of sunlight lit up the gash in the earthwork wall as if emphasising this singular chink in Bristol's armour, and the Royalists gauged the sides enough for infantry and then cavalry to pass through.

"Into the gap!" Francis led his company on. Jubilation did not penetrate the attackers' adrenaline-fraught and exhausted shells, for as soon as they passed through the wall they were confronted by Roundhead cavalry drawn up in wait. And not just a line of rested horsemen who seemed to have been patiently waiting hours for their prey, but another earthwork fort behind them too, with light artillery that would blast the Royalists to kingdom come. The sight left only one order for Francis to give: "Charge to horse!"

The pikemen of his group angled their eighteen-foot poles to the correct height to pierce the breasts of these apocalyptic horsemen. It was now approaching six of the clock in the morning. Despite 'Washington's breach' in the perimeter wall, all three Royalist tertias in the north were still held in check and the Cornish to the south were stuck behind a hedge. Time was a fickle turncoat and the next hour would prove its allegiance.

Chapter 37

"They're through!" The shafts of dawn's light wounded Governor Fiennes' confidence, pointing as they did to the Royalists at the breach in Bristol's defences. "Between Brandon and Windmill Forts," he said.

"Our weakest point." Major Lewis avoided saying 'I told you so', but his tone accounted for it all the same. "Out of artillery range."

"The enemy repulsed in every place but that one," Captain Bagnal agreed, but focused on the positive. "At least the Governor stationed cavalry there."

"Good job too, for even the ditches were shallower in that area." Lewis's pockmarked cheeks puffed out.

"It's the stony ground." Bagnal was quick to say. "My men found it impossible to dig any deeper."

"Let's hope we never have to bury any of our dead there," Lewis replied.

"As the good captain says, I have cavalry covering that weak point," Fiennes interceded.

"Now it's breached; it's breached. In my opinion, we should

set the whole garrison on Rupert and expel him immediately." Lewis advocated they leave the inner sanctum in a full-scale counter-attack.

"If we leave the inner city there is no going back," Fiennes responded and eyed the smoke plumes that tried to block sight of the breaking day. "Far better keep the garrison here fresh and safe."

"So, we lay all our hopes upon Major Hercules Langrish's cavalrymen?" Major Lewis had always been uneasy about the fellow. "I've said from the beginning that he's a coward at best, and a turncoat at worst," he said.

"We'll withdraw from the forts if Langrish doesn't drive them off. Pull the troops at the perimeter back into the city to join us." Fiennes had long ago decided against any risk-taking.

"What?" Lewis's nose screwed up into a hundred creases, one, it seemed, for each of the reasons he had to oppose this. "That would leave Rupert in possession of the high ground and all of the forts!"

"We cannot have the men in the forts cut off from us, otherwise they're as good as dead." Fiennes replied.

"Handing over the high ground would give Rupert a perfect crest from which his artillery could pulverise the city," Lewis argued.

"I have made my decision." Fiennes would not suffer any insubordination. "The men would be massacred if we left them in the forts. Far better they join us and make a stand here in the centre."

Footsteps interrupted the dispute of opinion and a man stepped out onto the tower. "A message from Major Wood, sir. One hundred of the enemy are through the breach and face Major Langrish's cavalry," the soldier said. "How about a charge from the entire garrison to see the enemy off?"

"What chatter is this from one of your station?" Fiennes said, taking exception to being lectured. "You are naught but a saucy knave!"

"Why has Langrish allowed so many Cavaliers to slip through?" Lewis pressed for an all-out assault and did not take his eyes off the Governor.

Fiennes, in contrast, watched the growing mass of Royalists swarm the earthwork line. This plague of Cavaliers would spread if not contained. Then, flaming, spitting sparks appeared at the breach and, like shooting stars, soared along it. A mere flicker in Fiennes' large eyes, but, he thought, does not every inferno start from a tiny spark? And Rupert knew all about fire, it being three months since he had burnt Birmingham to a cinder.

* * * * *

Fizzing sparks devoured the fuse of a firework strapped to a sixteen-foot pike. One of Rupert's cavalry officers levelled the pike as the walnut-sized charge of corn powder, sulphur and saltpetre took hold and then he bolted along the inside line of Bristol's wall. The shackled firework raged at its tethers, demarcating the earthwork wall to every Royalist and sending the Parliamentarian infantrymen manning it into spirals of panic.

"Wildfire!" The yells of the Roundheads jumped from mouth to mouth and they fled with tales of devilish flames ready to consume them all. Their retreat back to the centre of Bristol took them past Langrish's cavalry.

Major Hercules Langrish and his Roundhead horsemen bided their time and faced Rupert's men, near one hundred of whom had drawn up to make a stand.

"Everyone ready?" Langrish asked calmly and patted his horse's neck. Snorts and neighs abounded as he ordered their advance. He had his men ride at the one hundred and fifty Royalists now on Bristol's sacred ground, whose trespass was encouraged by yet another of Rupert's firepikes that flashed and glittered in defiance.

* * * * *

A waterfall of silver stars erupted from an exploding firepike that lit up the battleground.

"Charge to horse!" Francis and the other officers cried as the Parliamentarian cavalry came at them with levelled swords threatening to make this the last dawn for many a man.

The Royalist pikemen formed square, with pike butts resting on the instep of each right foot and poles extending outwards at forty-five degrees. Royalist musketeers with their backs to the earthwork also fired salvo after salvo as the horsemen closed in with a terrifying chorus of pounding hooves and thudding pistol shot. Into this mix were added the drums that transformed Francis's word of command into hurried beats that every soldier leapt to.

"Stand firm, here they come!" Francis barked, keeping one eye on his men and the other on the Roundheads. Then the bulging eyes of their giant horses looked down upon the Royalists; enemy riders larger than life beneath blood red streaks of sky. Rapiers blinded Francis's men with frenzied slashes, pistols picked holes in his ranks and beasts trampled them.

One rebel cavalryman blasted from his saddle left his horse rearing, leaderless and lost. A pike shaft was thrust into its chest before it could disrupt the Royalist formations.

When another Roundhead rode too close, some men grabbed his boot tops and buff coat to tug him down; the long tip of Francis's halberd finishing him off.

Crushed up into a square, shifting here and there and gripping their pikes like they were anchors, Francis's men burned with rage and their heads rang with terror. But their musket shot peppered the Parliamentarian cavalry until their leader eventually signalled a retreat, turned tail and led his men back towards the city centre.

Francis and the other officers encouraged their men to pursue, bellowing the code word of the day: 'Oxford'. With a foothold in the perimeter of the city, the attackers went on to storm the earthwork bastion standing between them and Bristol's inner sanctum, watched all the while by Bristol's cathedral and the castle turrets.

* * * * *

The fire of the Parliamentarian fort known as the Essex Work and its light artillery was brought to a halt; first by their own retreating infantry who yelled of wildfire, and now by their cavalry, who were in headlong retreat from the same peril. The defenders of this little island ceased fire, so as not to kill their comrades, and then they question their own fates, for none wanted to be marooned in a sea of Prince Rupert's soldiers.

More and more Royalists were making it through the earthwork wall and now their cavalry too. Rupert's cavalry; his famed horsemen who destroyed anything in their way; who charged furiously without stopping to fire a pistol but rode right over every obstacle. More fiery flashes heralded a wall of metal-tipped Royalist pikemen closing up on the Essex Work like a giant iron maiden. As a result, the Parliamentarians leaped over the walls of their fortress and every one joined the race back to Bristol, which, like a tolling church bell, seemed to call them to the fold.

Chapter 38

The fingertips of Governor Fiennes' hands came together like a clergyman's, so used to this posture of prayer that they appeared welded into position. At the head of a council of war in Bristol Castle, with a faraway look on his square face, he may well have called for divine intervention so impossible was his situation. It was two of the clock in the afternoon. Eleven hours of fighting had brought Rupert the Devil to Frome Gate, beating down the door to the inner city.

"If we'd attacked and forced the enemy back out of the perimeter line earlier …" Captain Bagnal had advocated this around seven in the morning.

"We made a sally out of the town and it didn't succeed," Fiennes replied, now aiming his fingertips at Bagnal.

"Aye, sir, but that was with only a few hundred men, and five hours after the enemy broke in." Captain Bagnall argued.

"I was facing mutiny at the time," Fiennes said, making complaint of Major Lewis, who had only withdrawn his men from the punctured earthworks when threatened by a death sentence.

"I can understand Lewis's apprehension," Bagnal replied, and leaned forward like an assize judge. "We had no reason to give up the forts and earthworks to the north. We could have done so much more," Bagnal gained supportive nods from many officers.

"Such as firing the suburbs?' Fiennes large nostrils flared like a thoroughbred. "I gave the instruction, but it was not carried out."

Captain Bagnal stroked his bald head. "I know of no such order. Indeed, it was proposed, but not approved."

Colonel John Fiennes, the governor's brother, got to his feet, scratching his chair along the floor. His blotchy skin reddened as he praised his brother's shoring up of morale by distributing both bread and Bristol's sweet wine. "May I remind you all that our governor was nearly killed by a bomb while visiting the soldiers manning the city gate?"

The applause of the mayor and some officers was countered by Captain Bagnal's blunt assessment of morale. "The men stationed at our earthwork line had been pulled back into the city with no encouragement, or explanation, and left to stand idle. As a result, many went on to reinforce the city's ale houses." He revealed. "Within this castle we have provisions aplenty for three months of siege. I say roll up the drawbridge and let us hold firm."

"Enough!" Governor Fiennes had been starved of his subordinates' support for too long. "This city and its castle go hand in hand. If the city be taken, then the castle surrenders too," he said, expressing his earnest desire to avoid unnecessary deaths and destruction. "Besides, the castle won't even hold half of my total force."

"The citizens are with us whatever the cost," Bagnal replied and spoke of the womenfolk who had stuffed sacks of wool against Frome Gate to keep back the Royalist hordes.

"I propose to parley with the enemy," Governor Fiennes said, noting that the earthworks, the suburbs and higher ground were occupied by the Cavaliers. "It will only be a matter of time before the King's men fire on the city from their vantage points. Further resistance will simply prejudice my men and the townsfolk."

With his more vocal officers at this time in the streets with the troops, Fiennes positively demanded a parley, a viewpoint adopted wholeheartedly by the Mayor who argued that to fight on threatened all the civilians of Bristol ... and the assets of its wealthy inhabitants.

Chapter 39

A long and drawn-out creak echoed, like the movement of a branch in the wind or the shifting interior of a galleon at sea. Only when John Pym's stout frame came fully to rest on the wooden seat did the noise peter out. He could be forgiven for pinning the cause on his tired body after a gruelling journey from London. He turned to John Glyn, one of two Members of Parliament accompanying him to army headquarters.

"The old man needs to get some fight in his belly," Glyn declared of Lord General Essex.

"He's too influenced by his cousin's peace party," Sir Henry Vane said with a thoughtful rub of his oversized chin.

"Such chords of discontent will never allow harmony within our high command," Pym warned, trying not to focus on his growing need for a chamber pot. He kept his black woollen cloak with its linen lining wrapped about him for warmth.

"Let us be purged of him," Glyn said. "A better commander could be found. You should have accepted his resignation when he so childishly offered it."

"Right now he's the best we have and will be given due respect." Pym's aim was to praise the Lord General to encourage his distance from the spineless advocates of peace.

"To cut free of Essex would be to cut Parliament in two: Lords on one side, Commons on the other." Vane was well aware of the true reason behind Pym's clemency.

"It feels like we've been on the road for days." Pym had other issues on his mind and adjusted his posture, his linen drawers being especially uncomfortable.

"You've not had much sleep, John." Vane had noticed the man's unease all the way to Kingston upon Thames. "Lord Essex may well be in the same predicament over worry that we might give an independent command to his rival," he said with a smile that made his arched brows rise.

"William the Conqueror." Glyn repeated the common-folks' name for Sir William Waller. "A tactician with more bravery, cunning and dynamism in his little finger than Essex possesses in his whole stout body."

Before Vane could respond, a soldier entered the room and announced that the Lord General would see them. Both Glyn and Vane held back for their leader, but Pym instructed them to go first and only after their backs were turned did he adjust his breeches. Once called 'The Ox' for his strength of resolve and character, he now noted a less than complementary similarity to the animal in the way he slowly plodded.

"Lord Essex," Pym said while removing his hat and ushering Vane and Glyn into the room.

"Mister Pym, pray explain why I am graced with such a visit?" Essex asked with a slow bow of his head. He eyed all three men with the look of an aged lion ready to defend his patch. Wisps of tobacco smoke rose from his smouldering pipe, infusing every crevice of the room with his presence.

"You can retract your resignation, my lord ..." Pym was cut short.

"You've changed your opinion?" Essex retorted and brushed some dirt from his ochre doublet of Italian silk.

"How so?"

Pym's question gave Essex the opportunity to vent his every grievance.

"Unfortunately, I cannot recall the exact allegations you made in your last letter, which in my anger was consigned to the fire. Yet I believe the phrase you used was that having Parliament's army under the King's command would be safer than having me at its head." Essex recollected, and Pym's gaze dropped.

"My lord, the flames were the best place for that letter," Pym replied.

"Yet it was not I who lost an entire army to the Royalists." Essex referred to William Waller. "But for this he is to be given ten thousand more men freshly raised to lose again?"

"It is your actions that support Waller's candidacy for command of these men," Pym said.

"How so?" Essex asked, so taken aback that he began to pace the room.

"You wrote to the Speaker of the House, proposing we reopen peace negotiations with the King," Pym said without taking a breath. "You appear defeatist while Waller, fresh from battle, courageously wishes to continue the fight."

"Charisma does not win battles." Essex raised his hands.

"And then there are your demands for enquiries," Glyn added. "One to examine the loss of Bristol, another to assess how the Queen managed to pass our northern forces and get to Oxford, and now you propose an enquiry into how Waller lost our western army." Glyn counted each point out on his stubby fingers. "Dwelling on all of this does not boost confidence in our cause and, in fact, suggests disillusionment on your part when instead you should be fostering hope."

"I cannot serve Parliament in the capacity of Lord General if Waller is given a command independent of me," Essex stated with hands clasped behind his back. "A man should not be honoured simply because he woos public opinion like a cheap whore."

"Then I will ensure that he is subordinate to you, Lord Essex. But he will still receive his army with orders to protect the south-east." Pym's decision removed Essex's argument in one fell swoop. "Of course, you will have to give me time to get all of this approved, but in exchange I expect your full co-operation."

"You find me satisfied with your compromise, Master Pym. Though I hope my pleas for reinforcements do not fall upon deaf ears," Essex replied.

"Demonstrate what you can achieve with the men you have and I'm sure your requests for more would be better received," Glyn said.

"I am Lord General of Parliament's armies and not a schoolboy who has to prove his worth." Essex slammed a hand down upon the table, which saw his pipe roll off. "Be damned!" He glanced down at the snapped stem as though it were a dead comrade in arms.

"My lord, your threatened resignation cast us into turmoil and gave extra strength to the peace party, who wish to sell out every one of us to the King." Pym warned. "The Cavaliers haven taken Bristol from us and now besiege Gloucester. That city cannot, and must not, suffer the same fate."

"My men are sick, unpaid and weary. I have barely three thousand infantry and two and a half thousand horse fit for duty," Essex said with a sigh.

"If Gloucester surrenders, then the whole of the West Country will fall to the enemy." Pym's expression was resolute. "Your actions will either save our cause, or sentence it to ruin."

"Then Gloucester will not be lost," Essex resolved, his gravelly tone now calm in the face of such a stark warning. Within the old general was a reserve of steel so deep that it didn't usually break the surface. After a marriage at thirteen years of age and a public divorce that saw his manhood mocked, this strength had been well-honed. Lord General Essex would therefore do his damnedest to ensure that he did not also succumb to accusations of military impotence. "The King has refused to storm Gloucester for fear of incurring similar losses to Bristol; a decision which may just give me enough time to get there and lift the siege."

"An outcome that would necessitate another set-piece battle." Pym prepared them all.

Chapter 40

"Can't you see him?" Sir Hamon Le Strange stood atop the octagonal Chapel of Our Lady of the Mount in Kings Lynn. His Majesty's newly appointed governor sheltered his eyes from the sun with a fine beaver-fur hat trimmed with braid and observed the Parliamentarian army besieging the town.

"Who, Father?"

The question prompted Hamon to release a sigh upon the summer air, determined not to demean himself by personally searching out the Earl of Manchester, commander of the enemy force.

"Manchester, of course," he replied, emerald ring glinting in the sunlight as he casually pointed in the direction of the enemy.

"I can see only his standard," Hamon's eldest son said.

"I suppose I should take it as a positive that they've sent a peer of the realm to besiege me and not that wart-ridden commoner." Hamon frowned.

"You mean Cromwell?"

"I believe so." Hamon sniffed. "Considering he failed to notice any disaffection here towards Parliament, I don't see why people speak so highly of his abilities." Hamon paced the roof, crowned by a cruciform chamber of Ancaster stone. The red-brick Chapel was a stopping point for many a pilgrim on the way to the shrine at Walsingham, and Hamon prayed for Lord Newcastle. If Kings Lynn was to be saved from its stranglehold, the Earl of Newcastle would be the one to do it as soon as he had managed to take Hull and continue his advance south.

"What do you plan to do about the eighteen thousand men out there, Sir Hamon?" The Mayor's elaborate lace collar draped about his shoulders much resembled the net that was closing in upon the town. "Relief is nowhere to be seen."

"Do not worry yourself, we will be rescued." Hamon had already chosen a suitable messenger to carry a letter pleading for assistance to the King.

"We cast off the Parliamentarians to escape their taxation, yet the cost could turn out to be twice as bad," the Mayor stammered with flushed cheeks.

"Every one of us has had to dig deep," Hamon replied with a withering expression.

Never one to stomach worriers, Hamon left him and entered the chapel and admired its fan-vaulted ceiling that sprayed out like an ornate, gothic waterfall. The town's gunpowder barrels now housed here stood sentry along the wall. The double staircase, which had once echoed to the footfalls of armies of pilgrims, offered one way up and a separate way down. It was by this means that Lucy Hungerford was escorted to him, and Madam Hungerford, as well as Our Lady, was to be tasked with the town's salvation.

"I have broken no laws," Lucy protested. Her high, peach-like cheeks were not rouged by her good humour, but from concern. Their ripe shine equalled the ruby of her plump bottom lip, now set with determination. "What is it you want of me?"

"I have a journey for you to embark upon." Hamon looked down his flat, thin nose.

"Why me?"

"It can only be you," he said as sunlight streamed through the little quatrefoil window. "To Oxford you must go with a message vital to the safety of this place."

"Oxford?" Lucy exclaimed, her long, black eyelashes blinking in shock. "I've no business there – my children need me here."

"Every person in this town is *my* child; needing my protection." Hamon held up one finger to ensure she remained focussed on his words. "Remember, if it weren't for me, your brother would still be languishing in prison." He removed his rose-scented gloves. "You and your family owe me a debt."

Lucy's eyes burned and her frown, which looked set to herald stern words, dissipated upon Hamon's statement. "For which I am most grateful to you, Sir Hamon, but to send me away ..." She was lost for words.

"You will carry a most important despatch to your brother, the successful delivery of which will mean the continued survival of all of those you leave here," Hamon instructed her.

"You mean my sons?" Lucy whispered with finality.

"They will be here upon your return."

"Will you provide everything I need?" she asked.

"You need little. Your coach leaves in an hour," Hamon told her and handed over a pass he'd prepared weeks before which would see her through Parliamentarian territory. "Your brother and his contacts can look after you when you get to Oxford."

* * * * *

Madam Hungerford next entered Hamon's thoughts as he made his way to church later that Sunday to pray for the town's deliverance. Saint Margaret's was his spiritual home and as long as he was governor, it was protected from Parliament, who were defiling every church. Beneath its towers, spire and central lantern, he stepped inside and passed the stone pillars that were the bulwarks propping up his entire world.

"Glory be to God." Hamon did the Lord's work. He took his seat in a pew separate from the common folk and near the carved busts of sixteen *misericords*, recalling how his mother of beloved memory had always pointed out the Black Prince.

"O' Almighty God," the preacher said with furrowed features. "King of all Kings and Governor of all things, to whom it belongeth justly to punish sinners and to be merciful to those that truly repent." The words were as crisp as the white ruff at the man's neck.

"Amen," Hamon whispered, for he had since repented his neutrality by declaring for the King, God's anointed sovereign.

"Save and deliver us, we humbly beseech thee, from the hands of our enemies. Abate their pride, assuage their malice and confound their devices, that we may be preserved evermore from all perils to glorify thee ..."

A low whine played about Hamon's ear, growing rapidly louder and more threatening until the arched, western window erupted into a mess of mullions, glass and tangled lead. Hamon yelled out, clawed at the wooden rail in front of him and fell to his knees. A decorative angel, whose face had adorned the huge window since time immemorial shattered, leaving but a lump of its harp remaining. The sound of falling glass and masonry was deafening and Hamon kept his eyes tightly closed against the din of what seemed like hellish, ghostly hounds.

"What treason and contempt for all things sacred!" Hamon yelled in a trembling voice.

"Father, you're bleeding." His son helped him up and attended to the small cuts that speckled Hamon's long, gaunt face, which further paled upon sight of the sixteen-pound cannonball smouldering in the aisle.

"We are facing rebels who have no soul and believe in nothing but greed and destruction." Hamon felt vulnerable, no matter how much he reassured himself that God, and indeed the King, would come to the aid of all those with loyal hearts.

Chapter 41

The crowd was as busy as ever, bustling with business and buzzing with tittle-tattle. The array of colourful attire was as diverse as the personalities of the ladies, gentlemen, ministers and officers that hummed with chatter in Oxford's Christchurch College. King Charles the First and his army were besieging Gloucester, but he'd returned to Oxford for a council meeting and it was to here that this vast army of attendants had followed him. Three other men also arrived, but their journey had been very much longer; it had taken them over one year to undertake, and they had left London that week. Yet, as they stepped into the college, they might well have been inmates of the Bedlam Asylum, such was the fascination their arrival prompted.

A wall of silence met the sight of the Earls' of Holland, Bedford and Clare. All faces turned to them, mouths smirked, eyebrows rose and, as they faced the tide of people, a whispering undercurrent started. Holland, his head held high, was dressed in an exquisite crimson silk suit, and he stepped forward with cane outstretched to lead the way. The courtiers parted before them, eyeing the trio as they drifted into the centre of the room to be gawped at some more. Only the arrival of Prince Rupert broke the awkward and uneasy proceedings.

"Ah, my lords, pray come with me." Rupert invited them to accompany him.

Holland's watery-blue ribbon of the Order of the Garter did nothing to smooth the currents in which he now found himself adrift. Nor did his past service, drawing up the King and Queen's marriage treaty, or his once close friendship with the Queen, matter to most here, for it was overshadowed by his having sided with the enemy. As he followed Rupert, he was oblivious to the whispers that the King had refused to meet them.

"I bid you welcome to Oxford, my lords," Rupert said as the antechamber doors closed behind him and blocked out the crowd.

"We are grateful for Your Highness's welcome." The Earl of Clare's pale face and sunken eyes looked nervously towards the royal presence chamber. As its doors opened, even Rupert stiffened upon the sight of King Charles and Queen Henrietta seated at a table.

Rupert strode across the black and white tiles to face the all-powerful Queen, who seemed poised to check-mate the advance of any who threatened her dominance.

"Rupert?" The King's large eyes narrowed at the sight of these arch-traitors.

"Your Majesty." The Prince greeted him with a grand bow.

"What disobedience is this?" The Queen stood and pointed an accusatory finger at the three peers.

"I present the Earls' of Holland, Bedford and Clare who have come to pledge their allegiance and crave Your Majesty's pardon," Rupert explained.

"His Majesty knows exactly who and what they are already." The Queen laid a hand upon her chest. "These rebels were not permitted an audience."

"Your Majesty, the peers wish to correct their errors of judgement and offer their support," Rupert said calmly. "I felt it would be a blow to our cause if they were shunned and left with no alternative but to return to London..."

"I thought I had made my position clear, Nephew." The King rose to his feet with a distant glance that seemed not to fall on any of the men before him. The five-foot Monarch stood on a dais and, although his light brown moustache twitched with distaste, he remained motionless. Expressionless too as he came to terms with this situation.

"Your Majesty, from the outset of this unhappy war we have always been loyal to your person," Holland said, insisting that they had never ceased to further his cause in their hearts.

"Such base lies are too much for me to bear." Queen Henrietta waved her index finger back and forth and sniffed at her pomander, as if to protect her nostrils from the stench of betrayal.

"Arise, my lords." The King acknowledged their submission with reluctance and hooked his thumb through the ribbon of the Garter around his neck.

"Well, you've got what you came for, so pray leave us," the Queen declared and then called forward a servant who dropped to bended knee and slid a silver platter onto the table.

"I think that by meeting them it will encourage others to leave the rebels," Rupert said, appreciating the enormity of the upset he had caused.

The three men took their leave as the Queen, fingers interlinked beneath her small chin, pored over the much more appetising sweetmeats. The leftovers of a frosty atmosphere was all Rupert was afforded – no place to seriously discuss his concern over Scottish events. King Charles merely reiterated his belief that his ministers could keep the country neutral.

"With good Catholics in positions of power, we shall be safe from the Scots," the Queen said with a wave of her hand and introduced Sir Arthur Aston as the new Governor of Oxford. Her porcelain features flushed with pleasure at the appointment of a second of her intimate circle to a position of influence. Sir Richard Warrington, she let it be known, had been detailed as deputy governor of Wallingford, one of the ring of towns that protected Oxford.

Chapter 42

Summer drifted lazily through the woods leading to Wallingford and offered up its fruits to any who wished to sample them. It buzzed on the back of bees, was scattered along with the blossoming flowers and sung about by the birds that fluttered across the azure sky. The acorns of the big, old oak trees browned in the sunshine and when ripe, dropped to the ground to sow new roots. But the wheels of one of the regular coaches that headed towards the town crushed the latest scattering.

Inside the coach, Talbot Berkeley was far from enjoying summer. He was hot, sweaty and uncomfortable cooped up in a small space with strangers who made him even more agitated and anxious. The leather flaps covering the windows were rolled up, yet the air outside was humid and offered no respite from the heat and noxious odours of the passengers. The air of Colchester, which Talbot had known all his life, didn't make him sneeze half as much as that of Oxfordshire.

"I told Hannah that she would be whipped," the old woman opposite said, continuing her story and only looking at Talbot when he tried to turn away. "Any child should know how to thread a needle, is that not so?"

Talbot ordinarily did not stomach anyone that he had no time for, nor listen to anything he didn't deem important. But, in his fifty-sixth year and after running an inn for two decades, he felt as vulnerable as a sapling and no longer a sturdy oak. His inn had become his latest loss. First his daughter disobeyed him and eloped; followed closely by his wife's death; his son then joined the army, and now the war had taken his livelihood.

"Hey, d'you hear me?" The woman sheltered her eyes from the light and looked at Talbot. "I'm talking to you."

"Apologies. My mind is not ..." Talbot wasn't allowed to finish.

"Nervous disposition, eh?" She mentioned his pale features and the way he sat forward. "Beetroot juice squirted up your nostrils will cure you of your ills. Mark my words."

"I do not recall asking for your advice," Talbot snapped.

"Good Lord, there's no need for that." She prodded him with her stick. "I've simply been trying to distract thy troubled mind."

Talbot grabbed her stick and only returned it after protests from the other passengers. Such an attack upon his person stoked raw emotions; having only just suffered at the hands of Colchester's mobs, which had rounded on him for his Royalist sympathies. They had been correct; he was a staunch King's man, so staunch and opinionated that he had been heading for an encounter within that Parliamentarian heartland for some time. When it finally came, he had barely managed to snatch his savings and flee.

The swinging and squeaking sign of Wallingford's Rose and Crown Inn was a welcome sight as it meant that he was barely one day's ride from Oxford and from his son, Sir Francis

Berkeley. His carriage had not even drawn to a halt when Talbot, impatient as ever, opened the door and stepped out.

"Wait there, old man." A red-coated soldier put his hand up. "Name and where you've travelled from."

"Talbot Berkeley from Colchester," he replied.

"Talbot? An unusual name."

"After one of the fireships sent against the Armada," Talbot explained with pride. "My father was a navy man."

"Papers?" the soldier demanded.

"I have this from the Governor of Colchester." He proffered the letter which his friend had written some weeks ago. "I'm coming to see my son, he's a colonel in the King's army, you know." Talbot exaggerated the rank, though even if the truth did matter to him, he was not certain of the facts. The letter was enough to secure a wave of the soldier's hand, a decision more than likely made all the easier by the attractive woman who was a little farther down the line.

Talbot marched to the Rose and Crown, his entrance disturbing several dogs lying asleep that rolled over from their slumbers to look at the interloper. Their masters' gazes in by comparison, never shifted from a game of backgammon, almost camouflaged from the local constable by a thick cloud of tobacco smoke. Being the first from the carriages, Talbot had already requested his room and was being shown up the stairs when behind him two soldiers accosted a woman and pulled off her hat and coif. Her hair was as black as the sea upon a moonless night and, although he only glimpsed her face, a foolish notion came to mind that she looked like his errant daughter, Lucy. But the innkeeper was calling him, and he dismissed his hallucination as most likely triggered by the traumatic events of late.

* * * * *

"How dare you treat me so ill?" Lucy's arm stung from the grip of a soldier. "You've already seen my pass."

"From Kings Lynn, eh?" The other soldier looked her up and down.

"Take her to the stables. We can question her there," he said with a grin.

"I'm not going anywhere with either of you!" Lucy resolved and struggled to free herself.

"A right feisty lass, this one," the soldier holding her exclaimed, and then proceeded to drag her through the inn and towards the yard.

"Wait till your officer hears of this," she cried, with racing pulse and spiralling fear. "I'm travelling by order of Sir Hamon Le Strange." Lucy was also petrified for the safety of her sons should her assignment be interrupted.

"A very *strange* excuse too." The soldier's snickering was soon cut short when she bit his hand and grabbed at his crotch, squeezing it excruciatingly tight.

"What is going on here?" Sir Richard Warrington took a sentry and came to investigate. "Restrain her," he ordered and then eyed his two soldiers with disgust. "I will not stomach such behaviour from you imbeciles."

"She grabbed his prick." The other soldier excused his colleague.

"That's nothing to what I'll do to both of you!" Sir Richard kicked the kneeling soldier in the gut and the slit of his downturned mouth did not register any of the enjoyment he seemed to derive from it. Next, he stepped in front of the other soldier and placed his baton under the man's chin. "Have them flogged," he commanded the sentry, and the wrinkles between his eyebrows seemed to draw them lower.

"But, sir …" the soldiers protested.

"And you, my dear, what can I do for you?" He swaggered over to Lucy.

"I'm here on behalf of Sir Hamon Le Strange of Kings Lynn," Lucy said, trying to compose herself, "with an urgent letter for His Majesty's council …" Still she trembled.

"You?" Sir Richard looked up at the tall woman. "Entrusted with a letter so important?"

"Might you help me?" Lucy asked. "I need to get to Oxford to find my brother."

"I am the deputy governor of this town." Sir Richard stroked his errant white locks into place. "Show me evidence of what you speak."

Lucy produced a letter concealed in her dress. "My brother Sir Francis Berkeley can help me get it to the right person."

"Your brother?" Sir Richard stood straight and took a deep breath. "I served with him at the siege of Bristol and prior to war, in the London Trained Bands. How is his lovely wife, Lady Anne?" He gave a wide smile.

"Well, as far as I hear," she replied.

"Might I suggest I look after this letter for the evening, after all, you seem weary and knowing it is in safe hands will allow you to rest easy." He warned her that places such as this were often frequented by dubious characters. "I can also take you to your brother in the morning."

"That's most kind of you." Lucy was pleased to find one of Francis's friends. How lucky that this man was in the right place at the right time and, considering his protection a good safeguard, handed him the letter.

Sir Richard fondled the paper between forefinger and thumb. In his grasp was the means to further ingratiate himself with the Queen by personally presenting her with the letter and, in Lucy Hungerford, a way of controlling Sir Francis Berkeley and securing satisfaction for his disobedience. "Arrest her." He pointed at Lucy before she had even made it back into the inn.

Chapter 43

Anne's stepmother sat in the bare room, sipping from a fluted glass that resembled a delicate flower. Her long fingers caressed the stem, while the wine turned it a burgundy rose, and her brother eyed the alcohol with a raised eyebrow.

"It is refined to drink wine. I do so with appreciation, whereas my husband would simply gulp it down," she replied, having read his expression.

"Where is George?" Cormac asked.

"Where else but sleeping off a befuddled head," she said pointing up at the crumbling plasterwork ceiling. "It's the beer again,"

"Beer?" Cormac's grin was framed by his black beard. "While you sip wine?"

"Yes, and why not? From the day we met I've cared for him and stomached his ways, so what's a little wine?" A knock at the door preceded a creak as it opened, prompting Mary's grimace.

"Pardon me, madam, but the master requests your attendance," the servant girl explained in a quiet voice while advancing towards the small gathering of furniture arrayed around Mary.

"I have told you before, speak up," Mary snapped, her Irish brogue stronger following Cormac's arrival.

"Sorry, madam ..." The girl repeated her message.

"Tell him I will come to him shortly," Mary instructed and promptly turned to her sibling. "Your time at sea has served you well, I see. No longer as slim as a beanpole, but solid as an oak."

"And more so, after seeing that innocent maid." Cormac's eyes followed the girl out of the room.

"Cormac O'Donnell, you will not bed my maid for I cannot do without her." Mary snorted. She eyed his lace collar, each side of it tied together with a black silk bow and scoffed. "Following Prince Rupert's style, are we?"

"Away with ye. I am no supporter of royalty. Unless, that is, they were to wipe Protestantism from Ireland," Cormac replied.

"There is but one thing to which you are loyal, brother, and I will not have any more little O'Donnell's running around this part of the world. I am a respectable lady."

"Not a word I expected to fall from your lips," Cormac replied as a growing beat of approaching hooves curtailed their laughter.

Mary gathered her silk skirt and dashed to the window, staring through the leaded panes at a cavalcade that swept past the overgrown gardens with a glorious burst of autumn colour.

"Holy Mother, orange sashes! And a tawny standard which can mean only one thing," Mary exclaimed.

She skipped to the door as if she were once more dancing the jaunty steps she had so enjoyed as a child. Stopping briefly at a small mirror, she checked her ox-bone false tooth, anchored to the others with silk wire, to ensure that she looked her best for the Earl of Essex. At the door she watched the noble dismount and pace towards her with heavy steps, whilst doffing a large-brimmed hat sporting white ostrich feathers.

"Good afternoon, madam. I hear you are a friend of our cause," Lord Essex asked, spurs jangling at his approach.

"I am so, sir. As well as my poor husband, who lies ill upstairs. Pray come inside," she said, eagerly prepared to overlook the dirt his leather boots left on the black and white tiles.

"You are Irish, madam?" Essex paused.

"I am so, though I fled the Catholic hoards long ago," she assured him.

"I see," Essex replied with a rattly cough.

"Now, would you like some wine to lubricate your throat, my lord?" she asked.

"No, thank you." Essex looked her up and down with a set jaw.

"Not every Englishman is a Royalist, sir, just as not every Irish lady is a Papist." She looked him in the eye. Yet Mary could not dismiss a silly belief that he could see her rosary beads through her blue dress.

"A valid point," Essex said raising his eyebrows.

"I can prove my loyalty is with you and Parliament." Her hand rested upon her bodice, and the vertical whale-bone stay that stretched down from her bust. She called for the maid to fetch some letters from her bedroom. "Would you care to be seated?"

She maintained a straight face at the stench of tobacco that reached her nostrils as the Lord General took his ease on a wooden chair and stretched out his legs. When the maid returned with the letters, Mary pulled apart the green bow with thumb and forefinger, as if undoing the strings of a corset, before holding them out in offering.

"What's their significance?" Essex enquired.

"A trusted officer of yours passed this way not so long back. I gave him a copy of one letter to pass to you." She watched Essex take them and his coat of arms, engraved into his gold signet ring, caught her eye. Mary's heart fluttered, and she was almost able to scent his power and influence.

"I do recall a letter, although my officers said it contained nothing of note," Essex replied and shuffled through the papers as though they were playing cards.

"Like panes of glass, each letter put together offers a window into the heart of the King's court. I present them simply as evidence of my connections." Mary moved slightly closer and lowered her voice. "My son-in-law is a well-connected Royalist. My daughter is an avid letter writer; therefore, I find myself quite informed, if you take my meaning."

"And his name?" Essex asked.

"Sir Francis Berkeley. There has been mention in other letters of discourse he has had with Prince Rupert, with whom he is close friends." Mary took a deep breath.

"You would betray your daughter?" Essex gave her his full attention.

"On the contrary. I aim to save her and she will thank me for it one day. Her husband has endangered her with his foolish allegiance to King Charles." Mary frowned.

"Then I look forward to reading more of your despatches," Essex said.

"I trust my sending those letters so long ago, before you even drew near this place, is sufficient proof of my loyalty and honest intentions," she said, and smiled at the Lord General to encourage the old man to reciprocate, hoping to secure his protection, and also his gold.

In fact, Mary was positive that she and Anne would be safer for her cultivation of the Lord General, because the King's cause, and her poxy son-in-law, had so far been of no benefit to the family and had instead seen off all of her husband's savings. Their financial position was so perilous, coffers so depleted, that Essex's money was the one thing that might tip the scales before the estate went under.

Chapter 44

Francis crept into the hall with a luscious afternoon sun following him and illuminating the oak panels. The golden light celebrated the fact that he was still alive and mimicked his joy to be back in Oxford. Gently closing the door, he caught the latch and then made his way through the passage towards the stairs, pausing when he heard Anne's sweet voice.

"O ne'er shall I forget the night
the stars were bright above me
and gently lent their silvery light
when first she vowed to love me."

The song was the one he'd sung to her before he left for Bristol; the same he'd sing whenever the war took him away. He delicately drummed the ochre painted wall to the rhythm of the next verse.

"But now I'm bound to Oxford camp
kind heaven then pray guide me

and send me safely back again
to the girl I left behind me."

He stood in quiet contemplation. The terror that had gripped him since that horrendous night before Bristol's walls had still not released its stranglehold. When a breath from behind reached his ear, despite being barely audible, it had him spin around and grab the person in a defensive impulse.

"Sir!" Jane gasped as he seized her arm and pushed her to the wall.

"My apologies." He frowned at the sight his eyes beheld: of sunlight that sparkled in her blond hair; that gave her eyes the softest of blue hues and the shadows that crossed her lips, neck and chest. Not a hint of any ugly, brutish Roundhead that he had so often had to anticipate.

"You startled me," she said, the nostrils of her delicately turned up nose flaring as she glanced down at his firm grasp.

"War does terrible things even to those who survive it." He loosened his grip.

"But, sir, I am not your enemy," she whispered and gave a curtsey.

"I have been fighting for many a day … perhaps too many." He found himself drawn to her eyes again, and her irises like a kaleidoscope of freshly cut sapphires. But then Jane demurely dropped her gaze and he followed it right to his hand, which still held hers.

"Her golden hair, in ringlets fair
her eyes like diamonds shining
her slender waist, her heavenly face
that leaves my heart still pining."

Anne's melodic voice almost called out to Francis. Awakening him from his daydream, it also prompted Jane to give a reluctant smile as she withdrew her hand. She interlinked her fingers, as if that would stop them straying again.

"My wife …" Francis gestured towards the stairs.

"Her ladyship sings beautifully if I may say so," Jane quickly added.

"She does indeed," Francis replied and headed for the stairs.

"Your son will be excited to see you too, sir." Jane trembled as she turned to make her way back to the kitchen.

"Jane …" he called her back. "What happened to your own child?"

"Alas," she replied with a sigh, "I know only that he was taken from me and given to a good family to raise, for I had not the means."

"Forgive my inquisitiveness." He did not know what else to say.

"That is why it brings such joy to my heart to be able to be of use to your son, sir." Her reply was followed by a quick bob and then she hurried away.

Francis was left to climb the stairs with an unexpected sadness for being unable to correct what Jane had been through. The sorrow was not entirely banished when, opening the bedroom door, Anne shrieked with delight and they embraced with a flurry of kisses. Holding his wife tightly in his arms, her head against his cheek, this was the moment when he realised he had survived the recent siege. To feel her warmth again, and all that it encompassed, was to know life.

"I hadn't expected you in view of your last letter." Anne laughed.

"Our detachment escorted the King here." He explained it was only for a few days, and then they would return again to the siege of Gloucester.

"Well, Son, I do not have such a tender welcome to offer thee," a gravelly voice warned, and Francis turned to see his father.

"Is this another hallucination of war?" Francis smiled and, with one arm he encircled Anne's waist, while the other extended towards his father, who swaggered over like a young brigand. "What brings you here?"

"I thought the King could do with the wisdom of an old navy man," Talbot replied and laid a hand on his son's shoulder. His lips, nestled between a neatly trimmed grey bread, curled into a wry smile. "You landlubbers let warfare drag on far too long."

"Things have moved on since the Armada days, even though it looks like you have not." Francis poked fun at Talbot, who still wore a small old-fashioned, starched ruff.

"Men!" Anne took Talbot's hand before he could put up any resistance. "Never ones to show any intimacy." She went on to reveal that Talbot had not been so reticent when he had held his grandson.

"I'll wager he's changed much since you last saw him." Francis drew immense pleasure from the three generations of Berkeley men being together.

"The lad's a strong one, just like his Grandfather," Talbot declared, folding his arms. "He has changed, but so too has everyone, me included," he said and gave Francis an abridged version of how a gang of rebels had turned him out of his inn.

"My God! Are you all right?" Francis asked, and then enquired as to what his father was going to do now. "That place was everything to you." It left Francis with a sting of resentment at the rebels who had done this. First his marital home in London had been attacked and now the place of his youth.

"You think the King can employ me?" Talbot asked, puffing out his chest and standing straight. But before Francis could answer, he added, "I trust you'll put a good word in. I cannot imagine him turning away experience."

"I have not the standing to directly influence the King." Francis couldn't help but stifle a smile.

"You always did have a negative tongue, boy." Talbot, as ever, was the stubborn optimist, unable to comprehend anything not going his way. "Then purchase a commission for me."

"I've just earned my own after months." Francis was not willing to be held responsible for his father's career.

"I have some other news too." Talbot paced to the window. "It concerns thy sister. I think I saw her on my way here."

Francis's body tensed at such an unexpected revelation. "Impossible, she is in Kings Lynn."

"Under siege, isn't it?" Talbot didn't turn around. "The more I think about it, the more certain I am that it was her, Francis ..." he hesitated.

"Where do you think you saw her?" Francis noted his father's serious expression.

"Wallingford."

"Was she with Ned and the children?" Francis grew more concerned as he recalled Sir Hamon le Strange's threats regarding Lucy.

"I saw not hide, nor hair of that whoremonger." Talbot raised his voice and glared at Francis, as if he'd been in the wrong to even mention Ned's name.

"Did you not think of approaching her?" Francis wondered why his father had not done so.

"There was nothing I could have done, and I had no reason to think it could be her." Talbot pointed at Francis and shook his head. "She was the one who vowed never to speak to me again after she eloped," he said and, after a pause, suggested they go to Wallingford.

Francis knew without a doubt that his father was correct. For all his bluster, defensiveness and his troublesome character, the man was as stubborn as an ox, and the topic of his daughter had never been mentioned in the six years since she married against her father's will. Yet the smooth skin of his father's cheeks and nose had developed a reddish hint that betrayed Talbot's fervent belief and concern. This was more than enough to have Francis summon a coach right away, for he had only two days in Oxford; two days in which to find his sister.

* * * * *

"Nothing to do with me, sir," the innkeeper of Wallingford's Rose and Crown said, wiping his hands on a cloth as if that was the end of the matter.

"With respect, sir, that isn't what I asked you." Francis's broad shoulders rose with growing impatience. "Now, shall we try once more?"

"The woman with black hair." Talbot stepped in and took control in a bid to sort it out.

"Listen, Francis Drake, I don't know what you're talking about." The innkeeper eyed Talbot's outdated attire.

"Did you see her?" Francis slowly repeated his question.

"I have plenty of women through here." The droopy skin of the innkeeper's eyelids seemed to block out anything he wished not to see. "As customers I mean, sir." He continued rubbing his fingers without looking up.

"The lady is my sister and she is in grave danger," Francis said, demanding he answer. "Would you prefer my whole company of soldiers search and tear this place apart?"

"Look here!" Talbot snatched the keeper's cloth, threw it aside, and then grabbed the man's black doublet. "You saw the commotion with the soldiers." Talbot's face screwed up and he tugged the innkeeper close enough that the man's beady little eyes were barely inches from his own. "Tell me what happened to her."

"Let go of me!" The keeper called for his wife to fetch the constable, and his long Roman nose could smell Talbot's anger.

"A man who receives no salary?" Talbot laughed in his face. "He'll be less inclined to help you than you are to help us!"

"Fetch the soldiers." The innkeeper changed tack and his wife hurried off.

"If you don't answer me I'll rip your tongue clean out," Talbot growled, shoving the keeper backwards against a wall. "Where is the lady?"

"The soldiers took her, you damned fool," the keeper yelled as his wife led in an officer.

"Jack Mandeville?" Francis gave a smile of relief at the officer whom he'd not seen in the nine months since Brentford. "As God is my witness, I'm so fortunate it's you." Despair rapidly gave way to hope.

"Sir Francis, what's going on here?" Jack asked.

"The man is not cooperating." Francis told his father to put the innkeeper down. "I'm looking for a black-haired woman who was taken by some soldiers. Can you help me?"

"She's gone I'm afraid, sir." Jack grimaced.

"Where to?' Francis asked. "She's my sister."

"I know not for certain, Sir Richard took her," Jack replied. "All I know is that he was headed to Oxford to see the Queen."

"Back to Oxford?" Talbot hissed with torment over his daughter's fate. "At least you can use your influence to get her released, Francis."

"I am in your debt, Jack," Francis was about to leave, but something troubled him. "You said Sir Richard?"

"Yes, Sir Richard Warrington, he's my commanding officer," Jack explained.

"God damn me!" Francis was shaken by every aspect of the dreadful situation before him; and the amount at stake.

Never could he have imagined that the siege of Bristol would bring him face to face with his old rival, Sir Richard, nor still that his disregard of the man's orders might well have compromised Lucy and, in turn, her sons. Nor could he explain any of this to Talbot; not until the bumpy blur of the carriage ride had Francis's fragile temper snap.

Chapter 45

Oxford Prison's dank and dismal reputation proved correct in terms of initial appearance, but that was as far as Francis had managed to get; the entrance. The cries of despair from the depths of the prison echoed from behind the gaoler and his guards; the same emotions that sprung from Francis's heart, which sank upon being refused entry. They also refused to answer whether his sister had been admitted.

The governor's hazy memory began to clear upon sight of a bright and shining golden sovereign, which led to deep, pondering breaths and many furtive glances. The man seemed to be undergoing an internal struggle on how to get his grubby hands on the coin whilst being pulled by some other factor. The walls dripped tears of slimy water, and the filthy stench was indicative of the Governor's morals when he finally revealed that a woman had indeed been deposited into his care. The use of the word 'care' prompted a grunt of sarcasm from Francis. Yes, the man confirmed, she was called Madam Hungerford and what's more, she had been detained by order of Her Majesty the Queen. This fact left Francis in a further quandary when he thought that the dire situation could not possibly get worse.

The officers who came to Oxford with the monarch a few days ago had departed once more for Gloucester. Every day, the King's men pushed that city closer and closer to capitulation, aiming to take it before Lord Essex could relieve the place. But the Royalist party making its way back there lacked one particular Captain Francis Berkeley. Francis, by remaining in Oxford, was risking everything he had done to secure his military post, but he had no choice. His blood allegiance must take priority; his sister and his nephews relied on him. Therefore, he made his way to the Queen's court at Merton College, desperate to find Sir Richard and drag him to Oxford Prison to first extract Lucy's release and, afterwards, his own retribution.

* * * * *

"My Lord Saint Edmondsbury," Sir Richard said in greeting to his friend. "Congratulations on your ennoblement."

"My thanks," the former Henry Jermyn replied with a smile. "At least now, if the rebels capture me, my position prevents me from being hung, drawn and quartered." He gave a deep chortle.

"Her Majesty would never allow you to be captured." Sir Richard pouted with absolutely certainty. "Neither would those to whom you owe money," he said in reference to Jermyn's gambling debts and, with a laugh, revealed a row of teeth like weathered gravestones.

"You, on the other hand, look set to be captured any day." Jermyn's revelation cut short Sir Richard's humour, and he went on to explain that there was a man searching all over Oxford for him.

"Sir Francis Berkeley, by any chance?" Sir Richard queried.

"Aye, that's him," Jermyn confirmed. "What have you done to upset him so?"

"Pulled him down to size, that's all," Sir Richard said with a wave of his hand, revealing that he'd imprisoned the man's sister.

"He's apparently apoplectic with rage." Jermyn's eyes widened. "What the devil was her crime?"

"It's more the crime of her insolent brother," Sir Richard said, explaining how he'd found her with a letter regarding Kings Lynn and passed it to the Queen, to earn her praise for his thoroughness. "I have suffered from Berkeley's insubordination for years. Most recently, his disobeying my word of command at Bristol!"

"Ah, so she is merely a means of punishing him," Jermyn smiled. "Well, you're right to teach him a thing or two."

"I'll most likely release her in a few days." Sir Richard was safe in the Queen's inner sanctum, which Berkeley, not being of the status or influence, could not hope to penetrate. Jermyn puffed on his pipe of tobacco and the two men moved on to the Queen's latest plans for a court masque, the antics of her two dwarves and tonight's card game. The smoke that surrounded the pair blinded them to events outside the little world of Merton College, which had become a cocooned microcosm.

* * * * *

The Gloucestershire countryside looked to be evaporating before Lord Essex's eyes, such was the smoke that spiralled heavenward. The dying light of day left a blood-red trace across the sky like a fleshy rapier wound, and he hoped that Gloucester was not fatally wounded by the Royalists' attempts to mine the walls. Only ten miles away, it would not be long before he would have an answer.

"Release the signal." Essex passed the order to Sergeant-Major-General Philip Skippon. "The firing of a demi-cannon should alert the city that relief is imminent whilst warning off the enemy."

"Either the Cavaliers have destroyed the city, or they're burning their camp and abandoning the siege." Skippon pointed out smoke on the horizon.

With his men strung out in the approach to Prestbury, where they were to quarter for the night, Essex gauged how long he would take to get to the beleaguered city; two days at worst, he estimated. Two days that would decide the future of Gloucester and the whole west of England, as well as his own reputation.

"Let us pray it's the latter," Essex muttered.

"We've encountered no evidence of a defeated citadel," Skippon assured him in his broad Norfolk accent.

"Twenty-six days they've been besieged," Essex reckoned, "which can surely only have made their resolve stronger." The positive musings of his astrologist went some way to reassuring Essex, but nothing short of defeating the King's men and entering the town would grant him release from his worries.

"That is surely the cathedral I see," Skippon exclaimed.

"A welcome sight to any pilgrim." Essex could not see it, but trusted Skippon's judgement and the resulting positivity it fostered, which was more important than the truth. "Promise each man extra beer once we reach Gloucester." He attempted to keep them happy, in advance of the intensive two-day march. The rubbing of his eyes, which watered from the oncoming wind, resulted in word spreading that the Lord General had shed tears of pride over the toil and devotion of his army.

"We spend the night at Prestbury, my lord?" Skippon asked.

"That is so. Your London brigade will escort the heavy guns, while we go on to prepare quarters," Essex instructed, riding ahead of the London Trained Bands and their standard bearer. The standard displayed an anchor coming out of the sky above the motto: 'Only in Heaven', and Essex knew that his own future was similarly tied to Gloucester's survival.

"As you command." Skippon's reply was drowned by the cannon salvo from the mouth of their six thousand pound 'sweet lips' – a twelve-foot-long demi-cannon.

"Hear that and stand firm, I beg you," Essex said and, as the sky drew darker, it seemed the shot had shattered the heavens, which released a light drizzle that invigorated his senses.

"Your Excellency!" Skippon caught the Lord General up, and with an excited cry, pointed out a second faint flash in the sky that preceded another light rumble; most certainly nothing to do with the weather.

"The city has returned our fire. It survives!" Essex's moustache and beard, fashioned into three parts like compass points, rose in a smile with his long nose comprising the north. Consideration of the Royalists' plans, should they abandon the siege, was the last thing on his mind, as was the one hundred and twenty miles his army would have to cover to get back to London.

Chapter 46

Prince James, Duke of York, opened the door to the royal carriage and alighted, inhaling as if he'd just surfaced from a swim in a river. It had been a long and arduous journey since leaving Gloucester. He stood with hands upon his hips, and his large, imperious eyes observed every man who surrounded the carriage. The nine-year-old walked right up to his cousin, who was discussing the location of the enemy, and interrupted him with a very serious frown.

"Rupert, how far is it now?" The Duke asked, rubbing his legs as if he'd come the whole way on foot.

"I should say at least another few hours, Your Royal Highness," Rupert replied and warned him that it was far from a short journey.

"Then I must take a short walk, otherwise I am sure my legs will stiffen up for good." the Duke resolved and marched across the middle of the waterlogged road, just as his father's head appeared at the carriage door.

King Charles stepped out, placed a black hat upon his head and glanced up to assess the beginnings of a drizzle that exacerbated the dreariness of the day. Such dull weather was indicative of the Royalists' fortunes of late. Dressed in a black satin suit with the watery blue ribbon of the Garter crossing his chest, the King looked at his son, and his splashed breeches, and shook his head in despair.

"Your Majesty." Rupert joined his uncle.

"What is wrong with the boy?" The monarch's eyes were more sunken than ever, the shadows under each as dark as the storm clouds overhead.

King Charles appeared ever more hypnotised by the creeping haze that crossed the fields and blurred sight of his poor, miserable realm. He frequently pondered what England would look like one day when the mist of war cleared.

"I hear there is good news from the south-west." Rupert stooped slightly to speak to the King, and he called over Sir William Legge. "Did we receive a message from Exeter, Will?"

"Yes, Highness, the town has fallen to His Majesty's armies." Legge's Irish brogue stirred the King. "The people give thanks for their deliverance from the rebels."

"So, with Exeter, Barnstaple and Bideford now ours, it shouldn't be long before our south-western army can join us," Rupert said with brimming confidence.

"Yet for all of these successes, the Cornish have deserted us and returned to their lands," King Charles replied. A momentary shaft of sunlight made the silver flecks in his beard sparkle before the clouds smothered it again. "They were the backbone of the army and their absence is as debilitating as an amputation."

"May I suggest we publish Your Majesty's good opinion of these men?" Lord Falkland, the Secretary of State, suggested after joined the group. "I could draft a document to thank your loyal Cornish subjects for serving you so heartily."

"A fine idea. See to it," the King commanded.

"Lord Falkland," Rupert called. "His Majesty desires the names of the captured towns also be published; listed like medals to the glory of these men."

The King had begun to pick his way along the roadside, coming to a milestone and, as if to highlight the chasm between King and Parliament, it gave London as being one hundred miles away. Slowly, the monarch sat down upon it, his head bowed as if in deep prayer and while the officers kept a respectful distance, none of them quite knew what to do or say. Rarely if ever had anyone seen the sovereign like this and only a little blackbird plucked up the confidence to bound over to the dark figure wrapped in a black cloak, chirping in its search for food.

"May we go home now, Your Majesty?" The young Duke frightened off the bird. His words moved his father, who lifted his eyes to the heavens and released the deepest sigh, sounding as if his last hopes were expelled with it.

"We have no home," the King of England, Scotland, France and Ireland replied.

* * * * *

Francis's horse struggled with the muddy Gloucester road as if something or someone was trying to prevent him from rejoining the royal army besieging that city. But what else could he do? The road slipped away perilously underfoot, as uncertain and shifting as life had proved to be in the last seven days. He could not get his hands on Sir Richard Warrington and could not, for Lucy's sake, waste any more time in Oxford without any result. So now Francis pinned his hopes of freeing his sister on Prince Rupert, who he prayed would overlook his absence from the army for the past week and assist him.

"God damn this weather!" Francis yelled, his burning face still dripping from the downpour that had pelted it earlier; wet clothes clinging to him as ruthlessly as insomnia. His horse lurched to one side and stuck fast in the boggy ground, forcing him to dismount, free it and continue on foot. Each step was a battle in itself and he diverted through a forest in hope of shelter.

To most people the route would have been a thoroughly miserable one. But the water that siphoned through the treetops, dripped from branches and bounced across leaves and undergrowth played a pretty tune that subconsciously soothed. Mother Nature had adorned the trees with leafy embellishments that twinkled in the wet weather; no less impressive than if they were jade, tourmaline or green sapphires. Even the vapour hanging in the branches offered a protective shroud from his woes. As he trudged along the track, left only with his innermost thoughts, he missed a rustle upon the carpet of leaves and the crackle of a snapping twig.

"Stop, you Roundhead dog!"

The shrill voice made Francis draw his blade with a scraping ring. "Hold it right there," he shouted, heart pumping furiously, only to discover a young boy barely a dozen paces in front of him.

"How dare you draw at me?" The lad looked outraged and brandished a thick branch in one hand.

"I'm not in the mood for games, boy," Francis said, keeping the point of his sword firmly levelled just in case the lad was a decoy. "I'll do more than draw my blade if you call me a damned Roundhead again." He finally lowered his weapon a little and looked around, but saw nobody.

"Sheath that sword, I say," the boy demanded. "Only a coward would threaten a defenceless opponent."

"You're quite an aggressive little imp, aren't you?" Francis replied with a shake of his head. "I'll sheath my sword in your scrawny gut if you don't close your mouth." He placed his rapier back into its scabbard.

"You dare to threaten the Duke of York?" the boy cried.

"I have no time to listen to your tales," Francis said and retrieved the reins of his horse. The sound of a sword being drawn had Francis leap aside and pull his own again, catching sight of the boy lunging forward; his cloak now across his shoulder to reveal the glint of both golden embroidery, and of a blade.

The lad inflicted a cut to Francis's arm before he could evade him. The boy would have nimbly sliced again with a very polished follow-up had not Francis dodged and spun around to take a swipe of his own. It was deflected with a clash that saw the tall trees weep more raindrops down upon the pair. But the timely arrival of another man running for all he was worth towards them brought an end to the contest.

"Your Royal Highness!"

The boy took the opportunity to point the tip of his sword at Francis's throat and left him peering down its length towards the golden hilt fashioned with a lion as proud as its owner.

"Jesus Christ! You are the Duke of York!" Francis dropped his weapon.

"Guards!" The man's holler was positively high-pitched with shock. "Are you hurt, Your Royal Highness?"

"Of course not. He was good, but he was no match for me." The Duke put away his sword, stood with hands behind his back and looked at Francis with a raised eyebrow. "A most enjoyable, though brief match. My attendants usually let me win."

"I can see you were never going to be as easy on me, Your Royal Highness," Francis replied. "Can I suppose that His Majesty's army is nearby?"

"Well, I wouldn't be here on my own, would I?" The Duke gave a sarcastic expression. "Your name, sir?"

"Sir Francis Berkeley," Francis replied with a bow, hoping to explain his reason for being here. "I'm a captain and have not long left Oxford to rejoin my men at the siege of Gloucester."

"Rejoin your men?" The boy's expression was one of mischief that upturned the very corners of his mouth. "A deserter?"

"Not at all." Francis's unease spilled over into outright fear. Fear that the last few confused minutes might have further destroyed his reputation. "My sister has been kidnapped."

"A good enough excuse that might just save your neck," the Duke replied.

"It's true. By order of Her Majesty the Queen, no less." Francis's serious expression seemed enough for the Duke to listen. "All she's done is to carry a letter all the way from the Royalist garrison at Kings Lynn."

"The town that declared for His Majesty?" The Duke asked. "She sounds like a brave woman just like the Queen."

"That she is, therefore I earnestly hope you see my predicament, sir," Francis said, while the officer interceded and urged the Duke to leave.

"Come with me, Sir Francis." The Duke led the way out of the forest, enquiring further into the circumstances of Lucy's imprisonment and, as they emerged from the trees, the boy's presence drew the attention of a number of flustered men.

"Where have you been, James?" The words of a distant, but exquisite, small man with a neat moustache and beard made Francis stop in his tracks, as if the water soaking his clothes had frozen.

"My apologies, Your Majesty," the Duke said. "I found one of your loyal officers looking for the army." He pointed at Francis.

The King's famous profile, the very same that adorned the coinage of the realm, turned in Francis's direction. Francis removed his hat and bowed. For a few seconds he was facing God's anointed sovereign, appointed by Him to rule over this land, and after the shock came a wave of euphoria as the King nodded politely and then left to get back into his carriage, followed part of the way by his talkative son.

"Sir Francis Berkeley?" Prince Rupert stepped forward. "We meet again."

"Your Highness, I must apologise for my absence," Francis stammered.

"And what is the cause of it this time?" Rupert asked, before his expression was taken to a bloody cut on Francis's arm.

"A token of the Duke of York's esteem," Francis pointed at the wound.

"Sir Francis," the Duke of York called out and marched across to him.

"Back to deliver the killer blow, Your Highness?" Rupert couldn't help himself, and the boy chortled.

"I will mention your sister's predicament to His Majesty," the Duke assured him, taking evident pride in his ability to intercede. "Call it compensation for your arm." He gave a firm nod of his head. "As well as a reward for brightening up such a dull day."

Chapter 47

"We may as well have no home, my dear." Mary stepped inside and sniffed, her small eyes reduced to pink pools ringed with wrinkles.

"What about Patrick Hall?" Anne asked.

"We just cannot afford to keep it up anymore." Mary closed her eyes and held the bridge of her nose, unable to bear even imagining the place.

"I don't know how your mother has made ends meet for the last six months on the meagre money we have," George said and took Anne's hands in his. "Now, how is my beautiful daughter?"

"I am fine, Father, but worried about you both," Anne replied.

"It's absolutely unbearable, sweetheart." A tear strayed onto one of Mary's high cheekbones laden with rouge, and she dabbed it gently with a handkerchief to avoid streaks. "Ever since Francis's men took our savings I knew this day was inevitable."

"You should have told us," Anne replied with a wince of guilt. "We could have helped."

"I didn't want us to be a burden." Mary sighed and, with a pause, tilted her head. "But I think we may need your help after all."

"Cormac is looking after the house and we've left the maid there," George said.

"He's making sure the local Royalists don't do any damage." Mary quickly interrupted to explain her brother's purpose. "We've been getting some negative attention."

"Your mother has been so strong and looked after me." George turned to his wife, and the prominent creases at either side of his mouth deepened as he smiled. "She's managed to put an array of delicious meals on the table in spite of our poverty."

"Oh, George, she doesn't want to hear about what I've done." Mary stepped between father and daughter. "He knows fine well I don't take well to compliments."

"The King should take her for Chancellor," George declared.

"Now that I would like to see." Mary gave a shrill laugh. "A woman would certainly sort out all of these squabbling men."

"Where's my grandson?" George's cloudy blue eyes looked lovingly for him.

"Before you fetch the boy, may your father have a seat?" Mary fussed. "His legs aren't so good these days," she said, and then leaned close to Anne, attributing this infirmity in faint tones to alcohol.

"Yes, come and sit in the dining chamber." Anne gestured. "You're looking well, Father."

"Really?" George paused, stretched his shoulders and went through to the other room. "Yes, I do feel good."

"Oh, he's such a handful, far from what he seems." Mary hung back, stroked her red hair and told Anne she hadn't wanted to admit as much. "He might change his ways if he is with you; that was my thought for paying you a visit." A stubborn curl refused to be stroked back into place by Mary's long fingers, seeming to emphasise her constant toil.

"I would never have guessed by looking at him." Anne embraced her mother. "You take care of him so selflessly."

"You know he adores you." Mary's smile turned her eyes to mere creases. "My pleasure is having the three of us together again. Perchance we can both help him cut back on his drinking."

"Let's hope so," Anne replied.

"I'm pleased you don't mind us staying for a while. Now, where is dear Francis?" Mary looked left and right, as though he could very feasibly be waiting at one end of the hall.

"He's away with the army," Anne replied. "They are pursuing the rebels and trying to bring them to battle."

"Oh, yes, of course he is. I had forgotten all about Gloucester." She stifled a false yawn. "Has the King taken all his men with him?"

"No idea." Anne was more concerned about her mother's fatigue. "Why don't you lie down?" She stopped Jane, who was passing, to ask her to prepare the spare bedroom.

"Who's that?" A frown of suspicion crossed Mary's pencil-thin eyebrows as the girl left.

"Henry's wet-nurse. Francis's brother-in-law hired her," Anne was quick to explain.

"I wonder at his reasons." Mary's downturned lips pursed. "Watch her, my dear."

Mary had no sooner delivered her warning than Anne looked away. Not only that, but her daughter reached for her pearl necklace and began to stroke the lustrous beads with the tips of her fingers, leading Mary to suspect that Francis was up to no good with the little harlot of a domestic. She placed a protective hand on Anne's shoulder and suggested they enter the dining chamber.

"My mouth is dry as a bone. Have you a little wine?" George asked, leading Mary to raise her hands and make the sign of the cross. "If it was good enough for Saint Patrick ..." George alluded to the saint's distilling of alcohol.

"Patrick never did create, drink, nor condone the use of alcohol." Two deep furrows appeared above the bridge of Mary's nose.

"Did he not call it aqua vitae?" George persisted with a wink at his daughter.

"I'm far too tired for this." Mary broke away from the pair and walked towards the hot charcoal brazier to warm her hands. Its orange glow cast shadows over her pale face as she watched it.

"Is there something troubling you?" Anne followed her mother.

"Sleep, my child, or lack of it," she replied.

"Then shall I have the maid mix up something for you to drink before bed?"

Mary shook her head and said, "It is what wakes me during the early hours that is the problem. Dreams have tormented me these past weeks even when I feel dead on my feet."

Mary groaned and wondered just why the good Lord should cause her to be so afflicted. Especially considering all she was doing to safeguard her husband, daughter and grandson by keeping the family home from the clutches of those to whom they owed money. But the flow of detail in her daughter's letters was drying up, along with Lord Essex's gold as a result. Anne's letters of late had been limited to nothing but family affairs and the plight of Francis's sister, who was of no interest to Mary – or to Lord Essex.

Chapter 48

An inmate of Oxford prison was offered up from within its deepest bowels. A note commanded the release of Lucy Hungerford, written by one of the King's secretaries and signed by the royal hand; a small sheet of paper with just eleven words, that upon being shown to the jailor, changed everything. Stepping into the daylight, Lucy squinted, and Francis hurried her to the waiting coach.

"Are you all right?" Francis hugged her tight, and then broke away for a few seconds to look at her and see for himself. Her long, black hair was loose about her shoulders, and Francis placed one of Anne's woollen mantles around her and lifted the fur-edged hood. His sister's skin was pale and tired, no longer rosy.

"You must help me Francis." The reflection she saw of herself in the pools of rainwater reminded her of her mother.

"Of course."

"My boys." Lucy's eyes, the whites of which were streaked with tiny pink lines, widened. "They are the ones in danger."

"I'm sure they will be fine," Francis reassured in an attempt to keep up her spirits. "Ned is still with them."

"You don't know how ruthless Hamon le Strange is," Lucy insisted.

All the way back to Francis's house, Lucy was agitated. When she walked inside, she began looking around, although for what, she did not seem to know herself. The only thing on her mind was her family and getting home.

"Kings Lynn is under siege. You won't be admitted even if you did make it back," Francis insisted and placed a hand on his diminutive sister's shoulder. "Take some food and drink. I will arrange for a letter to go to le Strange."

"Thank you, Francis, for not giving up on me." She glanced up at her younger brother, who she'd often looked out for in their youth. And with that, she stoically closed off the awful memories that had been Oxford prison and incarcerated them within the recesses of her mind, as only Lucy knew how. She embraced Anne, who stepped closer with Henry, and the boy recognised Lucy and beamed with happiness. In fact it was only hugging him that moved Lucy to the brink of tears, despite all that had passed.

"Sister, I want to say thank you for looking after Henry." Anne took the opportunity to express her gratitude in person. "Come through, you must be famished," she said and, placing an arm around her sister-in-law, took her to the dining room where Jane was laying out olive pie, pigeon pie and boiled mutton, along with delights such as gingerbread and bread pudding.

"Goodness, Anne, it was nothing, and certainly not worthy of all of this." Lucy seemed hesitant to even approach the table.

"If I'd never come to Kings Lynn you might not have been mixed up in le Strange's business." Francis cursed the man.

"The past is not worth dwelling on. We must focus only on the here and now, for that is all we can influence," Lucy thanked him again for rescuing her.

"Well," Francis said, folding his arms. "It wasn't just me." He stumbled over his words. "I would never have known about your predicament if I wasn't informed by another who has also made it their business to secure your release." He turned to the doorway as Talbot entered.

"I'm pleased to see you at liberty." Talbot stood still with a face that betrayed little, and looked right at his daughter.

"Father?" Lucy shook her head. "This is not the time, nor the place for any reconciliation!"

"It's not like that," Francis replied.

"You've chosen an occasion such as this to trap me?" Lucy removed the borrowed mantle and made to leave immediately. "Is having to meet him the price I have to pay for your brotherly support?" she asked Francis.

"I see your temperament has not changed in all these years." Talbot lifted his head. "The gaoler probably couldn't take any more of it," he said, and creases ran from the corners of his eyes as he smiled at his own remark.

"For God's sake, Father," Francis retorted and quickly took Lucy's hand.

"Just my humour, Son, you must know that by now." Talbot's piercing eyes were unrelenting.

"Lucy, please." Francis raised his voice. "He was the one who saw you being arrested and came here to get my help," he explained.

"He did?" Lucy frowned.

"Aye, girl, I recognised you instantly," Talbot replied but this time looked away. "I've only seen such vibrant raven hair ever belonging to you and thy blessed mother."

"He has been anxious to find you." Francis looked at them both in turn.

"Anxious to find me?" She couldn't help but laugh. "After five years of being cast aside and, because of his grudge, having never met his two grandsons, I'm led to believe that he suddenly wanted to save me?"

"It is all true, Lucy!" Talbot snapped with frustration. "You're right, I did bear a grudge, I have cut off my grandsons by casting you aside." He held a fist to his forehead. "But what's also true …" He paused to collect himself, "is that I do regret my actions. I was scared that I'd lost you for a second time."

Silence descended at this pivotal point. Not since Francis's mother had died had they all been together and, in the interlude, each one was left with poignant thoughts to weigh up; thoughts influenced by Talbot's emotional words, which had left him with closed eyes.

"If you truly mean that," Lucy replied, looking to the ceiling, "then I have been released from two unjust sentences in one day."

"Of course, I mean it, be damned!" Talbot exclaimed.

Francis put his arm around his father and eased him closer. Lucy couldn't reply, but upon finally coming face to face with her father, the two of them embraced. She cried, while he laid his cheek against her head and placed one of his large hands on her shoulder. At this point Francis and Anne left them. In an hour Francis would also be leaving Oxford, granted only the time to release Lucy before he had to rejoin the army in its pursuit of the enemy; a most vital pursuit, in which time was as much an enemy as the Parliamentarians. The King's army had to defeat them once and for all.

Chapter 49

The Royalist army scoured the countryside in search of the enemy. Engaged in a race with Lord Essex's Parliamentarians, they aimed to either reach London before him and seize the city, or defeat him on the field of battle. Either must result in the capital's fall. Yet that September night saw a very different competition playing out in a small stone farmhouse located in the expanse of the Cotswolds.

King Charles picked up twelve playing cards upon which the soft candlelight flickered. An Ace, King, Queen, Jack and Ten of Clubs were amongst them. He firmly believed with every fibre of his being that a great ruler was one who could exercise self-control, and when it came to the game of piquet, he made certain that he displayed no sign of pleasure at this hand to Lord Percy opposite.

"Let us pray that when we do catch Lord Essex, we hold all the cards," the King said.

"Rumour has it that they closed shops in London to encourage men to reinforce their army," Lord Forth commented and refilled his wine glass.

"And in their idleness they will go about the devil's work." The monarch referred to the apprentices. "Most probably the same ones who destroyed the Queen's chapel at Somerset House and imprisoned her priests."

After grumbling about the apprentices and agreeing with his royal master, Lord Forth checked that both the King and Percy were to begin the game. He declared the King first to go, seeing as he had dealt and left the monarch to ponder how many of his cards to jettison.

"I discard three." King Charles took a trio of replacements from the spare cards in the centre, two of which were queens.

"And I discard two." Percy carefully extracted them from his hand and picked up an equal number of new cards.

"See, Forth, how he grips his cards like a lady holds a fan?" The King laughed.

"A lady looking like that would certainly need a fan to hide behind," Forth replied, much to the amusement of the King. "Shall we declare ruff, sir?"

King Charles already knew the total score of his highest suit and watched Percy's head bob over every card he counted. Earlier that day the man had also reckoned up how many barrels of gunpowder they had, the meagre amount meaning that each shot would have to count when they tracked down the enemy.

"Well, I have a ruff of fifty-seven." The King said.

"And I fifty-four. So, well played, Your Majesty," Percy replied, conceding six points.

Forth asked if either had any sets, to which the King triumphantly held up three cards and declared none of the queens to be as beautiful as his own. King Charles then proposed a toast to Henrietta Maria and, after a suspenseful pause, revealed with a broad smile that he hoped her to be with child, though very early.

"Bravo, Your Majesty, most joyous news," Forth said and went on to declare that the royal family might soon have a set of four Princes.

Good humour filled this tiny farmhouse and relaxed the King, who took the laurels of the match; an omen he hoped, of things to come. The fire in the hearth had warmed the three men through and dried their cloaks and hats, but the rainwater that had soaked them had not altogether gone – just as the war persisted outside this little haven. Condensation hung in the air and clung to the panes of glass in the window where a face appeared.

"Ye Gods!" The superstitious Forth leapt to his feet.

The King's shocked eyes showed uncertainty as to whether they beheld an ethereal visitor or an enemy of this plane. As the distorted face peered inside, Percy raced to the door to alert the guards and, after less than a minute, the stranger was allowed to pass.

"Nephew?" The monarch watched Rupert enter the room along with the chill of night, which seemed as cold as his manner.

"Your Majesty, we have been awaiting your orders for hours," Rupert said, holding out his hands. "My cavalry are mustered on Broadway Hill waiting for your permission to ride ahead and harry Essex."

"Lord Essex trudges like a tortoise," Percy said. "Can this not wait until morning so that the King can rest?"

"Essex is fifteen miles ahead of us," Rupert explained. "Our infantry has no chance of catching him unless I take the cavalry and slow him down with a series of attacks."

"Have the scouts verified his position?" the King asked.

"They did not even know he'd moved until he was five miles away," Rupert complained bitterly.

"Your Highness, must we chase Essex like this?" Percy's frustration came over in a whisper. "If he does not offer battle, we would be free to pick up the siege of Gloucester precisely where we left off."

"That will involve losing time we do not have," Rupert replied.

"I concur that we need to do all we can to engage the enemy." The King suggested that Rupert's detachment should include mounted musketeers.

"A good idea," Forth agreed. "We could get a few hundred ..."

"I would need a thousand," Rupert interjected.

"Then take Sir George Lisle's musketeers from the Bristol garrison," the King replied, his hope refreshed by Rupert's dynamism. "Well, Nephew, to the chase! I will muster the infantry and follow, but I wish to be kept fully informed of your progress." He was determined that any new royal child should be born into a peaceful realm and into a royal family which was strong and secure. Therefore to achieve such a realisation meant that decisive action must commence immediately.

Chapter 50

Newbury was comfortably nestled by a blossoming wool trade, which also padded the purses of the inhabitants. But on the eve of autumn the town found itself in the path of the two armies. The silhouettes of its jagged rooftops, like dragon's teeth, bit at the Earl of Essex's wounded pride. Despite the town's sympathy for his Parliamentarians, the King's Cavaliers had reached it first and thus quartered there that night, while Essex's men were forced to sleep in open ground.

"You may have feasted on the town but, by God, you have bitten off more than you can chew," Essex said, looking down upon the town from high ground. He pictured the rampant Royalists bubbling in the depths below.

Attached to Newbury, the enemy camp was like a bulbous growth across the London road, while to the north and south dawn played out in the troubled waters of the River Kennet.

"My lord, yonder hills are ours for the taking." Philip Skippon cried with disbelief.

"And we shall have them, Skippon," Essex agreed. "Lead your men to Round Hill and I will advance upon Biggs Hill and thence to Wash Common which lies between the two." The Lord General turned his horse towards the morning light which had burst over the horizon with orange flames, burning Parliament's colour onto the land.

"They have not occupied the precious high ground, gentlemen." Essex told his officers. This was one occasion when he didn't mind being proved wrong, having yesterday predicted to his men that they would fight an enemy controlling the town, lanes, hills, hedges, and the river. But his intention had always been to paint a bleak picture, for he knew that his men fought best when their lives were at stake.

"The Lord of Hosts smiles down upon us," Sir Philip Stapleton replied to Essex, holding up his sword and signalling to his cuirassier horsemen.

"Follow me!" Essex was not to be outdone and drew his broad-bladed sabre, while the gilt rivets in his armour burned with zeal.

Three thousand troops marched off with vigour, leaving behind all the foreboding of the cold and black night. The Lord General's men drove off the pockets of Royalists that stalked the hills and common, sending them fleeing back to their masters with tales of woe.

Having won possession of these crowning landmarks, the jewels of the Parliamentarian army now proudly adorned them. Skippon's ruby redcoats lodged on Round Hill, and his standard, displaying a grasped sword issuing from a cloud, fluttered across the ridge with his advance. Sapphire bluecoats of the London Trained Bands dotted Wash Common, complementing the sparkling amber of Lord Essex's regiment and their coats of orange. The Parliamentarians were now in position; early birds who had risen to get their worms and whose lines buzzed with hymns and psalms in readiness to face the day. It would be with much recrimination that the King's men awoke to this vision.

Chapter 51

Francis gripped his pistol as though it were a talisman. Just holding it out in front of him and having its two-and-a-half-foot barrel point at the Parliamentarians offered some assurance of protection as he thudded across Wash Common.

His mind had raced all morning while facing this moment and awaiting the order to attack. His thoughts had been of Anne and Henry, as well as eagerness to be at the rebels, and it was only the trumpet call to charge that dispelled those. Now at one with his horse's pounding hooves, his head was filled with a thirst for survival; of killing any rebel before they killed him. The one distraction not shifted by his advance was simmering hatred of Sir Richard Warrington; a hatred that drove him with determination to the bloody task before him.

The oncoming wind chilled his face and the Royalist cavalry closed in on the Parliamentarians for a second time, hoping to dislodge them from the high ground they'd occupied since dawn. Rupert's horsemen attacked two thousand at a time, three rows deep, in an attempt to batter the enemy in relentless waves. Francis was part of the second attempt. In the centre, the King's infantry advanced with the same aim and, to their right, also the opposite wing of Royalist cavalry.

Francis's pistol rose and fell with his horse's momentum, but his eye never wavered from its line of sight. He aimed it as much as it aimed him. Closing up to the rebel horsemen who advanced to meet them, Francis's frozen trigger finger retracted to spin the metal wheel of his pistol. Contacting the pyrite, sparks bounded from the friction and leapt into the wheel-lock's pan to ignite the gunpowder charge. Now amongst the enemy, Francis followed on the heels of the bullet and launched himself at one rebel with a yell that had the veins in his neck stand out.

Lifting his second pistol from its holster, Francis fired at his foe, who was covered head to toe in the shiny steel shell of blackened cuirassier armour. The bullet merely ricocheted off it. The Parliamentarians resembled charred bodies that had risen from the fires of war and presented a formidable sight that had Francis panic when sword slashes also proved ineffective. Francis circled the iron-clad rebel, who struggled to keep him in his sights. With agility being his only edge, Francis went to dismount him with a jolt and a well-aimed slash to the horse's hindquarters.

The whinnies of beasts, yells of riders and crashes of gunshot fought for supremacy while flashes of fire and the blur of activity were dulled by smoking grey mist. A shot near Francis's head went unnoticed in the din. No man could ever know how close death stalked unless the Reaper actually took him.

Francis brought his backsword against the dismounted rebel, striking the man's gauntleted hand. A flurry of fire then revealed the rebels' mimicking of Rupert's tactics; they too, had withheld their shot until grappling at close quarters. It now became apparent to Francis just how the Parliamentarians had surprisingly managed to fend off the first charge.

A parliamentarian cavalryman spurred forward from the gloom behind Francis. The broad-shouldered brute was draped in a long grey riding coat, worn over burnished armour. He brought his blade against Francis's breastplate and nearly tipped him from his saddle. The killer blow loomed before Francis even comprehended it, but just prior, the rebel tumbled to the ground with his horse after it was felled by a bullet. A trumpet blare reached its climax and, digging his heels into his horse, Francis and the rest of the Royalists wheeled about and fell back to their lines.

The trumpeter's tune of retreat did not often dance in the ears of Rupert's men. Sweat streaked across Francis's face, such that he could barely keep his stinging eyes open and when his mount stumbled it seemed like his whole world was about to topple.

"They have you?" Frustration brought forth fury upon noting his horse's pink, fleshy wound. Nevertheless, while the valiant steed took him the last hundred yards to safety, another two thousand horsemen passed him for a third attempt at the Parliamentarians. Rupert's full wing of six thousand horse had now been engaged. Should his cavalrymen be defeated it would leave the Royalist infantry exposed and bring catastrophic defeat. A resounding rout that would allow Lord Essex's army to get back to London – something that the King's army were fighting to prevent.

* * * * *

"God has forsaken you all!" Sir Philip Stapleton cried. After holding off two Royalist charges, his passion was fired by this belief and beneath his cuirassier armour the Parliamentarian's hot body was equally fired. Stapleton pushed Rupert's men back towards their lines and then drew up in preparation to regroup and return to his own. His lifeguard had halted around him when he spotted a small group in the enemy ranks ahead.

"It cannot be ..." he said aloud and squinted at the standard over their heads. Golden lions seemed to snarl at him as they flapped on a background of midnight black. Silver and blue diamonds sparkled in Stapleton's eyes as if he had just opened a chest and set his eyes upon a treasure most priceless. "Rupert! The foreign mercenary himself."

Stapleton's hand instinctively went to his pistol. His eyes remained fixed on the prize. Tightly curling his fingers around the butt, he drew the gun and let it lie against his horse's neck, instructing his standard bearer to ride back towards Parliament's lines. With the absence of his pennant and the dropping of his visor, he became an anonymous assassin as he rolled his spurs against his horse to dart straight at Rupert's group.

"Show your face." One Cavalier called at the approach of this unknown rider.

At around fifty yards from the gathering, Stapleton drew up side-on. When he lifted his visor, his scowl prompted a repeated demand for his name; a name the Royalists would soon discover and never forget once he had shot Prince Rupert of the Rhine in the head. It didn't take a second to scan the enemy. Lord Digby's golden locks were not prize enough; it was tall Rupert in the centre who was the target of Stapleton's levelled pistol.

"Stop!"

Stapleton squeezed the trigger at the same moment his eye met Rupert's austere glare. The Prince had barely lowered his spyglass, clearly not seeing this coming, and with the gunshot the object dropped from Rupert's grip as he fell back. As Stapleton wheeled about to escape, the panic-stricken cries did nothing but give him hope that his shot had found its mark. The Prince's attendants rushed to his aid while Stapleton yelled encouragement to his horse and fled full-tilt with bullets flying around his head.

"Your Prince is as mortal as any man!" Stapleton's adrenaline-fuelled jubilation spilled over after eliminating the German Prince; the talisman that had secured so many victories, and whose demise must surely seal the King's defeat.

Chapter 52

The Royalist infantry pushed across a valley and to the slope of Newbury's fields which were enclosed by hedgerows. From the heights of Round Hill, the rebels' aloof artillery glared down at them. The noses of these ten-foot-long demi-cannons unleashed a storm of Parliamentarian projectiles at the rate of ten shots per hour; nine-pound cannonballs that tore gashes in the chalky soil to swallow many a corpse. Even Mother Nature appeared to oppose the King's men when the hedges ahead of them, lined by the rebels, lit up with gunshot.

"They must have nested in the damned things." Sir John Byron cursed the Parliamentarians, whose guns poked from the hawthorn like the beaks of hungry chicks. From the saddle, with his cavalrymen, Byron watched his infantrymen advance.

Commanded musketeers went ahead, using whatever cover was available to unleash a fire fight and desperately pave the way for the rest of the King's infantry. But the next scrub hedge they faced was higher and viciously manned. Pike poles jutted from it, muskets fired through it, while light field artillery bombarded any Royalist who dared approach, and as a result,

Byron's men were held in a deadly check. Three regiments and commanded musketeers failed to weed out the enemy, leaving the approaches to this natural and most formidable obstacle littered with bodies.

"Have my uncle's foot regiment reinforce us," Byron commanded, as case shot ripped through the infantry.

"Let's set those nesting rebels to flight," Lord Falkland said with a furrow of his delicate forehead. "Commit our cavalry."

"Cavalry, Lucius, will just hinder our troops," Byron replied in a slow, monotonous voice that expended little emotion. "The ground has too many obstacles."

Although he found the volunteer's ashen face mildly amusing, Byron's own displayed little more than a few creases, such was his antipathy for Falkland's type. It was his opinion that the Secretary of State would have been best limiting himself to battles in the council chamber.

"I grow weary of it all." Falkland's poetic tongue couldn't attempt to describe his misery over the war. Nor did his utterance receive a response from Byron, as a horseman had arrived, announcing himself as Sir Francis Berkeley.

"His Highness has expelled the enemy cavalry from Wash Common," Berkeley informed them.

"I knew Rupert hadn't been killed!" Byron's disbelief of the rumour was vindicated.

"The Prince is ready to attack the enemy infantry," Berkeley added. A decision that would see the Parliamentarians hard-pressed on two fronts. "He would have you do the same as soon as may be, so that we act in unison."

"Look at the obstacles I face," Byron replied, disdain accentuating the battle scar across his left cheek.

Flashes of fire sent the Royalist infantry to ground like animals, and their cry for cavalry support began to grow.

The single call for 'horse' was chanted until even the hardened Byron could not ignore it.

"The infantry is as ignorant of our predicament as the Prince." Sir Richard Warrington said, meeting Berkeley's glare.

"But I'm far from ignorant of the responsibilities heaped at my door." Byron knew that the reputation of his family depended on his actions. "If the infantry cannot dislodge the enemy from this godforsaken bush they can cut a way through it for my cavalry," he said, and turned to Francis. "You shall join us, sir, for I need every man I can get.

* * * * *

The Parliamentarians seemed at one with the landscape and mingled with the wiry claws of the hedges. Even their field sign was a sprig of greenery in their helmets and hatbands. Francis, along with the Royalist cavalry, watched every faltering attack upon this hedgerow and, as mesmerising musket flashes sparked along its length, a thinner gap became apparent.

"To the breach!" Royalist soldiers sprinted to the small chink, falling to their knees to hack at it.

"Christ, a few men will never widen it enough for our horses," Sir Richard Warrington said.

"Give them time." Byron held up a finger.

"By, God we are out of time," Falkland replied. "And they say it is I who lacks fighting spirit!" He lined himself up with the hawthorn not two hundred yards away.

Francis steadied his own horse over the distant rumbling of artillery which unleashed an iron downpour and watched Falkland's glazed eyes narrow and his back straighten. It was clear what the man was thinking and equally clear that he would be torn apart before he got anywhere near the small gap. Francis went to intervene. "My lord …"

"If His Lordship wishes to inspire the men …" Sir Richard had barely uttered the words when Falkland spurred his mount. "Then that surely is his prerogative."

Every hoof-fall of Falkland's beast roused the ranks of the Royalists he passed, as well as those ahead that he approached. Many took their lead from his example, and others followed in his wake.

Francis watched Falkland's thunderous advance and his receding figure with awe and bated breath. As long as the man's image remained in sight both their deliverance from this impasse, and their ultimate victory, became entirely possible, despite the odds being stacked heavily against him.

"A foolish way to prove one's manhood." Sir Richard shook his head.

Horse and rider leaped into the air and at the gap, although the flanks of Falkland's horse were too big and the spray of bullets too numerous. They couldn't clear the narrow opening in the hedge and fell right into it, but in death their corpses achieved the objective and widened the hawthorn by forcing it asunder.

"Charge!" Byron was not going to be left behind. If Newbury needed a victor he would be that man, outdoing all his six brothers in the process. But no sooner had he led his cavalry off than his horse was shot in the neck.

Francis needed no encouragement from the commander. His blood had been up ever since laying eyes upon Sir Richard, and he rode ahead of the man, making it over the hedge despite the wizened fingers of hawthorn that clawed at him. Now in Darke Lane, Francis and the other Royalists were cut off. With a shiver of shock, he could now see what they had been up against. The enemy were drawing off light artillery and retreating to the next hedge. Francis, and a growing number of Royalists, cut down as many of them as possible.

"Stop them retreating!" Byron cried.

With pike staffs threatening their horse's guts and lead balls blasting exit wounds as big as dinner plates, the King's soldiers fought desperately. Francis made for an eight-foot drake that had spewed grapeshot and halted its escape by running through one of the three gunners, who slumped over the artillery piece. The gun's remaining assistants held Francis and the group of Royalists at bay until the intervention of Sir Richard Warrington and his troop of cavalry overpowered them. Holding his sword aloft and crying out as if drawing energy from the grey clouds above, Sir Richard urged his men on.

Amidst the battle, Francis's horse was brought down by stray shot. On foot amongst snorting beasts, every cry and flash of steel was a threat as friend and foe became difficult to distinguish. Like a child, he looked up helplessly, wielding both his blade and pistol.

Sir Richard lashed out at a Roundhead standard bearer and made to take the enemy pennant. He rode over scattered bodies, and all one thousand pounds of horse and rider trampled anything in his way as he made to seize his prize.

The flow of Sir Richard and his men had Francis pinned helplessly against the cannon and he watched the old man take the enemy flag by its staff, his red face puffed with pride; perhaps the same pride that had consumed him after he'd kidnapped Lucy. Francis eyed Sir Richard's head while a dull ring filled his own, blocking out all else. Thoughts of revenge consumed him. His lip curled with hatred and, without thinking any further, he lifted his pistol and trained it on the man. Sir Richard turned, and his hook nose screwed up.

Francis's hands trembled, and he cried out at the top of his voice, "I'll kill you, you goddamned bastard!" Instead of firing a bullet, he could only let loose a verbal tirade and follow the influx of Royalist cavalry and infantry as they rushed to the next hedge. Francis's aggression spilled over on to all enemies encountered in this maze of enclosures, within which many more Royalists were set to be forever lost.

Byron's troops were held in check on the slopes of Round Hill. Within this stalemate Francis felt somehow imbued with a sense of immunity. The determination to live another day stemmed from a thirst for revenge, which drove Francis into a second and more personal war with Sir Richard. He regretted not pulling the trigger of his carbine; a reality that inflamed him.

Chapter 53

The wood-panelled walls were dotted with candle holders, and on each one a small piece of mirror-glass reflected the flickering glow into the room. Although assisted by some candles perched in pewter candlesticks, they were still not enough to brighten the sombre atmosphere. Even a fire in the hearth seemed to struggle for breath, leaving an ethereal haze.

King Charles sat at the head of a table crowded with counsellors and commanders. His heavy eyelids were poised to shield his gaze from the horror etched onto the faces of all present. Shadows played with the men's features and taunted the monarch, as if any one of them might turn out to be Lord Falkland, putting paid to the rumours of his death. The candlelight flashed up the earthy stains, torn clothing and dried blood of the commanders. This, coupled with the civilian counsellors' morose expressions, told everything about the battle which, having been sought for three weeks, had disappointingly resulted in stalemate.

"Lord Falkland?" the King asked, clasping his clammy hands together.

"I am afraid we haven't found his body, Your Majesty." Old Lord Forth's Scottish accent was without its melody.

"Have the enemy confirmed that they have him p-prisoner?" King Charles rubbed his large forehead.

"I'm afraid not," Forth said, holding his wounded arm.

"Conduct a search of the field." The King ordered as the door opened, and his eyes darted straight to it, as if the intelligent young Falkland was about to enter. But the newcomer was none other than Lord Percy along with a draught as cold as the two and a half thousand dead sown across Newbury's fields.

"Your Majesty, I propose we engage Lord Essex on the morrow." Rupert broke the silence and praised their troops for having held the rebels at bay, despite them possessing the best ground. "Our position here still blocks the rebels' return to London."

"What say you, gentlemen?" the King asked, holding out one hand and inviting comment. The resulting silence plucked at the monarch's nerves and had him look around the room with frustration. The elderly Lord Forth cupped his ear as if struggling to hear the question – never mind answer it – and others simply looked to the next man. It seemed that learned opinion, too, was missing in action.

"Your Highness, I fear we cannot afford such losses for a second time," Lord Digby eventually replied.

"Just as we cannot afford to let Lord Essex escape to London again," Rupert answered. "It's impossible to win this war without incurring more casualties."

"Why can't we pick a better field and a better day?" Digby asked.

"Pym is courting the Scots." Rupert reminded them with a stern glare. "It's nearly one year since our last opportunity of defeating the rebels in battle. If we give up the chance we have before us, the next occasion might see us facing a foe reinforced by Scottish troops."

The King blinked for a second longer than normal. The prospect of the country of his birth ever joining the English rebels was bleak enough to add further grey flecks to his beard. His first thought was to agree with Digby, but he was enough of a realist to acknowledge that this simply stemmed from a desire to put off the inevitable.

"Oh, Your Highness, I don't propose to wait for their next invitation." Digby's golden locks and his silver tongue made him sparkle. "Let us chase the rebels like a pack of hounds and bring them down on more advantageous ground. If they reach London, I'm positive we can lure them out once more by picking off their garrisons one by one."

"Would a lion pin down his prey only to let it scamper free again?" Rupert asked. "Why not have it done with now?"

At the mention of losses the King lifted his head. Seated bolt upright, he brought a hush to the council by the merest inhalation of breath as he made to speak. "If the rebels reach London, they will be strengthened both in morale and supplies." King Charles's thoughts turned to the heroic sacrifice of his commanders such as the twenty-three-year old Earl of Sunderland, a pearl now forever entombed in its shell. "I understand the enemy are presently short of both, most especially provisions."

"What they lack is made up for by the ground they hold. Let as many of those who fight for our victory survive to witness it." Digby uttered his words like a prayer. "The lie of the land is not in our favour here."

"Rupert, do your horsemen still hold Wash Common?" the King asked, drawing a resolute nod from his nephew. "And how did Byron fare in the centre against Round Hill?"

"They broke through several hedges, but remain stuck on the slopes, sir," Forth replied.

"And the enemy, I am informed, have been struggling to maintain their positions between those two points?" The King was for decisive action, the only action that befitted the reputation of his loyal army.

"That's absolutely correct, sir." Prince Rupert leaned forward. "And they have committed their reserves too."

"As have we," Digby added.

"Authors through the ages will immortalise our men's bravery this day," said Lord Percy, the General of Ordinance. "But I must add my own postscript and tell you that we do not have the means for another battle." Percy's revelation blew all debate apart.

"Explain yourself," the King instructed, gripping the arms of his chair.

"We have expended two thirds of our gunpowder and have but ten barrels left, Your Majesty." Percy's smooth features barely displayed a wrinkle at the revelation, and his sandy eyebrows were so light that when they dipped it was not even discernible.

"Have you requested more from Oxford?" Rupert glared.

"Of course, Your Highness," Percy replied.

"When might we expect it?" The King leaned forward.

"I estimate another day, sir," Percy answered.

"We cannot fight without powder." Lord Digby raised his hands.

"Then I see no option for us but to march for Oxford." The King was resolute.

"Rather than withdraw, let us occupy Newbury and continue to block the road to London while we wait." Rupert's proposal gained many a nod from the officers, but the King believed they would support anything his legendary nephew suggested.

"It is decided." King Charles's small lips pursed with stubborn finality. "We fall back to Donnington Castle and thence to Oxford. Have orders sent to the Mayor of Newbury to make provision for the dead and wounded ... of both sides."

A page proffered the monarch's hat and he paced into a corridor with short, fast steps, only pausing upon hearing the laboured rasps of the Earl of Carnarvon. Peering through the ajar door at the noble's lone battle, King Charles advanced into the room forbidding anyone to follow.

"Your Majesty," a physician whispered, bowed low and drew back.

The monarch stepped towards the bed and stood over Robert Dormer, Earl of Carnarvon, and looked down at his long face. It was as white as the sheet covering him. Sweat beads sat like evening dew upon his forehead or stuck his blond hair as the last vestiges of life seeped away.

"Your opinion?" the King asked, turning to the physician and looking him in the eye. "The truth, if you please."

The man gave a hopeless expression and an ever-so-slight shake of his head, a judgement that led the King to release him from his duties and have him leave. The Monarch dabbed Carnarvon's brow with a silk handkerchief; he would care for the peer during his final hours in a way that he'd been unable to tend to any of the others who'd perished fighting for him.

"O' Lord, I commend the soul of this man to pass to thy great kingdom and those of every man who fell in the service of your cause today. Let them suffer no longer," he whispered.

Sight of the peer stirred memories of their mutual childhoods. Carnarvon, orphaned at the age of six, had become a ward of King Charles's father and this long-lost world came to mind. People, places, sights and smells of old all returned in this final moment, as if a doorway to this long-forgotten land had become all that separated past and present. How had life come to this?

The King took Carnarvon's icy hand, closed his weary eyes and recited a prayer. No stammer interrupted this sad moment. A bitter sting rose to his throat and caused tears to drip onto the sheets and mingle with the bloodstains. The courageous actions of his loyal subjects gave King Charles inspiration, despite the immense burden he shouldered.

Chapter 54

Two men exchanged loud and angry cries. One drew a bollock dagger in a blur of movement. With a quick thrust, it was forced into the gut of the other up to the two spherical decorations on the grip.

The metal buttons, fashioned like spider's webs on the wounded man's doublet, were opened in haste. Beneath the jacket, his white linen shirt was soaked. Crimson blood rapidly increased in depth and tone and trickled onto a letter lying beside the body. Like an abundance of red sealing wax, it contrasted starkly with the paper.

In shock, Mary couldn't help but reach out and touch the blood. She stared hard at her tainted fingers and then held her face in despair. The creases of her wrinkled skin that remained untouched by the sticky blood were left to resemble white veins.

* * * * *

"Help me!" Mary shrieked, and sat up in bed with her head full of terrible images. She frantically rubbed her face to wipe clean the imagined blood and screamed again in her cold and confused state.

The only way her hands could stop trembling was if she kept them firmly pressed to her closed eyes. The more her breathing slowed, the more foolish she felt for being so alarmed at the vision that had plagued her for the second time that week. Now Anne was calling out and the floor outside the bedroom creaked as her daughter hurried closer.

"Mother, are you all right?" Anne opened the door, rushed to Mary's side and held her hand.

"Yes, my dear," Mary replied and began searching around the bed. "My pomander, where is my pomander?" She took the opportunity to dry her eyes while Anne retrieved it.

"Was it the same thing?" Anne asked as Mary drew comfort from the pomander's clove and orange.

"Just a bad dream." Mary sighed. She wished not to dwell on it, because every time she awoke with concern over the blood on her hands and a sensation of guilt.

Mary's mind returned to the blood-stained letter. The last letter she had written was to Lord Essex when she had passed on one or two useful snippets from Anne's correspondence. But through this Mary had garnered much needed cash that benefitted her husband and daughter, and this should instil, not guilt, but a sense of worth in being able to provide for them.

"What's worrying you?" Anne leaned closer, took an ivory comb and began gently combing her mother's hair.

"I've told you before, it's nothing," Mary said.

"You're missing sleeping with father, perhaps?" Anne explored every possibility as she worked on her mother's red tresses.

"What?" Mary shot a look. "He's snoring more often than not." She said that having a bed to herself was bliss. *Or it ought to be*, she thought.

"Do you see anyone die?" Anne's hesitation suggested she had suspected this for a while.

"Well ..." Mary never remembered much after touching the blood. "I see a man in a red coat stabbed, though I know not if he survives."

"A red coat?" Anne paused.

"Worry not, Anne, it won't be Francis." Mary sensed the concern in her daughter's voice. "Probably just my concerns about this war," she replied, finding herself now considering the awful plausibility of Francis as the victim, although she had never seen any indication of identity. The very chance of it made Mary doubly determined to give Anne and Henry her utmost protection. Lord knows, her son-in-law was far too reckless to care for himself, never mind them.

* * * * *

Two days after the Battle of Newbury, Francis's feet were firmly planted as he stood waiting in a small orchard enclosed by pear trees and hedges. The long grass shimmered back and forth like water lapping against his black shoes, while a breeze whistled that Sir Richard Warrington was on his way. The leaves on the trees were starting to turn. Some had paled to yellow, others blushed russet and had begun to crinkle; hardened by the season, they rattled in the wind as if their time was up. Francis's heart too was hardening through exposure to war, so much so that after contemplating killing Sir Richard a few days ago, he was not at all put off when faced with this second opportunity.

"Tell me you are fighting to first blood, and not death?" asked Jack Mandeville, Francis's friend from his time in Brentford.

"He chose first blood as well as the time and location," Francis replied and drew his rapier with a high-pitched ring. "He's used to making arbitrary judgments."

Francis placed his right foot forward and bent his knee, lunging forward with his blade levelled at shoulder height. Then, leading with his right foot, he bounded forward several times in succession, cutting and thrusting. The sword whooshed at his speed, but, careful not to waste too much energy, he stopped and began walking back to Jack, cutting the formation of an 's' in the air. He inhaled deep breaths at the thought of the risks, as duelling was forbidden by the King, and he'd been the one to lay down this challenge. But honour, injustice and revenge drove him.

"Remember you'll only have a handful of chances to get him," Jack said.

"One is all I need." Francis was not prone to over-optimism.

"Watch him at all times," Jack warned.

Francis bent down and retrieved a stray pear. "Despite his build and age, he's an able swordsman," he said of Sir Richard, and took a bite to quench his dry mouth. It was at this point that his opponent appeared with a second and began marching closer.

"Are we ready, Berkeley?" Sir Richard's grin bared his tombstone teeth.

"One question," Francis said, watching as Sir Richard drew a forty-seven-inch Dutch rapier. "You imprisoned my sister out of a desire to strike a blow at me?"

"You seem to have answered your own question," Sir Richard said.

"Well now it's my turn to strike at you, though I have the courage to do so to your face," Francis warned, curling his fingers around the leather grip of his English rapier which, although seven inches shorter, he aimed to make up for by curbing his anger and maintaining deep concentration.

Both opponents parted two paces and unfastened and removed their doublets. Sir Richard wrapped his around one arm. When Francis discarded his, he glared at Sir Richard, eyeing every detail of the man's face; from his flushed, saggy cheeks to the waves of white hair that curled down past a neat moustache and beard.

Outstretching his right arm, Francis pointed his sword at Sir Richard, while holding his left hand parallel. The weight of the pommel offered a counterbalance and Francis looked down the sword's double-sided blade, watching for the slightest movement in Sir Richard's body, or as much as a flicker in his eye.

"Begin!" Jack called.

The opponents shuffled closer to one another. With their levelled weapons at shoulder height, the two blades dipped slightly towards the tips, which kissed in first contact. Francis's brow was hot. Sir Richard's mouth was nothing more than an emotionless slit. For ten seconds they tried to anticipate the other or judge the other's tactic.

Sir Richard lunged forward first, raising his left hand into the air and slicing his sword out ahead of him. Francis parried it. The clang of blade meeting blade had barely sounded before Sir Richard grunted and attempted a riposte.

Francis leaped backwards twice in succession to escape Sir Richard's advance. Then both men stopped dead once more. They stood side-on to one another, watching and waiting.

Slowly they circled each other. Then Francis propelled himself forward, light on his feet, slicing from right and left. The rapiers flashed with silvery menace. Sir Richard met the blows, back-stepped three times and then lunged, so low that one of his knees practically touched the ground; low enough to avoid an incoming slice, and to catch Francis's ribs in a draw cut of his own.

"Aha! Defeated by an old dog," Sir Richard's raspy voice taunted. He stood up straight and stretched while Francis held the side of his chest.

"A pox on you," Francis yelled and went for him again.

Sir Richard barely escaped. The near miss drove him into a series of side-steps which had him orbit Francis just out of reach. With their swords outstretched, both men leaned back slightly to maintain a good view of the other.

Sir Richard swung in his rapier and made a pass, yelling when Francis parried it, as well as a second and third attempt in fast succession. Clinking blades resounded like a heartbeat of steel.

Francis took his chance and locked swords with Sir Richard. Once their blades untangled with a screech, Francis slashed the man's arm, making use of his foe's shock to kick him in the groin and send him to the ground. Two minutes since the contest had begun and Francis lifted his rapier, ready to stick Sir Richard.

"Francis!" Jack shouted and pointed at some approaching horsemen.

"Duelling is forbidden by order of His Majesty." One rider closed up. "Your names if you please."

"I know these two already, Captain." Prince Rupert was the other leading rider and he drew up within a couple of feet to peered down at the duellists.

"Your Highness ..." Francis breathlessly sheathed his sword and bowed.

"What is the meaning of this?" Rupert demanded. "On your feet, man." He turned and barked at Sir Richard.

"I had some business to settle, sir." Francis was ready for the consequences.

"Well, Sir Francis." Rupert shook his head. "You're honest, I'll give you that. Do I take it that honour has been satisfied?"

"Not quite," Francis replied.

"There was no honour here - he would have killed me." Sir Richard panted. "He struck like a coward after we had ended, and I was off guard."

"Hear this; if I catch either of you acting out your squabbles again, you'll both be thrown into Oxford gaol. Which I hear is a place that has distracted you both of late." Rupert went on to point at Sir Richard. "Had you not tipped my officers off about this contest, you'd be nothing more than a makeshift human scabbard."

Francis turned to Sir Richard and looked him up and down, but the Prince was not finished yet. He instructed Sir Richard to rejoin his men.

"My sincere apologies, Your Highness," Sir Richard replied. "I am most grateful for your clemency."

"Now you, Sir Francis, could do with some solitude to calm your hot head," Rupert said, and told him that he would have two days to prepare for a spell of isolation in Ireland. "Return to Oxford immediately and await further orders."

"Ireland, Highness?" Francis asked, barely able to utter the words.

"Aye, I have some business there you can assist me with. The distance will keep you out of trouble and allow this incident to be forgotten." Rupert raised his eyebrows, a sure sign that he expected no dispute.

"I am at Your Highness's command." Francis bowed and then watched as the Prince and his attendants turned about and rode away.

Chapter 55

Doublets lay draped over the lid of Francis's wooden chest. Black with silver ribbons at the waist and blue with silver embroidery, along with matching breeches, shoes, belts, and a pile of folded white shirts that leaned as much as the tower of Pisa.

When pulling a fresh shirt over his head, Francis knocked a pot of lavender from a table and it smashed onto the floor. It was one of the many aromatic plants littering every surface, in every room, as part of Mary's war against flies. But he kept his mouth closed and chose his battles carefully. The least he wanted on the eve of such a hazardous journey to an inhospitable land was to have Anne feel ever more protective of her mother's foibles and to part on a bad footing.

"Here is henbane and vinegar to promote sleep," Anne said as she placed a small wooden box into his travelling chest. "Now, if you're to be taken from me whenever the King wills it, then at least I deserve to know your destination," she pushed for a second time.

"Very well, Ireland, but you must tell no-one," he replied and watched her ringlets tremble with panic as she stood. "No-one, I say."

"What has Ireland got to do with this war?" She took hold of his arm. "I don't like it, Francis, it's full of cut-throats and murderers," she said, tightening her grip as if she would most certainly never get him back after he stepped foot into that country.

"A task for Rupert." He began gathering up his clothes. "I'm afraid I have no choice in the matter," he added, upon recognising the accusatory expression on her face. She watched him in silence. Francis could not explain his banishment in any other way, for the truth about the duel would have led to his damnation in her eyes.

"You always say we have choices in life." Anne vigorously flapped a newly washed nightshirt and folded it.

"Not when a prince of the blood gives a command," Francis replied and went to take his red doublet.

"Not that one," she interjected.

"Why not?" Despite his anxiety he couldn't help but shake his head at this irony. "Can a man not make a choice about his own apparel?"

"Don't make light of my remarks," she insisted.

"I'm sorry, sweetheart," Francis embraced both Anne and the nightshirt she still firmly held, for she did not reciprocate.

"How long will you be away?" She finally laid her head against his chest.

"That I do not know." He kissed her. "But I will return the moment I can," he said and stooped to pick up his clothes. "Now, why ever can I not take that doublet?"

"Mother's visions are of a man wearing red who gets stabbed." She did not look up as she offered her explanation, but instead ran her thumb over the metal buttons that resembled spiders' webs.

"Oh Lord." Francis sighed. "She has you believing those?"

"I choose to believe." Anne was quick to correct. "She's reluctant to speak of them. It's only because I comfort her afterwards that I've managed to find out what little I do know, and I won't tempt fate."

"You truly think that if I wear this it'll be the death of me?" Francis grasped one sleeve.

"I ask you to respect my opinion." Anne took hold of each of his arms.

"She's manipulating you." Francis buckled his sword belt around his chest and attempted to remain calm in the face of this meddling. "It's nothing more than an excuse to stay here so that everyone can rush around and cater to her every need," he said, regretting voicing this opinion as soon as he uttered it.

"Am I not permitted a little company while you're gone? From tomorrow I will watch every breaking dawn and worry about whether I'll end up as a widow by the time the sun comes to set. Can you imagine how upsetting that is?" Anne cried as a knock came at the door. Her mother opened it and stepped into the room.

"Anne, did you send out for a pippin tart?" Mary paused as she looked at each of them in turn. "Oh, my apologies if I have interrupted anything." Her gaze fell to the clothes strewn around.

"Yes, it'll be delivered this afternoon," Anne replied.

"Dear, dear," Mary said, and gingerly stepped into the room as if she had entered sacred ground. Yet nevertheless, she retrieved the broken pot piece by piece and suggested that they have at least two in each room, as that always served her well. "Basil also works just as well as lavender."

"Do these flower pots only ward off flies?" Francis bit his tongue and wondered how to get rid of Mary. Without sarcasm he'd have reached breaking point, having returned from battle to discover her invasion and occupation of his home.

"I think that after your last visit to our house, Francis, these pots were the only things your men left us with." Mary held the pieces close to her chest. She gave a confused expression and looked around silently at all the items of clothing. "Are you going somewhere?"

"I'll be away with the army for a while," Francis replied as Jane knocked and entered with his riding boots.

"Thank you." Anne took them before the girl had advanced more than a few steps.

"Well, it's fortuitous that I am here after all, for I can look after Anne and Henry while you're away," Mary said and then turned to Jane. "Especially as this girl will no longer be needed now that Henry has gone off her breasts."

"Jane will continue as our maid," Francis replied; his decision made firmer due to Mary's questioning of it. "Can you fetch my son, Jane? I will take my leave of him." He instructed and then closed his chest and locked it. As Jane left, Mary followed her.

"My entire heart will remain here with you, as will that deadly doublet." Francis kissed Anne and held her, desperately unwilling to leave. "I give you my word that I shall write daily and return to you."

"I only want one promise from you," she said, stroking the rough skin of his hand.

"Name it."

"The next time you leave for campaign, allow me to accompany you, like the other commanders' wives." She bid him not to answer now, but to consider it while he was away. "I would be just as safe, if not safer with you and the army."

"I will think it over." Francis gave a reassuring smile and wondered how his mother-in-law would play her hand while he was away. But for once all thought of Mary was of secondary importance to the Irish assignment and the items he'd been detailed to collect on Rupert's behalf. Goods that had not been elaborated upon, either verbally or in writing, but mentioned as if everyone except Francis must be aware of their inordinate value.

* * * * *

No sooner had Francis left than Mary paced the house in search of her daughter. She found Anne deep in thought turning a chess piece in her fingers.

"Remonstrating with the King, eh?" Mary sat beside her. She could sense the undercurrent and felt as if she had bided her time long enough. Now was the moment to make her move.

"I'd give him a piece of my mind if I could!" Anne complained.

"I do not like seeing you so afflicted, my darling." Mary fiddled with the ring on her little finger. "What is it that particularly troubles you?"

"Oh, it is nothing." Anne sighed and placed the ivory king neatly back onto the board. "I worry about Francis, that's all."

"That was a lot of belongings." Mary raised an eyebrow. But her daughter's response was not enlightening, and she was forced to be more specific. "To where is he bound?"

"I don't think he knows himself." Anne sighed.

Mary chased eye contact and held Anne's hand. "Ah, he's told you not to say?" She thought it inconceivable that it would be a short journey, and Anne seemed even more forlorn over talk about the destination. When their eyes met, an apologetic smile crossed Anne's face; the type Mary had seen many times in the girl's life. "You are precious, my daughter, please remember that."

"Thank you, Mother."

"But I fear all the things you hide from me …" Mary turned away and held a hand over her mouth. "My worry in life is only for you and thy father and it pains me to think that you are suffering in silence; not sharing your woes with me."

Anne hugged her mother. Anxious to reassure Mary, she revealed that Francis was destined for Ireland, sent by Prince Rupert, with no certainty of when he'd return.

"Tell me about Ireland, Mother." Anne asked if it was anything like the news-sheets portrayed.

"It is a most magical place." Mary's heart warmed and sparked a broad smile of recollection. "Magic and stories abound in every field, hill and vale. 'Tis only the Protestants who have spoiled it," she said and told Anne about the bonds of kinship and the music, which told the tales of Ireland's history that ran in everyone's blood. "One of my favourites is 'John O'Dwyer of the Glen', a new one."

"The stag is up in Carrick,
His antlers high as ever;
He can enjoy the heather,
But our day is o'er."

"Your voice is as sweet as ever." Anne smiled and dried her eyes.

"Oh, Anne, I am so pleased to see you a little more relaxed." Mary stroked her daughter's cheek. "But I sense your sorrow at losing your husband, and also your frustration at being stuck with that strumpet of a servant."

"Mother!"

"Even though you don't tell me things anymore, I saw the way you snatched those boots from her." Mary's pencil thin eyebrows rose. "Do not let the girl rule you. *You* are the mistress of this house."

"That's not true, I often talk to you about my problems." Anne did not deny Mary's comments about being stuck with Jane.

"Then let us always discuss our troubles and woes." Mary embraced her. "As long as I live and breathe, I will protect you." She told Anne that being her mother was her only meaningful purpose in life.

"I know you will, as you have likewise cared for father, too," Anne replied. "Now, tell me more about Ireland."

"It's always been a stepping stone to England, which is why the English insisted on conquering it," Mary explained. And then she told how the land had been confiscated and doled out to Englishmen, such as Sir Walter Raleigh. "The English have always been afraid the Spanish would invade via the back door of Ireland, you see." The way her stories soothed Anne, gave Mary a warm feeling of purpose. In the back of her mind, she pondered Francis's reasons for heading to Ireland.

Chapter 56

Agreed and concluded at Siggings-town, in the county of Kildare, the fifteenth day of September, in the nineteenth year of His Majesty's reign, by and between James, Marquis of Ormonde, Lieutenant General of His Majesty's army in the Kingdom of Ireland, for and in the name of our gracious Sovereign Lord, Charles, by the grace of God, King of Great Britain, France, and Ireland, &c.

And Donogh, Viscount Muskerry, Sir Lucas Dillon, Knight; Nicholas Plunket Esquire; Sir Robert Talbot Baronet; Sir Richard Barnwell Baronet; Torlogh O Neale, Geoffrey Brown, Ever Mac-Gennis and John Walsh, Esquires; authorised by His Majesty's Roman Catholic subjects, of whose party they are, to treat and conclude with the said Marquis a cessation of arms.

As the Marquis of Ormonde penned the large 'O' that began his signature, it resembled the open mouths of the onlookers whose awed silence was broken only by the scratch of his quill. Catholic and Protestant alike eagerly noted the indelible mark being left upon history, which brought a truce to the bloodthirsty rebellion that had ravaged Ireland for two years. Preceding the civil war in England, the rebellion had been one of the causes of it.

"The late Lord Strafford was correct when he said you're the greatest member of your illustrious family."

This was one of the many compliments heaped upon Lord Ormonde as he stood and passed the quill to the next signatory. As King Charles's Lord Lieutenant of Ireland, he headed the government and was feted as a monarch in all but name. He was a military leader too, commanding the King's army raised to suppress the Catholic uprising.

"He should have said greatest *Protestant* of the family." Viscount Muskerry, leader of the Catholic rebels, took the quill from Ormonde, his brother-in-law.

"Religion aside, every one of us is part of the same national family." Ormonde placed a hand on Muskerry's back.

"Just as long as your Catholic brothers are allowed to retain all the territory we currently occupy," Muskerry replied and held up the parchment with a triumphant smile.

"The terms of the treaty confirm it," Ormonde said, having been instructed by the King to agree to that point, despite two thirds of the country being in Catholic hands.

"We are His Majesty's loyal subjects." Muskerry raised a toast to the Monarch. "When we took up arms it was never against his person, but to defend ourselves from the English and Scottish Parliaments who are no friends of ours."

"This treaty doesn't bind the Scottish army in the north," Ormonde warned, for they were not under his command, but sent by Scotland's Parliament to safeguard their settlers. Uneasy as Ormonde felt about this delicate truce, its aim was a vital one: to allow his army to return home to England and fight for King Charles.

"We fear no man who wears a pleated skirt." Viscount Muskerry let out a rattling chortle. "The Scots simply cling to Carrickfergus like barnacles."

"Then I shall follow your progress with interest now that this truce affords me the chance," Ormonde replied. "When I am not hunting with my hawks and hounds, that is." He crafted a non-threatening image of his activity after the treaty, while considering how he would keep both Catholic and Scot in check.

"I hope your hunting outfit suits a blue sash, for surely you've earned the Order of the Garter." Muskerry turned to the gathering as if the King were present and his words a recommendation.

"Well, 'tis six of the clock," Ormonde announced – the time he always ate. "Shall we feast?" He knew his role in Ireland was far from over yet.

"Pray, not boiled mutton." Muskerry denounced Ormonde's favourite dish.

"*Go ro maih agad.*" Ormonde ignored Muskerry's remark and spoke to the assembled dignitaries, who roared appreciation at his grasp of Irish. "I am instructed by His Majesty to inform you that he has decided to take charge of the safety of every one of his Irish subjects, no matter their religion."

"*Hiberni unanimes Pro Deo, Rege et Patria*," Muskerry wished to have the last word, quoting the Catholic confederate motto – 'Irishmen united for God, King and country'.

Chapter 57

Construction work at Sigginstown House had ceased two years ago upon the death of its creator Lord Strafford, the former Lord Deputy of Ireland. That infamous politician had impressive plans for the house and for Ireland, but with his demise both remained unfinished. Sigginstown's red bricks flushed with embarrassment at its links to this most hated of men, and Francis, upon climbing its steps, paled with foreboding.

Sigginstown, a towering symbol of Strafford's ruthlessness, was as foreign as the Protestant settlers that England and Scotland had injected into the country. Even its distinct bricks had been imported. As Francis slowly approached the entrance, men still gossiped about Strafford having had his army form a human chain to transport the bricks from port to building site.

Francis had been present at Strafford's beheading in London along with one hundred thousand others. Parliament had brought the King's trusted minister to the chopping block, yet his long shadow survived to this day. And, newly arrived in County Kildare with all of these thoughts and sights – stuck here until God knows when, Francis felt severed from his family.

"I carry an urgent despatch for the Marquis of Ormonde."

Francis was allowed inside and escorted through the crowd. They weren't a crowd in a singular sense, more pockets of people split by religion and then quartered again by politics, but all were there for the purpose of witnessing the truce.

In Francis's mind were the woodcut pictures that had reported Ireland's rebellion; of babies skewered on pikes; Protestants stripped and left in the snow to die and a pregnant woman whose child had been cut from her belly. In London he'd seen grown men cry as they recounted tales of bloodthirsty Catholics who had their sights on England. And now Francis walked amongst them – in their den.

"Your name, sir?" A well-dressed Irishman approached.

"Sir Francis Berkeley. Here by order of Prince Rupert," he replied and, giving over his written credentials, was taken to a chamber where Ormonde was seated upon a chair on a raised dais.

Etiquette turned Francis into a mute. One agonising minute turned into the next as he waited for the great Marquis to grace him with a casual glance or flick of his finger. Francis straightened his lace cuffs, which contrasted with his mustard-coloured doublet. All the while, the eyes of those in the room burned into him, especially a raven-like priest in long black robes who seemed poised to fly to his flock and urge them to the Pope's bidding.

"Sir." A man nudged Francis, who had missed Ormonde's signal. A whispering struck up from those nearby and Francis promptly stepped forward.

"Sir Francis, I bid you welcome to Ireland," Ormonde said.

"Thank you, my lord. I come with a message from His Highness, Prince Rupert," Francis explained, reassured by Ormonde's warm smile and fair features, which enhanced his friendly aura.

"Pray follow me." Ormonde led Francis through a gap in the crowd. "Let's partake of some sweetmeats." The two men entered a small room and approached a table where Ormonde took some sugar-coated caraway seeds. "Now, what does the great Prince want of me?"

"He wishes to know when your lordship can hasten the first delivery of goods to England," Francis said, watching as Ormonde prodded a perfectly replicated marzipan walnut. "Though I was not given details of the cargo."

"You may be interested to meet Master Reed, another Englishman who hails from Bristol." Ormonde pointed to a man who entered the room. "You seem in need of company."

"Very kind ..." Francis could say little else, regardless of whether he was in the mood for socialising.

"I too, was born in England," Ormonde revealed, looking Francis in the eye. "So, here we are, three Englishmen together."

"The Marquis first sailed for Ireland in the year I was born." Reed eagerly pointed. "Via Bristol."

"I was but three years of age and carried in the arms of my nurse." Ormonde's doublet, breeches of blue silk and matching ribbons that tied his shoes, rippled like the Irish sea. His lace collar and cuffs were snowy white, like the caps of the swell that had carried him to his destined land thirty years ago.

"Very interesting." Francis wondered if Ormonde had actually heard what he'd just said about Rupert's message.

"Who could forget Bristol's fair city." Reed sighed.

"Sir Francis may wish to, having taken part in its siege." Ormonde's knowledge took Francis aback. "So, was there any more to the Prince's missive?" he enquired.

"His Highness hopes to receive your goods within the month." Francis recounted what he'd been instructed to say. "And he wished me to impart that he has the greatest respect for you."

"And I for him." Ormonde smiled appreciatively. "Inform His Highness that I shall entrust the first of the goods to your care and will do all in my power to send more as speedily as possible."

"My care, sir?" Francis had expected his responsibility to end with delivery of the message.

"That's correct. You are willing to be our courier, are you not?" Ormonde asked, but did not wait for an answer. "Master Reed will share the finer details." He took his leave and Francis and Reed followed him out not long afterwards.

"When do I depart for England?" Francis enquired of Reed when they had re-entered the noisy presence chamber.

"I shall deal with it all in due course," Reed declared with a confident nod. "I take it nobody has enlightened you about what you must convey to England?" He ushered Francis over to a tapestry upon which Apollo, swathed in cloth of gold, entertained numerous cherubs with his lyre.

"No. I'd be grateful if you could enlighten me." Francis waited to hear what tune he was expected to dance to.

"Do you know much about the treaty the Marquis agreed with the Catholics?" Reed asked.

"Only that Muskerry and his Confederates retained all of their territory." Francis considered this a victory for them.

"That's correct," Reed replied, taking his jutting chin between finger and thumb. "For which gift the King will receive some thirty thousand pounds."

" 'The sinews of war', as Cicero once said." Francis considered that the Catholics' blood money could no doubt end up paying his own wage.

"Let us discuss finer details over a drink," Reed suggested and left to fetch some wine.

The tight, crisp chords of a Gaelic harp fluttered across the room. Each note merged into the next like a bird's morning chorus, but it afforded Francis little reassurance as he considered his predicament - similar to that of a pawn pushed in one direction at the expense of everyone else. He turned his back on the room and took the opportunity to study the tapestry and the pink and gold features of a plump cherub.

"I can tell you admire our Irish harp." A stocky Irishman said with a light and breezy accent as he approached. "Carved from a single log of willow, with brass strings, yet nothing without a competent harpist. One begins learning it before the age of six." His accent was as melodious as the instrument he described.

"It certainly plucks at the emotions." Francis forced a smile despite the discord inside him.

"Connor O'Neale," the man said with a polite nod.

"Sir Francis Berkeley. From England, if you hadn't guessed."

"Aye, the drawl's unmistakable." Connor chortled. "But I've no quarrel with England, for your country took my estranged wife off my hands - if she still resides there, that is." He chuckled. "Ne'er trust a woman, apart from a whore, for she is up front with her price."

"I'll bear that in mind." Francis nodded in amusement at such stark honesty. "I do have a tenuous link to this country: my wife's step-mother is Irish."

"An Irish connection? I knew you seemed a decent Englishman." Connor pointed at him. "From which county does she hail?"

"I have no idea. Often it seems as if she's come from hell," Francis replied.

"Your father-in-law needs to keep her in her place." Connor stopped as a small man approached. After a few words, during which the newcomer eyed Francis with suspicion, Connor took his leave. "Nice to make your acquaintance, Sir Francis."

It was not long before Reed returned with an unusually serious expression crossing his smooth and oily features. "What business did O'Neale have with you?"

"Nothing of note." Francis shrugged.

"When you enter discussion with a leading Catholic, everything is of note," Reed whispered. "Fires of fervour burn deep in their bellies!"

"May we put O'Neale's belly aside and continue where we left off?"

"Perhaps he thought you a repentant heretic, dressed as you are in yellow," Reed said, his mouth rising at one side. "They were forced to wear the colour by the inquisition." He gestured to Francis's mustard doublet. "And repentant you must be, for you were sent here as punishment, let us not forget. Now, the cargo you are to convey is of a secret nature and could prejudice our new truce. Do you understand?"

"Pray, let's be plain." Francis couldn't abide courtly nuances. "I am the King's loyal subject and will do all I can to further his cause; the same cause which Lord Ormonde serves."

"You're to escort the first regiment of Ormonde's troops back to England to fight for King Charles," Reed whispered.

"What!" Francis was taken aback.

"I will try to secure suitable vessels for you, though I fear there may be delays." Reed cleared his throat. "However, your assistance with another matter may well speed up your departure. A mere conversation with your new friend O'Neale would be all it takes."

"A conversation about what?" Francis asked.

"Any topic that might reveal how many men the Confederates have in County Cork. That knowledge would take a great weight off my shoulders and help me focus upon your transportation," Reed said.

"I see I have no alternative." Francis shook his head.

"We all have choices to make." Reed fixed him with a steely expression. "And I would highly recommend you make the right one." He left no illusion that Francis's return to England would hinge on it.

Chapter 58

Francis entered a gallery where exquisite paintings hung on oak panelling in frames of burnished gold or bronze. Like crisp autumn leaves, each canvas was an array of colour, offering the eye a sight different from the last. Down to the very decor, the purpose of this house's construction was clear: to encourage the King to visit Ireland so that the nation could bask in the rays of his glory.

Connor caught Francis's eye. His thickset frame stood admiring a landscape in which men toiled with the harvest. A good omen. Francis hoped to gather in his own bounty after spending a restless night mulling over how to accomplish it. He ambled towards the oil painting nearest to Connor: Charles the First on horseback. An apt choice.

The lifelike image of the King held his marshal's baton as if to remind Francis of his purpose: to escort troops back across the Irish Sea. The horse's muscles rippled, and the mane curled down its neck like the locks of the monarch's flamboyant supporters. But, despite the beast's power, its colour was subdued, and it was King Charles's gleaming armour that drew the eye. For all the monarch's visual majesty, his urgent mission for reinforcements looked set to be delayed at the behest of Mister Reed, a minor official. Francis, knowing just who would shoulder responsibility for such delays, took a deep breath and turned to Connor.

"It represents his control over his realm." A young woman stepped up to Francis. "The horse signifies Britain, ready to respond to the King's every command and reined in by him." She smiled.

"As if he is about to ride forth from the frame," Francis said, gripping his hands behind his back and making small talk.

"England is one unruly mount at the moment." The woman's male friend raised his eyebrows. "I doubt the poor man can even master a donkey these days."

"Bartholomew... please!" she stammered. "My apologies, sir, his tongue runs on wheels."

"You're always afraid of the truth, Bridget," Bartholomew replied.

"The truth gets you hung," she retorted.

Francis was resigned to the expectation that Connor would pass him by after this inane banter.

"Bridget, is it?" Connor's rosy cheeks beamed, most at odds with his jet-black beard and wiry curls of moustache. "Will you not walk with me and share your valuable knowledge of these masterpieces?"

"Alas, I cannot today." Her cheeks dimpled. "Tomorrow, perchance, if you can make it."

"Meet me here at the King's side." Connor laughed heartily, as if his barrel chest was entirely hollow.

"Another stallion for you to break in," Bartholomew noted to Bridget as they left.

"If we were outside I'd drown him in the fish ponds," Connor muttered to Francis, and the zig-zagging vein on his temple plumped. "I recognise you, Englishman."

"Francis would do just fine," he said with a smile. "We met last night."

"My memory." Connor excused himself. "I'm afraid I no longer remember why you said you are in Ireland either.

Francis knew he'd not shared this information. "I was caught duelling, and short of being court-marshalled, sent to this ..."

"Nest of Papists?" Connor interrupted. "You'd think the King would have a greater need for his officers in England." He ordered them both a drink.

"Not how I was going to phrase it." Francis anticipated quenching his dry mouth, hoping it would take the edge off his apprehension and also loosen Connor's tongue.

"No doubt that's how most Englishmen see us." Connor's eyes betrayed his resentment at the stigma. "What is your opinion?"

"I expected darkness but found light," Francis answered. "A country whose towns, cities and people are no different to every other. My only problem with Ireland is the mother-in-law it gave me."

"Oh, yes, you told me about her." Connor ushered him into an adjoining room once a servant brought their drinks. "However, England produced Richard Reed, whom I saw you speaking with yesterday." Connor rolled his eyes. "Do you know him?"

"No more than I know you, although I gather he hails from Bristol," Francis said. "He told me enough times."

"Odious fellow." Connor screwed up his nose and then pointed at the tankards. "Tis brewed from a local house.

A tad stouter than English ale," he warned, moving towards the chimneypiece of Dutch brick and warming his hands by the fire. "Drink up, it will take thy mind off the voyage home."

"Whenever that will be," Francis replied and finally took a gulp.

"Takes some getting used to," Connor remarked. "But judging by your response I suspect you'll have time." He watched Francis grimace at the taste. "So, what other tales have you swallowed about the Irish?"

"The news-sheets are full of them." Francis thought Connor much at odds with the stereotype. "I have the impression you're an honourable commander. Where have you served?"

"Only ever in Ireland," Connor answered. "Did you expect us to be burning Protestants at the stake, or working for their conversions?"

"Befuddling my mind with this strong ale could be the start." Francis raised his tankard and clashed it against Connor's. "Now the truce has been signed, when will you return home?"

"Home? Abandon my men? We Catholics are fighting for our very existence." Connor rubbed his beard. "My men and I are as one and will be until we fully secure our country. I would never be separated from them as you have been from yours."

"My company is much depleted," Francis revealed, in the hope of furthering this avenue of conversation. "Recruitment is slow."

"The Virgin keeps our ranks swelled," Connor said and grasped Francis's shoulder. "Look at us, enemies in religion, yet conversing like old friends." His words were a reminder they were not on the same side, despite the Catholics' protestations of loyalty to the King. "Though I'd trust you as much as any of my subordinates."

"My thanks for your compliment." Francis had already taken a liking to his affable manner.

"Try not to worry about getting back to England," Connor said with a fixed look. "Your patron allowed you to evade goal by sending you here, so he clearly values you too much for your absence to be very long."

"I shall hold you to that observation."

"Let me draw upon your knowledge of English gossip," Connor said. "Tell me, have you heard that Lord Digby is considered the next Secretary of State?"

"He has the Queen's support," Francis replied. "And that counts for everything since her return, for she wields influence as much as any O'Donnell woman."

"O'Donnell, ye say?" Connor chortled at the coincidence. "Mary O'Donnell is my god-forsaken wife."

"And the name of my mother-in-law." Francis wondered at the match.

"My mother of blessed memory always used to warn me against gambling." Connor smiled wistfully. "Yet what are the odds of this?" He revealed that it was twenty years since his wife had left him.

"Perchance they are one and the same person?" Francis laughed.

"I doubt it, besides, there would be no way of proving it," Connor replied. "But, tell me more about your mother-in-law."

"You're right, my Mary O'Donnell is married." Francis shook his head. "Yet your wife's vows to you still stand."

"She stole my mother's ring when she left." Connor looked out of the window, his gaze lost in the sunken garden. "The only possession I had that was hers."

"Sorry to hear that." Francis hesitated. "What did it look like?"

"A round ruby." Connor held his head and narrowed his eyes. "Set amongst a cluster of small pearls, although the stone itself was practically pink," he said with a sigh and shook his head as if to dismiss the painful memory.

"Unique." Francis's mind conjured up an image of his mother-in-law's bony finger, upon which he immediately suspected sat the very same ring. "It fitted your wife?"

"Only her little finger, left hand."

"I ... suspect I know just where to find this ring." Francis frowned and looked Connor in the eye. "Though I would need your assistance in securing a ship home."

Francis told of Reed's reluctance to arrange his passage, omitting details of his assignment, and explained his shocked certainty that they knew the same Mary O'Donnell.

"I'll speak to Muskerry." Connor suggested that the Catholic leader could lobby Ormonde on Francis's behalf.

"My return home would suit us all." Francis felt sure that Ormonde would not wish to risk delaying the King getting his soldiers, nor have any whisper of it reach the ears of the Catholics.

Chapter 59

John Pym stood at his window, looking on to the London street. The church bell rang the hour, nine times. A scavenger approached a basket of rubbish on the doorstep below and poked through it for anything he could use or sell on. It was only a knock at the bedroom door that stirred Pym from his observations.

"A gift from Mister Saint-John, sir." The maid put a plate of roast pike on the table.

"Oh, I've no appetite, take it away," Pym instructed, holding a hand beneath his nose at the odour of claret and basted anchovy.

"But, sir, 'tis from the Solicitor-General," she replied, as if she'd face a trial should he not partake of it.

"It is of no consequence where it came from. Now, pray remove it." He turned back to the window and pushed open the casement for some air.

The gap admitted every squeak from the array of signposts outside, especially the glazier's opposite, whose painted cupid danced upon its board with a torch in hand – not to mention the noxious smoke of the lime kilns on Bankside. It was while he was pondering whether the smell of fish was the lesser of two evils that his physician, Geoffrey de Beauvois, entered.

"Good morrow, Mister Pym. Up and about I see?" the man noted with a nod of satisfaction. "As long as you don't overdo it."

"You must help me get through this momentous day," Pym demanded, worried that his decline in concentration levels, weakness and frequent bowel habits might join forces against him.

"I shall certainly do my best," Geoffrey replied, peering over the tiny spectacles clipped to the end of his nose.

"My pot's over there." Pym watched the man peer into the ceramic bowl to examine the liquid stool and its pungent stench.

"Blood," Geoffrey elongated the word, "which proves you are physically exhausted. Your body is rejecting it through the anus to alleviate your anxieties and temper."

"So, you think it down to temper?" Pym recognised his irritability of late.

"I suspect that your black bile is increased, thus causing melancholia." Geoffrey nodded in agreement with himself. "You must rest your mind. Dancing can do it, though you should not ..."

"Dancing?" Pym scoffed and lay down on the bed. "I have not sprung a jig since I was a boy and will not take part in such frivolous pleasures. I do the Lord's work."

"Your response is a further example of your hot head and addiction to a punishing schedule. One foreign scholar believes the symptoms you display may be contagious," Geoffrey warned and took Pym's arm, squeezed it a few times and then made a small incision with his knife. "I'll draw off some blood to help you."

"Isaac," Pym called his serving boy. "Pray do not send up Parliament's delegation until I give the signal."

Once the physician's work was done, Pym had Isaac show the man out. Left alone once more with his concerns, he saw shafts of afternoon light reach in through the half-closed shutters of the window. The outside world pried on Pym in his moment of weakness, yet nobody should know his true state of health. By the time his Parliamentarian colleagues arrived, Pym's world hovered between two planes, feeling neither alive nor dead. Anxious to see them whilst he had the wherewithal, he struck his stick on the wooden floor and, as if he'd conjured them, soon the men, all dressed in black, were in the chamber.

"Welcome, gentlemen," Pym said, after Isaac gave him some Scottish aqua vitae. Ironic, considering the tall visitor they ushered in was from that very nation.

"We come to deliver our wishes for your speedy recovery, sir, as well as to impart news of our great business," Sir Henry Vane explained.

Pym nodded his thanks to Vane, whom he'd appointed to lead negotiations with the Scots. The man's stolid appearance – his large eyes, and chin – reassured Pym that all was in sober hands.

"Are our two Parliaments closer to joining in the defence of liberty," Pym asked.

"The Solemn League and Covenant has passed the vote, so the Scottish and English Parliaments have wed themselves in a union that will be truly blessed," Vane replied.

"And the agreement was accepted in its entirety by your countrymen?" Pym enquired of Alexander Henderson, the Scottish representative. His tall figure, dressed in a black cloak, loomed over them all as much as Scotland's contrasting religious agenda.

"Aye, that's so, Master Pym. Our Presbyterian Church freed itself from the King's interference by abolishing Bishops. I hope the English Church will soon follow our example," Henderson replied in a deep, gravelly tone.

"The agreement affirms our intention to reform the Church of England according to the word of God." Pym carefully stuck to this deliberate wording, which allowed Puritan, Presbyterian and Independent alike to interpret in their own way.

"God bless our union!" Vane's cheer prevented any divisive questions on the subject of religion.

"When will your Scottish army cross the border?" Pym asked.

"We'll be in England in three months." Henderson's severe features seemed as if they'd been battered by highland winds his entire life.

"A moment that will be written into the history of our struggle for freedom." Pym raised one hand like a father blessing his sons.

"Without your efforts, John, this would never have come to pass." Vane spoke of the gratitude of all present. "When the day dawns, it will be yours."

"You are too kind." Pym told them. "Now, after such momentous news, I feel the need to rest." His eyes felt heavy.

"Would you like me to read, sir?" Isaac enquired as the men filtered out of the room. Pym could only nod.

"Lord Jesus I am blind, be my light. Ignorant,
be my wisdom and self-willed, be my mind."

Pym fixed upon the month named after Janus, god of the beginning and ending of conflicts, who would surely bring peace to the realm – and to Pym.

"Open my ear to grasp quickly your Spirit's voice
and delightfully run after His beckoning hand."

Pym's head rested upon his feather pillow and his eyes closed. He drifted into a deep sleep, perhaps one of the deepest in some time, with satisfaction that his toil was coming to an end.

"Melt my conscience that no hardness may
remain and make it alive to evil's slightest touch.
When Satan approaches may I flee to your wounds
and there cease to tremble at all alarms."

Chapter 60

Francis looked into Anne's eyes. Their misty joy glistening, their sparkle infectious. The happiness of husband and wife at being reunited needed no words. Their breaths became rapid, and slowly Francis brought his lips to Anne's. The moment they met was the point when their love, relief and fears fused and resulted in fireworks of kisses.

"You're not going out of the country again?" Anne asked between brief pauses.

"No," Francis said all that was needed and unloosened the cords that tied the front of Anne's cambric smock with the intention of lifting it over her head.

"I've imagined this moment many times." She raised her arms and gave an inviting smile.

"Anne, we have returned," Mary called from downstairs.

"Mother!" Anne caught her nightdress, but her warning didn't stop Francis, who kissed her neck and held her closer.

"Anne, are you up there?" Mary's shrill voice grew louder as she mounted each step.

"Stay silent," Francis said and scooped Anne into his arms. He gently placed her down by the door to the bedroom and planted one foot against it.

"Holy Mother, why does the girl not answer?" The curse from outside was too much for Anne and she stifled a giggle to which Francis placed a finger upon her lips.

Mary tried the door and gave three quick knocks, at which point Francis took his foot away and stepped back, anticipating his mother-in-law's impatience. It only took a moment for Mary to give the door a second try with added force, and this time it burst open and she stumbled into the room and fell to her knees.

"Mother!" Anne covered her mouth.

"You've returned?" Mary squinted up at Francis in surprise.

"Aye," he nodded.

"Help me up, Anne," Mary cried, and held up her hands like a child.

"You don't know your own strength, Mary," Francis couldn't help remark.

"I am often underestimated." Mary's eyes burned with resentment.

"Is Henry with his grandfather?" Francis asked of Mary, who was brushing down her woollen skirt.

"Yes, he enjoyed watching the birds in Christchurch Meadows," Mary replied with a look of satisfaction. "We're taking him back tomorrow."

"Let me go and check on him." Anne heard her son's cries and wrapped a cloak around herself. "And you two?"

"I shall regale thy mother with my Irish tales." Francis turned to Mary with a broad smile which prompted only a half one in return.

"I never thought I'd see the day." Anne raised her eyebrows and left them to it.

"Let us go next door," Francis instructed, leading Mary out of the bedroom and into the nursery.

"Henry is a darling." Mary's voice was strained, as if silence was unbearable to her.

"On that point you speak the truth," Francis replied and caught sight of her ring, whose pink ruby was like a sunset amidst a cluster of cloud-like pearls.

"Is your intention really to talk about Ireland?" she enquired breezily with a casual wave of one hand.

"Oh yes. I've been looking forward to it," he said, nodding.

"I see." Mary's downturned lips pursed.

"Especially seeing as you won't be staying with us much longer." Francis closed the door and watched Mary fold her arms.

"You must be mistaken," she said, and two lines appeared between her thin eyebrows. "Anne confirmed that we could stay as long as we needed."

"Are there no other homes you can go to?" Francis clasped his hands behind his back and paced to the far wall.

"You know ours is far too dangerous. Besides, I have seen much improvement in George's health now he is with Anne and Henry," she said, and rested both hands under her bust, as if the matter was closed.

"What about your other husband's house?" Francis asked.

"I beg your pardon?" she exclaimed, and her nose screwed up.

"My apologies. Let me elaborate." He coughed. "I had the fortune to meet Connor O'Neale, whom I believe you already know intimately."

"What?" She paused, and for once her heavily rouged cheeks looked pale. "Do you expect me to know everyone in Ireland?"

"Connor told me of his wife's adultery and her theft of his most valuable possession."

"You've lost your mind!" She spun on her heel and made for the door.

"Where did you get your ring, Mary?" Francis's question stopped her dead.

"This . . . ?" Mary raised her hand as Francis stepped closer. "A cheap trinket I purchased."

"O'Neale also beat his wife." Francis took her arm and the skin wrinkled under his grip.

"Stop this, I command you!" Mary spluttered and attempted to free herself.

"If you don't know Connor, it won't perturb you to learn that I've brought him to England." Francis let go of her. "He wishes to extract vengeance."

"I think war has turned your mind," Mary said with a deep frown.

"Connor found you sinfully lying with his friend and, this being the final straw, he beat you." Francis kept his voice monotone.

"My daughter is not safe with a lunatic such as you." Mary headed for the door once again.

"To highlight your sin, did he not strike you – with a crucifix of all things – right across your back?" Francis persisted and, with the side of his hand, he mimicked the blow. "Are the marks still present?"

"I will have no man touch me!" Mary turned, slapped Francis across the face, and then her eyes began to well up.

"Connor's mother must haunt your every move." Francis didn't so much as touch his burning cheek. Mary's agitated head swayed from side to side, as though tortured by his words, yet rooted to the spot by her demons. "The sole memento of the only woman he ever loved, and you stole it. Has it not burned its offence into your finger all these years?"

"You shall regret stirring this up ..." she hissed.

"May God take his retribution for your lies," Francis said and pointed as though cursing her. "My poor wife thinks of you as a devoted mother, yet you're simply a lying, thieving whore."

"You have no idea of the beatings I took ..." Mary said as tears rolled down her cheeks. "Have the cursed thing." She manoeuvred the ring from her finger and threw it at Francis. Then she wiped her eyes with her palms, her stoicism renewed.

"I forgot to add bigamy to your list of accolades," Francis added.

"George and I never sealed our union with marriage. But if you breathe any of this to anyone, I will not stop until I ruin you," Mary hissed.

"Leave my home," Francis demanded.

"I hope my visions are premonitions and it is you who is run through the gut." She glared. "Only then will my daughter and grandson be safe."

"If you are not ready to go in two days I shall reunite you with your husband." Francis leaned in close.

"That would destroy Anne and George. Would you have that upon your conscience?"

"Do not tempt me, woman, for I would stop at nothing to break your web of deceit." Francis's words caused Mary to storm out of the room.

Now alone, he examined the ring between his fingers. Liberated from the shadow that had dulled it for so long, the ruby blossomed and took on the delicate hue of a red rose. Francis hoped that in the same way, by weeding out Mary's poisonous behaviour, his family might also return to normal.

Chapter 61

A great roll of canvas was wrapped around a pole held by two servants. They unfastened the ribbons holding it and a map of England unfurled like a sail. Lord Digby, appointed Secretary of State yesterday, leaped to his feet.

"You pair of poltroons," Digby barked. "Now lay it on the table."

"Worry not. It isn't one of the King's art collection." Old Lord Forth got to his feet, drained his claret and nudged the glass for another refill.

A staff thumped the floor of Oriel College and the men of the council of war stood as King Charles entered dressed in a black suit of French silk. The fashionable slashes in his sleeves showed a lining of white as contrasting as the figures of the short monarch and his giant nephew, Rupert. On a blue velvet ribbon around the King's neck, hung the Order of the Garter, the reverse of which held a miniature portrait of his beloved wife.

"My most trusted commanders and councillors of state," the King said with a smile lighting up his long face. "I wish to share our grand plan with you." His warmth was as precious as the sixteen rose diamonds and multiple rubies which studded his Garter medallion and whose sparkle reflected his renewed positivity. He took time to look at each man in turn, securing their attention and further strengthening their bonds of loyalty.

"Baron Hopton, how good to see you." The King greeted this loyal commander, who had recently been wounded by an exploding powder cart. He'd have Hopton play a key part in today's council, as if the Almighty had saved the man for this purpose. "In better health I hope?"

"Much recovered, Your Majesty," Hopton replied.

"Your bravery and determination is an example to us all," the King said and sat at the table. He rested his hands one on top of the other and invited everyone to be seated.

The servants flattened out the canvas map and Lord Digby laid wooden flag blocks on it to represent the locations of the royal armies. The council opened beneath the hammer-beamed roof and the gaze of a portrait of King Edward II, who had also known the tragedy of civil war.

"At His Majesty's command, we are here today to revisit our strategic objectives and co-ordinate our armies," Digby told the assembled men.

Lord Forth, the army's Field-Marshall, got to his feet. "I have the pleasure of revealing that, following the treaty concluded with the Confederates in Ireland, we will be recalling our army back to England to fight for us." He chose his words carefully. With twenty-eight years' service in the Swedish army fighting Catholics, he knew how divisive a truce with them would be. "The first five hundred arrived today and we'll receive two thousand more within two months."

"Thanks to the courage and skill of the Marquis of Ormonde." The King's praise for his Lord Deputy reminded everyone that his Irish affairs were headed by a Protestant.

"Will these troops be the Englishmen that Your Majesty sent to Ireland at the outbreak of the catholic rebellion?" one counsellor asked.

"Aye, they are," Forth replied. "The men who established our strongholds in the east of Ireland and Dublin."

"Faith and nationality are immaterial in my view," Digby insisted. "What matters is the troops' loyalty to the King."

"Those two things are of extreme importance when printed in rebel news-sheets," Sir Jacob Astley said. "Deemed more important than truth itself, for they write that we are shipping over Irish Catholics to fight for us."

"A most important point," Prince Rupert agreed. "Perhaps we can reinforce their Protestant and English origins in our own publications."

"Let it be known that we would never ally with rebels of any faith." The King drew attention back to the map.

The flickering candlelight animated the ultramarine seas and verdigris land mass, covered by flags of Venetian red. Lord Digby selected one of the flag blocks clustered in Ireland and moved it across the Irish Sea to north Wales, where it was announced that they would reinforce the Royalists there.

"When Parliament's Welsh forces are subdued," Forth said, jabbing north Wales with his finger, "these men will move east and join our army besieging Hull." He went on to explain that upon the fall of Hull, the force would then strike at London.

Watching the representations of his armies appealed to the King's neat and orderly nature. As the flags were slid here and there across his painted realm, he felt the security of being in control. The political and military commanders who translated his vision into reality were his instruments to manoeuvre in much the same way.

"Lord Hopton, this is where you and your reinforcements come in," the King said, and watched as more flags were moved out of Ireland via Munster and across to Bristol.

"Sir Francis Berkeley will deliver five hundred men to you in the next few days," Forth told Hopton. He went on to push Hopton's flag down from Bristol to the south coast of England. "You'll then be tasked with securing Dorset, Wiltshire and Hampshire."

"Will there be any funding for my fresh troops?" Hopton's deep-set eyes met Chancellor Culpepper's. "I ask because of recent mutinies over unpaid wages."

"Six thousand pounds is allotted to you," Forth replied.

"There is only means to supply fifteen hundred." Culpepper puffed his cheeks.

"We will raise the money one way or the other," Forth asserted. "Have the college's plate melted down." He eyed the silver platters on the table.

"All twenty-nine pounds of their gilt plate has been coined to pay other armies," Culpepper pointed out.

"You will receive enough to cover what you need." King Charles nodded to Hopton with a confident smile.

The thirty thousand pounds from the Catholic Confederates was not disclosed to this council. Only the monarch's most trusted advisors were aware of such a contentious fact, which Parliament's scurrilous news-sheets would make much of if they knew. Yet his truce with the Irish Catholics paled into insignificance when compared to rumours that Parliament was inviting the Scots to invade England in their support. But even if this were true, the King's military plans discussed this evening would confound his enemies and bring peace to his people.

Chapter 62

Mary knitted furiously. Her needles methodically picked up and manipulated the wool with ruthless efficiency. Her thin eyebrows dipped, and her lips pouted with intense concentration.

"Another pair of woollen stockings for father?" Anne asked with a smile, hoping to discover what was on her mother's mind. But Mary barely gave an affirmative nod to the question.

Francis warmed his hands by the fire, attempting to protect himself from the effects of his mother-in-law's frosty mood. Silence ensued. It was a good job the woman would be gone tomorrow.

"I'll go and see if Father needs help packing." Anne sat on the edge of her seat and glanced at Francis.

"Oh, leave him be," Mary replied without looking up. "I've chased after him for too long, so no need for you to start. He should learn to stand on his own two feet."

"At least they will be warm when he does." Francis pointed to the stockings. He did not wish Anne to ask too many questions about her mother's temper.

"Mother, what are you going to do about Patrick Hall?" Anne asked.

"It'll be fine," Mary replied. "I have a few ways in mind to earn some money."

"If you need more time to make plans, you can stay longer." Anne turned to Francis. "Isn't that right?"

"Of course," Francis replied. "You know how welcome you'd be, Mary."

"There's no room here, especially with that wet-nurse," Mary declared.

"I've asked your father if he wishes to come to the inn with me this evening." Francis thought it best to avoid encounters with Mary on her last night under his roof.

"What?" Mary's knitting ceased and she looked up.

George's footsteps interrupted this second silence, and when he entered the room he looked at the three of them. "You're all very serious," he said and raised a glass of red wine to his lips.

"I hear you're wanting to go out tonight?" Mary remained motionless.

"Yes, such a kind invitation from my son-in-law." George took a sip of his drink and nodded to Francis.

Mary exhaled sharply, and her cheeks reddened. Getting to her feet, she didn't comment, but took some unravelled silver thread from her box and began winding it around her hand.

"Shall we be off?" Francis thought it as good a time as any.

"Heavens above, George!" Mary paced over as he drained his glass. "I will give unto him that is a-thirst, the fountain of the water of life." She quoted the scriptures and slapped his arm at such gluttony.

"Now look what you've done," George cried as spilled red wine stained his lace collar.

"Do not yell at me," Mary snapped. "I will not take that from any man," she said with a tremble in her voice.

"And I do not take kindly to your unexplained whimsies, such as ending our stay with my daughter." George's wrinkles, usually creased with humour, were instead deep chasms of frustration. "We do not have enough money as it is without you ruining my best clothes."

"We can help you with money," Anne interrupted and dabbed at George's burgundy stains.

"Thank you, Anne, but I'll make sure we get by." Mary sighed and turned to George. "Have I not kept us out of debt?" She suggested she fetch him another drink now that he would not be going out tonight.

"George, you can borrow some of my clothes if you wish." Francis suggested, feeling guilty at his father-in-law's upset over having to leave Oxford. "Getting out will surely do you the world of good," Francis said.

"On reflection, Francis is quite right," Mary said before anyone could comment further. "It will help take your mind off our worries." As George kissed her and left to get changed, she turned away from everyone.

"And what of you, Mother?" Anne gestured for her to sit down. "You worry so much about us all and don't think about yourself." She suggested they spend some time together while the men were out. "Would you like to play the virginal?"

"Let us talk about the old days," Mary seemed to perk up. "Fetch Jane if you like, and I'll look into the fire and see if I can get an image of who she'll marry."

"You'll be accused of witchcraft next." Anne took her arm.

"Well, if your husband doesn't protect you after we leave, he'll receive my curses," Mary replied and embraced her daughter.

"God damn the woman." Francis left the room and muttered as he walked to the front door and opened it.

He was confronted by a row of puddles that lined the road like mirror-glass into which every star above peered. Stepping out into the cold November evening, he recalled the fireworks that had lit up last night's sky in celebration of Gunpowder Treason Day and celebrated the thought being free of Mary's plotting.

"Sir, you had best take your cloak." Jane appeared at the door and handed it over. "I think it's going to be a frosty evening."

"Thank you," he replied and swung it about himself. Jane then pressed her hand to one of his broad shoulders and buttoned the cloak into place. She glanced up as she did so, and he found himself looking down at her.

"How is your smitten blacksmith? Is he still courting you?" Francis enquired.

"I'm not inclined to the match for he does not have my heart," Jane replied, but upon George's approach she bowed and retreated into the house.

"My thanks for the clothes." George, wrapped in a full-length cloak, gestured for Francis to lead the way. "Are we ready?"

"I have been for some time," Francis joked in response and the pair headed off.

Francis called to a young lad standing in the shadows. He held a long pole with wax wadding on one end of it that burned into the murky night. After Francis told him where they were headed, the boy held out the pole and lit their way across the dung-covered cobbles. Above them the silvery moon peered through the narrow gap between the houses like a shining sixpence tucked into the folds of a velvet sky.

"Sorry for losing my patience earlier." George inhaled the crisp air. "Sometimes I think Mary could do with a good strong drink or two."

"There's really no need to apologise," Francis told him. "Aye, some sort of distraction would stop her fretting over everyone else's business."

"Might stop her nightmares too." George shook his head.

"If that were the case, I'd take her to the Rose and Crown every evening," Francis replied with a laugh. "She seems to think Anne's in perpetual danger."

"Always has done." George gave a soft smile. "Mary is scarred by her past. I think her father used to beat her. So she has always wished for Anne to have a better life than she had." He revealed that this was one reason he fell in love with Mary.

"I see." The details did nothing to excuse Mary in Francis's eyes. "She still thinks she's the only one who can look after Anne."

"You're a good man. I know Anne's safe with you and that eases my mind. Dear Mary's just another overprotective mother, made doubly so by her background and mistrust of men."

"You're the exception," Francis replied. "She married you."

"Perhaps," George said after a contemplative pause. "Mind you, my gambling didn't help."

"Everyone has their guilty pleasures."

"You know, Son, nearly thirty years ago I played dice with King Christian of Denmark on one of his visits to England. I won a small fortune and that's where it started." George chuckled. "King Charles is prim and proper, but his father would put away enough alcohol for three men and it would take as many to get him back to his quarters." He drew satisfaction from reminiscing. "Any reverence I had for monarchy ended after that."

"There it is, sir." The boy interrupted what was proving to be a fascinating conversation and pointed out the Rose and Crown. Francis handed him some pennies.

"Sir Francis Berkeley?" A voice called from behind. "I am sent by Lord Hopton of Stratton."

"Why don't you get us a drink, George, and I'll follow," Francis suggested.

"I've fallen for that trick many a time," George chortled and folded his cloak back over his shoulder.

"Call it payment for the engineering your escape tonight." Francis smiled warmly and watched him enter the building.

"I was just on my way to your lodgings," the officer explained.

"How can I be of assistance?" Francis asked.

"His Lordship has a new command and is appointing officers." The captain handed over a sealed parchment.

Unfolding it and stepping into the light of the tavern window, Francis examined the neat writing to learn that Rupert had recommended him for promotion.

> Charles, by the Grace of God, King of Great Britayne, France and Ireland, defender of the faith, etc. To our trustye and wellbeloved Sir Francis Berkeley, Greeting.
>
> Wee doe hereby constitute and appoynt you to be lieutenant-colonel of one regiment of foote under the command of our trusty and well-beloved Ralph, Lord Hopton of Stratton. The which regiment by virtue of this commission you are forthwith to join and retain.
>
> Charles R

"This is indeed a great honour," Francis exclaimed, but was distracted by noise from the Rose and Crown. Not the ordinary din associated with the customers, but an aggressive yell and the protesting cries of those attempting to stop something quite terrible from taking place.

Chapter 63

Douglas Buchanan could remember little about anything. Copious amounts of beer had erased most of his memory, all except the one thing he wished to forget: his brother.

His taste buds were saturated, and he could no longer appreciate the honey, malted barley or hops, while the Rose and Crown had blurred into a sea of faces. They swirled around him as he drowned his sorrows. Some glared or shouted while others grinned, their heads rolling back with thunderous laughter that haunted him. It was three months since his brother was killed. Just under twelve weeks ago since he was left alone without a soul to call his family. His homeland of Scotland seemed as far away as ever, and the storm of war rolled on overhead.

Douglas had defended Basing House, a Royalist stronghold to rival Hampton Court Palace: a catholic nest, the Parliamentarian news-sheets had called it. A swelling bubo which two thousand of their best troops had been sent to lance.

Yet for sixteen months Douglas and his brother had called it home; had watched the windows and all but one door of the lower storey being bricked up in defence, and the perimeter buildings demolished. A thick fog arrived with the enemy that fateful day. The female defenders and children had refused to leave, so they cast bullets for Douglas and the garrison. God also stayed with them by lifting the mist and then lashing the enemy with rain which dampened the fuses of their muskets and artillery. Lady Winchester and the women threw bricks and slates from the roof and Douglas fired at the enemy from holes punched in the outer wall.

Seventy of Parliament's men had perished, while only two of the garrison died, one of whom was Douglas's brother. A musket ball had punctured his head, tore through his brain and ripped the back of his skull away. The haunting image had caused Douglas's heart to pump only ice-cold sorrow around his broken body ever since. Tonight, he just wanted the pain to be numbed by any means possible.

"Maggie, sit doun my bonnie bird." Douglas took the hand of the serving girl he'd frolicked with most of the evening. She'd barely sat upon his knee than a man made his way from across the room.

"Want a game of hazard, Douglas?" Peter asked.

"Begone, you bladderskate." Douglas had no time for the windbag and turned back to Maggie.

"I challenge you, Douglas, man to man." Peter was insistent. "If you prevail, think of what you could buy your new girl."

"Play, Douglas, win for us." Maggie gave a giggle.

"There's nane in Scotland plays sae weel as me." Douglas stood and squared up to Peter, towering above the man.

He'd seen Peter eying Maggie all night. Douglas had lost everything lately but wasn't prepared to have Maggie added to the list. Indeed, he needed her more than anything else, even for one night. Her intimate company was the difference between him retaining or losing his sanity.

* * * * *

George stepped into the Rose and Crown and some dogs sniffed his square-toed shoes. They watched him as intently as he eyed the other customers. From the corner plumes of tobacco smoke rose around a gaming table and, George's attention thus drawn, he sidled over.

"May as well, seeing as Mary will never know." George thought aloud.

Two bone dice gave a hollow rattle in a tankard. The noise stirred poignant memories and George's heart fluttered as he considered a little wager for old time's sake. Then he saw the little beauties, dice no bigger than fingernails, but upon whose authority alone the victor scooped every last silver coin. The crowd shuffled about and next up was a Scotsman, fumbling with his purse.

"He's too tight-fisted to unfasten it," a man yelled, making everyone laugh.

"I'll rip your heid off, Peter," the Scotsman roared, grabbing the man by the scruff of the neck.

"No, Douglas, play the game and have his money from him," the serving girl insisted.

"Only if you play your games with me later, Meg." Douglas grinned.

George smiled at the lively atmosphere he had once been so used to and which made him feel like a young buck again. The Scotsman's drawl amused him. For the most part he couldn't understand it, but it reminded him of another raucous Scot: old King James.

"I'll gan for eight!" Douglas emptied his purse while Maggie kept her eye firmly on the money.

Then Douglas grabbed her waist, pulled her close and kissed her for an uncomfortably long time. George knew girls like this of old; the type who'd fuss and flirt but would only stay as long as the stench of money hung in the air. And it was stale and hot air which saw George unfasten the little metal buttons of his doublet.

"Not too late for a wager of my own is it?" George found a space beside Peter.

"Six! So, I throw again." Douglas's fat fingers retrieved the dice that had rolled onto the floor before anyone had seen.

"Feel so threatened that you have to resort to cheating?" Peter thumped the table.

"It was a six, is that not so, auld man?" Douglas prodded George.

"Erm, I don't think so," George stammered, knowing it was a five.

Douglas's deep frown caused two vertical lines to divide his forehead and he bared his teeth as he was beset on all sides.

"Why don't you wager Maggie? Winner takes all, Doug, and I'll take her all right." Peter grabbed the Scotsman's wrist before he could cast the dice again.

The crowd were sucked closer to the tornado of rivalry. The more it escalated, the tighter they packed. George's mounting concern was only tempered on seeing Francis pushing through the crowd.

"Get your hand off me, you sodomite," Douglas demanded.

George's eyes widened as the two men went head to head. Peter was just to George's left, and both men's faces contorted into expressions of hatred. George put his arm on Peter's shoulder in a bid to get past and towards Francis.

"You'd like a bit of prick, eh?" Peter shoved Douglas. "With your brother gone, you'll need another arse to poke."

Douglas let out a cry that became deeper as it grew louder, like a wounded bear that had been torn down in a baiting ring. The raw emotions made George freeze; as if upon that instant he stood on a precipice.

Douglas grabbed the bollock dagger attached to his belt. The triangular iron blade was, without hesitation, lunged at Peter.

"Stop!" Francis shouted, grabbing Douglas and jerking him backwards, only to see the bloody dagger drop to the floor.

"I've been stuck!" A sharp pain had George double up.

The wound and torment quickly sapped George's strength. He dropped to his knees and collapsed as the room blurred. He tried to speak when he saw Francis bent over him but could only moan.

"Christ, his gut's been cut open," a voice cried.

George shivered with the cold. Icy hands of the dead seemed to grab at him, snatching and pulling him out of the living world. In the misty foreground Francis's features were fading fast. No sound plagued George's ears anymore; absolute silence brought peace to everything including his pain. And then a bright light from which a figure slowly emerged was all-enveloping. The beautifully serene face of his wife Eleanor was exactly how he remembered, and it filled him with jubilation.

Chapter 64

The narrow north ambulatory of Westminster Abbey was shrouded in deathly silence broken only by the feet of two rows of men shuffling across the slabs. Not ordinary men, but Members of Parliament. Resting upon their shoulders was a vast coffin containing the mortal remains of John Pym. After leading and supporting his Parliamentary colleagues for so long, they now did the same for him. In death, the King could no longer get his hands on the great man, whose spirit intertwined with the candle smoke that twisted and turned up to the arched ceiling of this magnificent edifice; the grand tombstone of many a national hero soon to have one more in their midst.

At the head of the procession was Robert Devereaux, Earl of Essex, who, as Lord General of Parliament's armies, was more used to leading infantry attacks than mourners.

The bird has now well and truly flown. Essex recalled the day two years ago when King Charles had burst into Parliament to arrest five members. As well as Pym, the wanted men had included William Strode and Sir Arthur Haselrigg, both of whom formed the entourage that wound its way slowly down the aisle. Lucky then that they had learned of the King's plans and withdrawn at the last moment, leaving the monarch not only empty-handed, but forever labelled a tyrant in the eyes of moderate men.

Following behind Lord Essex were those men he judged the 'new breed', such as Sir Henry Vane. Men who were ready to lay to rest not just Pym, but also Parliament's desire to establish a working balance of power with the King and bring him to his knees. Whilst the approaching void amidst the flagstones seemed ready to extinguish Pym's guiding light, Vane no doubt hoped that it would ignite his own. But shouldering the great leader's coffin was very different from shouldering his legacy. Essex was determined to hold them in check.

"Gentlemen," announced the preacher, Stephen Marshall. "Our leader has reached his final earthly destination, though his spirit will rejoice in heaven, where he now resides with his maker."

Essex gave the briefest of glances to the worn patchwork of stone beneath his feet but could not bring himself to look upon the dark void of the tomb.

"Woe is me, for the good man is perished out of the earth." Marshall clasped his hands together and watched the coffin. "God has deemed it fit that this good man shall have a place in heaven."

Propped against the wall was the tombstone and, to distract his mind from his own mortality, Essex scanned the Latin inscription to see that Pym would be laid alongside a medieval knight. Befitting indeed, for both Pym and Sir John Wyndsore had much in common in the form of their wounded bodies and great courage, but above all a strength of spirit that would live on in the eyes of God.

"And now we come to lament the fall of this choice and excellent man. I am ready to call for mourning such as that of Hadadrimon in the Valley of Megiddon," Marshall announced, raising his hands to God in despair and his voice increasing in volume; every word elongated. "Our Parliament is weakened, our armies wasted, our treasury exhausted and our enemies increased."

My army's not wasted, damn you! The words stuck in Essex's throat as he glanced along the lines of pale faces and picked out Saint-John, whose long thin nose and pursed lips were haunting.

* * * * *

Oliver Saint-John, the Solicitor-General, stood behind the front lines of mourners and in the shadows, a position he much preferred. Hands clasped behind his back, he remained detached from the emotions and, with his legal mind, thought only of the succession and how he could manage the front man who would replace Pym. Saint-John's air was as cool as the French stone of the Abbey and he considered Sir Henry Vane a suitable candidate.

"I mean not that we should mourn for him. His work is done, his warfare accomplished, and he is delivered from sin and sorrow and all of the evils which we may fear upon ourselves." Marshall extended his hand to the coffin as it was slowly and gently laid upon the floor.

Saint-John flicked his narrow eyes to Essex, whom Pym had indulged for far too long. The proud, sedentary old man seemed much more inclined to be engulfed in tobacco smoke than warfare these days. Ironically, Essex was leaning against the wall below the tomb of King Edward I, the 'Hammer of the Scots', which prompted Saint-John to consider how much the English Parliament now needed Scotland.

The coffin was swung over its final resting place and lowered into the depths little by little, all the while looked down upon by Pym's two sons. More candles were lit, casting a sinister flicker of yellow upon the walls like the fires that had once burned within the leader's belly.

Sir Henry Vane took a candle and lit it upon another, holding it as if ready to toast Pym's memory. He cleared his throat as the coffin was lowered into the tomb and came to rest with a muffled thud. With Pym now out of sight, it would only be a matter of time before he was out of mind.

"His toil knew no bounds." Marshall's lilt gave a melodious finale to the sermon that gave hope to the impatient and encouraged the ambitious. "Even in his final illness he tended to our vital business with the same energy and determination as ever."

The Puritan Saint-John stood straight and gave a sigh, which generated many echoes as others also released their pent-up emotions. But then Marshall was speaking again, stitching tributes together and weaving endless elaborate praise.

"Service to the public was his work, his meat and his drink, even his exercise, recreation, pleasure and ambition," Marshall said, his voice climbing. "His all."

"Very eloquent," Saint-John congratulated him to bring the rambling proceedings to an end before Lord Essex himself expired.

The stout Lord General's grey moustache, sallow features and double chin did not look any the healthier for having had a lit candle beneath them. Perhaps the Grim Reaper might remove him from his post before Saint-John needed to broach the subject of retirement. But the old dog had to plod on a little longer so that Saint-John's cousin, Oliver Cromwell, could gain valuable experience and promotion.

After entering the Abbey as a unified congregation with the purpose of paying tribute to John Pym, each man dispersed with a singular outlook as to the future of Parliament. They went off on their own merry ways into the new era that now dawned after such a great eclipse.

Chapter 65

The River Thames lay silent with frozen streaks forming a maelstrom of pale blues and greens lacquered with frosty ice. A biting wind took the opportunity to skate across it in the absence of the revellers who would have usually done the same, had not the city suffered a great loss. For today the sky was no longer full of snow, but the rhythmic peals of Westminster Abbey. To this dull tune the wind raced around the great river and up the embankment to infiltrate the narrow streets like a marauding Royalist army.

Howling an eerie, almost melancholy, cry, it whooshed past the Star Chamber building, whose cold and callous business stopped when the King left the city two years ago. Into Westminster it circled the fountain and on past Westminster Hall to slip between small streets towards the Abbey, where it found Lord Essex crunching snow underfoot. After toying with his black sash and plucking at his coarse woollen suit, it scurried off to leave the Lord General rearranging himself and considering his discarding of silk quite fortuitous; not only out of mourning for John

Pym, but also for his own protection against the elements. He had no intention of following his colleague into an early grave.

"I need you to be my eyes and ears around Parliament." Essex sought to protect himself. The scar-faced Captain James Jackson wasn't one of his most handsome spies, but certainly was one of his most able, and of the calibre needed to keep track of jackals such as those men he'd just left.

"My eyes are entirely yours, my lord," James replied, the machinations surrounding Parliament having always intrigued him.

"I don't trust a single one of them, least of all Saint-John." A fresh wind caught Essex's breath, as if for the sake of unity Pym's spirit was trying to silence him. But as the most senior and experienced leader left standing, Essex was certain of his right to say and think whatever he liked.

"Isn't he the cousin of Oliver Cromwell?" James asked.

"Humph." Essex searched for his coach amidst the jam of carriages filling the square. "You mean the one who's forever challenging Lord Manchester's command of the eastern army?" Essex disdained to answer, save only to mutter that Cromwell was nothing but Saint-John's pawn.

"That's him," James said. "A colonel with a growing reputation."

"Has more warts than admirers," Essex muttered under his breath. "Now, you know who to keep your eye on?"

"Yes, I'll send you daily despatches to Saint Albans," James replied.

"I will not be at my headquarters, as I need to block the King's advance," Essex replied. "Waller can't do it on his own, no matter how much praise the world heaps upon him," he said of his subordinate.

"Hey for old Robin!" A chimneysweep and his boy cheered Essex; the leader who had raised the first army to counter the King, and who had most recently saved Gloucester.

Their faces beamed through the blackened soot of their trade, which was under threat with Newcastle and its coal fields well within the Royalist grip. Two people's pure joy and belief soon generated a crowd who joined the praise, leaving the jubilant Lord General to forget all about Waller, Saint-John or Cromwell. Until, that is, a lady in black hurried forward, her brow and eyes covered by a fashionable dark mask, while a dark woollen mantle and hood sheltered her from the bitter chill.

"Lord Essex!" she called. "I crave but a moment."

"See to her." Essex was unwilling to be accosted by a flighty female at the best of times, never mind right now.

"I must speak with his lordship." She extracted a hand from her fur muff in an attempt to push James aside.

"Desist, madam!" James blocked her path.

The door to Essex's carriage opened and its painted coat of arms flashed before the lady's eyes as briefly as the moment she wished to secure.

"My lord, I bring news of Hopton's army," she said, prompting the Lord General to pause, and then grant her a morsel of his time. As she lifted her mask he recognised her as another of his agents.

"Be quick." He outstretched his arm and walking cane to keep her at a suitable distance.

"My apologies for not writing of late, but my daughter and grandson have been my focus," she explained and began to tell of her husband's murder.

"I have no interest in your domestic affairs, Madam Mercer, now get to the point."

"Lord Hopton's taken Arundel Castle and has been ordered to attack London as part of a three-pronged advance," Mary said. "It was taken on the ninth of December."

"I am well aware of Arundel." The news stoked Essex's concerns about the threat to the iron foundries of the Sussex Weald, as well as to London. "But tell me, where did you hear about this multiple attack?"

"My son-in-law is with Hopton's force," Mary replied. "Most fortuitous considering the information this presents to me."

"Then, by God, get me their numbers and locations." Essex seized the door to his carriage.

"I have those already." Mary discreetly held up Anne's last letter. "Lord Hopton has five thousand men, though he has them quartered in different locations." She sensed from the look in Essex's grey eyes that such information would bring in enough money to get by for another few weeks.

"His force is split, you say?" Essex's eyes narrowed.

"That's so, my lord, and Berkeley's contingent heads for Alton." The merest thought of her son-in-law engulfed Mary with anger and resentment. "And then probably for London."

"Very useful," Essex replied, deciding not to share this newfound knowledge with his subordinate, Sir William Waller, quite yet. "They'll be cast to hell before they get anywhere near London."

"I hope so, my lord," Mary replied as Essex climbed into his carriage and his features became ghost-like in the frosted window.

"Well, well." Essex watched his breath in the cold air. "We shall soon see if Waller deserves his array of accolades."

"Stand aside!" James grabbed Mary's arm as the horses pulled the coach away, "Or would you rather be trampled to death?" he asked.

"My time's not up yet," she assured James, and glared at him. "At least not until I safeguard my daughter and grandson."

"Isn't that your son-in-law's concern?" James asked.

"It is he who is putting them in danger," Mary shrieked.

"Then be about your business." James saw no point in arguing with her. "My sympathy goes to your son-in-law."

Chapter 66

Anne's vision blurred, such was the time she had spent absently staring at the letter before her. Gripped between her hands, its upper edge wilted backwards as if in a faint, much like Anne, who seemed barely able to concentrate on much apart from her late father. Each letter of the writing drew her further into a trance and spun her within their black loops, dominating the paper like nooses. By laying the letter flat on the desk she sought respite from the choking in her throat. Whenever she was overtaken by sorrow, which numbed every emotion bar despair, her father's murder felt as if it were only yesterday. Yet whenever she tried to recall his ruddy features, it felt like a lifetime since she had last seen them.

"Five weeks …" her voice trembled and broke. Silent tears rolled down her cheeks to hang upon her upper lip. It was a good thing that Francis was drilling his troops because she did not want him to see her like this. "Come on." A deep inhalation steeled her attempt to carry on and she picked up the letter again with the aim of properly digesting the contents of her mother's latest missive.

Thy poor father of blessed memory. I always said alcohol would see him off, but never once did I envisage such a brutal end. Sometimes it's as if I am the one who died, for my heart is filled only with emptiness.

Now, your last letter concerns me, Anne, for you tell me that you have quartered in Alton. Considering your father's death at the hands of a soldier, it terrifies me that you're living amongst five, or even ten thousand of Lord Hopton's men. Are they all near you? Are you safe? You also wrote that Henry was ill, which seals my resolve to travel to you with the balm I have procured for his headaches, and bring you both back to London. Rest assured, I am positive that dear Francis will understand, for he like me, cares only for your welfare.

"My son!" Anne looked forward to Henry's arrival tomorrow and sat back to release a deep sigh that began to ease her burden. Soon she could care for him personally and his presence would be her very own balm. Anne's motherly instinct flourished like a gently budding snowdrop amidst a winter of sorrow, and she cupped her hands together and blew into them. The very thought of Henry instilled her with drive, prompting her to take a goose feather and, with a knife, gently slit the centre and shape the end into a nib. Once prepared, she dipped the ink and channelled her effort into finishing her response.

Honestly, mother, you worry far too much! Lord Hopton is a kindly man. He's split his forces between four towns so they don't overburden any one place, which I think is a very compassionate gesture, don't *you*? Your estimates are most incorrect. We have only one thousand troops in Alton, but Francis commands them and they are good men.

I am quite safe.

Please don't travel here, for it will do more harm than good, though it is most kind of you to procure the balm. Send it on by all means, but Henry is recovering.

And so, I rest, your loving daughter.

Anne

With that, she folded the letter twice lengthways. Then, turning each end towards the centre, tucked one into the folds of the other. Such simple actions carried out so precisely gave her much satisfaction. Finally, she smeared the melted end of a block of red wax inside the join and pressed down upon the paper to seal it.

For a few minutes she sat looking at her handiwork, until the staircase's creak made her shove both letters into the drawer and stand up. The door opened and entering, Francis kissed her.

"Did you not hear me calling you?" he asked and looked at her trembling hand. "Are you feeling ill?"

Despite her reassurances, Francis strode to the charcoal brazier and jabbed at the smouldering remains as if they were somehow guilty of negligence towards his wife.

"I've no food prepared," Anne was quick to stress. "Midday seems to have turned into evening without me even realising it.".

"Don't worry," he replied. "I'll send out to the inn for some food."

"But there's ample in the larder," she said, stroking at her skirts in a bid to embrace normality; as if by smoothing them she might also smooth out her own troubled thoughts. For she must indeed, seeing as Henry's wet-nurse would be arriving too. It would not do for the servant to find her mistress in such a state.

"Been writing?" Francis looked at the ink on her fingertips.

"To mother," she answered, unable to cover up what she knew would be a point of dispute. "She's got some balm for Henry from the best apothecary in London ..."

"Does she know it's nothing serious?" He frowned. "Such a selfless errand to the capital cannot be the sole reason for her travelling so far."

"She just wants to help," Anne said, feeling light-headed and her heart thumping. She looked away and her eyes stung. The balance of her body and mind could not face any surprises, confrontation or upset.

"What time does Henry arrive tomorrow?" Francis asked, changing the subject.

"Midday." Anne hoped their son would be the only new arrival. The very thought that Mary might turn up on their doorstep filled her with dread. It wasn't so much the fact that Mary and Francis might meet again, but the conflicting loyalty she'd face that made her chest tighten. At the crux of it, Anne knew she could never turn her mother away.

"I'll return home in the afternoon and we can spend some time together, just the three of us." Francis embraced her. "Henry will make you smile again, sweetheart. I know it."

Anne's emotion was too much for her to reply. She suspected Francis was as adrift as she was, but she could barely look after herself let alone him. She felt powerless to put right what was wrong with her. His fussing, the questions and suggestions all seemed controlling, or else over-protective, and did nothing to alleviate the despair in which she continued to drown. Yet when he was not in the house, she craved his company. Tomorrow, she hoped, they could both turn a corner.

Chapter 67
Alton. 10 December 1643.

Walking briskly through Cut Lane, Francis's black bucket-topped boots splashed through a puddle and elicited a hiss from a milkmaid whose dress was besmirched by the mud.

"Watch where you're going!" A knife sharpener interrupted his door to door calls to join the girl's berating of Francis.

The townsfolks' frustration with the soldiers was far from unique, but hardly registered with Francis, who had more pressing matters on his mind. Dead leaves crunching underfoot certainly provided a vastly different carpet to the rose petals that had once graced them upon the King's entry into Oxford. Indeed, Alton's resentment towards the presence of troops seemed as strong now as it was six hundred years ago in the face of a Danish invasion.

"God's blood!" He was running late and peered down towards the bridge, wondering at Jane's urgency to meet him and where she might be. *She had better have a good reason.*

Prone to single-mindedness, Francis ignored the criminal whose head and arms were locked between the planks of a pillory, and who was the target of rotten eggs and a bucket of urine. On reaching the bridge, Francis leaned over the sandstone parapet to trace his eye along the margins of the pond below and the bare branches that clawed out into the water. Despite his certainty that he was in the right place, he was unable to see Jane and turned off the path to head down to the bankside. His sigh of frustration condensed in the cold air into tiny droplets of water, which left a misty trail behind him.

* * * * *

Jane, in her earnestness, had arrived much earlier and employed herself in the arranging of horsetail in her basket after a trip to the market. The wiry, green stems felt prickly within her gentle grasp; soothing her nerves a little as in her mind she again went over how to phrase her revelation.

"Might I have the pleasure of walking with you?" The gallant words were all she had hoped for, but she gasped upon meeting the gaze of a stranger. The sharp features, pleasing to the eye all the same, were not those she had expected.

"I cannot ..." she stammered and recoiled. The offer of his arm simply made her cheeks chill.

"I shall not hurt thee." The soldier stepped forward and hooked two fingers around the handle of her basket. "Plenty of pewter to polish?" He smiled upon eyeing the neat horsetail arranged side by side.

"You had best leave." Jane could not rid her memory of the last man who made such advances, and who had left her with nothing but a growing belly and the hostility of the entire community. Recollections of the man's wide nose that crunched up when he grinned still gave her goose pimples. "Leave me alone!"

"All right, lass, but pray share thy name at least," he said, seemingly taken aback by her response. " 'Tis not often a man finds such a beautiful rose along this old waterside."

"Jane," she whispered with the hope of pacifying him, and was thus obliged to listen while he introduced himself.

"I am Robert of Lord Hopton's army," he told her softly. "A soldier who finds his heart besieged by your unique beauty."

But still he did not take his leave. "My master comes," she warned and liberated her basket from his grip. "He's a knight of the realm."

"I have no title, but I would treat you as a lady." He stepped back and dropped her a bow.

"Sir!" She had never before been graced with such an honour.

"Well, Jane." He smiled. "I'd fight a hundred Roundheads for you, and then some more."

"Even then I would not be yours to conquer." She turned to leave, only for her hand to be grasped and her delicate fingers pressed to his moustached lips. Such an intrusion made her lash out with her basket.

"Be off with you, Hepple!" Francis yelled.

"Simply looking after the lady while she waited." Robert recognised Lieutenant-Colonel Berkeley. "Not that I'd ever trespass onto your territory."

"Do not bother my maid again." Francis marched up to him. "Now," he said, turning to Jane, "why are you not about your duties?"

"Please, sir..." Thought of his displeasure caused her to tremble, and doubly so at the reminder that she was nothing more than a servant. She dusted down her skirts and adjusted her linen coif while the soldier left.

"Come now, do not upset yourself," Francis said and at the sight of Jane's tears he embraced her. "Did that dog harm you?" No sooner had her body pressed to his than he froze.

"No, sir." A gasp of relief escaped her lips. "But if it hadn't been for your timely arrival," she whispered and looked up into his eyes, "there's no telling what might have happened."

"Some of these soldiers haven't seen their wives in months ..." Francis began to step back.

"But all soldiers are not alike." She sensed the inner turmoil that danced in his glistening eyes. "I feel safe when in your presence." Without prior design, desire impelled her fingers to curl about Francis's long hair. She kissed him. With eyes closed and lost in the divine, Jane realised that Francis could be hers both body and soul. His desire was equally matched as lip pressed upon lip and tongue upon tongue. It was a moment in which Jane might have been lost forever had they not been disturbed by the noise of a horse clattering across the bridge.

"Forgive me." Francis regretted his actions as the winter light faded.

"There's nothing to forgive," she reassured him, praying that he would not abandon her now, after she had laid bare her feelings.

"I have a wife and family ..."

"It is of that which I wish to speak to you, sir." In a bid to stop him from saying any more, she quickly recounted a letter that Lady Anne had recently penned to her mother. "Madam Mary wishes her ladyship to go to London with your son."

"You read private correspondence?" he asked.

"Oh, no, sir. I was in another room and overheard her ladyship talking aloud to your son about it some days ago. She sounded much troubled." Jane gulped, devastated that he thought her capable of spying on her mistress. "I was so shocked that I resolved to tell you. I felt you must know, sir."

"Are you sure of this, Jane?" He held a hand to his forehead.

"It seems your mother-in-law insists upon it," Jane explained in a hushed and sympathetic tone.

"The devil take that sorceress!" Francis exclaimed.

"Perhaps I shouldn't have continued to listen, but I could not let this happen behind your back." Jane's fear for his son's wellbeing was as genuine as if he was her own child.

"That woman has bewitched my wife," Francis cried with anguish. "I will stop this once and for all."

"My loyalty will always be to you." Jane was anxious to justify her actions and reached out as he paced to and fro.

"How could she?" He slammed a tree trunk. "I should have opened her eyes to Mary's lies when the opportunity presented itself."

"Tell me what you wish me to do." Jane's pale hand touched his.

Francis rested his forehead against the tree and Jane looked on as his spirit seeped from his body as if absorbed into the mist forming over the icy water of Cuts Pond. So numb did he appear that Jane thought he mustn't have noticed as she slipped her little finger into his fist, that is, until it loosened and he took her hand.

Chapter 68
Guildford, 11 December 1643.

"Where you 'eaded?" The soldier's voice was far louder and gruffer than it needed to be. " 'and over your documents."

"Alton," Mary replied. The man's grubby hand prompting her to avert her gaze. Her attention was instead transferred to a small blackbird that chirped vociferously at her predicament whilst hopping past the roadblock.

"What's your business?" he asked. But it wasn't the reply of medication for her grandson that prompted him to look up or the phial she produced, but her accent. "Irish?" His challenge was met by a nod of assent. "Another Catholic whore off to seek the King's protection, eh?"

"I know not which of those insults is worst!" Mary exclaimed. "I am here on Lord Essex's orders and I wish to speak to your superior."

"He'll 'ave you cut." The soldier alluded to the fate of the Irishwomen Parliament had recently captured.

"If Essex finds out, your throat will suffer the same," she said and thrust forward the Lord General's letter.

Sight of the recognisable, swirling signature was enough to make the soldier consider that discretion would indeed be the better part of valour. A silver sixpence sealed his conviction in passing on the necessary order, whereupon Mary was able to pass the roadblock and procure a coach to Farnham.

Crop-haired dog! The story of the Irishwomen who had their noses cut from bridge to tip incensed Mary, for after the brutality it had been found that they were actually Welsh. Proof enough, she thought, that the English were nothing more than mindless savages.

She boarded her coach and tucked Lord Essex's pass back into her purse alongside a recent missive from her daughter. Anne's short letter had announced her intention of following her husband to the ends of the earth. It was this more than anything that spurred Mary to get to Alton before the Parliamentarian army. She had hired a private coach for this reason, and a coachman who was driven by the promise of a whole silver crown if he could reach Alton by the morning of the thirteenth.

The jangle of bridle and clatter of hooves led her carriage through Guildford's streets and out on to a blurred monotony of countryside beneath a streak of blue sky as her coach raced onward to Farnham. Though Mary paid little heed to the view as she sat upon the hard wooden slat and prayed to the Virgin; praying for a miracle that she could persuade Anne to bring Henry and return to London with her. She turned to her brass crucifix and fervently kissed the Lord Jesus, holding it so tightly that its edges cut into her skin to have the Almighty seemingly bleed once more.

Chapter 69

Alton. Seven of the clock in the morning, 12 December 1643.

"Pray tell Sir William Waller that the seventeenth Earl of Crawford sends his thanks for this runlet." The Royalist noble stood over the cask of wine as if it were a felled deer from his Scottish estate.

"And the ox that was promised in return, my lord?" Simpson's words were drowned by the barrel rolling across the stone floor.

"I shall present it to him myself," Crawford replied, holding out his hand and yelling for a tankard. "Finally, something to replace the horse-piss that this town calls ale."

Sir Francis Berkeley, being closest, had no sooner fetched a tankard than Crawford ordered two soldiers to remove the cork and gave an appreciative snort at the full-bodied bouquet that trickled forth.

"Then I shall take my leave of you, sir," Captain Simpson said with a bow. "I will pass your assurances to Sir William that your ox will follow."

"You …!" Crawford barked, "… shall be the first to taste this gift." He kept his beady eyes fixed on Simpson.

"Alas, I do not drink." Simpson raised a hand.

"By God, man, even Jesus was not averse to a little wine!" Crawford's knee-high riding boots scuffed along the ground as he swaggered closer. "One of Waller's men will be the first to sample it."

"I must protest." Simpson stood resolute in spite of the spittle that accompanied this close-quarters intimidation.

"You would refuse a man's hospitality as if it were poison being offered?" Crawford asked.

"I simply wish for my abstinence to be respected," Captain Simpson said, "thus allowing us to debate an exchange of prisoners with a clear head. For that should have been the main purpose of our meeting, should it not?"

"Such impertinence!" Crawford yelled.

"I meant no such offence." Simpson held up his hands.

"Which jackanapes would refuse wine?" Colonel Bolle intervened with an offer to swig it himself and deftly moved Simpson aside.

"Let Taffy's dog at it, seeing as this one turns his nose up," Berkeley said and acted upon the Colonel's lead.

"Aye, he can hold his liquor better than me." Taffy's quip was met with much laughter, though not from Bolle or Berkeley, who both took the opportunity to counsel their commander's restraint. But Crawford dismissed his officers' advice.

"I simply offer this damned puritan a share in our bounty." Crawford slapped the table. "Would our own men not clamour to be regularly 'mistreated' so?" He demanded the Parliamentarian drink up.

"Forgive me, Oh Lord, for I do this under duress," Simpson muttered and drained the cup. Yet no sooner had he finished than Crawford roared with laughter and ordered him to be placed under guard. The firkin of wine was taken to Crawford's quarters for safe keeping whilst by the roaring fire he attended to a recent despatch from Lord Hopton.

"An update on the enemy, sir?" Bolle seemed to read the peer's expression.

"They're but ten miles away, at Farnham." Crawford chafed at his beard with the rolled-up letter and pondered both the enemy commander's resolve and the inclemency of the weather. "Though they've stopped there, have they not?" He was of a mind to believe that Farnham would be used as the enemy's winter quarters.

"For now," Berkeley said, having joined them. "Though I'm loath to second- guess Waller's unpredictability." He warned of the rebel commander. "On top of that, the quagmire betwixt Farnham and Alton has become passable to both man and beast, courtesy of a cold snap."

"I'd recommend doubling our patrols along the main Farnham road and have our scouts take a closer look at their camp." Bolle was ever the pragmatist.

"Yes, yes, see to it!" Crawford thought them two fretting old maids. "But I say, let the elements take care of them while we focus on our own men."

Lord Hopton's letter had also warned Crawford about the mutinous soldiers from the Irish contingent, two of whom he'd had to hang. But Crawford could never bring himself to focus long on anything that threatened to cause him concern and he left his two officers and struck up a song with the men.

"Waller and Hazelrigg, Stapleton, Scroop.
Way! Make way for His Majesty's troop!
Crop-headed Puritans durstn't deny,
His Majesty's gentlemen riding by,
With boot and saddle and tow-row-row!"

"Action would dispel any thought of mutiny," Berkeley said, watching Crawford as he finished his antics and returned for some beer.

"Shall I round up Waller's ox?" Bolle asked Crawford.

"Send word that if he wants it, he must come and wrest it from me." Crawford decided it was time to sample the wine and left to make sure the messenger was still alive.

"We're quartered over four different locations. This is pure folly!" Berkeley cursed.

"Dangerously so!" Bolle looked to the flickering grate for answers, but found only more questions amidst the logs that buckled and split in the rising flames. "It's imperative that we try and ascertain when and where Waller might strike, considering we have a front of twenty-seven miles," he instructed Berkeley just as another log cracked under the pressure. Yet Bolle seemed to shiver at the chill of its ill omen and basked in none of its warmth.

Chapter 70
Open countryside. An hour after midnight, 13 December 1643.

Beneath the soft lustre of the full moon, General Sir William Waller had already led his army two miles westward along the main road after leaving Farnham earlier that day. He'd started with Basing House right in his line of sight, yet, as clouds crept across the moon's face, the resulting shadows blotted out all trace of the Royalist stronghold. But that did not matter as it was not his target but simply a ruse to any enemy scouts who happened to have observed his bearing.

"Now!" His command was passed down the ranks by the clasping of hands on shoulders, resulting in the five-thousand-strong army turning due south. Each pikeman held on to the trailing fifteen-foot ash pole of the soldier in front – musketeers doing likewise with their guns – and, like a giant millipede, they cut across field and hedge, through the nocturnal homelands of many a hedgehog, bat, and fox. Waller could only hope that the warm beer in his men's bellies would fortify any superstitious heart against woodland spirits as they traversed this ghostly, silhouetted world.

Upon approaching the first of his men who had been posted along the route earlier that day, Waller afforded a nod and a sniff from his long, cold nose. He looked back over his shoulder towards his leather artillery. Their lighter design, which gave for minimal noise as well as manoeuvrability, drew from him a further nod of deep satisfaction. Amidst nature's rustling and scratching, his heightened state of mind became his only companion and he recalled Colonel Halifax's cautionary warnings of two days prior, which he soon hoped to disprove.

* * * * *

"Prince Rupert may have been the first to explode a mine in England, but I'll be the first to use leather-clad artillery." Waller aimed to punch a hole in the strung-out Royalist lines by capturing Alton.

"Well, I don't much fancy being the first to be blown to smithereens by one!" Colonel Halifax raised one eyebrow. "I've heard more bad than good about them."

"I'll blast Alton and every last one of its garrison into speedy submission and what better way than through the use of light artillery?" Waller replied.

"Defective artillery, might I remind you, Sir William," Halifax pointed out. "Prone to overheating and unusable after only a few shots."

"Only a few shots would be needed," Waller insisted, wishing only to list the positives. "So light that they can be drawn by a single horse and, if fired intermittently, of incalculable worth to our assault. Just picture it, my dear colonel, we can have them in place before Crawford even knows what's hit him. And then take him into custody lashed to the back of that ox he promised me."

"Well, when you put it like that ..." Colonel Halifax's shoulders heaved with mirth.

"I put it so because that is how it must be," Waller replied. "A lengthy encounter is out of the question. This needs to be a fast and hard strike."

* * * * *

Waller, who insisted on utter silence, was like every man present, left in the company of his own ponderings until reaching the great oak. Recognising it from yesterday's scout's report, the boughs did indeed hang over them like an old crone's hand ushering them all to the approaching forest.

He passed under the branches and hoped that the densely packed trees would provide some respite from the bitter winter chill. Coldness permeated his bones the longer their march went on, yet did not numb his innermost worries, which instead abounded; worries that everyday life usually silenced but now were given free rein. Aside from his battle plans, there weighed upon his heart a sorrow every time he thought of his good friend, Lord Hopton, whose forces he now aimed to obliterate. The man he'd served alongside in the Thirty Years War, and who but six months past, had been the recipient of Waller's most intimate thoughts courtesy of his own pen.

> Certainly my affection to you is so unchangeable that hostility itself cannot violate my friendship, but I must be true wherein the cause I serve.
>
> That great God, which is the searcher of my heart, knows with what a sad sense I go about this service, and with what a perfect hatred I detest this war without an enemy; but I look

upon it as an Opus Domini and that is enough to silence all passion in me. The God of peace in his good time will send us peace. In the meantime we are upon the stage and must act those parts that are assigned to us in this tragedy.

Whatever the outcome, I will never willingly relinquish the title of your most affectionate friend.

William Waller

And Waller, the central character, was brought back to his nightly stage by the gentle grasping of his shoulder and Colonel Halifax's whisper: "We should get there around eight of the clock."

The calculation fitted closely to Waller's own, although he had allowed an extra hour for the difficulties of a night march, to which he was well accustomed.

An enlivening scent of damp leaves and bark, mixed with the crisp breeze, infused his every fibre. He felt more alive than he ever did during the daytime. Alton was to be the scene of his comeback since gaining command of this army, and the hoot of a tawny owl seemed apt. Waller's nickname had been taken from this very bird, due to his ability to operate in twilight hours. Keen-eyed and especially keen of ear, the light tinkle of a few small wooden tubes that held the musketeers' measures of gunpowder struck up in his mind the tune his men had sang only the night before, favourably comparing him to Robin, the Lord General Essex.

"Robin's asleep, for Robin is nice,
Robin has delicate habits,
But 'whoo' says the grey night owl, once, twice,

And three times 'whoo' for the little shy mice,
The mice and the rats and the rabbits.
Whoo!"

The rising winter sun greeted Waller with vision and, along with it, the faint outline of Saint Lawrence's church spire; so sharp that it looked intent on bursting the sunrise like an egg yolk and rending asunder the Royalists' new day. Waller made all haste to secure his advantage.

Chapter 71
Alton. Eight of the clock in the morning, 13 December 1643.

Wishing to segregate herself from reality, Anne had retreated to one of the railed-off pews of Saint Lawrence's Church. Within this little shell she prayed for an end to her solitary inner battles waged against this war and the threat it posed to her loved ones. Awoken by Jane with a message to meet Mary in the church, she had rushed here to deal with her mother while Francis, thankfully, was with the army. Yet despite unburdening herself to the Almighty, Anne felt no more comfortable with Mary's impending presence.

"O' Lord, bring us peace," Anne whispered. "And let my husband remain ignorant of her sudden arrival, for never will he believe that I knew nothing of it."

* * * * *

"My child!" Mary's black figure, dressed in mourning, hurried past the only other worshipper, an elderly woman, and headed down the aisle.

"Your hood." Anne pointed, as upon its fall her mother's red hair was exposed to the sight of the Lord.

"The Forgiver understands my urgency," Mary said and jerked open the pew's small door to embrace her daughter.

"Why have you come here?" Anne asked.

"That's no way to greet your mother!" She sat and encouraged her daughter to do likewise. "I'd have you know that I've brought Henry's medication," she explained, hoping to get Anne into her waiting carriage and away before the Roundheads or Francis could stop it. "Let's go fetch him now." But Anne's raised hand dashed all hope of a speedy acquiescence.

"Please, Mother. Did I not make my feelings perfectly clear in my letter?" Anne asked.

"But there's to be a battle here!" Mary trembled. "War is upon us and you are misguided." She stood and excused her daughter to the Almighty. "He is the light and I his vassal come to save you."

"A battle in winter, with conditions such as they are?" Anne shook her head. "Francis assured me that the enemy would hole up until the climate improved," she replied.

"Waller will be headed this way soon," Mary remonstrated like a fiery preacher, "with his Parliamentarians." It might just as well have been the devil and his legions that were descending upon them, she thought.

"That's impossible," Anne replied. "They cannot march an army in these conditions."

"The roads may be passable by the frost." Mary took her daughter's hands and cursed her stubbornness. "Does that husband of yours tell you nothing? Doesn't he make you aware of the danger to both you and my grandson?"

"You're still overwrought about father," Anne said. "I also miss him terribly, but what are we to do?"

"Save ourselves while there's still time, that's what we can do," Mary replied breathlessly. "Not even the Holy Mother can protect us from soldiers who know nothing but murder and rape."

"Please ..." Anne squeezed her eyes closed.

"I've prayed for your safety every night and now been granted the opportunity of securing your salvation." Mary lifted her gaze to the beams and muttered an Ave Maria.

"I ... we will be fine," Anne reassured her with tears in her eyes.

"Do you not have any fear, girl? Fear of being robbed of your other parent so soon after thy father? Fear of every soldier who is guilty as charged for his murder?" Mary pressed.

"I fear for what troubles you," Anne replied.

"You think me a lunatic?" Mary spluttered.

"No ... I ..."

"Then why won't you listen, girl?" Mary revealed she'd learned of the coming battle from none other than Essex himself. "The Lord General, do you hear?"

"Essex?" Anne's frown was one of disbelief.

"No time to explain." Mary held out a pleading hand, then just as quickly seized her daughter and dragged her into the aisle. "Until my dying breath ..." She manhandled her towards the south door. "... I will do anything to save you and Henry."

Anne desperately attempted to grab a stone pillar from which an image of Pope Cornelius gazed down. Yet when a thunder of artillery fire rang out as if this saint had called for divine intervention, both mother and daughter froze. They were barely able to breathe as they tried to comprehend what had just happened.

In those few seconds, the red pigment that coloured the pillar shimmered like a river of blood. Another explosion ripped through the cool, morning air and across the roof of Saint Lawrence's, followed by a peppering of musket shot that gave chorus to Mary's worst fears. Battle had commenced.

"You see!" She lifted both hands and yelled that Anne must now believe her.

It was as if every dead soul in the graveyard had risen up around them, such were the gut-wrenching echoes of fighting men that seeped into the fabric of the building. Barrages of artillery. Ground-shaking thuds heralded a clattering of hooves that grew louder and louder.

Such repetitive clangs gave the image of all the houses being blown apart and each and every brick thrown into the air coming to land upon Alton. Despite having never before been physically caught up in the conflict, Mary's heart, its beat galloping, told her that civil war was upon her. The peril, from which she had fought so long to protect Anne and Henry, now engulfed them all.

Chapter 72

Lord Crawford had barely opened his weary eyes after another late night with his officers, than his sleepy mind was rudely returned to Alton. He reached for his wife, but found only a cold, empty space. He itched his head with curses at the lice who'd also wakened.

He was further irritated by the slits of harsh morning light that forced through the shutters and regretted Lady Margaret's absence. She had secured not only his love, but also his social standing just as effectively as her brother, the Duke of Hamilton, had courted the King's favour with bold assurances of keeping Scotland neutral.

Crawford rolled over to find solace in the empty embrace of his woollen blankets, but could sleep no more. He cursed the half-empty firkin of wine upon the floor, his foul breath, and what had become of his six and forty years. There was no making sense of the ways of the Lord, or the three tiny coffins he and his wife had consigned to the earth. So, with a sense of profound failure in his heart, he sat up, placed the soles of his feet on the cold floor and bemoaned his inability to sire an heir.

This unfulfilled desire had been much quenched by alcohol of late and would have had him drain the rest of the firkin that morning had not a distant rumble shaken him from his despair. A second rumble made him consider the impossible: artillery.

"My lord!" A banging at the door seemed to confirm as much. He opened it after pulling on his breeches and tucking in his linen nightshirt.

"What on God's earth is happening?" Crawford yelled and hurried to his boots, tugging them on with a panic that made the simple task almost impossible.

"The enemy are attacking the town." The captain's wide eyes met Crawford's. "Colonel Bolle is at his post and wishes to know your orders."

The shocking news prompted Crawford to run to the window and pull the shutters open to a bright eruption of wintery sunlight. Squinting afore its glory, its rays picked out every lazy dust particle that invaded the room, as if the brutal reality had burst into his sanctum.

"Where the hell are they?" Sheltering his eyes, he searched in vain for sight of the Roundheads, although the unmistakeable cracks of musket fire in the distance were proof enough.

"They are attacking from the north and heading towards the church, sir."

"Bolle is defending, you say?" Crawford stared at the captain as he imagined the layout of Alton and thought of what to do next.

"Yes, with his infantrymen. But Waller's men are rapidly pushing them back through the streets."

"Waller!" Crawford's tone was full of scorn. The roar of artillery, along with the cavalry officer who bounded into the room, unravelled all Crawford's thoughts.

"Your orders for our horsemen, sir?"

"How many men do they have?" Crawford asked.

"Three ... perhaps as many as five thousand," the man replied, drawing upon Sir Francis Berkeley's estimate taken from the sentry who raised the alarm.

Crawford rued the one thousand at his own disposal. Waller may have defied the season, but Crawford would be damned if he would let the man breeze through Alton and destroy both his infantry and his cavalry.

"Have Bolle's men use the buildings to hold the town at all cost," Crawford commanded.

"The rebels have torched a number already," the captain said.

"Damn them!" Crawford slammed a fist against the four-poster bed and shook its century-old framework to the core. "They should be in winter quarters."

"What about our cavalry, sir?"

"Prepare my horse." Crawford stamped his boot on properly and marched towards the door with his doublet still open. "I will lead them myself," he vowed resolutely as a boy hurried forward to fasten a sword belt about him. After that, Crawford swept outside to meet the resounding echoes of warfare in the only way he could.

Mounting up, he lifted his hands as if to encourage a huge flock of birds to flight. Certainly, Crawford intended to be swift. Grey smoke was already pluming above the town, soon to cut it off from all sight of God and the merciless acts taking place beneath it carried out in His name.

Chapter 73

Holding a piece of Spanish Paper covered in rouge between forefinger and thumb, Jane flicked her gaze to the small mirror-glass that beckoned her. With a momentary pause she remembered how she had seen her mistress, Lady Anne, applying the same cosmetic. Yet, try as she might, Jane could not imagine how she would look. Slowly, she brought the paper closer to her face, watching her reflection. With lessening reluctance she dabbed her cheek as gently as falling rose petals and, with a gasp, leaned closer to examine the result. No sooner had she admired the blossom of pink than a reverberating thud shook the house and made her drop everything in a flurry of guilt-ridden panic.

"Oh," she cried, quickly wiping her cheek, and a flood of emotion swept over her. A small glass jar smashed upon the oak floorboards, spilling egg-white at her unsteady feet. It was over an hour since she had prepared it for Lady Anne's face, though her mistress had still not returned from church. A series of muffled fizzing and cracking sounds made Jane rush to the window.

"Lord have mercy ..." The terrifying racket had her momentarily rooted to the spot, legs shaking. A flash of yellow emerged from the rooftops. Plumes of black smoke gushed heaven-bound like the last breaths of the dying home being devoured by flames. Just like the plague, this fire would spread quickly. In an instant her features flushed without further need of the discarded Spanish-paper. Then she heard a shout.

"Master Henry!" His cries impelled her to rush to his side and gather him into her arms. She returned quickly to the window to make sense of what was happening and beg God that she could catch sight of her master. But black smoke crept across the rooftops. It slithered up the window and, like a hand from the depths of hell, curled about the pane as if to reach out to her. She held Henry to her breast to protect him from the terror, while thunderous yells began to echo throughout the streets of poor little Alton.

They were under attack. Trumpet blares, drum beats and terrifying cries were unleashed with every flash of incendiaries. A dark congregation of soldiers edged into the narrow Millses Lane that led towards the armoury and on to the church. Saint Lawrence's offered Jane little reassurance. The building and its spire were like an island marooned by warfare, while closer to home everyone had abandoned the Crowne Inn. A block of enemy pikemen and musketeers edged further through the streets. So much so that Jane instinctively knew that what happened thereafter would be up to her.

"Be still." She sat Henry upon the floor and removed the line coif from her head. Lifting the fluted, pewter candlestick from the bedside table, she took the small key from the indent underneath and went to an oak chest by the wall. Kneeling reverentially before it, she inserted the iron key into the lock. It grated, clicking not once but twice before the heavy lid yielded to her quivering hands. Upon lifting it she peered down at a most marvellous gown within. Its satin waves of aquamarine all but extinguished the flames of doubt fanned by Jane's tormented mind. As a mere maid she would most assuredly be raped and killed; but as a gentlewoman she might just escape the marauding brutes. She stripped down to her linen smock and stays, took the new bodice and skirt which rippled around her and was transformed. It fastened at the front; perfect for Lady Anne's ease after having lost her maid. About her neck Jane tied a string of magnificent pearls secured by lace, before picking Henry up again.

"The enemy has entered from the north-west!" A man's voice cried when Jane opened the casement to get a better view. That, she assumed, would be where Sir Francis must be. A quiver of fear over his fate sprang from her heart to momentarily asphyxiate her. Then it just as readily stirred her into action, for she had to escape and find him. The world she had recently come to know was crumbling before her eyes and its boundaries blurred. She refused to be catapulted back to that former existence of mistreatment and poverty, having only just escaped it a mere four months ago.

"This is the only way." A glance in the mirror was met by glinting gold lace that decorated the gown. She was renewed and put on a neat black hat to finish the look. Now the lady she should always have been, she steeled herself against what was to come. For the first time in her life she felt her inner strength; that of Jane Aylesworth, formerly of Newark. The persona of Lady Anne Berkeley was but a shell, as was this gown and the lustrous pearls.

"I will protect thee, Master Henry." Her voice soothed the boy and when she retrieved him, he picked at the fur stole and its curious, bronzy streak.

Descending the staircase, creaking encouragement, she neared the door. Beyond this portal, and beneath the round-shot careering through the air like wailing banshees, were her master and mistress. The parents of this two-year-old boy, whose light brown hair she stroked as much for her own reassurance as his. With her other hand grasping the handle, Jane couldn't help but wonder whether her own baby resembled her, if it was still alive. For the second time this year all her hopes and fears rested with a child, but she would not be separated from this one except by the ending of her life.

Pulling the door open with a deep inhalation, she was confronted by a clatter of horsemen and a bellow of orders in deep Scottish. Hooves pounded the cobbles and brought tears to Henry, who buried his head in her breast. Hundreds of cavalrymen clattered by in a blur, streaked with crimson sashes.

"Save my master for me," she said, stepping into their wake and watching them depart. She spotted the illustrious leader, who was not even fully dressed, such was his desire to get at the enemy. A noble and larger than life man with whom went all her hopes for the future. Upon his disappearance, she looked along the houses in the distance. The hollow windows of one in particular stared back at her like a corpse with sunken eyes. When fire lit up the casements, it was as though Lucifer himself looked her in the face with evil assurance that death stalked the street upon which she stood.

Chapter 74

Like the delicate hop of a sparrow across dew-soaked grass, twitching hither and thither and then plucking a worm, Waller had also arrived with the early morning to extract Crawford from his den.

Orange flames burst from one house like a fiery tongue, licking higher and higher up the walls and leaping to the next wood-framed abode. Musket fire exploded all around Francis's head. Like kindling spluttering for survival amidst an engulfing collaboration of heat and air, he felt close to combustion himself. It was unclear how many Parliamentarians had swooped down upon the five hundred infantrymen of Colonel Bolle's regiment barracked in Alton, but what was clear was that Bolle's men were badly outnumbered.

"Artillery, be damned!" Bolle exclaimed as an iron cannonball decapitated the garret of one house. "How have they got them here?" he asked. The Royalists secreting themselves in every building must have asked the same question. Some, like Francis, would have realised the terrible answer.

"We know what this means," Francis declared, knowing that artillery had blown apart any notion that this was to be a mere skirmish.

"As promised, Waller has come for his ox," Bolle said through gritted teeth.

"Let's hope Crawford and his cavalry disperse them." Francis prayed the enemy could be prevented from getting into the heart of town, especially Normandy Hill, the street commemorating a treaty between William the Conqueror's sons, where Francis's family were quartered.

Charred tears fell from the burning houses, bursting into black splashes of charcoal upon hitting the ground. With a hiss, they settled upon the cold layer of excrement and animal innards that littered the butcher's alley; a gasp that seemed as though Alton too had glimpsed the enemy soldiers emerging from the far end of Millses Lane.

"Colonel Bolle." A young trooper hurried as fast as he could in cavalry boots. "A message from Lord Crawford."

"You've forgotten your horse, lad." Bolle's remark caused laughter amongst those close enough to hear. Mirth which eased a tiny pang of the shock that gripped them all.

"I tethered it yonder, sir ..." The boy's explanation was soon waved aside by the colonel.

"Your message, man?" Bolle prompted.

"Lord Crawford wishes you to hold the enemy back building by building."

"In that case, we should fortify the church, sir," Francis suggested. "Its commanding position is a natural defence."

"Good point, Sir Charles," Bolle agreed. "Take command of the lunette and hold them off long enough for me to marshal the men to the church."

"Aye, sir." Francis left for the earthwork.

"Return to Lord Crawford," Bolle ordered the messenger. "Ask him to take his horsemen and attack the enemy's rear."

"His lordship has left with the cavalry to fetch reinforcements from Winchester," the young man explained.

This news precipitated a multitude of desperate orders from Bolle. Extra men were to be posted in the large brick building near the church. Still more to line the redoubt and the lunette, which, built of compressed soil and resembling the bow of a ship, pointed right at the invading rebels.

* * * * *

Captain Matthew Shepherd of the Green Regiment, London Trained Bands, eyed the Royalist earthwork with hatred for all those manning it. The threatening flashes of gunpowder, followed by clouds of smoke that evaporated upon the breeze, fuelled his resentment. It was the butchering Irish, who he'd heard made up more than half the enemy force, that stoked the most anger; the same Irish Catholics who had massacred thousands of good Protestants and who had now come to England to try and kill more. All in the King's name.

"Damn 'em all," Shepherd growled, vowing to give no quarter to any one of the Papist whoremongers, nor their women. "Let us attack now," he urged the major, Owen Roe.

"Nay, we have to wait for the guns," Roe warned his friend.

"But when will ..." Shepherd's question was answered by an explosion that sent a whizzing ball hurtling towards the earth wall in which it became deeply embedded. The sight left a bad taste in the former sugar baker's mouth and a whistle escaped through the gaps in his blackened teeth.

"Patience, Matthew." Major Roe attempted to convince him that it was a virtue. But knowing his subordinate for many a year, the words would be no more effective than the cannonball which, like an earring, merely adorned the lunette.

"There go our beautiful guns!" Shepherd pointed at the tall, brick building near the church, the top of which crumbled away after a direct hit and cascaded like a waterfall of masonry. "Jack!" he yelled to a wiry sixteen-year-old whom he treated as though he were still his apprentice. "Set afire that thatched house."

The boy was obedient after tasting many a whipping during the five years he'd been indentured to Shepherd. He crouched low and made for some burning timbers. After a precursory glance about, the lad took a smouldering piece and ran to a small house and hurled it unto the thatch with all his might. It caught light so quickly that the sweet smell of burning straw clung to his nostrils before he had even returned to Shepherd, who gave him a hearty slap on the back. As the smoke swirled towards the lunette, the green regiment followed its lead and stormed the Royalist defences.

"What's that?" Shepherd's jubilant praise of the Almighty was interrupted by a dull clatter of monotonous sound that grew louder. "Cavalry?"

Soon enough, word of mouth revealed it to be the cowardly hoof-falls of Ludovic Lindsay, Earl of Crawford, whose cavalry had clattered out of town in full retreat. Captain Shepherd cheered, not knowing whether it was Crawford's arrogant behaviour over the ox, or his history in having raised cavalry for Catholic Spain that galled him most.

Shepherd charged under the green regiment's ensign, which waved with a great swish of bravado and encouragement. Up the steep incline to the lunette they went, crying out with fierce and determined voices while their colleagues in the Red

Regiment joined them. Musketeers picked off any exposed Royalists, while pikemen rushed around the steep crescent earthwork to attack the rear.

* * * * *

"Crawford's reinforcements can help bury us!" Bolle muttered as he watched the strongholds manned by his men fall one by one. The tall, brick building nearby was first and now the lunette, which not even Sir Francis Berkeley could hold against the increasing number of swarming Roundheads. Spitting out a mouthful of gunpowder-thick mucus with a resolve to fight to the end, Bolle watched as Francis and his retreating men approached the churchyard.

"Any news from Crawford, sir?" Francis asked upon his arrival, wiping his sweaty brow and the dirt that streaked it.

"Formulating an attack with his cavalry as we speak." Bolle's high cheekbones seemed gaunter. His arched black eyebrows and white face were a stark and serious monochrome. "We need more time to fortify the church."

"I'll keep some men in the churchyard and hold the rebels off," Francis replied.

"Fall back to the church!" Bolle cried to his contingent with sword aloft.

In that second, when Colonel Bolle grasped Francis's arm and wished him luck, Francis wondered if they'd see each other again. More and more of the street fell to the invading soldiers around the beacon of Saint Lawrence's. Soon, its entrance doors and graveyard were swamped by an arc of Royalists eager to claim sanctuary. The grassy mounds, where not one soul could any longer rest in peace, were covered by a thick and creeping haze.

"Line up behind the cemetery wall," Francis instructed his detachment. All the while the last vestiges of Royalist troops burst into the graveyard, some running, some crawling. One man lay in a mangled mess, though his howling did not penetrate the relentless crashes of debris, musket fire and the undertone of cries, moans and laments.

"Truth and Victory." The Parliamentarian war cry meant they were closing in.

This repeated call tempered the hypnotic panic that had gripped Francis in the last few seconds. He ordered the gates to be closed and barricaded with pews that had been thrown out of the church to make room for the influx of refugees. Some of his lads began to knock loose bricks out of the graveyard wall and through one he watched the red and green standards of the London Trained Bands, whose coloured taffeta flapped menacingly amidst the dour surroundings.

"If these dogs want to come to our church, lads." Francis's veins stood out at his neck. "Then be sure to let your muskets sing out in praise of the Lord." He instructed them to make ready and lean their weapons on the top of the wall, or through any gap they could find, while he glanced back to assess the swelling crush at the church. "Stay with me until our lads are inside and then we follow."

"Wait till our cavalry cut the buggers down!" one of his men yelled.

The noise began to abate, at least enough to bring the fact to Francis's consciousness. A chorus of tinkling glass fell upon the stones and a gun poked out of one of the church's stained-glass windows. Small pieces of burnt paper and thatch floated across them like blackened snow to emphasise just how much this world had been turned upside down. Francis held his breath.

The enemy artillery was silent, although for how long remained to be seen. Their musketeers too, only fired an occasional warning shot to prove their still-looming presence. Now released, a cacophony of secondary noises came to the fore, fluttering like crows across the desolate landscape.

"I need a score of you on either side of the gate," Francis ordered, recognising their weak spot. "The rest of you, go behind the gravestones."

Bolle's pikemen crushed at the church doors as if they were packing up against enemy lines, some of the long poles jamming and sending shards of wood across their heads as they snapped in the jostle.

"Front rank, make ready," Francis cried as his stinging eyes peered through the grey pall.

"We'll be safe in God's house, sir." One man's certainty caused a cheer, albeit a half-lived one. It was quickly countered by Parliamentarians singing hymns, who, outnumbering the Royalists ten to one, still called on the Lord's assistance.

The scraping of hundreds of ramming-sticks in musket barrels provided a chilling warning of the chorus yet to come, though Francis pre-empted their intentions with a yell of: "Give fire!"

The short-lived cascade of lead shot took out a few of those in the enemy's front line before they returned a volley of their own that peppered the thin, wooden gates to within an inch of its framework and bowled Royalists into oblivion. The Parliamentarian pikemen soon set upon the King's men to finish the job and before long the gates were down and frantic shooting and hand to hand fighting encroached upon the eerie graveyard. But by the grace of God, the small band of men under Francis's command pushed the Roundheads back amidst a wave of sorrowful cries.

"Draw swords or turn your muskets," came the brutal order of one enemy officer, who had his troops transform their guns into makeshift clubs.

"Full of bluster!" Taffy, one of Francis's men, did not let the situation kill his positivity.

"And of lead soon enough." Francis paused to reload.

Upon fresh shooting, the rebels emerged from the dank air and penetrated the graveyard again. Francis holstered his spent pistol and lunged forward to slice his sword at the first man he could get at. His repeated bellow of the code word of the day – the King's name – was all he could utter as he pulled his blade from one foe's gut. Francis stabbed the next Roundhead and another of their number was almost cleaved by a halberd whose blade sliced down the back of his skull. Every ferocious cry and vengeful oath was accompanied by growing screams and tortured cries of pain. Gradually, the rebels were prevented from realising their goal a second time as every bullet fired from the walls, or from behind the crooked weather-beaten gravestones, became too much to bear. But dwindling reserves of powder and bullets threatened a break in the fortunes of the defenders, and Francis knew it.

"Have every pikeman lean his weapon against the wall in unison." Francis discreetly passed on the order and then his pikemen headed for the church.

From beyond, the Parliamentarian musketeers kept up resistance while seeming to ponder their next move, and no doubt reconnoitre the perimeter. They were not to know that the pikes that poked out above the wall were but a ghostly army. The butts were wedged in the graveyard soil as if the corpses below had taken them up to support the King's men.

"We have perhaps a few minutes to get inside," Francis whispered to his captain.

Chapter 75

The sound of bellowed orders and demands rang throughout Anne's head and she was jostled by dozens of men that funnelled through the west door of Saint Lawrence's. Each man was a link in a chain being dragged along by waves of panic - sheer desperate panic - that prevented her every attempt to exit the church to find Francis. Anne had never before witnessed expressions that so disfigured men's faces and made them so inhuman. Deep creases pushed down upon their eyes, which no matter how wide, fixated on nothing but the arched entrance to this holy refuge. She lost count of her attempts to break through; unable to make sense of the blurred crush that cast her aside like a stricken ship upon a reef.

"Francis!" Her cry was immediately neutralised. Not that she was calling for help, but merely to reinforce the last vestiges of her will against this relentless tide. Then came a pause. A gap opened through which someone tugged the sprawling carcass of a broken horse.

"Make way." A shot rang out from Colonel Bolle's pistol to temper the storm.

Anne's exhaustion was such that she was left staring at the carcass, whose head had begun to tuck under its chest from the drag; as if in its final moments the beast had tried to shield its eyes from the unfolding carnage. The mound of its once powerful hindquarters, pulled by the front legs, slid past her and, without further thought, she scrambled over it. The soldiers tried to stop her; to appeal to reason and prevent her from going to her death, but she shrieked her resistance to being manhandled in the same manner as the unfortunate animal. Colonel Bolle then intervened.

"Let me out!" Anne yelled.

"Lady Berkeley," Bolle cried, and had the soldiers grip her. "It is no place for a woman out there."

"My husband," she shouted at him. "Where is he?"

"He'll be here soon enough." Bolle ordered the men to escort her into the centre of the church, unwilling to have any further disruption to an already perilous operation. The horse was manoeuvred across the aisle, joining others to form a defensive bastion of corpses, beyond which came the wails of another woman.

"In the name of God!" Mary rushed forward and seized Anne.

Outside, a shot sent another horse tumbling into a heap. Anne did not see the killing for Mary stood in front of her, making small the gap through which the stench of death and dismay drifted. If she had, perhaps it would have had her think twice about going out there.

"Get scaffolding up at the windows so that we can fire from them." Bolle left Anne to her mother's care.

"He's out there!" Anne argued with Mary as the next horse plugged the flow of soldiers.

Seizing a man's doublet, Anne propelled herself through the narrow gap, losing her black bonnet in the process. The cold air pricked at her cheeks immediately, it too was impelling her to desist, but she was out now and there would be no going back. Behind her, Mary could only watch with horror as Anne was enveloped by smoke and vanished.

Anne fled her captors and the west door, calling out her husband's name as she raced to who knows where. Her footfalls, uneasy and troublesome, struggled to find even ground, yet she continued onwards. Her sight was blurred and sporadic, and her eyes only registered what was before her with each step. The millisecond in between was simply dark and unfathomable until a tree loomed ahead and she fell to its trunk. Clinging to the bark, she steadied herself.

Dazed and confused she no longer recognised the graveyard and, no matter which way she turned, what little she registered with each glance seemed no different from the last. Her hearing, assaulted on all fronts, commuted every last noise into a dull, hollow ring. Then her sense of smell, once frozen, was hit by a sudden thaw; putrid excrement, the musky scent of flesh and blood intermingled with gritty gunpowder.

"Francis Berkeley?" Anne called out. "Where is he?" She finally relinquished her grip on the tree, dropping to her knees to be level with a seated soldier. Leaning forward onto all fours she looked desperately into his eyes. Where she imagined they should be, she found only the bulbous ruby of raw flesh, as though they had dissolved from their sockets and, like molten lava, bubbled down his face. Amidst this barren wasteland the wide-open mouth revealed rotten teeth streaked with blood which trickled down his jaw and dripped onto her hand.

Anne screamed, fixated upon the grizzly remains. Holding up her hands, she desperately tried to cover her eyes. Each finger attached to her face like a limpet and clawed into her skin, taught, unrelenting.

The rapports of musket fire couldn't stir her, nor could a trio of men running past her. A musket butt clashed across the head of one man, while a poleaxe pierced another man's belly and sent a spray of blood towards Anne, trickling into the roots of her hair and down her forehead like the warm raindrops of a summer squall. She curled into a ball as the poleaxe then swung in an arc and lodged in the man's neck, cutting arteries like a scythe through grass.

Yet despite her brokenness, she was being lifted. Scarred, she was somehow ascending to heaven and out of this chaos. An arm went about her waist. Deep chords resembling a voice boomed in her ear. The support firmed her legs once more; turned her about like a lifeless leaf upon a breeze and that was it.

Abandonment. Only the door to the church was visible in the distance, seeming to be edging ever further away, yet she shuffled forward.

The sight of her mother, hands raised, brought tears to Anne's eyes and animated her blood-smeared cheeks, while rekindling a desire to escape whatever pit she had fallen into. Mary's features contorted; her eyes widened; her open mouth stretched her skin every time she called her daughter's name and waved her closer. The thump of Anne's heartbeat pounded in her head, her rasping breaths securing barely enough oxygen to drive her towards her saviour.

* * * * *

"Come to me!" Mary watched as her daughter came closer, like a fleeting shadow in her black dress. With sobs of joy she held out her arms to receive her daughter back.

"They've broken into the graveyard," an officer cried. "Close the doors."

"Let it be known that I'll kill any man who surrenders to the rebels," Sir Richard Bolle threatened all waverers. "I will fight side by side with every last one of you in defence of our families and the laws of the land."

The men tugged at the doors of this last bastion, prepared to seal their fate. Closing off from the chaos beyond and standing shoulder to shoulder in God's antechamber, they would await his salvation and eternal peace.

But Mary, devout as she was, would sacrifice all these people, rather than allow them to shut Anne out and leave her to be torn to pieces. She jostled, cried out for mercy, lost sight of Anne, and then found her again, barely an arm's length away and framed within the doorway that was about to be closed.

The Almighty lit up the sky and a tinge of yellow flashed around Anne as He showed her the way. Upon that glorious, golden tint Anne fell forward. Her body slipped through the opening in time to be embraced by Mary as the oak timbers clashed together and the swell of men ushered the pair into the inner sanctum. Still holding her tight, Mary whispered the Lord's prayer.

"Deliver us from evil ..." Mary struggled to grip her daughter, who seemed heavier by the second, collapsing with her to the floor. But whereas Mary manged to sit upright against a pillar, Anne's arms lay limp and her body folded onto the stones.

Crawling forward on all fours, Mary stroked her daughter's cheek, which caused her head to roll aside, hair covering her closed eyes. Mary held her hand. She called Anne's name; shook her body, all to no avail. She brushed back her hair. Was this her daughter? Could it be someone else?

"Anne?" She barely managed to say her name.

Her beloved daughter was unresponsive and Mary's throat choked. Frantic, she felt Anne's body, fervently rubbed her arms as if she could stimulate the flow of her life-blood, restore her from the shock, or waken her from this faint. Then, from beneath the body, oozed a pool of blood. It extended from each side as if her daughter were sprouting deathly wings.

She had gone. It was too late. Anne's angelic face paled, its glow never to be seen again as a cold, matt hue took over, very like the slabs upon which her mortal remains now lay. Mary's heart was seared with pain, as though torn out and tossed through the smashed windows like one of the grenadoes being hurled at those who had taken from her the only person she had ever truly loved. She felt nothing but emptiness. Her stepdaughter – nay baby – who, aged only nine months upon their first meeting, had looked up into Mary's eyes and stirred emotion within her soul that she'd never imagined possible. An enduring love that now, twenty years on, laid waste to all Mary had ever believed in, for she would never meet those eye's sparkling emerald gaze again.

Chapter 76

The churchyard teemed with activity. Not since Alton fair was held here in the fourteenth century had the place seen such numbers, though this time the appearance of a frantic Bishop with his posse of abbots and deacons would certainly stand no chance of bringing proceedings to a close. Lead shot, fired from all angles, ricocheted against every object – human or otherwise – that happened to get in its way. Gravestones became ideal rests for muskets. Their flints scratched down frizzens upon the depression of triggers to create a cascade of sparks that ignited gunpowder charges. It was ironic that the walls of Saint Lawrence's were decorated with local flint; the stone that was aiding its destruction.

The shock of seeing Anne was momentary and fleeting. The array of Roundheads coming at Francis's small band, who lined up to block access to the church, did not allow time to think. Yet his wife's presence – shocking and unexpected – gave impetus to every blow that Francis doled out. Falling back to where he'd raised Anne to her feet and pushed her towards the church, he glimpsed her outline slipping through the grizzled oak doors, which enveloped her in a flash.

"Fall back." Francis commanded, knowing that Anne was now safe. "Let's get inside!"

Francis banged the door with the hilt of his sword, calling out his rank and name and demanding those inside admit the remaining men. Now stalled, his neurons sparked life into a cluster of desperate worries that flooded his mind Where was Henry? Why had Anne come to the church?

The door finally opened. With the defenders' musket barrels poking out to keep the enemy at bay, as many of Francis's men as possible squeezed inside with him for the last time before the doors were slammed shut and barricaded. Francis gripped his sword and stood facing a pile of dead horses and scaffolding rising up to each window, atop which soldiers lay with piles of grenades. The windows were pierced with holes; shards of coloured glass hung limply from their lead roots, while below men swarmed around both aisle and nave.

Where is she? Francis desperately made his way through the building to find Anne.

"Francis!" A smile of relief crossed Bolle's features as he told his lieutenant-colonel of his defensive plan. "We've cut small holes in the doors through which to fire." The details were endless, gritty and determined. "If I'm killed, you must take over the defence. There's to be no surrender."

"You have my word," Francis replied. Though at that moment he would have agreed to anything. "Have you seen my wife?" He asked while there was still opportunity.

"Yes, I believe she is hereabouts." Bolle nodded.

"Then grant me but a few minutes to search for her."

"You have as long as it takes for the enemy to storm the building."

Leaving the colonel, Francis headed through the church and the ranks of soldiers in his search, until he came to the heart of the building. Beneath the four Norman arches that formed the tower, he paused with growing desperation.

She has to be in here. He questioned himself as to whether it was Anne he had assisted. Albeit fleeting, the doubt left him as cold as the stone pillar he thumped with the palm of one hand.

"Taffy," he called to one of the lads who had defended the graveyard. "Have you seen a woman in here?"

"Tis not the time, nor the place, sir." Taffy snorted.

"My wife, damn you," Francis growled.

"Sorry, sir, I ain't."

Pacing to the other corner of the archways, Francis saw only men milling around. One doled out musket balls from the stone Anglo-Saxon font that fed an array of men and their guns. From floor to scaffolding troops lay in wait. Carved into one arch above Francis was a wolf gnawing on a bone, who looked down upon his fruitless search and watched as his hope was devoured.

"God's blood!" Francis stormed towards the north aisle, almost missing the sight of a woman near prostrate on the ground. Sobbing desperately, she lay across a body dressed in black, which he immediately recognised as his dear wife. Anne's clothing was so dark that, like an eclipse, sight of her corpse shut out everything else.

This certainty, so brutal and unrelenting, assaulted Francis's senses. His heart seemed to stop feeding his body. Every starving muscle ached. His limbs grew cold at the terror and his sight burst into a black and white haze that did its best to shut out the image before him.

"Anne!" His cry was that of one abandoned. As if her soul still teetered in this life, or he had the power to prevent the inevitable. As if she had not already died many minutes ago.

He stared, bewildered as the crouching woman turned about and he beheld Mary's face. He wished in those seconds that it was his mother-in-law who was dead, and that for some reason he was simply hallucinating. But now the old hag was clinging to Francis's clothes, shaking him and screaming.

"You killed her!" Mary trembled so violently that her movement was jerked.

"She's dead?" Francis's eyes were blurred with tears and he felt a lead weight inside his stomach.

"I was ... too ... late." Mary held her head in her hands.

"Get out of my way." Francis pushed her aside and dropped to his knees. He could only stare at Anne's body, for to touch her would mean it was real.

"Too late to save her from you." Mary sobbed and spat the last words with venom.

"Me?"

"You brought her here," Mary hissed. "Your selfishness."

Francis turned back to Anne. Her head lay to one side and her features didn't look like those of the woman he loved. They were white as a phantom's and speckled with pinpricks of crimson. He gasped for air and, with a deep yell, lashed out at Mary, striking the very centre of her face with his fist. Now exorcised of the tormenting evil spirit, he collapsed beside Anne in a breathless heap and took her hand in his.

"I brought you here." Had his body not been numbed, he would have felt the chill of death touch his lips as he kissed her. His eyes streamed with tears that rendered him speechless, senseless and blind.

Senseless, he failed to notice the shots above him as the soldiers fired upon the Roundheads now outside, nor the grenades that tore open new graves. Blind to the Royalists who barricaded the south door against the rebels and shot at them through small holes, or took up position behind the dead horses. Speechless, he was unable to give his men any direction, order or reassurance.

"Look at me." Bolle kneeled and took hold of Francis's shoulders. "Your men need you."

"My wife." Francis groaned. "Let me die next to her."

"If we hold out here, it gives others the chance to escape." Bolle's thoughts went to his own wife and child far away in Lincolnshire. "Consider all the women and children in this town we can assist by holding out."

It pained Francis to consider fighting anymore. But when Bolle exhorted him to action, an image of Henry came to mind. Francis covered his face with both hands at the lad's absence and a seed of hope floated softly across the desolation of his barren soul. A lone seed, clinging to a downy dandelion head that impelled Francis to fight, if only to see his boy safe.

"The cavalry?" Francis struggled to his feet, and blood seemed to flow through his veins once more.

"Crawford fled with them much earlier," Bolle revealed.

"Damn him!" The fire in Francis's stomach burned with condemnation that implicitly linked Crawford to this catastrophe. It was he who had goaded Waller and ignored warnings. He, who had left them all outnumbered, and fled like a coward, allowing the enemy to swarm into Alton, and therefore he who had caused Anne's death.

"We fight with God's protection, in His house," Bolle cried. His voice carried through the beams of the church and shored up the morale of his men.

"They'll never take us alive." Francis vowed and, shortly after this, a stained-glass window erupted into a rainbow of twinkling shards, and the statues of Virgin and Child in the niches above were peppered with gunshot.

Having repulsed the rebels at the south door, now the western one was under pressure. The Roundheads' battering soon burst it open and a torrent of enemy troops forced their way into the church. Too many to hold back. Each used the full extent of their firepower and the Royalists fell back to the horses, leaving a trail of dead.

Colonel Bolle withdrew to the wooden pulpit. He mounted the steps and began a deadly sermon that saw him cut down one, two and three of their number with his rapier. A fourth was pierced in the belly after the colonel jumped down in an instant with bellowing oaths. Parrying further blows, he sent a fifth to join the other corpses at the foot of the pulpit. A sixth was dispatched after Bolle's rapier cut the man's sword arm, and then his torso.

The seventh Roundhead came at Bolle so quickly that he could not catch his breath. The colonel's aching arms were as heavy as lead and two of his men who fought alongside him were now dead. Bolle was alone, facing this Roundhead who had half a dozen more ready to replace him. Their attack was swift and, although meeting one blow, it took all Bolle's energy and he tumbled back onto the steps whereupon a blade was stuck firmly into his gut. Whatever else they did to Colonel Richard Bolle brought him no further pain.

Now in charge of the remaining defenders, Francis only became aware of the fact when a great cry went up that the colonel was dead. The voices of both sides joined in unison for very different reasons. Responsibility was now his. Francis would have to bring this brutal battle to a close. He bellowed at the rebels coming at him, fully prepared to carry out Bolle's final order to the letter, and the last man. His small group of men formed an arc and cut, thrust and stabbed at the Roundheads in any way they could. Despite gut-wrenching anger, Francis faced his last moment with tears, knowing that he would never again see his son or know his fate. The pain of this was far worse than any death blow waiting for Francis.

A cannonball smashed the arch above the window behind him and his field of vision narrowed immediately as a stone struck him down. The absence of command brought demoralisation to the Royalists, with some calling for quarter over a pointless and bloody death. One by one they gave up the struggle, and their Parliamentarian attackers became more eager to end the carnage and take whatever booty Alton had to offer.

Chapter 77

Jane stood at the window looking out onto the deserted alley at the back of the house. Her mind churned over the possible actions she could take to find her master and mistress, as well as the endless dangers that confronted her and Henry. The grey tint of the glass emphasised the bleak sky. Not knowing what to do, nor where to go, she had remained in the house, it being the only place that offered any semblance of safety and, most importantly, the first place Sir Francis would return to. For he, surely, would never abandon her.

With a prayer for deliverance upon her lips, her view was blurred by the appearance of a face passing the window which made her draw back. A face it had to be, yet the colour resembled the dying embers of a fire. As warnings rang in her head, a tumult of clattering almost finished off her nerves, and she turned to find Henry knocking down his oak ninepins with a small wooden ball. As the pins flailed helplessly around the floor, she heard raps at the door that led her to instinctively pick him up.

"Jane, let me in!" A voice called.

"Who is it?" She had her suspicions already.

"Mary. Now, quickly, there's no time to lose."

"Go play with little Tom," she instructed Henry, who complied as soon as his feet touched the floorboards. He headed towards the stairs, atop which, in his nursery, he would find the straw horse. Jane, meanwhile, hesitated before walking slowly to the door. She had no alternative but to unlock and open it with a clunk. Mary stepped inside. Her face was bruised, one eye ringed with ripples of rouge, as well as congealed blood at her nose.

"Lady Anne sent me to fetch Henry," Mary said and spotted her grandson ascending the stairs. Her wide eyes watched in what looked like fear as he got farther and farther away.

"Where is Sir Francis?" Jane fixated upon Mary's hollow smile, so at odds with the circumstances in which they found themselves, although it was short-lived.

"I am instructed to take Henry …" Mary turned to Jane. After a moment she shrieked at her at an almost unintelligible pitch. "What are you doing in my daughter's clothes?"

"It's not what you think," Jane stuttered.

"Is that so?" Mary's face screwed up. "You try to steal my daughter's husband, her son and even her apparel."

"Please let me explain." Jane began to sob.

"Ironic you're thieving silks and jewellery after spending so much time in a state of undress with Francis – the cheating bastard." Mary howled and ran at her. "Well your lover is dead and rotting in hell!"

Jane turned tail and rushed up the stairs with Mary wailing and screeching as she raced after her. Jane's steps were short and fast. The crone's hand scratched at the silk of the dress in a bid to pull Jane back down the stairs. But rushing through the door and slamming it shut, Jane turned the key in the lock, ran over to Henry and fell to her knees before him. There was no relief, for this was only the beginning. They were trapped with Mary on the other side banging, threatening and clawing at the door like a rabid dog. Henry's nursery was much smaller than the other bedroom, tainting Jane's fear with claustrophobia.

"Mama." Henry's big brown eyes looked up. His downturned mouth quivered so much that Jane scooped him up and ran to the window. Lifting the curled iron handle, she flung it open to the stale air of war outside. From across the back alley another house peered at her with open windows and a washing line spanning the four-foot gap.

"I want my grandson!" Mary insisted.

"We're going to have an adventure." Jane widened her eyes at the child and put on the biggest smile she could manage. "Will you be as brave as your father?" she asked, to which Henry nodded enthusiastically as she placed him on the floor and frantically looked around.

"I'll tear you limb from limb." Mary pounded.

"How to bridge the divide?" Jane's eyes landed upon a wooden bench which she dragged towards the window, turning it over to rest its surface upon the windowsill.

"Henry, open the door for Gamore," Mary urged, mimicking the boy's crude attempts at 'grandmother'.

"No, let's hide from Gamore!" Jane pushed the bench out of the window so that it rose at an angle; manipulated it across to the ledge to the house at the other side, and guided it down like a drawbridge. Flipping it over had the legs at each side lock it firmly in place against the ledges of both houses. "Now Henry." She stopped him going to the door.

"Gamore," Henry repeated with agitation.

Jane lifted him up and held him to her bosom; stepped onto a chair and climbed up to sit astride the bench. Her legs dangled in the air and as much as she knew not to look down, the harder it became to avoid the drop compounding her fear.

"I'll shuffle us across and hold you tight," she told the boy and kept a tight grip of him with one arm. With her other hand, she eased them both slowly across.

* * * * *

Mary darted into the main bedroom and rummaged through chests. She needed something, anything, to use to beat down the door. Clothes, belts, shoes were all she could find. *What about the kitchen? There must be something in the kitchen.* She hurried down to seize a poker from the fireplace. On her return, determined not to lose her grandson, she beat the door half a dozen times, each blow accompanied by a howl that released a portion of the anger, pain and desperation that consumed her as she fought for her and Henry's existence. Without him she had no life. Nothing to live for; nor anyone to love. So on she went. The poker lodged into the wooden panels to stick fast until, with a fierce tug, she removed it and continued. Very soon the wood was pierced, each subsequent strike further compromised the door and shed splinters as the hole grew bigger.

* * * * *

"Don't move," Jane said slowly as her smooth silk skirt eased her along the bench. From behind, the repetitive clashes and clattering were, thankfully, less distracting than they could have been. Her concentration blocked out most of it, in a bid for self-preservation. Her legs were numb with cold, but she had forgotten all about them while she focussed on keeping

Henry tight to her chest and maintaining her balance by leaning forward as far as possible.

The form creaked now and then, and each time Jane regretted risking them both like this, but it was the only way out. The worst part came when they were half way across; when both houses were out of immediate grasp. In Jane's peripheral vision a vacant expanse swirled around her. The wind taunted her by flapping her dress and blowing her hair across her face. Onwards. She continued relentlessly until the opposite window ledge was near her fingertips, which were white from clinging on.

"Go inside." She eased forward and grabbed the window with one hand, guiding Henry with the other. "Wait for me." Jane pulled herself closer and stuck her head and torso through the window and tumbled inside head first with a squeal of relief that lasted only a second or two. She stood up and lifted the bench, reversing it to come away and fall to the street below, where it exploded with a reverberating roar.

Mary was at the other window. Her poker, thrown across the void, smashed panes next to Jane and, if she needed any prompting, this was it. Grabbing Henry, Jane left the room and rushed down the stairs. Once into the hall, they ran its length and burst out of the front door and onto the main street right into the tight ranks of a column of soldiers.

"What have we here?" Sergeant Foster licked his lips upon sight of the exquisite pearls adorning Janes heaving bosom. "An Irish harlot?" He grabbed her wrist and made comment about how well used she must have been to be dressed so. "Lord Crawford left his plaything here, has he?"

"I'm no such thing!" She cried that her husband was a knight of the realm, though to no avail. The man's hands were bloodstained, as was the green fabric grip of his poleaxe, leading her to wonder if she'd leapt from the pan only to land right in the fire.

"A high-class harlot then." Foster would concede no more than this.

"I wouldn't complain about any night march with 'er in tow, sir," one of his company acknowledged.

"Let go of me!" Her scream set Henry crying, causing some of Foster's men to cheer.

"And a brat, too?" Foster laughed. "Breeding is Crawford's only way of getting new recruits."

"I am Lady Anne Berkeley!" Jane insisted.

"Then I'll be sure to kiss your hand first," Foster replied and dragged her close. "Get in there." He pushed her back towards the building she'd just exited.

"And this?" One soldier pointed at the child.

"Kill him if she resists."

"What's this commotion?" An officer stopped his horse's monotonous canter and looked down on the sergeant.

"A prisoner, Sir William," Foster said.

"With a child, I see." Waller frowned. "Get your column moving, man!" He turned to the lady and her loveliness elicited his smile. His eyes widened at sight of her blue eyes and perfect lips, which revealed the tips of two teeth that gave her an air of innocence.

"Sir William Waller?" Jane had seen his engraving in the news-sheets and knew of him from Francis and Colonel Bolle's conversations.

"Yes, indeed." Waller lifted his hat. "And who might you be, madam?"

"Lady Anne Berkeley, wife of Sir Francis."

"Oh, Crawford's lieutenant-colonel?" Waller's features changed.

"Yes, Sir William, that's correct. You know of his whereabouts?" She managed to control the urge to rush at Waller and cling to his leg to beg for news. "Please, tell me if you have seen him. For his son's sake if nothing else."

"Well, Lady Anne." Waller took a deep breath. "The last I heard, your husband was alive." He pursed his lips and turned away deep in thought.

"I beg you tell me where he is." Jane assumed Waller's rumination meant that he was hiding something. "Would you have Prince Rupert hear of this?"

"Rupert?" Waller snatched his hat from his head and let out a roar of laughter. "I care not one jot what reckless Rupert thinks about me," he replied. "But my interest in what your husband might know is another matter entirely. He could speak of the Prince's plans all day and still not test my patience."

"Please." Jane had no tears left to cry.

"Take them both to the rear with the other prisoners," Waller instructed.

Jane lifted Henry into her arms to comfort him, and also drew reassurance herself from holding another person close in a time of utter peril. She had veered from one crisis to the next, but the boy's presence gave her determination when otherwise she would have been spent. His affection kept her sane, when all she faced were cold and callous men.

"It'll be all right … my son," she whispered and kissed his head. As his stifled sobs began to ease, she would do well to heed her own words as she walked down a line of ghoulish Royalist prisoners. Blood-stained, dirty and weary, she felt their exhaustion; she too had faced a battle and survived, but would any of them ever be the same again? A few Parliamentarians ogled, laughed or grunted some comment or other.

"Come on, woman!" a corporal shoved her onward.

Jane kept her head high, as any lady would, turning away to ignore the man. It was then that her sight came upon a tall man whose head was bowed. His hair hung forward, so matted with dirt and blood that it seemed as black as sea coal, and Jane's heart almost stopped. She could just make out his square chin, glanced at his broad shoulders and then the bloody gash on his head.

"Sir Francis?" Her footsteps halted and she stood open-mouthed.

The man slowly looked up as if the movement was painful, or if he did not wish ever to look again at the world around him. His arms hung limply by the shell of his body and she met his empty eyes, which seemed like two deep wells dry of all emotion. His body tensed. A frown crossed his dirty features and, whereas Jane began to shed tears of relief at finding her master, Sir Francis remained silent and motionless.

"Who's this, y'er husband?" The corporal took the back of her dress in his grasp and pushed her onward.

"Yes." Jane kept her eyes on Sir Francis, her heart pounding in her chest as she walked past him, desperately hoping he would understand; that he would realise why she was dressed this way and just why she claimed to be his wife. And, although Francis remained speechless, he looked at his boy in her arms and tightly closed his eyes, as if thanking God for his survival and praying for their future.